FROM
Sydney
With
Love

With Love
COLLECTION

February 2017 February 2017 February 2017

March 2017 March 2017 March 2017

FROM
Sydney
With Love

KELLY
HUNTER

ROBYN
GRADY

LINDSAY
ARMSTRONG

MILLS
&
BOON

First Published in Great Britain 2017
By Mills & Boon, an imprint of HarperCollins*Publishers*
1 London Bridge Street, London, SE1 9GF

FROM SYDNEY WITH LOVE © 2017 Harlequin Books S.A.

With This Fling... © 2011 Kelly Hunter
Losing Control © 2012 Robyn Grady
The Girl He Never Noticed © 2011 Lindsay Armstrong

ISBN: 978-0-263-92760-3

09-0217

WITH THIS FLING...

KELLY HUNTER

If wishes were fishes, beggars would fly.

Kelly Hunter has always had a weakness for fairytales, fantasy worlds and losing herself in a good book. She is married with two children, avoids cooking and cleaning, and despite the best efforts of her family, is no sports fan! Kelly is however, a keen gardener and has a fondness for roses. Kelly was born in Australia and has travelled extensively. Although she enjoys living and working in different parts of the world, she still calls Australia home.

PROLOGUE

THERE was a lot to be said for fictional fiancés, decided Charlotte Greenstone as she settled into the saggy vinyl hospital chair for yet another night-time vigil by her dying godmother's side. The room had seen decades of sickness and death but the elderly Aurora refused entry to gloom and opted instead to remember a life well lived and speculate quite outrageously on what might come after death.

Ashes seemed inevitable given that Aurora wanted to be cremated, but, if not dust, Aurora pondered the layout of heaven, the hierarchy within it, and how long the waiting list for reincarnation as a house cat might be.

This night, unfortunately, wasn't shaping up to be one of Aurora's better nights. Tonight Aurora was morphined-up and fretful, her main concern being that once she was gone Charlotte would have no one. Not nothing—for when it came to worldly possessions Charlotte had more than enough for any one person. But when it came to family and a sense of belonging…when it came down to the number of people Charlotte could turn to for comfort and company… Aurora's concerns weren't entirely unfounded. Hence the invention of Charlotte's tailor-made handy-dandy fictional fiancé. A wonderfully useful man if ever there was one.

Dashing.

Deliciously honourable.

Modest yet supremely accomplished.

And, last but not least, absent.

Once the awkwardness of the initial deception had passed, the fictional fiancé had provided endless hours of bedside entertainment. More to the point, his presence— so to speak—had provided valuable reassurance to a god-mother who needed it that Charlotte would be loved. That she wouldn't be lonely. Not with the likes of Thaddeus Jeremiah Gilbert Tyler around.

Not that anyone actually called the man Thaddeus to his face, oh, no. His research colleagues called him Tyler, and they uttered the name respectfully given his status as an in-dependently wealthy globetrotting botanist, humanitarian, eco warrior, and citizen of Australia. His mother called him TJ. Always had, always would. Thaddeus Jeremiah Gilbert's father called him son, and bore a startling re-semblance to Sean Connery. The adventurous Mr Tyler had no siblings—easier just to make him like Charlotte in that regard.

Charlotte called him Gil and laced the word with af-fection and desire, and Aurora believed.

Gil was in Papua New Guinea, somewhere up the Sepik River where phones were few and contact with the outside world was practically non-existent. Charlotte had managed to get a message through to him though…finally…and he'd sent a tribesman back to Moresby with a message for her. He hoped to be there soon, for he'd missed Charlotte most desperately and never wanted to be parted from her again. He wanted to meet Aurora, for he'd heard so much about her: accomplished businesswoman, artefact col-lector, godmother and all round good fairy; he wanted to meet the woman who'd raised his beloved Charlotte.

Aurora wanted to meet *him*.

The wonderfully eccentric Aurora Herschoval being

the closest thing to family Charlotte had ever had, for her parents were long dead, over twenty years dead now, and little more than a glamorous memory.

The cancer-ridden and increasingly morphine-medicated Aurora had a tendency to confuse Gil with Charlotte's father. Easy enough to do, Charlotte supposed, seeing as she'd modelled the man on the bits of her father she remembered.

Gil, aka TJ, aka Thaddeus Jeremiah Gilbert Tyler, in other words her fictional fiancé, also paid homage to Indiana Jones—complete with hat; Captain Kirk—probably best not to try and figure out why; and a swaggering Caribbean pirate or two—minus the hygiene issues. Yes, indeed, Charlotte's fiancé was quite a man.

She'd miss him dreadfully when he was gone. His zest for life and new experiences. His tenderness and his wit. His company, as daft as that sounded, for he *had* kept her company these long anxious nights. He'd helped her keep the tears at bay and given her the strength to face what was coming.

Aurora passed away right on time. Two months from the discovery of the cancer to the finish, just as the good doctor had predicted.

This time, the thought of Gilbert did not hold Charlotte's tears at bay. She wept with relief that Aurora's pain had finally ceased. She wept with grief for the loss of a mother and friend.

She just wept.

Gilbert didn't make it home to Australia in time to meet Aurora—an unforgivable act of negligence as far as Charlotte was concerned. Poetic justice came swiftly.

Gilbert, in his haste to return to her, had ventured into territory he had no business venturing into. Once there, the reckless—yet noble—fool had tried to prevent the kidnapping of tribal daughters by a renegade hunting party, so it was said. Authorities had little hope of recovering his remains. The words *'long pig'* had been whispered.

It was a double blow, his demise coming so soon after Aurora's, and in the wee small hours of the night Charlotte mourned for him.

She really did.

CHAPTER ONE

'CHARLOTTE, what are you doing here?' Professor Harold Mead's panicked expression didn't quite fit his soothing fatherly tone. Then again, a lot of things about her boss didn't quite fit. Like his version of Ancient Egyptian history as opposed to everyone else's, for example. Or his idea of a regular working week, which was somewhere in the vicinity of seventy hours as opposed to, say, the fifty everyone else put in.

Granted, it was seven-thirty on a Monday morning and she didn't usually start work quite this early, but still…she *did* have every right to be here. 'Charlotte?' he repeated.

'Working?' she offered helpfully. 'At least, that's the plan. Is there something wrong with the plan?'

'No, but we were hardly expecting you in today. We thought you might take a few days to come to terms with your loss, what with your godmother's funeral yesterday.' Which he'd attended. Which had been nice of him, seeing as he hadn't known Aurora well at all.

'It was a good funeral,' she said softly. 'A celebration of a life well lived. That's what I think. That's what I know. And thank you for attending.'

'You're welcome,' said the Mead. 'And if you do need to take a few days' leave…'

'No,' said Charlotte hastily. 'Please. No leave. I'm fine.' She tried on a smile, and saw from the deepening concern in the Mead's eyes that he'd seen it for the falsehood it was. 'Really. I'm ready to work. I think I have a lead on what the pottery fragments coming out of the Loess site might be.'

'It can wait,' said the Mead. 'Or you could pass that work on to someone else. Dr Carlysle, perhaps? Seeing as he's on site? Dr Steadfellow values him quite highly.'

'I'm sure he does.' Steadfellow's reports had been full of the man. 'But I'd rather not.' The Loess site had been one of her finds. Hers and Aurora's. She'd *given* Steadfellow that site—co-ordinates, preliminary work, everything—on condition that she took part in the analysis. Alas, the good Dr Steadfellow seemed to be in danger of forgetting their arrangement now that the highly valued Dr Carlysle had joined the team. 'Harold, I know Dr Steadfellow and Dr Carlysle feel they can take it from here. I know they're eminently qualified to do so but that's not the point. I feel like I'm being sidelined and that wasn't the arrangement.'

'Charlotte, be reasonable,' said the Mead soothingly. 'Everyone knows you pulled together the funding for the Loess dig. No one doubts your claim to significant project input, but is this really a good time to be challenging your colleagues? Might they not simply be trying to help you through a difficult personal patch?'

Charlotte heard the words. She wanted to believe in them. Wanted to trust that Steadfellow would honour his word and acknowledge her contribution to the discovery, but in all honesty she just didn't know if he would. Her judgement was shot, these days. Too many sleepless nights. Too much weaving in and out of imaginary realities because it had hurt too much to stay in *this* one. 'I'll talk to

Steadfellow. And Carlysle,' she said quietly. 'We'll sort something out.'

'Excellent.' The Mead beamed. 'I knew you'd be generous about this. You already have more publications than most archaeologists three times your age. A tenured position is just around the corner for you.'

'Even if I'm seen as a pushover?' she asked quietly and Harold had the grace to flush.

'Charlotte,' he said. 'I know your godmother was of great assistance to you when it came to contacts in the archaeology world. I know your family name engenders a great deal of goodwill. God knows, I've *never* seen an archaeologist pull funding from the private sector the way you do. But your godmother's gone now, and a lot of people will be looking to see if your legendary contacts went with her.' He took a breath and fixed her with what he probably thought was a kindly gaze. 'Charlotte, you're a wonderful asset to this department, but if you'll take an old man's advice—and I do hope you will—losing ground on the Loess dig is the least of your problems. You need to think about taking to the field for a while and renewing your contacts in person. You need to think about getting back out on site and heading up your own digs. That's what I'd be doing if I were you and I *really* wanted to get back in the game. Your position then would be unassailable. If that's what you want.'

If that's what you want.

Truth was—Charlotte didn't know *what* she wanted any more, when it came to her work.

And the Mead knew it.

'Charlotte, I know you're not given to discussing your private life with your work colleagues,' the Mead began awkwardly. 'But I heard what happened to your fiancé in PNG. Bad business, that. Terrible.'

'You, ah…heard about that?' Charlotte's heart thumped hard against her chest, and if her smile was a little strained it was only because the situation warranted it. Thaddeus Jeremiah Gilbert Tyler was supposed to have lived only in her mind and Aurora's. No one else's. 'How?'

'One of the palliative care nurses up at the hospital is married to Thomas over in Statistics. He's been keeping us abreast of various…things.'

'Oh.' Charlotte offered up another sickly smile, dimly registering the collision of planet fiction with planet reality but having no idea how to wrest them back apart. Why couldn't she have simply broken her fictitious engagement to her fictitious fiancé in a sane and sensible manner, rather than killing him off? That way the formerly useful Gil could have gone paddling up the Sepik for ever, and she and Harold would not be having this conversation.

'At least with your godmother you were prepared for her death. But with your fiancé, and without the body… Anyway, enough of that. Charlotte, I reiterate—if you need to take some extended leave, please do.'

'I—thank you.' Charlotte's voice shook alarmingly. The Mead took a giant step back, as if downright horrified at the prospect of Charlotte in tears. He wasn't the only one to be horrified by such a notion. *Stop it, Charlotte. Shoulders back. Don't you dare break down. A Greenstone never breaks down. Chin up, Charlie, and smile.* The last was pure Aurora.

Slowly, very slowly, Charlotte collected her composure and offered up what she hoped would pass for a smile. 'Thank you, Harold. I appreciate your concern and your advice, I really do. But right now, I'd really rather work.'

If Charlotte thought her early morning conversation with the Mead had been bad, morning tea in the staffroom was worse. Kind words cut deep when they weren't deserved, and there were a *lot* of kind words for Charlotte this morning on account of her loss.

Loss*es*.

She cut out fast, back to her little corner office, taking her cup of tea with her. Once there she slumped into her chair and stared at her computer screen without really seeing it. Surely things would be better tomorrow? Surely this overwhelming sense of loss on the one hand and guilt on the other would fade? All she had to do was ride out these next few days. Maybe she could resurrect Gil and then dump him? Or have him dump her. Mutually agree to part ways…

'How're you holding up?' said a voice from the doorway. Millie, seeking entry, offering solace. Millie, who deserved better than lies from her.

'So-so.' Charlotte offered up a weak smile. 'Sympathy on account of Aurora's death I can handle. I'm not so sure I can handle any sympathy on account of Gil.'

'It's not so much sympathy as rampant curiosity,' said Millie as she came in and perched her skinny rear on the edge of the table. 'We've been friends and co-workers for, what, almost two years now? Why didn't you *tell* me you were engaged? And why aren't you wearing his ring?'

'It was a fairly loose arrangement,' said Charlotte awkwardly. 'Really loose.'

'How long since you'd seen him?' asked Millie.

'A while. Gil was very independent. Adventurous.' For a moment, Charlotte let herself dream. 'Gil was a law unto himself. Passionate and focused. Energetic. Patient…'

'Stamina?'

'That too.'

'I'm beginning to see the appeal,' said Millie. 'Unless you actually happened to want him around.'

Charlotte snapped out of her Gilfest with a wry smile. 'Well, there was that.'

'Do I sense a shred of relief that you're no longer tied to such an independent adventurer?'

'You might,' murmured Charlotte. This was what she wanted, wasn't it? Millie and everyone else to think that she'd recover quickly from her fiancé's demise? Why on earth, then, should she feel so disloyal to *Gil*?

'Do you have a picture of him?' asked Millie.

'What?'

'A photo. Of your fiancé.'

'Somewhere I do.' The lies, they just kept coming. 'Honestly, Millie. I'm okay. I may have embellished Gil's importance for Aurora's benefit. Just a little.'

'You should dig out a picture,' said Millie gently. 'Put it up. Swear at it if it makes you feel better. Even if he wasn't the marrying kind, even if your engagement was a colossal mistake, you should celebrate the time you spent with him. It's *okay* to feel conflicted about his death, Charlotte. It's okay to get *angry* with him for putting himself in a position to get eaten. It's all part of the grieving process and it's perfectly normal.'

'It's really not,' said Charlotte faintly. Nothing about these last two months had been normal. 'Everything's gone a little bit crazy. Starting with me.'

'That's because prolonged bedside vigils will do that to a person. Which is why you shouldn't be here,' said Millie earnestly. 'Seriously, Charlotte. Why don't you take a few days' leave? Head for the coast. Rent a lighthouse. Refresh your spirit. Allow yourself to grieve.'

Charlotte shook her head, hot tears not far from falling. 'I can't.'

'Why not?'

'Because I need to keep busy.' She gave Millie the truth

of it, and felt marginally better for doing so. 'I need to be around other people, people I know, even if they do think I'm a spoiled archaeology heiress with fading networking skills and no brains.'

'Says who?' said Millie sharply. 'Did the Mead say that to you?' And without waiting for Charlotte's reply, 'Moron.'

'He didn't say that.' Charlotte felt obliged to defend him. 'He was really very kind. He just…'

'Implied it,' said Millie darkly. 'I know how he works.'

'Maybe he didn't imply it,' said Charlotte. 'Maybe I did. Maybe it's just a big day for self doubt.' And loneliness. It was a hell of a day for that. 'Thing is, I need to feel as if I'm part of a community today, and this community is the only one I've got. Does that sound needy?'

'No.' Millie's smile came free and gentle and washed over Charlotte like a balm. 'It sounds like your community needs to lift its game.'

For all her inquisitiveness, Millie Peters had a good heart and for the rest of the day she did everything in her power to ensure that Charlotte had company. Half the archaeology department went to the cinema with them that evening. The following evening Millie and her latest beau, Derek, invited Charlotte to dine with them at a local pub.

Derek was an archaeology student with a builder's licence in his back pocket, a double degree in geology and ancient history, and a blissfully practical outlook for someone bent on becoming a field archaeologist.

They found a small round table over by the window, not too sticky, not too wobbly, and settled in for the duration. Derek bought the first round of drinks and the barman went back to filling his fridges, and the pool players went back to smacking their balls around as lazy jazz played softly through oversized speakers. Not bad. Infinitely better than being at home.

'The crispy pork sounds good,' said Derek, and Millie glared meaningfully at him.

'The crispy pork does *not* sound good,' countered Millie. 'Have the beef. Or the duck. No mistaking duck for anything but duck.' Millie's face disappeared behind her menu. 'Remember what I told you about the *long pig* incident,' she muttered to Derek as quietly as she could, which wasn't nearly quietly enough.

Derek slid Charlotte a lightning glance and promptly disappeared behind his menu too. 'Where's the duck?' he said.

'Halfway down the specials list,' murmured Millie. 'Have it braised.'

'Why not barbecued?' Derek whispered back. 'You're just *assuming* he was barbecued. They could have braised him. They could have *boiled* him.'

'You're right,' muttered Millie. 'Order the vegetable combo.'

At which point Charlotte reached across the table and pulled Millie's menu down past eye level. 'Psst.'

'What?' Millie eyed her warily.

'Millie, let the poor man eat pork. I don't care if he wants it crucified, I promise I won't see it as a metaphor for him eating Gil.'

Derek's menu dipped slowly. Derek's eyes appeared, followed by a nose, very nice cheekbones, and a wide wry smile.

'I knew she was saner than you,' Derek told Millie and barely winced when Millie's menu clipped his shoulder. They were very broad shoulders. Millie might just have to keep this one.

'So what was he like?' asked Derek. 'Your fiancé.'

'He's hard to define, but if I had to sum him up I'd probably go with *useful*,' said Charlotte. Nothing but the truth.

'Useful as in "Honey, could you fix the hot water system?"' asked Millie.

'I'm sure he *could* have fixed the hot water system,' said Charlotte. 'Had it needed fixing.'

'Can't everyone?' countered Derek.

'Sadly, no,' said Charlotte.

'I dare say Gil was modest too,' said Millie, glancing pointedly at Derek.

'What?' said Derek. 'I can be modest.'

'Of course you can,' murmured Charlotte, eyeing Derek's frayed shirt collar and shaggy hair speculatively. 'Gil was a snappy dresser too, in a rustic, ready for anything kind of way.'

'Window dressing,' said Derek. 'It's the body beneath the clothes that counts and don't either of you try and tell me different.'

'Wouldn't dream of it,' said Charlotte. 'But just for your information, that was superb too.'

'Well, it would be,' said Millie. 'What with all that paddling up the river. I bet the man had fabulous upper-body definition.'

'I was a lumberjack once,' said Derek.

'Of course you were,' murmured Millie consolingly.

A youthful waitress stepped up to their table, smile at the ready as she asked them if they were ready to order.

'I'll have the pork,' said Derek. 'But could I have it beaten first?'

'Chef runs it through a tenderiser,' said the waitress. 'You know—one of those old-fashioned washing-machine wringer things with the spikes?'

'Perfect,' said Derek.

'Unlike some things around here,' murmured Millie.

'No man is perfect,' said Derek. 'Especially in the eyes of women. A determined woman can turn even a man's *good* qualities into major flaws of character given time and motive, and half the time the motive is optional. It's just something you do.'

'There's got to be an ex-wife in your past somewhere,' murmured Charlotte. 'C'mon, Derek. Spill.'

'Never.'

'Maybe an overcritical mother,' said Millie.

'I'm an orphan,' said Derek. 'Never knew my parents. Never got adopted. Ugliest baby in the world, according to Sister Ramona.'

'That explains a lot,' murmured Millie. 'Though it doesn't explain how you got to be quite so handsome *now*. In a craggy, hard-living kind of way.'

'Thank you,' said Derek blandly.

'You're welcome.'

They finished ordering their meals. They started in on their drinks.

'Here's to the wonderful Aurora Herschoval,' said Charlotte. 'The best godmother an orphan could have.'

'Hear hear,' said Derek. 'Good for you. And here's to Useful Gil. May he be blessed with more brains in his next life.'

'*Derek!*' said Millie, aghast. 'We can't toast to that.'

'Why not?' said Derek, aiming for an expression of craggy, hard-lived innocence. 'Sweetie, he may have been handy, handsome, modest, and built like Apollo, but let's be honest here...the man got eaten.'

CHAPTER TWO

A WEEK passed, and then another, and Charlotte kept busy. She applied herself diligently, if not wholeheartedly, to her work. She considered the merits of Harold's suggestion to hit the archaeology road again for a while and came to no firm conclusion. She inherited Aurora's wealth and her Double Bay waterfront estate on Sydney Harbour.

And when it came to dead fictional fiancés, she kept right on lying.

Was it too late to tell Millie the truth about Gil? To tell everyone the truth?

The question plagued her. 'When, when, *when*?' her conscience demanded. And, 'Too late, too late, too late,' the devil kept saying smugly. Bad friend to Millie. Too late to tell the Mead that Gil had been nothing more than a figment of her imagination. That time had passed. Her detractors within the archaeology world and the university system would flay her if she did.

'What did I tell you?' they would say smugly to each other. 'I always knew she was too reckless to hold down a position of responsibility, no matter *what* pull her family name has in high places.' Then they'd shake their heads and say what a loss Charlotte's parents had been to archaeology with one breath, and castigate them for being too bold on the other. 'Crazy runs in the family,' they'd say.

'And the godmother was cut from the same cloth. Always chasing rainbows. No wonder poor Charlotte has trouble separating fantasy from reality...'

'*Charlotte!*'

A distant voice, sharp and concerned.

'What?' Charlotte blinked and there was Millie. Tortoiseshell glasses framing earnest hazel eyes set in a heart-shaped face.

'You didn't hear me come in. You didn't hear me calling your name.'

'Sorry,' murmured Charlotte. 'Must've been daydreaming.'

Millie winced. Probably because she thought Charlotte had been spending a little too much time in that state of late.

'What's up?' said Charlotte, determined to forestall any actual complaint about her not entirely firm hold on reality.

Millie hesitated. Millie fidgeted. Millie was not in a good place right now and Charlotte didn't quite know why. Time to ask Millie what was wrong and see if there was any way in which she could help. Good friend, Charlotte. *Good* friend.

'Don't kill me,' said Mille anxiously.

'O-kay,' said Charlotte carefully. Not quite the response she'd been expecting.

'I was only trying to help,' said Millie next.

'And?'

'And I emailed the Research Institute in PNG to see if they had a photo of Gil anywhere that they could send to you. A memento. Something tangible for you to remember him by. I, ah, signed it in your name.'

'And?' said Charlotte, with an impending sense of doom.

'And his secretary wrote back and said she'd see what she could find and was it okay to send everything to your university address. To which I said yes.'

'And?'

'And there's a huge packing box downstairs, addressed to you from PNG. I think it might be Gil's effects.'

Charlotte blinked. 'His...*effects*?'

Millie nodded. 'I swear all I asked for was a photo. I never once implied that you were his next of kin or that you wanted all his stuff. I mean, he does have other family, right? Parents and so forth.'

'Right,' said Charlotte faintly.

'And you know how to contact them, right?'

'Er...right.'

'So, do you want the box up here or in your car? At the moment it's sitting by the stairs on the ground floor.'

Charlotte blinked again. 'I think I need to see it.' Hopefully the trip down two flights of stairs would give her time to *think*.

A dozen flights of stairs would have been better.

All too soon, Charlotte and Millie stood at the bottom of the stairs, staring at a large removalist box with her name and university address on it. A nervous giggle escaped Charlotte. She countered by putting one hand to her mouth and the other hand to her elbow. The Standing Thinker pose.

'So...' said Millie. 'Where do you want it?'

'I'm thinking we take it upstairs for now,' Charlotte muttered finally. 'I may need to send it...on.'

There was no lift in the building.

'I'll get a trolley,' said Millie. 'And Derek.'

'Thanks,' murmured Charlotte, still staring at the box.

* * *

They got the box upstairs and into Charlotte's office eventually. Neither Millie nor Derek seemed of a mind to linger. They fled.

Charlotte tried ignoring the box, at first. That didn't go well.

The compulsion to open the box and find out exactly what the good souls at the PNG Research Institute had seen fit to send her took control. A pair of office scissors later and the flaps on top of the box sprung open. Tentatively, Charlotte folded them back.

The first thing she saw was a man's collared business shirt, the really expensive wash-n-wear kind of dress shirt that didn't need ironing and always looked fabulous. Size: Large. Colour: Ivory. A hat came next, an honest to God, Indiana Jones-style Akubra that looked as if it had been trampled by a herd of elephants and then dragged through a river backwards. Well-worn jeans came next, the kind that had earned their faded knees and ragged hems the old-fashioned way. Then some scuffed leather walking boots and thick socks. No other smalls whatsoever. Commando Indy.

Books came next, an extensive library of botany books and journals. Then came file upon file of research papers in haphazard order. A laptop had been tucked in between them. There was a round wall clock that still worked but told the wrong time. A handful of USB storage devices had been sealed inside an envelope. She unearthed a plastic takeaway container full of the stuff one might find in an office drawer. There were no photos.

The last thing she pulled from the box was a door tag with the name Dr G Tyler printed on it, the lettering no-nonsense black on a white background. A similar contraption graced her own door, and almost every other door in this building.

Charlotte stood back, ran unsteady hands through already wayward curls and surveyed the items strewn around her. She didn't need to be an archaeologist to know what she had here.

Heaven help her, they'd sent her someone's office.

The first thing to do was not panic.

So what if Dr G Tyler was going to be mighty unhappy when he discovered that his research wasn't where he left it? That someone had packed up the contents of his office and shipped it off to…her? Belongings could be returned. Repacked and returned to sender with a brief note of apology for the confusion. Email! His computer would have his email address on it. She could send him an email and let him know that his office was on its way back to him. Of course, said email might not be received by him given that she also had his laptop, but surely the man would be accessing his emails from another computer. He'd be doing that, surely?

Unless the man was dead.

'I did *not* wish you dead,' she muttered. 'Please don't be dead. You'll get your stuff back, I promise. Or if you *do* happen to be dead, I'll make sure this gets to your family.' Only…what if he had a wife? Children! 'I'll explain *everything*,' she said fervently. No way would she allow G Tyler to emerge from this mess with a reputation as a cheating, lying husband with a mistress on the side. 'I *will* come clean.'

I promise.

Greyson Tyler wasn't an unreasonable man. He understood what it took to get scientific research done in remote locations. He tolerated inefficiency in others, applied leeway when needed, and pressure when needed too. He took his time, worked his way calmly and methodically through the red tape associated with such endeavours, and eventually he got his way. He always got his way, eventually, and he always got results.

He'd known he was tempting fate when he'd boxed his office effects up, ready to ship back to Australia, and hadn't personally delivered the box into the hands of the freight carrier. He'd thought twice before leaving that task up to Mariah, the latest in a long line of temporary secretaries. Mariah had potential. She might even make a halfway decent administrative assistant one day. Presuming, of course, that she mastered the art of punctuality.

He'd left her a note with the name of the freight company he wanted to use. He'd left 'Please Send To' details right there on her desk. He'd set his misgivings aside and departed on his final field trip up-river without talking Mariah through the process.

Bad move.

She *had* used the freight company he'd recommended, that was something.

But she swore blue that she'd never seen the mailing address Grey had left for her, so when the email from his fiancée had come in—asking for a photo of him—and said fiancée had also been agreeable to Mariah sending the rest of his things her way, well… Problem solved.

A chain of events that showed initiative and even sounded halfway reasonable, except for one small anomaly.

He didn't have a fiancée.

He did, however, have a shipping address, and a phone call to the University of Sydney's information line gave him a work phone number for his beloved intended.

Charlotte Greenstone was her name, and she was an Associate Professor of Archaeology, no less.

He'd never heard of her.

He was prepared to be considerate, given that there had clearly been a mistake, and that she presumably did have a fiancé in these parts with a similar name to his. He was prepared to give her some leeway when it came to the return of his possessions. And if she *didn't* have his office effects already in her possession, he could warn her that they'd be arriving soon and that he'd be by to collect them.

He'd just completed his final set of measurements. Three years' worth of research all done, which meant he could be out of here.

Not a moment too soon in the opinion of some.

He could be back in Sydney by tomorrow. He could collect his office contents, head for his catamaran moored on the Hawkesbury River just north of Sydney, find a suitably secluded cove to anchor in, and analyse his data from there. His cat was ocean-going and had all the amenities he would need. He'd lived on her before.

He could kiss goodbye lawlessness and brutality and live for a time in a place where one's possessions had a halfway chance of staying *in* one's possession.

Tempting.

He put a call through to Charlotte Greenstone's number and got her answering machine. A warm and surprisingly youthful voice told him to leave a message and she'd get back to him.

It was six-thirty on a Friday afternoon, Sydney time. Chances were that Associate Professor Charlotte had skipped for the weekend already, which meant the soonest he could reasonably expect a call back was Monday morning, her time. By which time he could be *at* her office collecting *his* office. He could be on the catamaran, set up and working, by Monday afternoon.

Aspro Charlotte had left a mobile phone number on her

answering machine for urgent requests. Probably a good idea to check with her before he left PNG that she hadn't turned his belongings around already.

This time when he called he got her in person. Same smooth velvety voice. The kind of voice that slid down a man's spine and reminded him that he hadn't had a woman in a while. He cleared his throat, nonplussed by the notion that he'd responded to the voice of a woman his mother's age. Associate professorship took time.

'Hello?' she said again, and damned if his body didn't respond again and to hell with her advancing years.

'Professor Greenstone, my name's Grey Tyler,' he said hurriedly. '*Dr* Grey Tyler, botanist. I'm calling from PNG.'

Silence at that.

'We're not acquainted but I'm hoping you can help me.' There. He was politeness itself. His mother would be proud. Charlotte Greenstone would be impressed. 'I'm based in Port Moresby, although I spend a lot of time travelling between research sites in the country's interior. I've just returned from such a trip to find that the contents of my office have been shipped to you by mistake.'

'Yes,' she said faintly. 'Yes, Dr Tyler, your belongings arrived today. Did you get my email?'

'Email?' he echoed.

'The one I sent you from your computer in the hope that you were still accessing your emails,' she said. 'Although judging by the several hundred emails that subsequently popped *in* to your inbox, I wasn't all that hopeful.'

'You accessed my *computer*?' What about his password protection? The supposedly unassailable drive he kept his research files on? *'How?'*

'Actually, it was the IT guy who did the accessing,' she confessed. 'He's very good. And we only accessed your emails and we only did that to get your contact details. I tried calling the number in your signature line but you no longer seem to have a functioning phone.'

'Forget the phone, you accessed my *computer*?'

'Dr Tyler, why don't you just tell me where you want your box sent?' Not so mellow now, that gorgeous voice. Impatience had crept in, firing up his own.

'Nowhere. Don't send it anywhere. I'll pick it up on Monday.'

'What?' For some reason, Charlotte Greenstone didn't sound overly enamoured of the notion.

'Monday,' he repeated. 'Preferably Monday morning.'

'No!' she said. 'That plan's really not going to work for me.'

'Then outline a course of action that will,' he countered. 'I need my office back, Professor. I've work to do.'

'Will you be in Sydney on Sunday?' she asked.

'I hope to be.' Plane ticket willing.

'I'll go and get your box from work tomorrow, Dr Tyler. You can pick it up from my private address on Sunday or I will drop it in to wherever you're staying. Does that suit?'

Decisive woman. And yes, it suited him just fine. She gave him her address. They arranged a collection time.

And when he got off the phone, the memory of her voice stayed with him and refused to go away.

'Keep it simple,' Charlotte said to herself for the umpteenth time that morning. Sunday morning, to be exact. Sunday morning at Aurora's, no less, for that was the pickup address she'd given Grey Tyler.

Dr Greyson Tyler was a water weed control specialist. She'd discerned this from the research papers he'd authored and co-authored. Lots of them, and he didn't bother submitting to the smaller journals either. Quality work, all the way.

Maybe she'd read one of his papers years ago and filed his name and that larger than life persona of his somewhere in the dim recesses of her mind. Maybe that was why, when she'd needed an absent fictional fiancé, she'd picked the name Tyler, only she'd used Gil for a first name instead of Greyson. Greyson being far too formidable a name for any fiancé, fictional or otherwise.

Not that it mattered, for within an hour his box would be gone and so would he, and after that there would be no more fictional fiancés *ever* and certainly no doing away with them. 'This I pledge,' she said fervently.

By the time the doorbell finally rang, a good two hours later than expected, Aurora's house was spotless and Charlotte had taken to fretting that Dr Greyson Tyler wouldn't come for his box at all today but would turn up at her workplace tomorrow, thus exposing the entire fictional fiancé debacle to all and sundry, thus sealing her reputation as a complete and utter nutter, and ruining her professional reputation along with it.

She opened the door hastily and found herself staring straight at a broad and muscled chest. She dragged her gaze upwards and finally came to his face. A tough, weathered face, not young and not yet old. Strong black brows framed eyes the colour of bitter coffee, easy on the milk. His hair colour hovered somewhere between that of eyebrows and eyes. He had excellent facial bone structure and an exceptionally fine mouth. A mouth well worth staring at. She had a feeling she'd stared at it before, but where?

Eventually the edge of it tilted up a little and she remembered her manners and stepped back politely and fixed a smile to her own face.

'I'm looking for Professor Greenstone,' he said, his voice a perfect match for the rest of him. Rough around the edges but with a fine baritone centre. Gil had also been in possession of such a voice. A voice to make a woman swoon.

'That would be me,' she said. 'Dr Tyler, I presume?'

'Yes.' His eyes had narrowed. His mouth twisted wryly. 'You're young for an associate professor.'

'My parents were archaeologists,' she said. 'I was raised by my godmother, who was also an archaeologist. I grew up chasing lost cities and ate breakfast, lunch and dinner at tables covered in maps. I was working dig sites by the time I turned six. I had a head start.'

'Sounds like quite a childhood.'

'Worked for me,' she murmured, although it hadn't exactly provided her with an altogether firm grip on reality. Not when there were so many ancient and different realities to choose from. Where *had* she seen his face before? A glossy magazine ad for something sumptuously male and decadently expensive? A magazine article? 'World's Sexiest Scientists', perhaps? Oh, hell. *New Scientist.*

Charlotte sped back in time to a hospital waiting room, and an old waiting room copy of *New Scientist* magazine with an article on water weeds in it. There'd been a picture of the weeds. A picture of this man. She'd skimmed the article while waiting for the specialist to finish with Aurora.

Gil Tyler—fictional fiancé extraordinaire—hadn't been a figment of her imagination at all.

The parts of Gil that hadn't been based on movie superheroes and a long dead father had been based on *this* man.

'Your box is here in the hall,' she said, stepping back and opening wide the huge slab of petrified oak that doubled as a door. 'I taped it back up for your convenience but you're welcome to go through it while you're here if you want to. It's all there.'

The good doctor stepped into the hall and eyed the box balefully.

'Okay, let me rephrase,' she murmured. 'Everything they sent me is in that box, and I'm really sorry if it's not all there.' Charlotte's dismay hit a new low at the thought of Greyson Tyler losing important possessions on her account. 'Extremely sorry.'

Greyson Tyler studied her intently. Finally he put his hand to the back pocket of his trousers, stretching fabric tight across places no well-brought-up woman should be looking. Charlotte averted her gaze and watched the unfolding of the paper instead. He held it out to her. 'I understand you have a fiancé working in PNG and that he and I share a surname.'

Charlotte took the paper from those long strong fingers and reluctantly scanned the email printed on it. The request was a simple one for a photo of the late TJ (Gil) Tyler, botanist, if there was one about. Just as Millie had explained it to her.

'Thing is, PNG is a small place,' he continued conversationally. 'Especially for scientists. I know my colleagues. Your fiancé wasn't one of them. I checked the records. No sign of him there either.'

'It's complicated,' she said, queen of the understatement. 'This email, for instance. Unfortunately, one of my work colleagues sent it on my behalf, without my knowledge, but with the very best intentions.' Charlotte felt herself shrinking beneath that penetrating dark gaze. 'To be fair, the information I gave her about my fiancé wasn't quite correct.'

'Exactly how wrong was it?' he asked silkily.

'You mean on a scale of one to ten with one being almost correct and ten being a whopping great lie with a momentum all its own?'

'If you like.' He could be droll, this man, when he wasn't so busy being stern.

'Ten.'

'And the lie?'

Charlotte shoved her hands in her pockets and moved past him, back through the door so she could stand on the top step of the portico and look out over Aurora's immaculately kept grounds. 'My godmother was dying,' she said, her voice surprisingly even. 'She was the closest thing to family I'd ever had and she was worried about leaving me alone in the world. I invented a fiancé. A botanist, working in PNG. His name was Thaddeus Jeremiah Gilbert Tyler.'

'You named your fiancé Thaddeus?'

'It was 3 a.m. I wasn't exactly thinking straight. Yes, I named him Thaddeus.'

'Go on,' he said.

'Aurora lasted another month. Gil became a regular topic of conversation.'

'Gil?' he queried.

'Thaddeus.' Charlotte closed her eyes, shook her head. Felt her lips curve in memory of some of those late night conversations with Aurora. 'You were right about the name. No one called him Thaddeus except his mother when she was annoyed with him. I called him Gil.'

'Go on.'

'There's not much more to tell,' she murmured, coming back to the present with a start and shooting Greyson an apologetic sideways glance. 'Aurora died. Two days later I did away with Gil, only by that time someone had told my work colleagues about him so the lie continued to grow.

Everyone now thinks I'm mourning both Aurora *and* a fiancé. My colleague Millie went in search of a photo of Gil that I could put up somewhere. To help me grieve, or maybe to help me rejoice in the time I'd spent with him. Something like that.'

'And then?'

'Someone in PNG sent me an office.' Charlotte risked another glance in his direction. Greyson Tyler was staring back at her as if reluctantly, unaccountably fascinated. 'And here you are. I'm not usually this…' She stopped, lost for words.

'Batty?' he said. 'Irresponsible?'

'Like I said, your belongings are in the box in the hall-way,' she muttered. 'I'll reimburse you for the cost of your airfare and your time. I'll make a considerable donation to your research fund. There won't be any more confusion. I'll be telling my boss and my colleagues the truth of the matter tomorrow. Your PNG colleagues too, if that's what it takes. And then there'll be no more lies.' No more good reputation or friends either, but the devil would have his due and Charlotte only had herself to blame. 'You're not married, are you?'

'No.'

'Excellent,' she said faintly.

He'd heard madder explanations. Not often, but it could be done. Grey vacillated between wanting to comfort the apologetic Charlotte and wanting to strangle her.

'Excuse me for a moment,' he muttered, and headed back inside towards the box. The tape gave way easily beneath his hands. Probably his temper showing. Clothes came first and he tossed them aside as befitting their im-portance. Hard copies of various research papers came next—it looked as if they were all there. He pulled out his laptop and his back-up drives. Reference books, all of them. It was all there.

'What's missing?' Associate Professor Charlotte had joined him, she of the velvet voice and excessive imagination. The horror of losing work was something she appeared to understand.

'Nothing,' he muttered. 'I've decided not to strangle you.'

'You're a rare and generous man,' she said.

'I know.'

'Humility too.'

Sexy velvet voices could be dry as dust and *still* make his blood stir. Who knew? 'Let's not get carried away.' A warning, and not just for her. He started piling books and references back in the box. The good Charlotte retrieved his clothes and handed them to him at the end.

'I've packing tape in the library,' she said, and Grey glanced down the hallway towards the innards of the house. The library. Of course. It was the kind of house that ran to libraries, a billiards room, conservatory, tennis court, pool and gym. Family estate, he figured. Unless she'd made her fortune *before* embarking on a career in archaeology. Possibly as a novelist. *Thaddeus.* Grey snorted. Possibly not.

'Don't worry about the tape. You'd do better worrying about how your work colleagues are going to react when you tell them there's no fiancé, dead or otherwise. You *do* realise that your personal and probably your professional integrity is going to be called into question? Assuming you had some in the first place?'

Charlotte's eyes flashed. Temper temper, and it looked very fine on her but she held her tongue. Not a big woman, by any means, but fragile wasn't a word he would have used to describe her either. Slender, she was that, but she had some generous curves and an abundance of wavy black hair currently tied back in a messy ponytail. She also possessed a heart-shaped face and a creamy complexion that would put Snow White to shame. A wanton's mouth. One that turned a man's mind towards feasting on it. Big doe eyes, with dark curling lashes. 'Are you *really* an archaeologist?'

'Yes,' she said grimly. 'And before you start making comparisons between me and a certain tomb-raiding gun-toting female gaming character, I've heard them all before.'

And been neither flattered nor amused, he deduced. He hefted the box. She held the door open for him.

'Do you need any travel directions to wherever it is you're heading?' she asked. 'Provisions, so you can be on your way? Can of drink? Box of crackers?'

'How did he die?' asked Grey. 'This *fiancé*.'

'Heroically. Very honourably.' No need for details, decided Charlotte. Details were bad. 'It was the least I could do.'

'Has anyone ever told you that your grip on reality's a little shaky?' he murmured.

'Hello,' she said dryly. 'Archaeologist. It's part of the job description.'

A smile from him then. One that chased the sternness right out of him and left devilry in its place. Charlotte stared, drinking in the details. Greyson Tyler was a dangerously handsome man when he wanted to be. Handsomer than Gil.

'Hnh,' she said.

Greyson's smile widened. 'You'll let me know if anything else of mine happens your way?' he said.

'Of course.'

His gaze had shifted to her lips and his smile was fading.

Something else started moving into place. Something fierce and heated.

'Will you be staying in Sydney long?' she all but stuttered. 'Is there a contact number or address I can reach you at?'

'I'll be here for a while,' he said. 'And yes, there is.' Not that he seemed inclined to part with that information. 'This predicament you've got yourself in...'

'Which one?'

'The fake dead fiancé. The lie that just keeps getting bigger.'

'Oh. Right. That predicament.'

'There *is* a way around it without necessarily having to come clean about the lie,' he offered. 'You'd be indebted to me, of course, but I figure that's a small price to pay, and I do happen to know of a way in which you could repay me. All strictly above board and harmless, more or less.'

'What are you suggesting?'

'Resurrection.'

'Pardon?'

'You're not the only one with an ex-fiancé,' he murmured. 'Although mine happens to be real and she's not yet dead. She's also been welcome at my parents' place since childhood. She's part of the family, the daughter my mother never had.'

'No wonder you went paddling up the Sepik afterwards,' said Charlotte. 'Who ended the engagement?'

'I did.'

'Were you heartbroken?'

'Do I look heartbroken?'

'I really don't know you well enough to tell. Was *she* heartbroken?'

'The engagement was a mistake,' said Greyson Tyler curtly. 'Sarah wants a conventional husband. One who's home more often than not. One who's ready to settle down and start a family.'

'How unusual,' murmured Charlotte and wore Greyson's steel-eyed glare with equanimity.

'That's not me. I don't know if it'll ever be me, only Sarah—' He gave a tiny shake of his head. 'Sarah wants to pick up where we left off. With my family's blessing.'

'You're a big boy. Just say no.'

'I have. No one seems to believe me. No one *wants* to believe me. I'm running out of gentle *ways* of saying no, but maybe you can help me. Maybe I can help you.'

'How?'

'I need a woman at my side for a family barbecue next weekend. Preferably one who's ecstatic about me, my way of life, and what I can give her—which is, needless to say, not a lot. A free spirit who can make Sarah and my family believe that everyone should just move on. In return, I'll play your back-from-the-dead fiancé whom you can produce, bicker with, and shortly thereafter cut loose in good conscience. No need to admit your original lie at all. Do we have an agreement?'

Charlotte hesitated, a twinge of something that felt a whole lot like wariness riding her hard. An ex-fiancée who wanted Greyson still, maybe even loved him still. A barbecue at which he—they—would dash her hopes as gently as they could. Except that there would be nothing *gentle* about his ex-fiancée coming face to face with proof positive that Greyson was indeed serious about Sarah needing to move on. 'Are you sure you wouldn't rather have another shot at discussing this between yourselves?' she said. 'Somewhere nice and private? Bring out the steely resolve. Maybe you could say no louder this time.'

'I have,' he said darkly. 'It's not working. Bringing you along might.'

And still Charlotte hesitated.

'Never mind.' His face was closed, his voice clipped. 'Bad idea.'

'Wait,' she said tentatively. 'How long is it since you broke up?'

'Two years.'

'And you really think there's no other way to dissuade her?'

'Look, I don't want to hurt Sarah. I don't want her to feel that she's no longer welcome at my parents' place. I just want her to *see*...'

See being the operative word.

'Couldn't you just *tell* her that you've found someone else?'

Silence from Greyson Tyler. Silence and a bleak black glare. 'You already have,' said Charlotte slowly. 'And now you have to produce her.'

Bingo.

'You're as reality challenged as I am,' she said next.

'Hardly.'

'Oh, give it time.'

Another glare from the behemoth. The one who was offering to help with *her* fiancé problem if she would only help him with his. 'I don't do animosity,' she said firmly. 'If we do this, we do it with as little *hurt* as possible.'

'Agreed.'

'You arrive at my office tomorrow and things seem a little strained between us,' she continued. 'I can take it from there. I attend your family barbecue next weekend, thus providing Sarah with visible evidence that you've moved on, and you can take it from there.'

'Agreed,' he said. 'So do we have a deal?'

More lies aside, Greyson Tyler's suggestion really did seem to solve a multitude of problems. 'We do.'

CHAPTER THREE

THERE was something about waiting for the eminent Dr Greyson Tyler to arrive at her workplace that set Charlotte's jaw to clenching. Correction: the waiting part wasn't the problem. He set her on edge regardless.

She'd been expecting a scientist—a no-nonsense man of formidable intellect and optional physical prowess. Instead she'd encountered Action Man in the flesh, a man so physically fine, quick thinking, and composed in the face of complications that a woman couldn't *help* but wonder what life would be like with a man like that in it. Not steady and predictable, she wagered. Anything but.

Not boring or empty either.

Greyson Tyler was a living, breathing reminder of a life she'd left behind in her quest for inner contentment, security, and peace of mind. Hardly his fault that for all her efforts to settle down, the jury was still out on whether staying in Sydney was making her happy. Where the hell *was* he?

Charlotte had plenty of work to be going on with. Satellite images to look at for a dig site that showed promise. Third-year essays to correct, a lecture to prepare, and no patience this morning for any of it. Greyson was twenty minutes late already. He'd been late yesterday too. The man had a punctuality problem.

That or he'd decided that he didn't need a fake fiancée after all.

Rapping on her open door signalled a visitor and Charlotte turned to see who it was.

Millie.

'Morning tea time,' said Millie.

Indeed it was, and the perfect time for introducing a formerly dead pretend fiancé to her colleagues, but Greyson Tyler did not put in an appearance during the break.

Gil would have *never* been so tawdry.

But when she and Millie walked back along the corridor after the break, Charlotte discovered she had a visitor. A visitor who felt at home enough to plant his rear in her chair and his boots on her filing cabinet while he browsed through one of her archaeology journals.

Millie stopped. Stared.

Greyson Tyler glanced up, nodded to Millie, and favoured Charlotte with a deliciously slow smile; an invitation to come play with him if she dared.

'You made it,' she said icily.

'Of course.' Greyson's smile widened. Lucifer would have been proud. 'I always do. Eventually.'

Millie was still staring. Charlotte figured introductions were in order. 'Millie, this is Tyler. He arrived home yesterday, rather unexpectedly. Tyler, meet Millie. Historian, map muse, and friend.'

'But…' Millie slid Charlotte a lightning glance before returning her attention to the figure in the chair. 'You're not dead.'

'No,' said Grey. 'Well spotted.'

'Apparently there was some confusion on that score,' murmured Charlotte.

'But…that's *wonderful*!' said Millie on firmer footing.

'I'm glad *someone* thinks so,' said Grey.

Greyson Tyler played the part of antagonist exceptionally well, decided Charlotte. The man was a natural.

With fluid grace, Greyson found his feet and held out his hand towards Millie, his smile a study in warmth and friendliness. 'Charlotte's had a rough few months, what with one thing and another,' he offered in that chocolate coated baritone. 'Thanks for helping her out.'

Millie shook his hand as if awestruck. Millie blushed, caught Charlotte's eye and blushed some more.

'How long are you planning on staying angry with him?' Millie asked her.

'A while,' said Charlotte.

'Good luck with that.' Millie slid another helpless smile in Greyson's direction. 'I'm so glad you weren't eaten by marauding tribesmen,' she told him. 'Did you manage to prevent the village daughters from being kidnapped as well?'

Grey blinked. A muscle ticced beside his mouth. 'Yes,' he said finally.

'Hard to stay angry with a hero,' said Millie.

'Oh, it's not that hard,' said Charlotte.

Stifling a grin, Millie left.

Charlotte shut the door in Millie's wake, took a steadying breath, and turned to face the man currently dominating her office space. His charming friendly smile had disappeared. The formidable Greyson Tyler had returned and he seemed out of sorts.

'I think that went well, don't you?' she said lightly.

'You told them I'd been *eaten*? By *cannibals*?'

'Not *you*,' she said soothingly. 'Gil. And of course nothing was ever *certain*.'

'And they *believed* you?'

'It happens,' said Charlotte.

'Sixty years ago. Maybe.'

'What's a few decades? Besides, it's a moot point. You're back, alive and kicking and about to become my ex-fiancé. You need to embrace the bigger picture here.'

'I'll refrain from mentioning what I think you need,' he said.

'Greyson, all is well. Your work here is done and I do sincerely thank you for it,' she said earnestly. 'I'm still prepared to attend this barbecue with you but if you'd rather not… If you've decided you no longer need a fictional fiancée, or that I'm too irresponsible and that no one's going to believe we're an item anyway, it doesn't have to happen. Your call.'

Greyson's gaze grew intent. Whatever other flaws he had, there was no denying that the man could focus intently on something when he wanted to. 'You welshing on me, Greenstone? I come through for you and you don't reciprocate? Is that how you repay your debts?'

'I didn't say that,' she said evenly, never mind the erratic beating of her heart. 'I'm simply giving you the opportunity to reconsider your options. Fictional fiancés are more trouble than they're worth—trust me on this. I'm doing you a favour by pointing this out.'

'You're very kind,' he said smoothly. 'I propose an experiment. Something that lets me decide if bringing you along to meet the family is going to work.' He drew closer. Close enough for her to feel the heat in that big lean body of his. Close enough for her to catch the scent of him. Tantalisingly male, undeniably appealing. And then there was his mouth. Such a tempting mouth.

'Kiss me,' he murmured, and her eyes flew to his.

'Excuse me?'

'That's the experiment,' he said. 'If there's no chemistry we're square. Finished.' His lips moved closer. 'Through.' Greyson's lips brushed hers, and Charlotte drew a ragged breath. 'No barbecue.' And then his lips were on hers, warm and coaxing, not demanding, not yet.

Teasing, those lips of his.

Practised, the hand that came up to cradle her skull and position her for deeper invasion, only he didn't invade, not yet.

Torture first.

Slow, savouring torture as his tongue traced her lips, only to withdraw once she'd parted them for him. His lips playing at the edge of her upper lip now while she gasped for breath and clutched at his forearms for balance, only to have his skin beneath her palms play havoc with those senses too.

His eyes stayed open, observing, always observing, coolly watching her come apart beneath his ministrations.

And then he closed his eyes, slid his mouth over hers and simply took.

He wasn't supposed to devour her, thought Grey with what little coherent thought he had left. He'd only meant to test her, not match her uninhibited response and raise the stakes by tabling a whole lot of mindless hunger as well. Too long without a woman, that had to be it, as he buried his hands in her silken tresses, his lips not leaving hers as he took what he needed and what he would have by way of supplication and desire.

She didn't protest. The ragged husky sounds she made weren't sounds of protest. The way she gave her mouth over to him, as if savouring every last drop of his invasion, wasn't objection. She wrapped her arms around his neck as he lifted her up, both hands on her buttocks urging her legs around his waist and she obliged him and kept right on kissing him. Another gasp escaped her, one he echoed as hardness found a home. Too many clothes. Way too much urgency. He wasn't a small man, not by any means. He usually had more care for a woman's comfort. He usually made sure to harness his strength and turn it to tenderness.

There was no tenderness here, just sensuality unleashed and Grey wanted more, and more again, and Charlotte gave willingly. Locking her legs around his waist she rode his hard length through two sets of clothing and slayed him with her abandon.

It was Charlotte who guided them back to reality.

'Enough,' she muttered, and when he bared his teeth against her cheek on a groan of pure frustration, 'Greyson, stop.' Grey's body protested but he gentled his hold on her and held still while she nestled her forehead into the curve of his shoulder, her body trembling as she sought to master her desire and his. 'I'm not saying no.' Her lips and breath were warm against the skin of his neck, that sex-soaked voice doing nothing to aid her cause. 'I'm saying not here, and not now. Let's not be insane.'

Rich, coming from her.

But he slid her down gently, let her find her feet and step away and put some distance between them. One foot and then another until reason and caution returned.

'What just happened?' she asked warily.

'You want the standard biology lecture or shall we just summarise and say that the dopamine and adrenaline kicked in? Hard.'

'In other words, just an ordinary everyday biological response to sexual stimulus,' she murmured and leaned against her workbench. 'Nothing more.'

'Exactly.' Thank God for analytical minds. 'I may be a little overdue for release in that particular arena. I've been out of touch with female company for a while. Nothing for you to worry about. Nothing I can't control.'

She sent him a look, dark amusement running deep.

'So I'll pick you up Sunday morning at around eleven thirty,' he said, ignoring his growing unease when it came to spending any amount of time with the delectably loopy Charlotte Greenstone. 'It'll take us an hour to get there. Barbecue starts at one. I figure we can be gone by three.'

'You're sure about this?' She folded her arms across her slim waist.

'I'm sure.' More or less.

'How would you like me dressed?'

Greyson blinked. 'Do you normally ask a man this question?'

'Normally, I can figure it out on my own. With you, all bets are off.'

He still didn't have an answer to her question.

'I'm not asking you for your colour preferences, Greyson. I'm asking you for your social status. I realise it doesn't show, but I'm not without wealth. The kind that takes generations to acquire. You want me to wear it or not?'

'Up to you,' he said with a shrug. 'My family is solidly middle class. My mother's a paediatrician and my father's a mechanical engineer currently contracted to the Australian Defence Force. My ex is a psychiatrist. We're heading for a holiday house on the banks of the Hawkesbury. It's private, sprawling, and comfortable in a totally different way from the showpiece you inhabit. There'll be good wine, home-cooked food, and enough conversation to fill any gaps. Is that enough information?'

'Plenty,' she murmured, her gaze turning speculative. 'Believe it or not, I just want to get this right and hopefully get the job you want me to do done with as little bloodshed as possible. Do you have any siblings?'

'No.'

'Anything else I should know in advance? Your ex-fiancée, Sarah. Will she be protective of you?'

'Not without analysing the situation and every possible response to it first.'

'Marvellous,' muttered Charlotte, with the lift of a sweetly pointed chin. 'You do realise that a psychiatrist will probably have a field day with me. I'm not without my eccentricities.'

'Really? Who'd have guessed?' Time to leave before he closed the distance between them and set his lips to the slender curve of her neck. 'Look at it this way, it'll give her something to do. Oh, and before I forget your what-to-wear question,' he said as he opened her office door, 'my favourite colour's green.'

CHAPTER FOUR

GREEN it was, and a vibrant tree-frog green at that, shot through with yellows and vivid reds, pinks, and purples. Okay, so maybe calling her silk spaghetti-strapped sundress green was a stretch. Maybe green was only *one* of the colours splashed on it, but it was suitably bohemian, flattering to the figure, and inviting to the touch.

The matching manilas or Portuguese slave bracelets Charlotte wore at her wrists were a particularly nice touch, considering her services for the day had been bought and paid for. Part of Aurora's eclectic collection of antiquities, the beaten brass bracelets could almost be classified as green and would hopefully give Sarah the psychiatrist something to dwell on.

Just one more reason to make Sarah reconsider whether she wanted to renew a relationship with a man whose current paramour indulged his every whim.

Tedious business, the indulging of a man's whims.

Charlotte's make-up was subtle and she'd decided against perfume. Her demeanour was obliging; she'd been practising all morning.

Time to get this over with. This task she had no taste for.

This dashing of another woman's hopes and dreams.

* * *

As far as anthropological experiments were concerned, Grey had a strong suspicion that this one was ripe for failure. Too many variables. Far too many unknowns. Social interaction between him and Charlotte had been volatile, at best. Add the pretence of a relationship, his parents, and an ex-fiancée to the mix, and the impending family barbecue had all the hallmarks of social disaster.

When he drove up Charlotte's gravelled circular driveway and she looked up from her watering of the plants beneath the portico and smiled, he groaned aloud.

He'd ordered a free-spirited woman. By Charlotte's translation, this seemed to mean a golden-limbed goddess wrapped in a slip of a dress that dazzled the eyes. A wild profusion of wavy black hair tumbled to her waist and showcased her dress to perfection. Completing the outfit were flat sandals that looked suspiciously like ballet slippers, and huge grey-tinted sunglasses courtesy of someone's Elton John collection.

Bring on the circus.

He brought the car to a standstill. A hired, late-model four door Toyota, nothing special, hopefully reliable. Charlotte cut the tap, rolled up the hose on its reel and tucked hose and reel into a low cupboard, seemingly built for that purpose. Money, and lots of it, thought Grey. Enough to make conforming to society's rules optional, never mind the tidy hose arrangement. It might be worth discussing a few rules of engagement before they reached his parents' place. Spell out just what he expected of an unconventional yet perfectly acceptable partner in deception.

Charlotte collected up a handbag and wrap from beside the front door. She made sure the door was locked and made her way towards the Toyota. She bent down and smiled at him through the window, showing even white teeth and an abundance of free-spirited cleavage.

She made no move to get in the car.

Gritting his own teeth, Grey slid from the car, strode around it and hauled the door open for her. 'Why couldn't you have been a feminist?' he said.

'Why on earth would I want to be a feminist?' she muttered as she slid into the seat and waited for him to close the door. 'Where's the power in that?'

He shut the door. Gently. He got back in the car.

'You'll notice I'm not currently wearing a bra,' she said briskly.

Oh, he'd noticed.

'That's because the bodice of this dress fulfils that function, not because it's a feminist convention of the late last century.'

'Noted,' he said.

'I would, however, have made a wonderful suffragette,' she told him. 'There are *many* principles of equality that I adhere to.'

'Wonderful,' he said dryly. 'Power-based selective feminism. Can't wait to experience that.'

'Oh, I dare say you already have,' she murmured. 'How long were you engaged?'

'One year. And Sarah opens her own doors.'

'As is her choice,' said Charlotte magnanimously. 'Did you live with her?'

'No. I spent most of that time in PNG. In my defence, Sarah knew I'd committed to a three year project there *before* we became engaged.'

'Perhaps she thought she could tolerate the wait,' said Charlotte. 'And discovered otherwise.'

'Yes,' he said heavily, and won several points for honesty. 'That's pretty much what happened.'

Not a comfortable topic of conversation for Greyson Tyler, decided Charlotte. Plenty of skeletons in that cupboard.

'Sarah's a smart woman,' he continued. 'Capable. Loyal. Lovely. I want her to be happy. I want her to realise that calling off our engagement was a good decision and that one day she'll meet someone who *can* fulfil all her needs, not just some of them.'

'Idealistic,' murmured Charlotte.

'Practical,' he countered.

'If you say so. You know what's interesting when you speak of your Sarah?' said Charlotte. 'You never speak of passion. Or longing. Or needing to wake up beside her. Did you never feel that? Not even in the beginning?'

Grey stayed stubbornly silent.

'I see,' she said gently. 'Then I guess she *is* better off without you.'

They drove the next twenty kilometres in silence.

'So when did we meet?' asked Charlotte, determinedly breaking the silence.

'Three months ago when I was in Brisbane for a conference. I stayed a fortnight longer than planned because of you. We kept in touch. How does that sound?'

'Plausible. I'm liking the implied passion. Let's face it; you're not offering commitment, progeny, or fiscal support. There's got to be *something* in it for me.'

'There is. A back-from-the-dead fiancé who suffered the ignominy of almost being eaten by cannibals.'

'Something else,' she said, not above a little needling of her own. 'I'm thinking that if I really was the free-spirited type, I'd probably only want you for the sex. Outrageously intimate sex of the most delectable kind. The kind of passionate tour de force a woman would go out of her way to

encounter.' Charlotte lifted her sunglasses and favoured
him with a sultry glance. 'How does that sound?'

'I've no complaints,' he said gruffly.

'Excellent,' she murmured. 'I *do* hope you can keep
your end of the pretence up.'

'It's up.' God, what was it about this woman's voice
that had him reacting like an oversexed schoolboy? Grey
suffered that knowing gaze of hers drifting down his body
in silence. He suffered the lift of her elegant eyebrow and
the tiny tilt of generously curved lips.

'Stop it,' he muttered.

'Practice makes perfect,' she said airily. 'I'm a method
actor.'

He put the radio on, a man in need of a diversion. 'Tell
me about your work,' he said, and then just as quickly
decided against hearing it. Given the effect of her voice
on his body, it was probably best if she didn't speak at all.
'No. I've changed my mind. Don't speak. Take a nap or
something. Pretend you had a tiring night.'

'I *did* have a tiring night,' she said. 'I dreamed of
you.'

Greyson Tyler quite unknowingly brought out the worst in
her, decided Charlotte as they drove up a steep and winding track to his parents' weekender on the river. Tall gums
and rocky undergrowth stretched before them and a vast
river flowed behind them, placid and serene. None of it
could stop the butterflies from starting up in her stomach.
None of it could match the man beside her when it came
to arresting views. He'd dressed casually in old jeans and
a white linen shirt with a round neck. The shirt *could*
have looked effeminate, but not on those shoulders, and
not with that face.

No, with those shoulders and that face and that lean

and tight rear end of his, the metro shirt served only to emphasise the blatant masculinity of the body beneath.

'Ready?' he asked gruffly.

'Ready,' she said with far more confidence than the situation warranted. 'Just as soon as you open the car door.'

He got out and came round to her side of the car and opened the door. He put his hand out to assist her graceful exit. He even managed to hide his impatience with the whole antiquated process.

Almost.

'Thank you, Greyson,' she said magnanimously as she flowed out of the car and into his arms, one hand still in his and one hand covering his heart as she pressed her lips to that strong square jaw. 'You'll figure out this game yet.'

'I already have,' he murmured. 'It's about torture, and touch, and it's dangerous.' His mouth hovered over hers. His eyes promised retribution. 'Don't say I didn't warn you.'

'And a gentleman is born.' Charlotte smiled in slow challenge, but peripheral movement made her glance beyond Greyson. A trim, well-preserved older woman had come out onto the deck of the house and stood watching. 'I think your mother's watching us.'

'Good,' he murmured, and kissed her. Not swiftly or perfunctorily, but with a sensual abandon that a mother probably didn't need to see.

'How am I doing so far on the led-astray-by-passion front?' he murmured when he'd finished with her.

'Quite well,' she offered, her words little more than a strangled squeak. 'Mind you, Gilbert would never have subjected me to such kisses in front of his mother. Gil had more sense.'

'Pity he wasn't *real*,' said Greyson silkily.

Cheap shot. So was the hand she deliberately let brush across the well-packed front of his jeans as she sailed past him and summoned up what she hoped was a meet-the-parents smile. Charlotte wasn't all that familiar with parents, hers or anyone else's, but mentioning this tiny snippet to Greyson *now* would only alarm him.

'You must be Charlotte,' said the older woman with a smile. Not entirely friendly, not exactly brimming with antagonism either. Greyson's mother was reserving judgement. 'We've heard a lot about you of late.'

'She's lying,' said Greyson, coming up the deck stairs behind Charlotte and putting his hand to the small of her back as he leaned in and pressed a light kiss to his mother's perfectly powdered cheek. 'I told her you lectured at the university and that she'd be meeting you on Sunday. That's *all* I told her.'

'Thus ensuring a week's worth of rampant speculation,' Greyson's mother said dryly before turning her attention back to Charlotte. 'Call me Olivia,' she said. 'And I promise to limit my curiosity to the basics. Age. Weight. Intentions…'

Charlotte twirled on the ball of her ballet slippers and ran smack bang into Greyson's chest.

'The door's that way,' he rumbled.

'I know.' She stared up at him, more than a little panicked. 'I really don't think I can do this.'

'Coward,' he said next. 'Think of your reputation.'

'I'm thinking it's shattered beyond repair anyway,' she said to his shirt covered chest.

'Then think of mine.'

'Yours seems pretty robust from where I'm standing.'

'Not if you run out on me.' Greyson put his lips to her ear. 'Please, Charlotte. Just follow my lead.'

Charlotte didn't stand a chance against a pleading Greyson Tyler. Charlotte straightened. Charlotte turned. Greyson's mother stood waiting by the sliding door into the house. Maybe intimidation came naturally to her. Or maybe Charlotte was just oversensitive when it came to mothers and wanting to impress them and knowing instinctively that she wasn't going to. 'I'm sorry,' she said, summoning a smile. 'Slight moment of panic on my part. I hadn't really thought through my intentions towards your son. Nothing to worry about though. I'm pretty sure I only want him for the sex.' Nothing but the truth.

Olivia blinked, and turned her gaze on her son.

'What?' he said blandly and ushered Charlotte through the door. 'It's a start.'

There were more people inside. Neighbours and family friends, Greyson's father. Half a dozen faces in all. Someone handed Charlotte a frosty glass of white wine, and Greyson a beer.

'Thank you,' murmured Charlotte, and promptly drained half of hers. Greyson was far more restrained. He only took one mouthful of his.

'I hope you're not lactose intolerant or allergic to seafood,' said Olivia, offering up what looked to be trout dip with rosemary flatbread on the side. 'Grey didn't seem to know.'

'I eat almost anything.' Charlotte tried a mouthful of bread and dip. Nodded as she chewed and swallowed, with every eye still firmly fixed upon her. Perhaps they were assessing her manners. Perhaps they'd overheard the sex comment. 'This is delicious. Thank you.'

Grey's mother smiled warily and moved on, offering the plate around to all her guests. Conversation resumed. Gazes drifted away. Charlotte took a deep breath. Follow his lead, Greyson had told her, only Greyson was now being talked at by a grey-haired gent who seemed wholly disinclined to include her in the conversation. Charlotte sipped at her drink more cautiously now and surveyed her surroundings. Large covered deck, an array of comfortable chairs. Stainless-steel gas barbecue groaning with sizzling seafood kebabs. Lots of older couples and one other younger woman around Charlotte and Greyson's age, standing a short distance away. A beautiful buttoned-down blonde with forest-green eyes and an air of quiet suffering.

Probably Sarah.

Bohemian, Greyson had requested of Charlotte. Free-spirited. Now she knew why. The contrast between herself and the lovely Sarah couldn't have been more extreme.

Sarah smiled tentatively at her. Charlotte smiled back.

Awkward.

'Hi, I'm Sarah,' said Sarah, in the absence of anyone else willing to make the introduction. 'The ex-fiancée.'

'Charlotte,' said Charlotte. 'Greyson's…friend.'

'I know,' said Sarah quietly, and that was that. Or maybe not, because Sarah was still speaking. 'How long have you known him?'

'A few months.'

'Not long.'

'No, not long.' Not when compared to a lifetime.

'Long enough to fall in love with him?' Sarah asked next.

'Sarah…' said Charlotte, helpless to reply in the face of the other woman's pain. Where the hell was Greyson? When did it become *her* job to break this woman's heart?

'It's okay,' said Sarah. 'Heaven knows he's easy enough to love.'

'Oh, not at the moment,' murmured Charlotte. 'At the moment I'm more of a mind to wring his neck. You?'

Sarah looked startled. Then a tiny smile appeared. The shrug of an elegant shoulder. 'Now that you mention it...'

'Exactly.' Charlotte smiled in full. 'The man's a menace.'

The man in question looked up from his discussion with the white-haired patriarch. The man in question paled a little when he saw them together. Kudos to him when he rapidly excused himself and headed their way.

About damn time.

'He minds you,' said Sarah. 'He's nervous.'

'How can you tell?' asked Charlotte.

'Shoulders,' said Sarah. 'His carriage. The way he keeps glancing at you. He can't read you. He doesn't know what you want.' Greyson's ex glanced back at Charlotte. 'That's interesting.'

'No, I'm pretty sure that's just me,' said Charlotte. 'Hard for Greyson to know what I want when I hardly know myself. I really can't blame him for that one.'

'Blame who?' said Greyson, reaching them.

'You,' said Charlotte and smothered a smile when his eyes narrowed upon her. 'It's okay though. I've decided not to. For now.'

'Good of you,' he murmured.

Sarah was watching them closely. Sarah the psychiatrist who'd known how to read Greyson since childhood and who in the space of a three-minute conversation had already unearthed Charlotte's greatest flaw. 'Sarah and I have been getting acquainted.' Charlotte bestowed on him a very level look.

Greyson bestowed on the lovely Sarah a very level look. Sarah blushed and looked away.

'I might go and see if Olivia needs any help with serving the food,' said Sarah finally, after a long and awkward pause. 'Nice meeting you, Charlotte. Grey.' And then Sarah was gone.

'Nice manners,' murmured Charlotte.

'What did she want?'

'I guess she wanted to meet me. Get it over and done with.'

'Don't underestimate her, Charlotte.' For a moment Greyson looked troubled. Concerned, and not for Sarah. 'For all Sarah's good points, she's not without claws.'

'Greyson. Sweet man.' Did he really think he was telling her something she didn't know? Charlotte smiled, really smiled at him and had the pleasure of seeing Greyson relax and smile back. 'No woman is.'

'So...' he murmured. 'You know what you're doing, then.'

'Hardly,' she murmured. 'Do you?'

'Sometimes. Right now, for example, I'm about to introduce you to my father. He's the one over there captaining the barbecue.'

But Charlotte hung back. 'Is he a Sarah fan too?'

'He's very fond of her, yes.'

Great.

'Relax. He'll be fine,' said Greyson as if reading her mind. 'And so will you.'

For an Associate Professor of Archaeology, with all the staidness the position implied, Charlotte Greenstone didn't hold back when it came to playing the part of free-spirited bohemian. She could tell a story of old bones and bring to life the heat and the dust and the excitement along with it. She could open a person up and rifle around inside until she found something they could both discuss with passion and verve. She had manners, and a great deal of charm, some of which was polished, and some of it innate.

Grey watched Charlotte bespell his father within minutes of her starting up a conversation with him about the vagaries of catapults versus castle walls. He watched her as she talked oysters with his father's fishing buddy and recipes with his wife. He watched his mother's friends tread carefully with her, wanting to find fault with her manners or her demeanour, and discovering to their consternation that they could not.

His mother remained aloof, never mind Charlotte's many attempts to initiate conversation and find common ground.

Chillingly, publicly unimpressed.

The meal came and went and the hours ground by. People began to make noises about leaving. Charlotte asked if there was anything she could do when it came to the clearing of tables or general tidying up. Grey frowned as Sarah immediately stepped in and began clearing and Olivia waved Charlotte away, telling her to sit and relax and continue telling tales.

Telling tales…

As if nothing she'd said so far could be trusted.

Charlotte smiled politely. She didn't so much as flinch as she settled back into playing the role of carefree companion and confident lover, and doing herself a disservice in the process, for there was more to her than that. Far more depth than he'd ever suspected.

Maybe it was time to leave.

Grey eased Charlotte away from the other guests until they reached the deck railing. He pointed out the various landmarks and she leaned her shoulder against his and showed every indication of hanging on his every word. He hadn't touched her since their earlier kiss. He hadn't been game. Now he turned his back on the view and spread his arms along the railing. Not quite an embrace, but an invitation for Charlotte to take what she would from him. Shelter, if she wanted it. Protection if she felt the need. Or anything else she might want to avail herself of.

Charlotte traced her fingers along the inside of his arm, up to his elbow and back, and when she reached his hand she covered it with her own, so soft and slim against the rough squareness of his. He liked the contrast. He liked a lot of things about this woman.

'Ready to go?' he murmured.

Relief crossed her face and was gone in an instant but this time he saw it. Charlotte Greenstone was more than ready to leave the family embrace and probably had been for hours.

'Yes.'

'C'mere,' he murmured and drew her towards him, touching his lips to her hair as she nestled against him as if she'd been there a thousand times and would be there a thousand more before they were through. 'You should have said.'

'It's your show.'

Yes, but it was *her* identity that was taking the battering.

They made their farewells after that. Sarah receiving Grey's guarded goodbye with a tight-lipped smile and eyes that wished him to hell. He hadn't encouraged Sarah's attentions over the course of the afternoon. Sarah hadn't given chase, hadn't made a scene, hadn't singled out Charlotte again. Sarah waited, that was all, and Grey wished to hell she wouldn't.

'Where to next with your work?' asked his father as he and Olivia saw them to the door.

'Could be Borneo,' said Grey. 'Could stay here a while.

Plans are pretty fluid at the moment.' He slid Charlotte a quick glance. Charlotte picked it up and responded with a smile.

'Borneo's lovely,' she enthused, playing the Boheme and playing it well. 'Wonderful place to visit and to work. My godmother and I spent half a year there once, when I was a child. Think of the history.'

'Think of the malaria,' said Olivia dryly. 'What were you and your godmother doing there?'

'Just looking,' said Charlotte. 'We did that a lot. Thank you for having me to lunch.' She didn't say she enjoyed it. Olivia didn't say, 'Do come again.'

Women.

Grey wasn't used to a pensive Charlotte Greenstone. A woman who wore her beauty effortlessly, almost unconsciously, but who'd grown quieter and more reflective with every passing kilometre. As if lunch with his parents and Sarah and all the rest had drained her dry.

'I'm sorry about my mother,' he said, after another fifteen kilometres of silence.

'Mothers are protective of their young,' she said quietly. 'You don't have to be a biology major to get that. Anyway, it's not as if I'll be seeing her again.' Charlotte closed her eyes as if to shut out reality. 'May I offer up a little bit of advice?'

'Go ahead.'

'When you *do* find a woman who interests you, introduce her to your family gradually. Try one limb at a time; or one family member at a time. Don't involve Sarah, not at the start. It does no one any favours.'

'Noted,' he murmured. 'And thank you.' He'd do well to keep his eyes on the road and off his companion. His wildly beautiful companion with hidden depths. 'Are you hungry? We could stop somewhere on the way home. I did promise you dinner.'

'I can't eat any more today,' she said. 'Your mother sets a fine table.'

'You have to eat something later on.'

'I might have a cognac nightcap.'

'That's not food.'

'Want to bet?'

They drove in silence after that, apart from a murmured comment here and there. When they got to the outskirts of Sydney, Charlotte surprised him yet again by requesting that he drop her at an inner city Rocks address rather than the one he'd picked her up from.

She directed him into a steeply descending driveway, dug a set of keys from her handbag, and pressed a remote switch attached to the key ring. The eight-foot wrought-iron driveway gates began to ease open. A heavy-duty garage Roll-A-Door began to open further down the drive. 'Who lives here?'

'Me,' she said as Grey drove down into a spacious underground car park with room for a dozen or so vehicles. 'The house at Double Bay belongs to Aurora. At least, it did. Now it's mine, only I couldn't face going there tonight. She'd have been disappointed in me today, I think. In the hurt I caused, no matter how much better off Sarah's going to be without you. Too many lies. Far too many lies of late, and they just keep getting bigger. You can park there.'

He did as suggested, brooding over her remarks as he strode around the car to open the door for her.

She smiled, briefly, as she got out of the car and he closed the door behind her, but there was no leaning into him as there had been for his parents' benefit. No playing of power games.

'I'm sorry about today,' he said gruffly. 'I shouldn't have dragged you into this.'

'You didn't. We had a deal. A good deal—one I entered into willingly.' She offered up a small smile. 'Don't mind me if I seem a bit morose. It'll pass.'

He hoped so.

'Would you care to come up for a coffee?' she said next. 'I've no agenda, no ulterior motive other than I don't think much of my own company these days and I do my best to avoid it. You could tell me about your research. About what you hope to find in Borneo.'

Grey hesitated.

'Never mind,' she said quietly. 'It's not mandatory. We're square now. And you probably have other places to be.'

Somewhere between this morning and now, Charlotte's confidence had taken a hammering and self-derision had found purchase. His doing, not hers, and he cursed himself for not seeing, not giving any thought whatsoever to Charlotte's feelings about the role he'd asked her to play and the hits she would take on his behalf.

'You should know that a research scientist never misses an opportunity to expound on his work,' he offered gravely. 'You don't even have to be an appreciative audience. You just have to be awake. And, yes, I'll join you for coffee.'

They stepped into a lift and went up a few floors and came out onto a landing with only two doors leading from it, one of which was labelled 'Fire Escape.'

Charlotte's penthouse apartment boasted a million-dollar close-up view of Sydney Harbour Bridge, framed by enormous, double—or triple—glazed tinted windows. White was the predominant colour in the apartment; white walls and ceilings, white marble floors, white kitchen fixtures and benches and a snow-white leather lounge. And then, as if someone had taken exception to the designer palate and vowed to melt it down, an eclectic array of paintings, sculptures, books, tapestries and floor rugs in every imaginable colour and from every imaginable historical period had been added to the mix.

He stopped in front of a painting formed entirely of various coloured oil paints dripped onto a canvas in no particular order.

'Do you like it?' she said.

'What is it?'

'Abstract art. Jackson Pollock's finest. It's whatever you want it to be.'

'Handy,' he murmured. 'You *own* this?'

Charlotte nodded. 'It was my grandmother's. Lots of rumours about how she came to own it. My favourite one is that she and Pollock were friends and that she won it from him in a card game. Rumour has it they were initially playing with coins from the Roman Empire. As the stakes got higher, the currency of the realm went twentieth century.'

'What exactly does a person throw in the pot to match a Jackson Pollock painting?' he asked.

'Could have been the Dali,' she said.

Of course. The Dali. 'Family wealth, you said. Just how much family wealth is there?'

'Plenty,' she said dryly. 'My great grandfather was in shipping. My grandmother added luxury liners to the mix and then divested herself of the lot when she hit her fifties. Said it had sapped the life out of her. She turned philanthropist, gave a lot of her possessions away, but she still left my mother extremely well provided for. She urged my mother to follow her heart. My mother took her advice, chose my father and archaeology, and by all accounts was ecstatically happy with both. My parents died in a light aircraft crash in Peru when I was five.'

'Long time ago,' he murmured.

'So it was. I usually went everywhere with them but that day they decided to leave me at the hotel with Aurora.'

'This is the Aurora who died recently? Your godmother? The one you invented a fiancé for?'

Charlotte nodded. 'Aurora was an archaeologist like my parents. Fortunately for me, they'd also named her as my guardian in their wills. From then on, I went where Aurora went and that was everywhere. You take milk in your coffee?'

'No, thanks,' he said. 'How long have you worked at Sydney Uni?'

'Five years.'

'And this associate professorship, it allows for the kind of travel you're used to?'

'No, it's a desk job.'

'And you're not fed up with that?'

'Not yet.' She set spoons and a bowl of sugar on the counter. A pewter sugar bowl with dragonfly handles. 'I like the stability. I like the people I work closely with. I even like the routine, and I can usually tolerate the politics. And what with communications these days, field teams can get photos and data to me and I can make comment within minutes if required.'

'You wouldn't rather *be* there?'

'I've been there,' she murmured. 'I travelled that road for twenty-three years. When Aurora retired, I lost enthusiasm for it. It just wasn't the same without her and I didn't want to continue on alone. I hate being alone.' Charlotte absent-mindedly brushed dark curls from her face. 'I can play your free-spirited bohemian friend to perfection, Greyson. I have many role models I can look to for inspiration. Heaven knows, my boss would be ecstatic if I went back out into the field for a while. Problem is, I'm very fond of my settled existence. Of being among familiar faces. I think that in the absence of family I look to the community for a sense of belonging. Of place. I need to feel connected to something, whereas you...you need to be free. It's why we'd never gel in real life. It's why, deep down inside, I'm no better suited to you than Sarah is.'

'Thanks for the warning.'

'My pleasure,' she said gravely. 'Doesn't mean I can't enjoy your company. Doesn't mean that when it comes to a short-term liaison I couldn't be tempted to take my fill of you. You *are* a spectacularly beautiful specimen and you have some very fine qualities.'

Charlotte murmured something else but Grey's brain had ceased functioning the moment she'd mentioned the words *short-term liaison* and *tempted*.

He tracked Charlotte's every move as she set the coffee machine to working. Moments later a steaming cup of fragrant coffee-beaned joy sat on the gleaming granite-topped kitchen counter in front of him. Too hot for drinking, so he added sugar and stirred and Charlotte did the same to hers. The porcelain teaspoons had porcelain ladybirds on them.

'So, Borneo next,' she said eventually.

'Maybe. There's write-up work to do on the PNG project first. Reports. Papers. Probably some presentation work.'

'Ah, yes. The Glory,' she murmured. 'A scientist's pleasure.'

There were other types of pleasure.

'About your thoughts on short-term liaisons,' he muttered, and suffered her knowing gaze and her delicately raised eyebrow with dogged determination. 'What are they?'

'Would you like an in-depth analysis or just the summary?' she enquired sweetly.

'Just the summary.'

'Okay. Assuming that both participants are free from all other romantic entanglements, I'm reasonably in favour of flings as a legitimate means of providing temporary companionship and sexual satisfaction.'

'That's a very bohemian outlook for a woman who eschews a carefree life.'

'If you say so. Of course, even a temporary partner has to fit certain criteria. A different set of criteria from that expected of a life partner.'

'Of course,' murmured Grey. 'Do you have a list?'

'Of course.' She didn't elaborate, just smiled. Charlotte Greenstone knew how to make a man work for what he wanted.

'Let me guess,' he murmured as he set his coffee aside and leaned over the counter towards her, his mouth mere inches from her own. 'You need to be attracted to him.'

'Well, naturally.'

'He needs to satisfy you sexually.'

'Goes without saying.' Her gaze had settled on his lips. 'I'm thinking we'd be good to go in that respect.'

'Does he need to be wealthier than you?'

'No, but he does need to feel secure enough in his circumstances for my wealth not to intimidate him. I don't need to dine at the most expensive restaurant in the city. I don't need to be lavished with expensive gifts. What I do expect, when a temporary liaison invites me out to dinner or drinks or a show, is that he pays for it. When I do the inviting, payment will naturally fall to me.'

'Sounds very fair-minded for a woman who insists on having her car door opened for her.'

'I'm a woman of contrasts,' she said. 'Also a big fan of gentlemanly manners. A short-term liaison candidate would require those too, or at least be willing to learn some.'

'Anything else?' he asked silkily.

'Yes. A temporary lover would have limited input when it comes to my long-term plans and how I choose to live my life. There'd be no trying to turn me to his way of thinking. No major compromises required. Asking for such would almost certainly signal the *end* of the liaison.'

'Have you a position on time limits for such an association?' he asked. He'd never met a woman quite so fond of rules and regulations when it came to personal interaction. The scientist in him was intrigued by the need for such protective barriers. The suitor in him regarded it as a challenge.

'How long they're going to be in the area usually dictates the length of the association,' she murmured. 'I don't encourage long distance relationships, temporary or otherwise.'

'Yet you still invented long-distance Gil.'

'Well, I could hardly invent a fiancé who lived in Sydney. I'd have had to produce him. And lest you get the impression that I enter into temporary liaisons lightly and without careful forethought, I don't.'

'I'm getting that,' he said dryly.

'So what about you?' she said. 'What do you look for in a fling?'

'Well, I need to be attracted to her,' he said.

'And?'

'And what? That's it.'

CHAPTER FIVE

GREYSON TYLER didn't strike Charlotte as a particularly cavalier individual. Not when it came to his research. Not when it came to his relationships. He was, however, male—which probably went some way towards explaining his limited thought processes when it came to bedding a woman and walking away.

'Are you attracted to me, Greyson?'

His gaze locked with hers, boldly direct. 'Yes.'

'Do you respect me?'

'Is this another one of your fling criteria?' he murmured.

Charlotte narrowed her gaze.

A hint of a smile tilted Greyson's extremely kissable lips.

'For what it's worth, I have a great deal of respect for the way you conducted yourself at my parents' this afternoon. You did the job I asked of you. You withstood my mother's disapproval with dignity and grace. You were gentle with Sarah. I'm grateful. And I'm impressed.' He set his coffee on the counter, out of harm's way. 'So, do I qualify for a fling? Do I meet your criteria? Because from where I'm standing, I think I do.'

'Modesty's not really one of your strengths,' she murmured.

'No.' Those dark brown eyes lightened a little. 'But then, you didn't specify the need for it.'

'Gilbert was very modest,' she said on a sigh.

'Gilbert was a figment of your imagination,' he reminded her. 'I think you'll find me far more satisfying in any number of ways.'

'You really want to do this?' she murmured.

'Yes.' Not an indecisive bone in this man's superbly sculpted body. 'Do you?'

Did she? Would a night spent in the arms of a man she barely knew chase her loneliness away, even if only for a little while? A man who made her feel warm and protected. One who, for a moment there, back on that deck overlooking the water, made her feel valued and loved. 'Yes.'

His smile came slow and warm. 'As in now?'

'Yes.'

'Noted,' he said silkily. 'But if you don't mind, I might wait a while. What with all this arranging of events, we seem to have lost a bit of spontaneity. I do enjoy spontaneity within lovemaking.'

'You should have said,' she murmured. 'I'd have left the slave bracelets off.'

'Slave bracelets?' His gaze cut to the bracelets at her wrist, and that big body of his became unnaturally still.

'Oh, yes. Did I not mention them? I'm pretty sure I mentioned them to everyone else at the barbecue. The slave bracelets, that is. Signalling possession and worth. A certain willingness to oblige.' Challenge, not submission, and Greyson responded, as Charlotte knew he would, for this man fed on challenge and always would.

He stalked around to her side of the bench and trapped her against it, his hands either side of her on the counter.

Perhaps he'd decided not to take his time after all. Oh, well…

'I'd ask for your thoughts on submission within love-making but I wouldn't want to endanger the spontaneity. So…' She deliberately leaned forward and let her chest brush against his; her nipples responding instantly to all that hardness and heat. He noticed. Charlotte breathed in deeply, savouring the scent of him. He noticed that, too.

'What would you like to do while we wait?' she asked in dulcet tones. 'Would you care for a drink to go with your coffee? Cognac? Brandy liqueur?'

'No.' Greyson's lips were at the spot on her neck, just below the base of her ear where a woman might put perfume only she hadn't worn any perfume. Not today. Next time, if there was such a time, she would apply a scent this man would remember with a deep and abiding pleasure.

He touched the tip of his tongue to her skin next and she gasped her approval, arching her neck to allow him better access. Spontaneity was all well and good but when it came to the act of making love, she far preferred a man who was thorough. One who would not be rushed. One who knew how to take his time.

'Scotch?' she murmured.

'Yes.'

'Now? Or shall I wait for spontaneity to strike?' That earned her a husky rumble that set her hands to his chest and his lips to curving, lips she couldn't help but find with her own. The kiss started out as fleeting and rapidly grew ragged.

'I like it neat, no ice.' Greyson's hands were at her waist. Wide warm palms and long strong fingers, he slid those hands down the sides of her body until he reached her thighs. When he slid his hands back up to her waist he dragged the fabric of her dress with him.

'And the glass?' She closed her eyes and shuddered as the hem of her frock inched higher. 'Square or round?'

'Round.' He lifted her effortlessly and sat her on the bench, stepping in between her legs, forcing them open to accommodate him. The skirt of her dress pooled at her waist. His fingertips slid under it, while his thumbs traced slow circles against the tender flesh of her inner thighs.

'You want that drink now?' she whispered and stifled a gasp as a wayward thumb brushed against the delicate silk of her panties.

'I'm a little busy right now,' he murmured. 'So are you.' His fingers had reached the top of her panties but he didn't try to ease them down her body, not Greyson. He liked his fingers right where they were, with his thumb at her centre, sliding over silk and over nerve endings already swollen and sensitive.

'Aurora would have my hide for being a bad hostess,' she whispered as she covered his wrist with her hand, unsure whether she intended to make him press down deeper or drag his hand away. In the end she did both, one first and then the other as she slid from the countertop, dug an unopened bottle of Scotch from the cupboard, linked fingers with Greyson and led him towards the couch.

Watching Greyson make himself comfortable on the pristine white couch, draping his arms along the back of it and owning the space so utterly, brought a smile to her face.

The swig of Scotch she took straight from the bottle before handing it over brought a smile to his.

He drank his fill and then tilted the bottle towards her. When she shook her head he leaned forward and set the bottle on the low table in front of the couch and reached for her again, drawing her down onto him. She went willingly, straddling his thighs, finding the hard ridge of his arousal and sinking down onto it with a gasp. Plenty to get excited about there. Just *plenty* as his fingers curled into her buttocks and positioned her for best effect.

Arousal bit deep as his lips parted beneath hers, whisky tinged and ravenous as she slid her fingers through his hair and gave herself over to that expert mouth.

Too many clothes and to hell with going slow. One could be both thorough *and* fast, Charlotte decided hastily. Grey's shirt buttons came undone beneath her ministrations. A heartbeat later and the shirt was gone. Beautiful. So very, very beautiful, this man. Charlotte set her hands to his chest and afforded herself the pleasure of dragging them down over rippling muscles until she reached his belt buckle. She made short work of that, and the zipper too, and that which had been encased in denim jutted free.

She rose up onto her knees, rose because she knew exactly what she wanted to do with all that hardness and heat, but her movements put her breasts in line with Greyson's mouth, and he knew what he wanted too. Within the space of a breath he'd eased the spaghetti straps from her shoulders, the silk covering from her breasts, and taken them in his mouth. Such a wicked, teasing mouth. She shuddered against him, straining, whimpering, and he suckled harder and sent a lightning stroke of desire straight to her loins.

His hands were beneath her dress, beneath her panties, testing for slickness and finding it. Only her panties in the way of him now but not for long, one side parting beneath his insistent tug, and then she was sinking down onto him, fast at first and then more slowly as she realised just how much of him she would have to accommodate.

'Easy,' he rumbled against her throat, and then again. 'Easy.' Right before his mouth captured hers for another of those all-consuming kisses.

He didn't rush her. He let her take her time, and if his

breathing came harsh and his hands went to the cushions on either side of him and stayed there, rigidly immobile so as not to hasten her along in any way, it was only to his credit.

'Distract me,' she murmured, fighting her body for every thick and pulsing inch of him. It had been so long for her. She was beginning to doubt her ability to accommodate him.

'You don't need distracting,' he muttered, and brought the fingers of one hand to rest on her abdomen and set his thumb to her centre as he'd done once before. 'You need focus.'

He started off with slow, lazy circles and she focused, heaven help her she did, and slowly, and with infinite patience on his part, she took all of him in.

She stilled his hand, holding onto his wrist with her eyes closed and her lower lip between her teeth as she adjusted to the fullness of him. 'You should come with a warning,' she muttered.

'You should come,' he whispered back, and set about making it happen.

He knew how to move inside a woman slow and easy, this man. He knew how to use the friction of penetration to drive her higher. He knew when to lave and he knew when to bite, and when she came for him and sweet moisture came with it he tumbled her onto her back on the floor and kept her there, his thrusts coming harder now because she wanted them harder, and faster, his every stroke a lesson in ecstasy as she crested around him for the second time in as many minutes.

Grey knew he was a tight fit for a small woman. Holding back was second nature to him, being patient, taking his time—it was the code he lived by, the rule he made love by. But when Charlotte clenched around him again, when her nails dug into his shoulders and she cried out and slammed against him, milking him, coming apart for him, he abandoned all thought of restraint and followed her willingly into madness.

They stayed joined together in the aftermath. Grey rolled to his side and brought Charlotte with him, still buried deep inside her, still trembling. He groaned as she moved but she was only throwing her leg across his hip to keep that connection in place as she eased her upper body back against his outstretched arm.

'I've sworn off lying,' she murmured, and the lazy satisfaction in that velvet voice of hers had his body twitching and threatening to go another round. 'And it's probably not quite the time for teasing either. Maybe later.'

'Is there any particular point to this train of thought?' he queried, and got a not quite accidental elbow in his solar plexus for his efforts.

'Has anyone ever told you you're a very impatient man?'

'No,' he said dryly. 'Never.'

'How unusual.'

'Charlotte,' he said evenly. 'Get to the point.'

'Oh. Right. The point.' She brought her arms above her head and slid him a laughing glance, every bit the wanton gypsy she purported not to be. '*Damn*, that was good.'

Charlotte Greenstone had a God-given talent for understatement, decided Grey upon hearing her words. She also possessed a bone-deep sensuality that he wasn't about to forget in a hurry. One could only hope that in offering him a taste of it, she hadn't taken possession of *him* in the process.

He didn't *feel* as if he'd just met his soul mate.

More as if he'd walked upon a precipice and slipped twenty metres down a hundred-metre cliff and was holding onto his current position by the tips of his bruised and bloodied fingers.

He didn't *think* he was in love with Charlotte.

More like he'd been run over by a truck.

Nothing to worry about though. He'd be up and about again soon. Gone soon enough, as specified by their initial agreement regarding the nature and properties of temporary liaisons.

It occurred to him, fleetingly, that he might want to run.

And then Charlotte slid her hand up and over his chest and around his neck and urged his mouth down to meet hers for a kiss so intensely erotic and full of promise that he immediately fell another twenty metres down that cliff.

'Greyson?' she murmured, and there was absolutely no denying that the sound of his name on her lips was going to haunt him from here to eternity. 'You want to do that again?'

CHAPTER SIX

WAKING up to a sleeping man in her bed wasn't a regular occurrence for Charlotte. She knew his name and she knew where his parents lived. She knew he had a doctorate in botany and that he'd just returned from a three-year research stint in PNG. She knew he made love like a fiend and that she ached in places she'd never ached before. That was about it for what she knew about Greyson Tyler.

It didn't seem enough.

Not for her to have allowed him the liberties she'd allowed him to take with her last night. Not that she remembered a conscious decision to allow him anything once the touching had started.

Spontaneous, that was the word she was looking for. Last night's spontaneous lovemaking had been a revelation. What a woman should *do* with this new information regarding lovemaking and her own hitherto unknown capacity for abandon remained something of a mystery.

She spared a glance for her bed partner. Still sleeping, thank you God, because she could feel a blush coming on just looking at him. He slept on his stomach, with one hand beneath his pillow and the other reaching towards the bed head. He had one knee bent, and he looked for all the world as if he were trying to scale a mountainside.

He seemed to take up an inordinate amount of space in her bed.

Charlotte slipped from the bed and reached silently for her robe. Butt naked was not a regular state of being for her, though she might have to get used to it with this man around. She risked a glance back at him, he was still sleeping so she allowed her gaze to linger on those broad bronzed shoulders and the way the muscles fitted together across his back and tapered down towards his waist. White cotton sheets covered the rest of him, possibly the best of him, but she'd seen it last night and the memory was engraved on her brain.

'Morning,' said a deep and sleepy voice from further up the mountainside and Charlotte dragged her gaze upwards to meet his eyes.

'You're thinking,' he said next.

'No, no, not at all. I think you'll find that I'm just looking.'

'Good,' he said. 'Come here.'

Charlotte raised a sceptical eyebrow.

'Please.'

Much better. She crossed to the empty side of the bed and perched on it, grateful for her breakfast robe, a vivid red silk wrap with a golden dragon embroidered on the back. Kitschy and glorious, and very much her style.

Grey reached up and slid his hand around her neck and drew her down into a kiss that surprised her with its tenderness.

'You okay?' he asked.

'Is this a regular morning-after question for you?'

'Yes.' Long and silky black lashes came down to curtain his eyes as he bussed her lips once more. 'You could try answering it.'

'I'm quite well,' she murmured. 'Possibly even invigorated. I'll know more once I've showered.'

Greyson's lashes came up and he regarded her warily. 'I wasn't always easy with you last night.'

'No.' Her turn to initiate the kissing this time. Her choice to linger. 'You weren't. Still…a woman might choose to be grateful for that fact.'

He didn't look reassured. Charlotte stifled a sigh. Perhaps he wasn't as confident in his size and sexuality as she expected him to be. Perhaps he hadn't always… fitted in.

Perhaps a demonstration of her sincerity was in order.

She slid from the bed and headed for the bathroom suite, shedding her robe along the way. Bare butt and a tumble of waist-length tangled black curls—that was the view she afforded him. 'Shower time.' She glanced over her shoulder and offered up a siren's smile. 'It's a big shower.'

She'd been under the spray for only a few minutes before he joined her. Long enough for her to get wet and soapy. Just long enough for her to start wondering if, when she stepped back out of the bathroom, she'd find him gone.

'I'm not normally so careless,' he said gruffly as she turned to face him.

'By careless, do you mean passionate? Fevered? Lost?'

'Yeah, that.'

A woman couldn't help it if her smile turned somewhat smug.

'I usually make a concerted effort to please,' he said next.

'Really?' Now there was a pretty picture. 'Do tell.'

'Why don't I just show you?' he murmured.

Charlotte's smile widened. 'I want you to know that I

really am doing my best to convey to you that last night was an intensely erotic and pleasurable experience for me, with absolutely no apology necessary on your part. Just so we're clear on that point.'

'Consider it clarified,' he said. 'Now turn around to face the tiles.'

'Please.'

He smiled, but he didn't say please. Just turned her gently around and then stepped in behind her and slid his hands down her arms and his fingers over hers before taking her hands and placing her palms against the tiles, shoulder height and body length apart. 'Like this,' he said.

'Please.'

But he didn't say please. Instead, he slid his hands down her body, down to where she was tender and swollen. He parted her legs, caressed her with knowing fingers. 'You okay?'

Did a groan qualify as a yes?

He slid his hands around to her buttocks, filling his palms with them before sliding his hands up the length of her back in one long massaging caress. Arms next, out to her wrists, and then all the way back to where he started.

He kneed her legs open, she braced herself against the wall and stood on tiptoe, waiting for his entry. Expecting it.

'Don't move,' he whispered.

'Don't move, *please*. Alternatively, you could say please don't move. Do you have no manners *at all*?'

'Sometimes, I do,' he countered and there was laughter in that dark, delicious voice. 'I'm very impressed by yours. But just in case you feel obliged to interrupt me any time soon, you can thank me later.'

And then he was kneeling down and wedging broad water-slicked shoulders between her legs and twisting his torso, one strong powerful hand at the small of her back, tilting her pelvis forward, his other hand high on her thigh, as he set his mouth to her centre and feasted.

Charlotte managed to keep her hands to the tiles.

She managed to keep all curses, pleas, and oaths to a minimum.

Later, much later, she remembered to thank him.

Breakfast wasn't a leisurely affair. Charlotte ate grapes from one hand while setting the espresso machine to brewing with the other. She'd dressed for work in her usual working attire—smart trousers, plain shirt, boring shoes—and she'd kept the make-up light, aiming for elegant minimalism. Greyson had shrugged into his clothes of yesterday and followed the creation of Associate Professor Charlotte Greenstone with some bemusement.

'Why the disguise?' he asked finally as she set his coffee in front of him, finished her grapes, and began smoothing back her wayward hair in readiness for a hairclip.

'Who says it's a disguise?' she murmured.

'Seems a little Plain Jane for you,' he said with a shrug. 'Correct me if I'm wrong.'

'I'm a relatively youthful female giving undergraduate lectures and gunning for tenure within an antiquated and patriarchal employment system,' she said with a shrug. 'Respect comes a little easier to some if I look the part.'

'What do you do about the ones who don't respect your abilities, no matter how you dress?'

'They get to learn the hard way.'

Now she'd amused him.

'What?' she snapped. 'Over twenty years of hands-on fieldwork and analysis not enough? Get back in the field, Charlotte, before your godmother's contacts forget you,' she mimicked grimly. 'We wouldn't want you to lose those, now, would we? Or the goodwill that comes with your family name. You are aware, Charlotte, that your ability to pull more funding than the rest of us put together has nothing to do with any actual talent for bringing particular projects and interested parties together? You have a brand name that implies excellent connections, inspired thinking, quality work, and exceptional results, that's all. Don't you be thinking that your success has anything to do with *you*.'

Greyson said nothing.

'You want to know the sad thing about it all?' she said with a frustrated sigh. 'They're not entirely wrong. And now that Aurora's dead, the naysayers are just *waiting* to see how much goodwill towards me died with her.'

'How much goodwill towards you do *you* think died with her?'

'I don't know.' Charlotte wouldn't meet his eyes. 'A lot of these people have known me since I was a baby. They knew my parents. Many of them tutored me in their various areas of expertise. They've followed my career, smoothed the way for me many times over. Because of the brand or because of me or because Aurora called in favours, who knows? I certainly don't. And you really don't need to hear any of this,' she finished with a grimace. 'Sorry. Touchy subject.'

'So who *do* you run all this stuff by?' he asked mildly.

'Well… Gil happened to be a *very* good listener,' she offered, which earned her one of *those* looks.

'Would you like some advice?'

'I'm not sure,' she said warily. 'I might.'

'Don't let anyone tell you that your success is due to

your birthright or a brand you have no influence over. Yes, you had a head start, your upbringing saw to that. But your parents have been dead for, what, twenty years or so? And your godmother was retired for the last five?'

'Something like that,' she murmured.

'And the funding for the projects just keeps coming?' Charlotte nodded.

'Figured as much.' He sipped his coffee. He kept her waiting. Charlotte hated waiting. She had a sneaking suspicion that Greyson knew it. 'The way I see it, Professor, you *are* the brand and have been for some time,' he said at last. 'Your godmother knew it. I dare say she traded on it, added her own to it, taught you how to build it. And you have. Get back out in the field if you want to—if that's where you want to keep your brand based. If you'd rather stay put, all you need do is continue to grow your brand at the management and funding level. It's *your* brand, Charlotte, your life, and you're in the enviable position of being able to choose exactly how you live it. Tell your naysayers to look to their own effectiveness, not yours.'

'You want to know something?' said Charlotte as his words put another chink in her carefully constructed armour.

'I'm not sure,' he offered dryly. 'I might.'

'You're much better at giving advice than Gil.' She glanced at the kitchen clock. 'And I have to get to work. You want to let yourself out? There's a spare set of driveway keys around here somewhere.'

But to that, he shook his head. 'I'll follow you out.'

'Will you call me?' she asked tentatively. 'Or are we done here?'

Greyson got to his feet. Charlotte adjusted her gaze skywards. He looked even bigger than he had last night and a whole lot more lethal. Maybe it was because he hadn't shaved. Maybe she was simply applying her newfound knowledge of how this man thought and what made him tick. What he was capable of giving to a woman by way of encouragement and support. And pleasure.

A shudder ripped through her and it felt like a warning. Just how was she supposed to keep this liaison carefree and temporary when every move he made and word he spoke brought him closer?

'We're not done yet, Charlotte.' Greyson eyed her a little too grimly for comfort. Call it a hunch, but he didn't seem to be embracing their temporary liaison with a whole lot of lightness and joy either. 'You can expect me to call.'

He probably hadn't meant to make it sound like a warning.

Or maybe he had.

'I tried calling you yesterday afternoon to see if you wanted to go to the movies,' said Millie at morning tea time as they raided the biscuit tin for biscuits that weren't a hundred years old. 'Couldn't get through to you though.'

'What did you go and see?'

'I didn't see anything,' said Millie. 'The offer's still open for tomorrow night.'

'Done,' said Charlotte, never mind what films might be playing.

'It's fine if you want to bring someone else along too,' said Millie.

Charlotte shook her head and smiled.

Millie sighed heavily.

'Subtlety will get you nowhere,' said Charlotte archly. 'Ask.'

'Thank you,' said the long suffering Millie. 'What's going on with you and Gil?'

'He's hoping to go and work in Borneo soon. We've

ended our engagement. It was a mutual decision based on many factors.'

'Fool,' muttered Millie. 'Have you seen him lately?'

'I have.'

'Sexy as ever?'

'Alas, yes.'

'Attentive?'

Charlotte felt her face start to heat.

'Feel free to enlighten me,' said Millie. 'Really. I mean it.'

Charlotte smiled again; it was that kind of day. Blue skies above, body sated, mind still trying to work its way through the sensual haze Greyson's lovemaking had left her with. Hard to concentrate on the bigger picture, namely Greyson's—no, *Gil's*—impending exit from her life and from her co-workers' consciousnesses. 'He'll be gone again soon, and that'll be the end of it. Really. It's for the best.'

'What's Borneo got that you haven't?' said Millie.

'Novelty value. Research possibilities. The call of the wild.' Charlotte reeled off the attractions. 'Rainforests. Temples. Orang-utangs.'

'Trifles,' said Mille. 'Though I will confess a fondness for orang-utangs. Have you considered going with him?'

'No,' said Charlotte, and a little bit of brightness went out of her day. 'That's really not an option.'

'Why not? There are opportunities for archaeologists in Borneo. You're wasted here, Charlotte. You know you are. The Mead dangles tenureship in front of you and turns you into his lackey. Carlysle and Steadfellow mine your knowledge and then try and take the credit for it. You could do such brilliant work but you don't. You could tie yourself so lightly to this place and go anywhere. Everywhere.'

'Everywhere's overrated,' said Charlotte lightly, and suffered Millie's puzzled glance.

'I thought it was your godmother's failing health that kept you here,' said Millie. 'But that wasn't it, was it? There's something else. Something bigger than Gil, bigger than love, only I don't know what it is.'

'It's hard to explain,' said Charlotte.

'Try.'

So Charlotte tried. 'I like stability. I like the connections I've made here. I feel like I'm part of something, even when I'm being used up.'

'I still don't get it,' said Millie. Millie, with her big and loving family all around her, brothers and sisters, and parents and cousins, all scattered across a city she knew and loved. Millie didn't know how lucky she was to have that safety net of people who cared for her, people who'd *be* there for each other in times of need.

'Millie—' Charlotte searched for just the right words. Not wanting pity, she'd never wanted that. 'It takes time to get to know a place, to make friends, but I've done that now. Here. And I won't give that up lightly. I feel—I feel that for the first time in my life, I'm starting to belong.'

Grey left it until Friday morning before phoning Charlotte. Never mind that he'd wanted to call her earlier... He hadn't. Self-control had been applied. Restraint. The restraint required of a man embarking on a casual, no-strings affair.

The presence of one Charlotte Greenstone in his life should have made his time between jobs very pleasant. A smart and sensual woman of independent means and a gratifyingly strong sexual appetite wanted to spend a little time with him. Riveting to look at, and with a voice fully capable of coaxing angels downstairs to play in the pit a while—what more could a man *want* from a short-term sexual partner?

A little less perfection of form wouldn't have gone astray, he decided bleakly. She could have at least given the women who were to come after her a fighting chance to measure up.

A little less abandon in the bedroom wouldn't have hurt either, for exactly the same reason.

And would it have killed her to have led a normal life instead of some fascinating life of money, privilege, and discovery? How was a man supposed to do his own work while continually wondering how *hers* was going? The Internet was for instant access to research papers, not for Googling Charlotte's family name to see if he could get a better feel for this *brand* she'd inherited. A glamorous brand, by all accounts. The Greenstones were to archaeology what the Kennedys had been to government. Dazzling, immensely successful and supremely ill-fated. And the only one left was Charlotte.

Who hadn't called.

Or texted.

Or emailed.

Not that he was obsessing. Not that it would do him much good if he were.

He placed the call. Confidence was key. That, and knowing exactly what he wanted from this woman. Right now, he wanted her on *his* turf and he wanted it with an intensity he usually reserved for his work.

'I'm moored at the marina at Hawkesbury River,' he said without preamble when she answered. 'I can offer fresh seafood, cold beer, and a berth on my boat if you've a mind to stay over.'

'Hello, Greyson,' she said, and there was rich amusement in that whisky voice. 'I'd almost given up on hearing from you.'

'I said I'd call.'

'So you did,' she murmured. 'I was hoping you might have managed it a little earlier.'

'You have my number,' he reminded her. 'You could have called me.'

'Ah, but a lady wouldn't,' she murmured. 'Not before you renewed contact and initiated another meeting. Now I can.'

'What particular book of etiquette are you working from?' he said.

'Mine.'

'Don't suppose you have a spare?'

'It's all in my head.'

'That's what I was afraid of. If it's any consolation, I wanted to call you on Monday, Tuesday, and Wednesday, and I almost caved and called you yesterday. There was the small matter of proving to myself that I could wait and work in the interim, not to mention letting you get your own work done.'

'You're very kind.'

'I know. And now it's Friday and the work is done and I'm done with waiting. I want to see you again.'

'Have you heard from Sarah lately?'

'Yes, we've spoken on the phone.' Not a topic he felt inclined to discuss with a woman he wanted in his bed tonight. Even if Charlotte *had* been part of his efforts to deter his former fiancée. 'I've made it brutally clear to both Sarah and my mother that I can't give Sarah what she wants. I've also made it clear to my mother that I was disappointed in her treatment of you.'

'I bet that went down well.'

'It needed to be said. Even with you attending that barbecue with no emotional attachment to me whatsoever, they managed to hurt you. Imagine how much damage they could have done if you *had* had feelings for me.'

'Hence our discussion afterwards about introducing a new partner to Sarah and your family,' said Charlotte. 'I'm glad you took those thoughts on board, Greyson,' she said softly. 'To be honest, I didn't expect you to take them on board on *my* account. They were intended for the women who came after me.'

'What? You don't think you deserve to be treated with respect or given a fair go?'

Grey waited for some wry and clever comeback but Charlotte stayed strangely silent.

'My mother wants to know my intentions towards you.'

'What did you tell her?' Wariness in Charlotte's beautiful velvet voice now. A reserve he didn't want to hear.

'I told her I'd never met a more fascinating woman.' Truth. Bare and unvarnished and Charlotte could make of it what she would. 'I wasn't lying, Charlotte. I want to see you again. Have dinner with me tonight. Stay over if you like or head home afterwards but come. Come spend some time with me.'

'Okay.' Nothing cool about Charlotte now. Her voice had gone husky, bringing with it memories of whispered entreaties and outrageous sexual pleasure. 'I figure I can be there around seven. And Greyson?'

'What?'

'Thank you for championing me, and, yes. I'm of a mind to stay over.'

Charlotte's commute home from work took time. The drive down to the Hawkesbury involved getting across the bridge and through the city during Friday night rush hour, and took considerably longer. She'd called Greyson to inform him of her delay in case it affected the dinner plans. He'd assured her it wouldn't. He'd told her to take her time. She'd told him he'd better be worth it. Not his decision to make, he'd told her, and hung up.

One slow and crooked smile of welcome from Greyson as he took her overnight bag from her and held out his hand to help her up the stairs of his gleaming catamaran went some way towards making Charlotte glad she'd said yes to his plans. The way he filled out his grey canvas long shorts and had left his white shirt unbuttoned went further.

'In my defence, I'd forgotten all about the traffic,' he said, and mollified her some more.

'So had I,' she said as she slipped off her shoes to go barefoot on his deck. A very high deck, she decided as she straightened and glanced over the side of the catamaran. 'Nice boat. I should have realised you'd be a sailor, what with your folks' holiday house on the water and your water-weed work.'

'I was five when I got my first catamaran,' he said affably as he guided her along the craft towards an enclosed area that spanned the twin hulls. 'It was love at first sight. I wanted to sleep on it. My mother said I could when I got a bit older.'

'How old were you before you got your way?'

'Eight.' No sign of the formidable Dr Greyson Tyler in the grin he shot her; he was all boy and finally living his dream. 'Longest three years of my life.'

Greyson opened a sliding glass door into a spacious living area, compact galley with plenty of bench space and sitting areas to one side, a lounge area to the other and more seats and a table to the fore. 'I usually eat in here,' he said. 'Sleeping quarters are down in the hulls.' He set Charlotte's bag at her feet and his smile turned wry. 'Guest hull is to your left, mine's to your right, and I've no idea what etiquette demands. You choose.'

'Where do your women friends usually sleep?'

'Not here,' he said gruffly and continued with the tour. 'Bridge is above us and there's a little cove where we can anchor for the night about fifteen minutes away. Your call which comes first, food or more travel. There's a plate of seafood starters in the fridge. We can take it up to the bridge if you're inclined to multitask.'

'You eat on the bridge?'

'I do when it's past dinner time and I want to appease a beautiful woman,' he murmured. 'I can be flexible.'

'And I can be grateful,' she said. 'I'm for getting under way and I'll bring the feast to you.'

Greyson nodded and headed back along the cat, casting off and heading for the bridge. They weren't under sail and moments later an engine purred to life. Charlotte made herself at home in the little galley, opening the fridge and pulling out a high-lipped flat-bottomed bowl crammed with shelled king prawns, oysters, and various types of dipping sauce.

Not a dish that required hours of fiddly preparation, but effort had been made nonetheless. Point for Greyson.

Dish in hand, Charlotte headed out of the cabin and climbed the stairs to the bridge as Greyson eased the craft slowly away from the dock. Once clear of the marina and other craft, he throttled up and the cat responded with surprising alacrity. Plenty of horsepower at Greyson's fingertips, and as for the catamaran itself, a great deal more luxury than Charlotte had expected. This wasn't just a pleasure craft; it was a home, and one that reflected the wanderlust of its owner.

Charlotte reached Greyson's side and smiled at the dark eyed devil who greeted her with a swift and potent smile of his own.

Terrible fiancé material, this man—as the patient, still-smitten Sarah had discovered.

But on a night like this, for an outing of this nature, he was damn near perfect.

They motored past the small township of Hawkesbury River, past tree clad ridges rising up from the riverbanks. They motored under an old railway bridge and on to where solitude and natural beauty held sway.

The catamaran rode high in the water, and looking out over the wide expanse of glassy river held plenty of appeal. Leaning back against the instrument panel and watching Greyson's eyes darken as she fed him a prawn held more. From her hand to his lips, and if feeding him took on a savagely sensual edge, well, it was only to be expected in such a setting and with such a man.

'Tell me about your work,' she said.

'What would you like to know?'

'What inspires you the most. What a regular day is like for you. Where you think your research will lead. Just the usual.'

He took an oyster on the half shell from her outstretched hand. 'That's not the usual.'

'It's not?' Charlotte briefly wondered what *was* the usual, and what type of woman Greyson would normally choose to spend time with. Sarah hadn't been a shallow woman by any stretch of the imagination and Greyson's mother had been downright formidable. Perhaps his taste ran more to sweetly obliging types these days. 'Sorry.'

Greyson devoured the oyster and set the shell to the side of the plate where Charlotte had been neatly stacking them. 'I like the element of discovery that comes with the research,' he said at last. 'I like exploring the applications that stem from such a discovery.'

'Ever think of being an archaeologist?' she asked dryly.

'I prefer the living world,' he murmured. 'Ancient cities can be dazzling but they aren't my passion. Plant interactions are.'

'And then there's the travel,' she said.

'Exactly. As for a regular day, it varies. At the moment I'm here on the boat, sitting in front of a laptop for most of the day, running the stats on experimental results. It's data entry at its most pedestrian—until you find something. And I never know what I'll find until I find it, or where it will lead until I get there. That's the beauty of it.'

'A man who savours the journey.'

'Don't you?' he countered.

'I used to.' Charlotte stared past him, out over the water and the increasingly dusky sky. 'And then somewhere in my mid twenties I started wondering what it might be like to stay in one place for a while. So instead of scraping away at how other people lived, I took the Sydney uni job and tried to put something of what all those ancient civilisations had taught me into practice.'

'What did they teach you?'

'That sooner or later everyone needs a home. An environment they can control. A place to retreat to. Somewhere that brings them peace.'

'And does your apartment by the bridge feel like a home?' he asked quietly.

'I've been asking myself the same question for a while now.' Charlotte shrugged and looked out over the water. 'Sooner or later I'm going to have to decide what to do about Aurora's house. I really don't need two.'

'Which one's closer to your workplace?'

'The apartment. But Aurora's has more sentimental value. It's the closest thing to a childhood home that I've got. We used to make a point of going back there at least once a year.'

'For how long?'

'A couple of weeks,' said Charlotte. 'A month if I was lucky.'

'What about school?' asked Greyson.

'We used the New South Wales distance education system,' said Charlotte. 'Tailored for children who travelled, children who roamed. Aurora supplemented it, of course. She had a knack for making the past come alive so the histories fast became our passion. I studied the Battle of Waterloo by walking the battlefield. I sat in the Colosseum and dreamed of gladiators and the roar of a Roman crowd.'

'It sounds idyllic.'

'It was richly rewarding,' said Charlotte quietly. 'And sometimes it was incredibly lonely. It's why I resist the notion of taking the archaeology road again. At least here I have friends and a place that's mine.'

'Two places, in fact,' murmured Greyson dryly.

'Exactly.' Charlotte fed him another prawn. 'I like *your* home, by the way. It's very you.'

'Thank you. We're almost at the cove.'

And then they *were* at the cove and Greyson was cutting the engine and dropping anchor as the last shards of light from a long gone sun surrendered to the night.

Charlotte smiled and let Greyson take the near empty food tray and lead her inside. He fetched some drinks—a white wine for her, beer for himself. He took two cheese-sauce-covered lobster halves from the fridge and shoved them in the oven. He looked comfortable in the kitchen. At home.

Charlotte had never once pictured Gil in the kitchen. Certainly not in a ship's galley. Nor had Gil ever been quite so delectably dressed.

'You're smiling,' Grey murmured.

'I know.' She set her wine on the bench and flowed into Greyson's arms, burrowing beneath his open shirt in search of warm skin over rippling muscle. She touched the tip of her tongue to his collarbone and tasted salt. He put his hand to her head and held her there for a moment, breathing in deep, before tilting her head back and covering her lips with his own in a kiss that spoke of welcome, and wanting, and a man who intended to savour every moment of this particular journey.

'Miss me?' he whispered, between kisses.

'It's really not part of the plan,' she countered and kissed him again. She didn't tell him that sinking into his kisses felt a lot like coming home. She didn't say that she'd thought about him far more than she'd wanted to this past week. That she'd envied him his overprotective mother and his lovely ex-fiancée, the work that was his passion, and the surety with which he moved through life. A smart and sexy man who knew exactly what he wanted was a very attractive proposition for a woman who did not.

He filled a gap, as Gil had filled a gap. He fed a need Charlotte hadn't known existed.

'I think I'm using you,' she murmured.

'That's okay.' He kissed her again. This time she moaned her approval. 'Blame it on the endorphins.'

'You don't recommend that I take at least *some* responsibility for my behaviour?'

'We have a short-term liaison agreement, remember? Your behaviour is entirely appropriate. You could even—just a suggestion—increase your enthusiasm for my company.'

'You called, I came,' she countered, stepping out of his embrace and retrieving her wine. 'Undress me, make love to me, and I guarantee I'll come some more. How much more enthusiasm do you want?'

'Maybe enthusiasm wasn't quite the right word,' Greyson said smoothly. 'Never mind.'

He reached for his beer, leaned back against the tiny galley sink, and studied her intently. 'My mother phoned this evening to ask me what I was doing this weekend. I told her I was spending it with you. She wants you over for dinner again, some time. Just the four of us, my father included.'

'Why?' asked Charlotte warily.

'Perhaps she feels that she didn't give you a chance.'

'She doesn't have to.'

'Alas, she doesn't know that.' Grey studied her some more. 'I'll tell her you're busy.'

Charlotte lowered her gaze. Had she really been involved with Greyson, she'd have grasped the olive branch extended. As it was…he could tell his mother whatever he liked.

'It's one of the drawbacks of having a nosey family,' he said next. 'My mother's been after grandchildren for years.'

'Grandchildren?'

'What's your position on that?' he asked and Charlotte glanced back towards him to find his gaze more intent than ever.

'On grandchildren?' she said lightly. 'I can see the appeal.'

'On children,' he said. 'And you having them.'

'Yours?'

'Anyone's.'

'Again, I can see the appeal,' she said. 'And were I in a loving and stable relationship, I might consider children an option.'

'What if your partner had a vocation that required travel? Would you consider joining him on his travels? You and the children?'

'Are we talking about a partner much like yourself?'

'Let's assume yes,' he said.

'It's not a question I've given much thought to,' she said. 'Mainly because the plan is to avoid becoming involved with such a man. I've a lot of experience when it comes to unorthodox childhoods, Greyson. I know what worked for me, and what didn't. I'll not be repeating what didn't.'

'Wouldn't that make you the perfect partner for such a man?' he said silkily.

'That would depend on his ability to forfeit his needs and desires for the greater good of his family when the time came for him to do so,' she said, equally silkily. 'Could *you*?'

'Good question,' he said blandly and peeked into the oven. 'I think they're done.'

They ate on deck, bypassing the perfectly prepared table in favour of a starry sky, a playful breeze, and balancing their plates on their knees. It fed Greyson's need for freedom and Charlotte's need for escape from difficult questions and impossible compromises. When they were done with the food she relaxed back against the moulded bench seating and stared at the sky. You couldn't see the stars from where she was in Sydney. Not many, at any rate, and not often. 'I'm not *against* travel,' she murmured. 'I'm very fond of new horizons and experiences.'

'I see that,' he murmured.

'Just not as an ongoing way of life.'

'Have you ever made love beneath the stars?' he murmured.

'Are you changing the subject?'

'Yes,' he said. 'I've had enough of the old subject. I'm hunting a new one. Have you ever made love outside, under the stars?'

'No.'

'Want to?'

She rose and straddled him, pushing his shirt from his shoulders as she'd wanted to do all evening, glorying in his size and his strength and the lazy intensity he could bring to a moment. 'Yes,' she said. 'I do.'

He didn't mean to devour her. He hadn't meant to bring up his mother's dinner invitation or the subject of children either. Hadn't meant to make love to her half the night and then again come sunrise because he couldn't get enough of her. But he did all those things to Charlotte Greenstone and she matched him, passion for passion, and warned him that last time, before her eyes had fluttered closed, that if he didn't want her committing mutiny, her breakfast had better be bountiful and could he please serve it some time after ten.

'What did your last Sherpa die of?' he'd muttered.

'Boredom,' she'd mumbled and promptly fallen asleep.

Greyson wasn't bored.

Exasperated, at times. Astonished by the sexual pleasure he found in Charlotte's embrace. But not bored.

He had a plan, formulated last night in between one bout of lovemaking and the next. A stupid plan, half baked and wholly crazy and one he wasn't at all sure he'd be able to sell to Charlotte as a viable option, given her soul deep aversion to traipsing around the globe according to someone else's whim. Still, he did have a habit of getting what he wanted. Eventually.

Grey waited until ten-thirty to wake Charlotte from her slumber. He used a mug of the finest highland coffee PNG had to offer to rouse her. He told her the pancakes would be ready by eleven, and that there were fresh towels and toiletries in the bathroom. He thought he heard the words *slave driver* mumbled by way of reply, along with a few other odd words like *incubus*, *sadist*, and *dead man*.

Perhaps she'd been comparing him favourably to Gil.

'I have a plan,' he said when Charlotte was wholly awake and halfway through her pancakes and coffee. 'Will you hear me out?'

'Does it involve your mother?'

'No, although I dare say she'll have something to say about the matter. It involves me going to Borneo next week to scout locations for the new project. And you coming with me.'

Charlotte chewed slowly and swallowed hard. She reached for her coffee, deliberately stalling for time. Grey kept his mouth shut and let her stall. Press her and he'd lose her. Rush her and she'd bolt. Challenge her and he might just be able to persuade her around to his way of thinking.

'Why would I do that?' she said finally.

'Because it'd give you an opportunity to test your feelings about travel,' he offered. 'You'll get all the vagaries of working a remote location without having to involve your own work. Then if the lifestyle still holds no appeal for you, your work will be exactly how and where you left it. Face it, Charlotte. You're a little hazy right now when it comes to the direction you want your career to take. A trip like this can't hurt and might even help clarify your thoughts on the matter.'

She didn't deny it. 'What's in it for you?' she asked warily.

'You mean apart from the insanely good sex?'

He won a tiny smile from her. 'You have a one-track mind.'

'So I've been told. Usually by people who fail to comprehend the bigger picture.' He sent her his most reassuring smile, not particularly wanting to discuss his big-picture plans with her at the moment. 'I'll pay your way, of course.'

Just like that, her smile disappeared. 'Don't be daft.'

'Why is that daft? My invite, my expense. Your rules, remember?'

'Those rules aren't applicable to this situation.'

'My mistake,' he said smoothly. 'You presented your position on the matter of who pays for what strongly enough that I naturally assumed there was no room for movement. You present your position on careers that require extensive travel with equal conviction, but again, I sense uncertainty as to *why* you consider them not to your liking. I leave on Wednesday. Sydney to mainland Malaysia, then a couple of regional flights to get to a little river city called Banjarmasin.'

'I know it,' she said flatly.

'I've an interest in the conservation forests there.'

Charlotte picked up her fork and cut into her pancake with the edge of it, deftly liberating a chunk before stabbing it with the end of her fork. She put it to her mouth, chewed, swallowed, and smiled. 'I'm sure there'll be plenty there to interest you.'

'And to interest you?'

'Well, the monkeys are very sweet,' she murmured. 'When do you need my answer by?'

'No rush. Although some time before Wednesday,

obviously.' He sipped his coffee. 'Anywhere you need to be today?'

'Not really. I often spend Sunday afternoon at Aurora's house. It appeases the neighbours.'

'If I dropped you back at the marina tomorrow morning, you could be there by lunchtime. Would that work?'

'I didn't bring two days' worth of clothes.'

'Wear mine.'

'Are you asking me to sleep over again tonight?'

'Yes.'

'So you can convince me to come traipsing with you?'

'Because I'm enjoying your company and I'm not quite ready to let you go.' He gave her the truth of his thoughts in that he gave her what he thought she would bear. 'A short term affair doesn't by nature have to lack intensity.'

'So I'm discovering,' she murmured.

'Will you stay on another night?'

'Will you try and convince me to come travelling with you next week if I do?'

'No.' Greyson shook his head. 'My offer stands but I'll not badger you into accepting it. That's not my way. I'm quite happy to leave the question hanging there if you are.'

'The old elephant in the living room,' she said with a wry smile.

'Exactly.'

'So what would we do with the day if I stayed on?' she said at last, and watched Greyson's eyes lighten and brighten with possibilities.

'Wind's picking up,' he said. 'Have you ever raced a cat under sail?'

* * *

They raced the day away and made the most of the night.

Greyson kept his word. He never once mentioned his offer. Instead he made love to her with a focus no other man had ever matched. Passion ruled him, ruled them both, along with greedy abandon in Charlotte's case, liberally laced with desperation at the thought that this night might be their last.

Morning came too soon for Charlotte but she savoured it regardless, delighting in being wooed awake by wicked promises and exceptionally good coffee. A woman could get used to such treatment, but only a foolish woman would allow herself to depend on it.

She'd thought about joining Greyson in Borneo for the week. One week, what harm could it do? She had holiday time owing. Time her boss had urged her to take. She had no commitments to pets or to people—no responsibilities at all in that regard. She was a free agent and why shouldn't she follow her heart—or at least her libido for a time—and see where it led?

Tempting, so tempting, this man's kisses, as she and Greyson stood on dry land later in the day, saying their farewells beside her baking hot car, and stealing kisses where they could. Charlotte stole a lot of them, a woman bent on gorging herself before a famine.

'Safe travels, Greyson Tyler,' she murmured, and if her heart felt as if it was breaking, well, perhaps it was. She stood back and took one last look at him, storing up the memories for later. A big beautiful man with tousled black hair, intelligent brown eyes, more charm than was good for him, and an air of command and purpose that clung to him like skin. 'I'll think of you with pleasure and I'll think of you with regret, but I'll not be going with you to Borneo.'

'Why not?' His turn to move forward, to reach for her and coax every last drop of pleasure from a kiss. 'We're good together, Charlotte. Better than good.'

'I know. And maybe in another lifetime, one shaped by a different upbringing, I'd have followed you and never looked back.' She stepped back, out of his arms and the solace she found there and regarded him pensively. 'You think I don't know my own mind or that you can change it. Somewhere along the way, I've given you the impression that I don't know what I want from a partner or from this life, and maybe I don't. Not fully, not with certainty. Thing is, no matter how often I examine the notion of travel or of being with a partner who travels, there's a resistance there that runs soul deep.'

'Call me,' he said gruffly. 'When I get back.'

'Greyson.' She looked away, down at the suddenly blurry steering wheel of her car, anywhere but at him. How had she come to care for him so much in such a short time? Two weeks. Less than half a dozen meetings, and already he was tearing her in two. 'I can't.' Nothing more than a ragged plea for mercy, for he seemed bent on making this farewell so much harder than it should have been. 'I can't,' she whispered again.

'Then I'll call you.'

'Greyson, please…' She pressed her lips to his, one final farewell. She stepped back and smiled through her tears. Time to go before she begged him to stay. 'Don't.'

CHAPTER SEVEN

GREYSON TYLER wasn't always an easy man to deal with. He had his fair share of dogged determination. He knew exactly how well persistence paid off. He hadn't wanted to walk away from Charlotte Greenstone when she'd asked him to. His body had screamed no and his brain had assured him that he could overcome her protests eventually. Only honour had stayed his hand.

Charlotte hadn't refused him in haste—she'd thought about his offer, thought hard about where their fledgling relationship might lead and what he could give her that she wanted. Her conclusion had been a valid one.

Not enough.

He'd heard that tune before. He knew all the words.

This time round, they hammered home hard.

He went to Borneo. He stayed the week and decided he had all the skills required to do good work there—if he had a mind to. Living conditions would be perfectly adequate. The seafood was exceptional. He'd be on the water a lot, and that always endeared a project to him, for the water was his home. He knew of half a dozen funding opportunities coming up. He should have been busy writing and sending out proposals.

And yet…a week passed, and then another three, and

he still hadn't written an outline for what he wanted to do in Borneo.

He tried telling himself it was because the PNG data had proved so richly rewarding, and he'd been distracted by that, and by all the research papers to be had from it. He even wrote some of those papers and was pleased with his efforts. Dr Grey Tyler was doing good work—work that, when reviewed and published, should make finding grant money for future projects easy.

Six months was all he'd allowed himself when it came to mining the PNG data for papers and two of those had already passed. He needed to get another project in place soon or he'd be out of work.

Being out of work held no appeal whatsoever.

Neither, he finally admitted to himself, did spending the next three years in a tiny fishing village in Borneo.

Something else, then. Something fascinating and captivating and a little more civilised would surely command his attention sooner or later.

And he wasn't talking about Charlotte Greenstone.

With Greyson—and Gilbert—out of the picture, Charlotte attempted to settle back into her normal routine with joy, and, if not joy, then at least some measure of contentment. Alas, embracing her inner contentment really wasn't going so well.

Restlessness plagued her. She couldn't settle to her work.

For the first time in five years, the congestion of inner city Sydney got on her nerves, and the charm of her nose-to-girder view of the Harbour Bridge, and the vibrations that shook the windows with every passing passenger train, wore thin.

Life didn't shine so brightly these days. Emptiness had

crept back into her life and this time it stayed. Dreariness and weariness had crept in too—ugly unwanted companions that she couldn't seem to shake.

Crankiness... Heaven help her, she had a short fuse these days.

The Mead had requested a meeting this morning to discuss a dig he was keen to find funding for. No guesses required as to whose job that would be. Following that, she had two undergraduate lectures scheduled for ten and twelve, and a doctor's appointment to go to in the afternoon.

It was seven a.m. and all Charlotte wanted to do was crawl back into bed and relive a morning or two when she'd woken up in a strong and loving man's arms and been treated to coffee in bed and pancakes with syrup, and a day of sailing and sunshine that she'd never wanted to end.

'Damn you!' she muttered to the man who'd given her that day. *'A curse on you, Greyson Tyler.'* A really good curse, for having the temerity and the God-given *attributes* to worm his way into her psyche and stay there.

Greyson the gone—be he in Borneo, PNG, roasting over hot coals...wherever.

Gone.

Charlotte's meeting with Harold Mead didn't start well. She was ten minutes late, the smell of the coffee he handed her made her want to throw up, and there were two other suits in the room—one of them the head of university finance, the other one the Dean of Geology. She smelled collaboration and coercion and they came through on that in spades. A joint dig involving every geologist, archaeologist, and currently aimless dogsbody on the payroll of three different universities. Charlotte would not be in charge, of course. She wouldn't even be required to step foot on site, if that was her preference. Nor would they utilise her field expertise, nor, by extrapolation, did they intend to credit her with any of the research.

No, Charlotte's sole task was to shake the loose change from the private sector in order to fund the project.

She declined. Politely.

She damn near resigned. Not so politely.

'Charlotte, I don't know what to do with you,' Harold Mead told her after the other two had left, his frustration and disappointment clearly evident. 'You won't commit to any field work, you pick and choose which projects you'll support with no clear research direction that I can discern, you *say* you'd like to move into project set-up and administration and yet here I am offering that to you on a plate and you refuse. What exactly is it that you *want*?'

'How about we start with some small level of *input* into the projects the Greenstone name is expected to sell,' she countered hotly, knowing her words were unprofessional but powerless to stop them tumbling out. 'An assurance that my experience might, at some stage, be *valued* when it comes to modifying a project plan, and not swept aside because I'm young and female and couldn't possibly know better than you.'

'Sometimes you don't,' said the Mead curtly.

'And sometimes I *do*,' she said. 'You want to know what I *want*? Fine. I'll have a proposal on your desk tomorrow morning, outlining my thoughts on project funding and administration in detail. I suggest you look it over rather closely, see if you can bring yourself to accommodate at least *some* of my suggestions, because if not I'll be moving on and taking my family name and my cashed-up connections with me.'

Two lectures, a salad sandwich, and a hasty drive

through the city centre later, Charlotte arrived at the Circular Quay surgery near her apartment. Twenty minutes after she took a seat in the waiting room, the doctor called her in.

The affable doctor Christina Christensen sat her down, looked her over and asked her what was wrong. 'Lethargy, loss of appetite, and a tendency to get a wee bit emotional over the strangest things,' she said.

'What kind of things?' the doctor asked as she reached for the blood pressure bandage.

'Well...this morning I was howling along to a piece of music,' said Charlotte.

'It happens,' said the doctor. 'You should see me at the opera.'

'It wasn't that kind of music.'

'What kind was it?' asked the doctor.

'Beethoven's Ninth. Seriously, I'm getting more and more irrational of late. Short-tempered. Opinionated.'

'Anything else?'

'Cross,' said Charlotte.

'You already said that.'

'It probably bears repeating.'

'Tell me about your appetite,' said the doctor as she pumped up the pressure wrap around Charlotte's upper arm to the point of pain and then abruptly released the pressure.

'What's to tell? It's gone.'

'Any uncommonly stressful events surrounding you lately?'

'That would be a yes,' muttered Charlotte. 'But I'm either getting on top of them or coming to terms with them.'

'Lucky you,' said the doctor. 'Your blood pressure's fine. How much weight have you lost?'

'A couple of kilos in the past couple of weeks.'

'Scales are over there,' said the doctor.

And when Charlotte stepped on them and the readout settled, 'You're a little lean, but nothing to worry about. Periods regular?'

'I'm on the pill,' muttered Charlotte. 'I went on them *because* of irregular periods.'

'Any chance you could be pregnant?' asked the doctor, gesturing for Charlotte to return to the patient's chair.

Charlotte didn't answer her straight away. She was too busy counting back time and fighting terror.

The doctor opened a desk drawer and pulled out a box full of little white individually wrapped plastic sticks. She set one on the desk in front of Charlotte. 'Ever used one of these?'

'No.' *Hell*, no.

'Bathroom's two doors down. Pee on the window end, shake off the excess moisture, and bring it back here.'

'I really don't thin—'

'Go,' said the doctor gently. 'If it comes up negative, I'll order you some blood tests to see if there's another reason for the changes you're describing, but first things first.'

Right. First things first. Nothing to panic about.

Charlotte held to the 'first things first' motto all through the long walk to the bathroom and through the business with the pregnancy-kit stick. A blue line already ran across the window of the stick—that was good, right? It was the crosses you had to worry about.

'Just pop it on the paper towel there,' said the good doctor when Charlotte returned. 'It'll only take a couple of minutes.'

Longest two minutes of Charlotte's life.

The doctor chatted. Inputted data into Charlotte's patient file. Asked her if she was currently in a steady relationship and whether she'd been considering mother-hood, of late.

'No,' said Charlotte, and, 'No.' While another little line grew slowly stronger and transected the first.

Eventually the doctor looked down and then back up at Charlotte, her gaze sympathetic. 'We can do it again,' she said. 'We can take a blood test to confirm, but I think you'd best brace yourself for unexpected news.' The doctor's smile turned wry. 'Congratulations, Ms Greenstone. You're pregnant.'

Charlotte sat unmoving, her gaze not leaving that ter-rible little stick.

'I want to see you again in a few days' time,' continued the doctor. 'We'll talk more then. About options. What happens next. Until then, take it easy, don't skip meals, and be kind to yourself.' The doctor studied her intently. 'Do you have anyone you can talk to about this? Family? Friends? The father?'

Charlotte didn't answer straight away. Mainly because her gut response had been no. There was no one to talk to or turn to. No one at all.

'Charlotte, do I need to refer you to a counsellor?' Dr Christina Christensen's eyes were kind and knowing. She'd probably seen this response before. 'I can pull some strings and get you in to see one this afternoon, if need be.'

What was the doctor saying now? Something about a counsellor? Charlotte stared at her uncomprehendingly. She had no words. There were no words for this.

'Charlotte.' The doctor's voice was infinitely gentle. 'I'm going to make an appointment for you to talk to a family counsellor this afternoon.'

'No!' Another emotional outburst in a morning filled with them. 'No,' she repeated more calmly. 'I'm fine.' Not shattered, or terrified beyond belief. 'Pregnant, right? But otherwise fine.'

The doctor sat back in her chair and steepled her fingers, her gaze not leaving Charlotte's face.

'I have people I can talk to,' said Charlotte next. 'I do.' Imaginary Aurora. Back from the dead, fictional ex-fiancé Gil.

'Your call on the counsellor,' said the doctor. 'But I still want to see you in three days' time. Make the appointment on your way out.'

Charlotte made the appointment and made it to her car. She didn't make it home to her apartment. Instead she drove to Aurora's and went to the kitchen and made herself a cup of tea, black because there was no milk in the house because she'd cleaned out and turned off the fridge, and sugared, because there was sugar in the cupboard and sugar was good for shock. She sat in Aurora's conservatory-style kitchen and stared out over the gardens to the harbour beyond and tentatively tried picking her way through her chaotic emotions.

A baby. Dear God, a baby to love and to care for. Loneliness in exchange for motherhood. A child to teach. A child who would learn what she had learned, what everyone learned eventually. That life was glorious and unexpected and too often brutal. A child who had no one. No one but her.

Only that wasn't quite true, for this was Greyson's child too.

Greyson the magnificent, with his loving family and his travelling life.

What now? What on earth was she supposed to do now?

I miss you, Aurora. I wish you were here. I wish...

A memory started forming; a vivid picture in her mind.

A lamp-lit private library and an overstuffed leather arm-chair. Aurora in her thirties and Charlotte at five. A leather bound children's picture book rich with story and life. Aurora's fine voice; such a marvellous sound.

If wishes were horses then beggars would ride…

Drawing her knees up to her chest, Charlotte wrapped her arms tightly around herself, and wept.

'You need to be at work,' said Millie two days later, while sitting in Charlotte's sunny apartment kitchen beneath the bridge. The bridge still loomed large and the windows still shook when the trains went by, but those things had ceased to annoy her. These days Charlotte was all about simply being grateful that she owned her own homes, that she didn't need to work to support herself, and that when it came to the things that money could buy, neither she nor this baby would ever go without.

Reason had returned to Charlotte, or, if not reason exactly, at least a functioning awareness of how fortunate she was. She had an education and a great deal of wealth. She had stability and a good life.

She even had friends who cared enough to call in on their way home from work, seeing as Charlotte *hadn't* been in to work these past few days. Millie was here, bearing flowers and cake, and Charlotte was ridiculously glad of her company. Grateful that Millie had thought enough of their friendship to drop by. Glad that Millie brought with her gossip from work.

Charlotte had almost tendered her resignation the afternoon she'd received news of her impending motherhood but she'd dredged up a thimbleful of professionalism from somewhere and put together a 'Greenstone Foundation' proposal instead and emailed it off to the Mead.

A proposal that—the more she thought about it—didn't

really require the university's participation at all. One that outlined her preferred project set-up, co-ordination, collaboration, and financing practices. One that granted the university beneficial ties to the foundation and in return requested that the university provide her with a management assistant. Preferably one eager to travel with or without her to dig sites in order to oversee operations. Preferably one who'd worked outside the academic arena and had real world skills in place as well as the necessary archaeology qualifications. Preferably Derek.

'Seriously, Charlotte,' said Millie, from her spot at the kitchen counter, where she'd taken to slicing up the walnut loaf she'd brought with her, 'the entire department's in an uproar about this foundation of yours and what's in it for them—Derek loves the idea, by the way—but you not being around to explain your vision isn't helping any. You need to get in there and get forceful if you want it to happen.'

'I want it to happen,' said Charlotte simply.

'So you'll be back at work on Monday?'

Charlotte nodded. 'You want some coffee to go with your walnut slice?'

Millie nodded.

Charlotte set the coffee maker to gurgling. She headed for the fridge. Out came the milk for the coffee and double dollop cream for the cake.

'So what prompted this Greenstone Foundation idea?' asked Millie.

'Aurora's death,' said Charlotte. 'More money than I know what to do with. The need for a challenge. Not getting the leeway or the recognition I wanted from the university employment system. Take your pick. Life lacked purpose. The foundation will give me one. And flexibility as well. Happens I'm going to need that too.'

'What does Gil think of your newfound purpose?' asked Millie.

'I've no idea.'

'Ah.' Millie's eyes turned sympathetic. 'Guess you two didn't sort out your differences, then.'

'No. Some people never lose the wanderlust. Grey's one of them.'

'Who's Grey?'

'Gil,' said Charlotte. 'Thaddeus. Only he's not Thaddeus either. He's Greyson.'

'The man has more names than a birth registry,' muttered Millie, and bit into her now cream-slathered walnut slice.

Charlotte smiled and toyed with her own food. 'So it seems.' What to tell and what to withhold from a woman whose friendship she'd come to value? 'Millie, will you keep a confidence for me?'

'Is it likely to impact negatively on my work, my relationship with others, or my ethics?' asked Millie.

'Not really,' said Charlotte. 'Maybe a little. It's probably not going to do a whole lot for your opinion of me.'

Millie put down her slice, wiped her hands on the napkin, sipped her coffee, and set it down gently. First things first. 'Okay,' she said cautiously. 'What's up?'

'Gil Tyler was a figment of my imagination. Grey Tyler is the man who came to collect his office. They're not one and the same. And I haven't finished yet.'

Harder than she'd thought, this unburdening of her sins. So many, *many* lies. It was time for them to stop.

'Okay.' Millie's eyebrows had risen considerably. 'Continue.'

'Grey and I slept together a time or two. It was...intense. Amazing. But strictly short term. We parted ways relatively amicably.'

It seemed as good a summary as any, even if it did downplay the intensity of the real thing.

'Sounds like a good time was had by all,' said Millie.

'And now I'm pregnant.'

Millie blinked, nodded slowly, and kept her mouth firmly shut.

'Not deliberately,' said Charlotte hastily. 'This would be one of those extremely unexpected pregnancies. As opposed to a planned one.'

Another slow nod from Millie.

'Millie, say something.'

'Yes,' said Millie. 'Yes, I believe that *is* the custom. I just need a moment's processing time. And we're definitely going to need more cake.'

'I have mountains of cake,' said Charlotte. 'Also ice cream, pickles, and caramel tart, just in case. All I'm after is your uninhibited response to my news.'

Millie sent her a speaking glance.

'Although any response will do.'

'Does anyone else know?' asked Millie.

'Not yet. You're my practice run.'

'Oh, the pressure to say something you might actually want to hear,' murmured Millie. 'I feel like I'm on a game show and you're the host, waiting for my reply to the million dollar question.' Millie put both hands to her head and groaned. 'Can I phone a friend?'

'Who?'

'Derek.'

'Only if you're planning on inviting him over,' said Charlotte. 'I may need him for my second practice run. I think I've blown the first.'

Millie ran her hands over her hair and looked back up at Charlotte, her eyes imploring. 'I don't know what to say.'

'Say I can do this,' pleaded Charlotte, brittleness giving

way to uncertainty in the face of Millie's continued hesitation. 'Please, Millie.' Before Charlotte's tears started in earnest. 'I need someone to tell me that I can do this and that everything's going to be okay.'

'Oh, Charlotte. Sweetie.' Millie was on her feet, wrapping her arms around Charlotte. Contact and comfort. Charlotte gulped back a sob. 'It *will* be okay. I know you. There's nothing you can't do when you put your mind to it. You'll make a wonderful mother. You'll see.'

'What am I going to tell Greyson?' whispered Charlotte.

But to that, Millie had no answer.

Derek arrived an hour and a half later, bearing Thai take-away for three and a six-pack of beer. 'I don't do feel-good films and I don't do tears,' he said. 'I'm here strictly to get the low-down on the Greenstone Foundation proposal.'

'Of course you are,' murmured Millie soothingly. 'Shall we eat first?'

'We should definitely eat first,' said a freshly composed Charlotte.

Derek eyed the sweets laden kitchen counter sceptically. 'You're into the crisis food,' he declared. 'I've lived in enough foster homes to know crisis food when I see it and crisis phone calls when I get one.'

'This crisis doesn't involve you directly,' said Charlotte.

'Then why am I here?'

'We needed a test male,' said Millie. 'And by *we*, I mean Charlotte. Strictly speaking, this isn't my crisis either—lucky for you.'

'Millie's going to observe and take notes,' said Charlotte. 'Derek, would you like a cold glass for your beer?'

'Hospitable,' said Millie. 'Nice touch.'

Charlotte poured beer for Derek with a relatively steady

hand, wine for Millie, and sparkling mineral water for herself.

'The mineral water could raise questions,' said Millie. 'Maybe you should pour yourself a glass of wine as well, even if you don't touch it. Derek, what do you think?'

'Huh?' said Derek.

'My mistake,' said Millie. 'Proceed.'

Charlotte set three places at the kitchen counter for eating. She set serving spoons to Derek's Thai offerings. 'You think I need to be more formal?' asked Charlotte. 'Because I can always set the dining table?'

'No, this is good,' said Millie. 'He needs to feel comfortable and relaxed. Derek, do you feel comfortable and relaxed?'

'I might if I knew what was going *on*,' muttered Derek.

Millie nodded sagely. 'Proceed.'

'I'm going to ask him about his work,' said Charlotte. 'Derek, how's the work? Research coming together well?'

'Is this a job interview?' asked Derek, hoeing into the food. 'Because if this is about the sidekick position for the Greenstone Foundation, I want more prep time. Seriously, Charlotte. You could do worse than consider me for the job.'

'Interesting,' said Mille. 'The man has his own agenda.' She turned to Charlotte. 'Greyson may well have his own agenda too.'

'Who's Greyson?' asked Derek.

'Formerly Thaddeus,' said Charlotte. 'In other words Gil. Gil Tyler. Of long pig fame. Millie can fill you in on the details later. The important thing is for you to put yourself in the role of dedicated research scientist and world traveller. We didn't think it'd be too much of a stretch for you. As for the foundation position, if it goes ahead you'd damn well better apply seeing as I wrote it with you in mind.'

'Seriously?' said Derek.

'Seriously.'

Derek beamed.

'Excellent work with the compliments,' said Millie, and to Derek, 'How are you feeling? Are you feeling relaxed?'

'Well, I *was*,' murmured Derek.

'I think it's time,' said Mille.

'Are you sure?' Charlotte didn't feel at all sure. 'I mean, he's hardly touched his beer.'

'It's time,' said Millie. 'It's just a practice run. Master the fear.'

'Okay.' Charlotte took a huge breath and reached for Millie's wine, only Millie was faster, holding it up and out of the way before Charlotte could get to it. Derek had his beer halfway to his lips so no joy there either. 'Derek, I'm pregnant.'

Derek's beer went down wrong. Derek surfaced all a splutter.

'I'm thinking you should probably wait until Greyson's *between* beers to make that particular announcement,' said Millie.

'Will do,' said Charlotte nervously. 'Derek? Anything to add?'

'Not a word,' wheezed the beleaguered Derek.

'Put yourself in Greyson's shoes,' said Millie encouragingly. 'Anything to add *now*?'

'Am I the father?' asked Derek. 'No, let me rephrase. I can't say those particular words without breaking into a cold sweat. Is Greyson the father?'

'Yes,' said Charlotte.

'And also your fiancé.'

'No,' said Charlotte. 'I'm currently fiancé-less. As is Greyson.'

'And you want him back?' asked Derek.

'Hard to say,' murmured Charlotte. 'I never really had him in the first place. Let's just assume that I don't really know *what* I want from him at this particular point in time.'

'Do you want financial assistance when it comes to raising this child?' asked Derek.

'No.' Charlotte shook her head emphatically. 'I don't need Greyson's money. That's the last thing I need.' She picked up her glass of fizzy water, wishing it were wine. 'Is that really one of the first things that came to mind?'

'Yes,' said Derek grimly. 'Not everyone can afford to be blasé when it comes to ongoing monetary commitments, Charlotte, and raising a child very definitely qualifies as that.'

'So maybe she tells him she doesn't want his money *before* she tells him she's pregnant,' said Millie.

'How?' asked Charlotte. 'How do I do that?'

'Maybe you start with what you *do* want from him,' said Millie. 'Which would be…?' And when Charlotte remained silent, 'This is your cue. What do you want from him?'

But Charlotte didn't know. 'Maybe, apart from the knowing…maybe some level of participation?'

'You mean marriage,' said Derek.

'No! Not necessarily.' Charlotte was starting to tremble now. She countered by crossing her arms in front of her. 'I don't know. This isn't going well, is it?' she said in a small voice.

'You're telling a man he's going to be a father, Charlotte,' muttered Derek. 'How do you expect it to go?'

'Better,' she said and choked down her rising panic. 'I just assumed that breaking the news to him in person would be better, but maybe it's not. I could email him with the news, or text him, and *then* arrange a meeting…'

But Derek was shaking his head. 'I didn't say don't give him the news in person. I said give him some thinking time once you do. Don't analyse his initial response. Like as not, it won't be the one you want. Give him some space with this. Let him know *your* thoughts on marriage and motherhood, and then *let him be*.'

'I can do that,' said Charlotte faintly, and turned to Millie. Millie who'd been judging her presentation and hopefully taking notes. 'Millie, so how did it go?'

'Fine. Just fine,' said Millie a little too readily. And then, 'I need another drink.'

Charlotte waited until the following morning to email Greyson. A beautiful late-summer's morning with not a whisper of a cloud in the sky. A good day, she decided, for sharing unexpected news. Nonetheless, her email to Greyson still took her all morning to construct and finally consisted of three short words. 'Where are you?'

Greyson's reply pinged back within ten minutes. 'Hawkesbury river.'

'Dinner at my place this evening?' she wrote back, before she lost her nerve entirely. 'Seven p.m.?'

This time his reply came almost instantaneously. 'Why?'

Not a man bent on being amiable. Not entirely unexpected, given that her parting words to him two months ago had been, 'Don't call me and I won't call you.'

'Need to talk to you,' she wrote back. Now there was a phrase guaranteed to send a chill up a man's spine.

Charlotte sat back and stared at the computer screen after that, sat there for ten minutes with her heart in her throat, waiting for a reply that did not come. When the phone rang, she almost slipped her skin. Charlotte reached for it gingerly, hoping it was Greyson, hoping it was not.

'Charlotte Greenstone,' she said as evenly as she could, while her hands shook and her knees shook and she tucked her free hand between her knees in an effort to stop the trembling of both.

'So talk.' Greyson's voice; deep and gravelly and riddled with wariness.

'Hello, Greyson,' she said, in a voice that wobbled only faintly. 'I half expected you to be in Borneo.'

'No.'

'No.' She ran through the script she'd prepared in her mind. Some sort of compliment was supposed to come next, but her brain had gone blank the minute she'd heard that familiar deep voice.

'What do you want, Charlotte?'

'Not money.' She remembered Derek's words of last night and figured she might as well get that one out of the way. 'You don't ever need to worry on that score.'

'I wasn't,' he uttered dryly.

'Because money's not the problem here.'

'So what *is* the problem here?' he said. 'I'm assuming you're not ringing because life felt empty without me and you want to pick up where we left off? Am I wrong?'

Charlotte closed her eyes. She hadn't armoured herself properly against Greyson's thinly veiled hostility. She should have. 'Never mind,' she said raggedly. 'This was a really bad idea. I'm sorry. I shouldn't have bothered you.'

'Charlotte, wait!'

She waited in silence. Trembling. Quailing.

'Dinner, you said,' he muttered, and his voice was as ragged as hers.

'Yes.'

'You should know that I'll not be able to keep my hands off you if we have it at your place. You should know not to be with me in private right now. I'm telling you this as a courtesy.'

'Somewhere else, then,' she managed, while his words seared through her, bringing equal parts heat and apprehension. 'There are dozens of restaurants nearby.'

'Name one.'

She did. A steakhouse slash cocktail bar. Nothing fancy but there was privacy to be had in darkened booths if conversation demanded it, and this conversation surely would.

'I'll meet you there at seven,' he said. 'And, Charlotte?'

'What?' she said faintly.

'If you want me to be at all civilised, you'll be letting me pay for the meal.'

Greyson Tyler was no stranger to trouble. He knew the ways in which it crept up on a man. He knew how it smelled. He knew without a shadow of a doubt that meeting Charlotte again for a meal and whatever else she had in mind spelled trouble for them both. His needs were a little too intense when it came to delectable yet thoroughly unsuitable Charlotte Greenstone. There was no telling what he might demand of her, or the concessions he might make in order to get those demands met.

He'd stayed away. He'd been the gentleman and kept his distance. He'd done everything she'd asked of him and, *dammit*, he'd been hurt in the process.

Cancel.

That was what he *should* do. Tell her she'd been right all along about them wanting different types of lives, and that he couldn't see any reason to meet up with her again. No reason at all.

Cancel.

But he did not.

Greyson arrived fifteen minutes early to the restaurant Charlotte had suggested: a scarred and bluesy corner bar with a blackboard menu promising quality fare that didn't cost the earth. A quick glance around told him that Charlotte hadn't yet arrived. He ordered a beer, found a shadowy corner booth with a view of the entrance and settled down to wait.

Charlotte the wilful, the reckless, the vulnerable. Best lover he'd ever had. Unstinting in her responses and mesmerising in her sexual abandon. Not a woman any man would forget in a hurry and he cursed her afresh while he sat with his beer and waited, and nursed the scars she'd given him.

He didn't know why he was here—lining up for another serve of nameless sorrow—except that she'd asked him to meet her and she'd sounded so unsure of herself and that in itself signalled trouble. Maybe her workmates had found out about her fictional fiancé. Maybe she'd lost her job and her reputation—*her* problem, not his—but he would hear her out and help if he could. He could do that much without letting bitterness hold sway.

They'd only been on a handful of dates. Hardly her fault if her withdrawal had come too late to save him from going under. He could give her that much.

Honour demanded it.

Grey saw Charlotte before she spotted him. Small

woman with generous curves and a waterfall of wavy black hair pulled back off her face with a vibrant silk headband. She wore tailored black trousers, dainty high-heeled sandals, and a sleeveless vest top in the same pinks, purples, and greens as her headband. A purple leather handbag completed the outfit, and she looked more like the pampered socialite he'd taken to his mother's barbecue than the experienced Associate Professor of Archaeology he knew her to be.

He stood as she approached him. Stood because a woman who expected a man to open car doors for her would surely expect that as well. Stood because the fighter in him demanded he pursue any advantage he could with her and size was one of them.

She cast him a quick smile and slid into the bench seat opposite. A waiter materialised and took her order for mineral water. Greyson's beer stood mostly untouched and he left it that way.

'Thank you for coming,' she said politely.

'I'm a sucker for punishment.' Nothing but the truth. 'I'm also curious as to what you have to say to me.'

'Ah,' said Charlotte. 'Yes. That. I kind of need to work my way up to that particular discussion. How's your mother?'

'My mother's well.' Not where he'd been expecting this conversation to go. 'Why?'

'No reason. How's the Sarah situation?'

'I've seen her once since we spoke after the barbecue. We talked. She left. She blames you, by the way, for my newfound insensitivity.'

'Handy,' she said quietly.

Charlotte's drink came and the waiter directed them to the blackboard menu. Neither he nor Charlotte was ready to order. 'You've lost weight,' he said. She still took his breath away with her perfection of form and features, but there was no denying she'd dropped a few kilos from her slender frame. Kilos she could ill afford to lose.

She'd lost weight; she looked wan. He was the son of a doctor. 'Charlotte, are you sick?'

Grey watched in horror as tears swam in Charlotte's eyes and threatened to overflow.

Oh, God, she *was* sick. 'What is it?' Information. He needed information.

'Not sick,' she murmured. 'Not sick.' She put her hand to her forehead for a moment, then changed her mind and put both hands in her lap. Not once did she meet his gaze. She stared at her coaster, the tabletop, the entrance to the bar as if she'd rather be anywhere else but there with him. 'Pregnant.'

'*What?*'

Charlotte glanced up at him then, startled and terrified and apologetic all at once and he had his answer.

'Mine,' he said.

'Yes.' He could hardly hear her for the thundering of his heart. 'There's tests we can do if that's what you want,' she offered. 'But there's been no one else.'

'Forget the tests.' Satisfaction flooded through him, as unexpected as it was savage.

Mine.

In which case… 'Shouldn't you be putting *on* weight?' he said silkily.

'I'm working on it,' she said in a low raw voice. 'I've also been thinking about what we might do. Greyson, I don't want to raise this child all by myself. It's not enough. *I'm* not enough. A child should have more than that. More family. More security.'

'You want a termination?' Hard to keep his jaw from clenching or his dislike of that notion from colouring his words. 'Is that what you brought me here to tell me? Because it's not going to enamour you to me, Charlotte. Not by a long shot.'

Mine.

'That's not why I asked you here,' she murmured. 'I've not considered that course of action. I don't think it's for me.'

'Good.'

The waiter approached them again, took one look at Grey and kept right on walking.

'I'm not asking for marriage or monetary support either,' she said earnestly.

'Tough.' From one have-it-my-way child to another. 'You're getting both. And food. We're ordering food *now*. Pick something.'

'I'll have the chef's salad.'

'Now pick something *else*.'

'And the teriyaki chicken kebabs,' she said with a roll of her eyes. 'But only because I'm humouring you.'

Grey glared at her. Better that than leaning across the table and kissing her senseless. Or was it?

In the end he did lean across and kiss her, terrified that she wouldn't respond to him, equally terrified when she did because it was still there, this all-consuming need to lose himself in her. 'Pick a date,' he murmured when his lips left hers. 'Any date.'

'I'm not marrying you, Greyson. There's no need for that. Not in this day and age.'

'If you really think I'm going to let my child be raised a bastard, you really don't know me very well,' he said grimly.

'My point exactly,' countered Charlotte. 'Greyson, we hardly know one another. What I do know of you suggests that marriage is the last thing on your mind, and that you'd start to feel trapped within five minutes of taking that step. You've already broken one engagement because you weren't prepared to settle for a life based in Sydney.'

Grey stared at Charlotte broodingly. He couldn't deny it. He liked his freedom, and he loved to travel, but, dammit, was it so wrong to want this child to be born within marriage?'

'The baby could still have your name,' said Charlotte. 'Access wouldn't be a problem. I *want* you in this baby's life. But we don't have to get married for that to happen.'

'You think I'll take it, don't you?' he said bleakly. 'The easy way out. The half measure. You think I'll be content to stand at the periphery of this child's life, never quite giving or getting enough.'

'Greyson, I—'

'You're wrong.'

'Lofty words for a man who intends to spend the next three years of his life in Borneo.'

'I didn't take that job,' he said tightly. 'Something you would have discovered weeks ago had you thought enough of me to stick around.'

'I thought enough of you to bring you back, didn't I?' She looked mutinous, and scared, and sorry, and she made his heart bleed.

'No. You're scared enough of your inadequacies as a single parent to bring me back. You're looking for a back-up plan for this child in case something happens to you, and, unfortunately, I'm all you've got.'

If Charlotte had looked wan before, she now looked positively waxy. 'This is never going to work,' she said faintly.

'Are you going to faint?' Dear heaven, she looked fragile, and anxious, and perilously close to tears. 'Don't you dare faint!'

'I'm not going to faint.'

'Or cry.'

'Or cry,' she said in a voice that threatened exactly that.

Greyson eyed her grimly. 'You should know something about me, Charlotte. I never give up. I make things work. It's what I do.' He cupped her neck in his hand and touched his lips to hers again, hard and fast and ruthless. 'I'm free next Tuesday. What say we get married then?'

CHAPTER EIGHT

DINNER wasn't going well. Charlotte hadn't anticipated that Greyson would see straight through to her fear of leaving this child all alone in the world should something happen to her. She hadn't planned on his kisses reducing her to jelly and she certainly hadn't anticipated that his heated insistence on marriage would wash over her like a panacea, or that the thought of marriage to this man would be so very tempting.

'Greyson, I thank you for the offer,' she said raggedly. 'Truly, I do, but *think*. You're talking about a marriage of necessity, not a union based on love. Is that really what you want?'

Greyson remained silent. Such a beautiful man, so hell-bent on doing the right thing by her and this baby, that he couldn't see through to what he might need, and what he would lose if he insisted on a marriage of convenience.

'What about your work?' she continued. 'If not Borneo this time, you'll want to go somewhere else down the track. Greyson, you know my feelings on that kind of life.'

'We'll compromise,' he said, in a voice that promised anything but. 'I don't have all the answers for you, Charlotte. I have three more months' work here. After that I had planned on taking on a new project but it doesn't have to be out of the country. Maybe it's time I looked to my own backyard and reassessed my future direction. Maybe it's time you did the same.'

'I want to finish up at the university and set up a Greenstone Archaeology Foundation,' she offered. 'One that finances and manages archaeological projects and gets key people working together. I'd start small. One project at a time. If I can get the right people in place, I'll be able to work part time from home.'

'Or anywhere else,' he said silkily.

'Is that your idea of compromise? We traipse the world with you?'

'Of what use is a father to a child if he's never *there*? Jesus, Charlotte. What is it you *want* from me?' Greyson glared at her, a man trapped.

Trapped because of her.

'Not marriage,' she said, and her heart bled for herself and for Greyson, and the baby they'd unwittingly made. 'Not without love. Something else. Something that love doesn't necessarily have to play a part in. I'm arranging for my own work to become more flexible so that I can be a hands-on mother. You've no idea how relieved I am that you want to be a hands-on father. I'm just saying that there's no need to rush into marriage. Truly. We have the time and the resources to come up with a solution that doesn't necessarily involve for ever and ever, amen.'

Greyson closed his eyes, shook his head. Probably wishing himself halfway up the Sepik River. Anywhere but here.

'My work's probably going to get a little chaotic over the next few months while I set up a foundation blueprint,' she began, and Greyson's eyes snapped open.

'As long as it's not a dangerously exhausting plan, I'm all for it,' he said smoothly. 'Could you base your foundation headquarters at the Double Bay house?'

'Yes.' This was where she wanted this conversation to go. Exactly where she wanted it to go. 'It's the logical choice, especially if the baby and I lived there too.' Tell him what you want, Derek had told her. Not marriage, not without love, but something that might suit them both and allow them to raise a child and still partake of the work they loved. 'I don't know that you've been around the back of Aurora's place but the grounds flow all the way down to the harbour. There's a boat house down there—big enough for a speedboat, nothing more. There's a jetty and a deepwater mooring there too.'

Charlotte thought she saw a flicker of interest in Greyson's dark eyes but if he had any thoughts on how that deepwater mooring might best be put to use, he kept them to himself.

'You'd be welcome there. Living in the house or on your boat. You might not always be there, what with your work and your travels, but you could base there. We could all base there. That's kind of as far as I've gone with the thinking.'

'It's sound thinking,' he murmured. 'God, Charlotte. You're going to have to give me some time with this.'

'Of course.' Charlotte picked up her mineral water and sipped it through the straw. She looked to the bar. She looked at the artwork on the walls. She'd known this meeting would be a hard one. But she'd seriously underestimated just how hard it would be, or how bad she would feel about being the tool of Greyson's entrapment. 'Greyson—I'm so sorry.'

'Don't,' he said gruffly. 'Please, Charlotte. Just... I need some time to think.'

She gave him time. Seconds that felt like hours. Minutes that stretched into eternity. Much more of this and she was going to start rocking back and forward keening, such was her nervous tension.

'All right,' he said finally. 'I accept your offer to base myself and my operations at the Double Bay house with you, under one condition.'

'What's the condition?'

'Marry me. Tie up your money and your possessions so I can't get to them if that's what you're worried about, but marry me.'

'No.' He wasn't the only one around here with a stubborn streak the size of the pyramids. 'Not without love.'

'What makes you think you won't get that too?' Greyson at his most formidable, but the chill in his eyes was at odds with his words and a perfect example of what she *didn't* want their relationship to be.

'You won't love me if I trap you into a life you loathe, Greyson. You'll hate me.'

He was back to scowling at her. Back to brooding.

'Three months,' she bargained desperately. 'Give us three months, and during that time we live together in the house on the hill and we sort out our work and we try and make space in our lives for this baby and for each other. Surely you can see the sense in that?'

But he shook his head. 'Half measures don't suit me, Charlotte. They never have, and truth be told I don't see much sense in postponing our marriage at all. But…' his beautiful mouth twisted into a mockery of a smile '…in the spirit of compromise, I'll give you these next three months free of matrimony. With one caveat.'

'Which is?' she asked warily.

'That if we live together, we give it our best shot. No holding back. No behaving like polite strangers. And no separate bedrooms.'

'That's three caveats.'

'No, it's not.' His knuckles were white as he reached for his beer. Charlotte wasn't the only one around here so tense she could snap. 'It's just three different ways of saying the same thing.'

Charlotte's food intake was abysmal but Grey coaxed and connived and eventually she cleared her plate. He put his mind to amiable conversation. He stayed away from topics like parenthood and work commitments because, frankly, he was still processing their earlier conversation about those. He paid for their meal and insisted on walking Charlotte home. He bought her a gelato along the way and Charlotte rolled her eyes and protested that she was too full for ice cream, but she ate nearly half of it and Grey finished off the rest.

He took a fair stab at pretending that the world beneath his feet hadn't just irrevocably shifted out of his reach.

He kept his hands to himself until he got to Charlotte's apartment door, and when she unlocked it, and asked where he was parked and whether he wanted to come in, he shoved his hands in his pockets and leaned against the wall. He'd bargained hard for this very concession: no holding back, no distance between them. He hadn't bargained on being afraid to take advantage of it.

'When do you want me to move into the house?' he asked gruffly. 'I figure I can get the cat there in a couple of days, weather willing.'

'I can be there from tomorrow onwards.' She looked so beautiful standing there in the doorway to her apartment. Hard to believe that such a small frame could contain a will that more than matched his own. 'I'll get removalists in at the weekend to pack up and shift all this stuff across.'

'You won't keep your apartment as a bolt hole?'

'No. You wanted all in, remember? If I keep this place I *would* be tempted to retreat here when the going got tough.'

Charlotte looked nervous. He far preferred her not. 'Pessimist,' he murmured. 'It might not even *get* tough.'

She sent him a disbelieving glance. He countered with a slow smile. 'There are benefits to having a man around the house that you haven't even dreamed of yet,' he said.

'Oh, really?'

'Oh, yes.'

'We'll see.' She leaned against the door, more relaxed than he'd seen her all evening. 'Do you cook?'

'Not often, but I hunt and I can gather.'

'Do you clean?'

'No, but I do appreciate a tidy house.'

'Do you iron?'

'That's what laundry services are for.'

'Do you mow?' she asked silkily.

'What? And do a groundsman out of his job?'

'Greyson, you've spent the last dozen or so years living out of a suitcase, eating hotel food and answering to no one. You're not even housebroken. I'd go easy on the promises of domestic bliss if I were you.'

'If you say so, dear,' he murmured. 'Little phrase I picked up from my father. Like it?'

'Yes, but it's a little early in the relationship for weary resignation, don't you think? You need to keep that in reserve.'

'Noted.'

'Are you coming in?' she asked again, so Greyson stepped inside and she closed the door behind him, and he stood there.

All in.

Same priceless painting on the wall. Same wickedly expensive furnishings.

Totally different situation.

'Coffee?' she offered.

'No.'

'Cognac? Liqueur? Scotch?'

He remembered the Scotch from last time, and the raw and desperate lovemaking that had followed. 'Absolutely not!' He needed no encouragement in the raw and desperate department. He was there already. 'And none for you either.'

Charlotte's sandals came off. Her eyes had narrowed. 'Someone's having a panic attack around here,' she murmured. 'And it's not me.'

'I'm not panicking.' It was more of a cold sweat and it had nothing to do with the enormity of the changes he was about to make to his life. No, he was far too busy sweating the small stuff. Like that for all his expertise in the area of biological interactions, he didn't know the first thing about making love to a pregnant woman.

'Are you going to sit down?' she murmured.

'Probably not.' Not the lounge. Probably best to avoid the lounge. God, his nerves were shot. He crossed to the window and stared out at the view.

Charlotte crossed to the sidebar and poured a hefty belt of Scotch into a glass and brought it over to him, and placed it in his hand. 'Drink,' she said gently. 'You don't want to ruin all your fine and heroic rhetoric by going into shock.'

Greyson grimaced, but he put the glass to his lips and drank it down in one long swallow.

'Oh, the *envy*,' she murmured, and he smiled a little at that but his eyes remained guarded. A woman looking for joy in their depths would be disappointed. A woman looking to Greyson to hold her and make everything feel all right—if only for a little while—was disappointed too.

'Are you scared?' he asked gruffly.

Such a simple question from a deeply complex man.

'Terrified,' she whispered, and exposed her soul and all its flaws completely. 'Absolutely terrified.'

And then his arms came around her, strong and infinitely gentle. His lips were gentle too, and his taste was one she'd tried hard to forget. 'It's okay,' he murmured, as he slid his hands through her hair and cradled her head to his chest. 'It's going to be okay. I promise.'

Charlotte wanted to believe him. She wanted to believe that her baby would have a father to look to, and that she wasn't alone in this. She wanted badly to believe that Greyson was here for her now and here he would stay. That he would domesticate easily and be content. That she would find the home and the family she'd been searching for all her life.

She desperately wanted to believe all those things.

But she could not.

Two days later, Greyson moored his cat at Charlotte's jetty in Sydney Harbour. His view of the Bridge, Circular Quay, and the Opera House was one to make angels weep. The turmoil Charlotte's steadfast refusal to marry him had instilled in him would have made Satan crow.

Grey *knew* the value of family. Of marriage, solid and binding. Hell, Charlotte only had to look to herself to see how insecure not being part of a family unit made a child feel. So why wouldn't she just do the right thing and *marry* him?

So what if he hadn't lived a regular life for a while? He'd grown up in a house, gone to school in the suburbs, he knew how it worked. He knew how to mow lawns and unpack groceries and take out the garbage. He knew how to peg out washing and clean a bathroom—his mother had seen to that, bless her iron-willed soul.

He could do this.

And then there were the things Grey didn't know how to do, he admitted reluctantly.

Like how to convince a stubborn woman that marriage was the only option for him and that love would come easier to *both* of them once a commitment had been made.

And how to make love to a woman with his baby in her belly, which was something he hadn't done yet but would, soon, just as soon as he got over his fear of doing something wrong.

By bedtime that night, Greyson was a mess and Charlotte was no better. They sat in the informal living room, watching the late-night weather together in silence. Charlotte, sitting on the couch with her legs tucked up beneath her, Greyson commanding one of the man-sized single chairs. Greyson cloaked his nervousness in stillness. Charlotte tried to do the same but her eyes followed his every movement, watchful and wary, and she jumped at every unexpected sound. Damn near drove him nuts with her quick smile and panicked eyes. Terrified—just like him—of what they'd begun.

'I might have to bed down on the catamaran tonight,' he said after the weather report had finished and he'd got to his feet. 'I really should make sure of the mooring this first night. Wouldn't want her to drift away on the tide.'

'No. No, of course not,' said Charlotte quickly, and stood as well. 'That would be bad.'

Charlotte nodded. Greyson nodded too. A festival of nodding, followed by a long and excruciating silence.

'Can I get you any bedding?' Charlotte's words came out rushed and nervous. 'Blankets. Pillows. Stuff like that?'

'No. No, I have everything I need.'

'Of course.'

More silence. Pregnant woman nodding.

'So...goodnight?' said Charlotte finally. Did she look relieved that they wouldn't be sharing a bed? Hard to tell beneath the panic.

'Yeah, I'll see you in the morning. I'll come up before you go to work. We can do newspapers. Or breakfast. Something.'

'Sounds good,' said Charlotte. 'So...goodnight?'

'Night,' he muttered, and cursed himself for his fears and his awkwardness as he turned on his heel and fled.

Maybe Charlotte was right. Maybe these new living arrangements *would* take some getting used to. Maybe Charlotte's notion of easing their way into each other's lives hadn't been such a bad idea after all.

On day two of Greyson's incarceration at the mansion, he banished the crow on his shoulder to the farthest tree and started taking stock of the house and where he might fit in it. He needed an office, spacious and light filled, and he didn't think the second-floor sewing room would mind. The day came and went as treasures were found and ruthlessly vacuum sealed and boxed for storage. Greyson worked solidly and made hardly a dint when it came to the contents of that room. He was sorting and bagging yet another monstrous pile of brightly coloured cottons when Charlotte walked into the room, looking tired and not altogether pleased to see him. Or maybe it was just the chaos he'd created that offended her.

'Busy day?' she said from the doorway.

'No.'

'Don't you have papers to write?' she asked next.

'Yes.'

'But you've decided to take up patchwork quilting instead?'

'No, I'm stealing office space and banishing your godmother from the premises. I'm sure she was a wonderful woman, not to mention all the way eccentric and richer than Croesus, but I can't live with her. And while we're on topic, I'm not sure I can live with being a kept man, either. Somewhere along the line I expect to contribute towards this household's upkeep. I don't know how but it's something we need to talk about.'

Charlotte leaned against the doorway, and crossed her arms in front of her, all neat and tidy, as if she'd stepped straight out of *Businesswoman's Vogue*. It didn't escape Grey's notice that she looked completely at home in the luxurious surroundings. He really didn't know if such surrounds were ever going to suit him.

'You know, somewhere among all those dreamed-of benefits of having a man about the house was a dream where he greeted me cordially when I came home from work, asked me how my day had gone, *listened* when I told him, and maybe even poured me an icy cold handsqueezed apple juice and soda with a dash of lime,' said Charlotte sweetly.

'What was he wearing?' asked Greyson.

'Not a lot.'

Grey peeled off his T-shirt and dropped it to the sofa, perfectly willing to oblige. 'That better?'

'Well, it's a start.'

Grey looked around at the chaos he'd created with his emptying of cupboards and drawers. All that storage space, and every inch of it crammed full. 'It's a work in progress.

And I'm guessing you probably had a bad day at the office. You've got that look.'

'I either got fired or I resigned,' she said reluctantly. 'Depends who you ask.'

'You don't need them anyway.' Grey abandoned the cottons in favour of closing the gap between them. 'And I guarantee they're going to regret losing you.'

'I'm beginning to appreciate your appeal,' she said with a smile that was way too small for her.

'Wait till you try my hand-squeezed apple juice with soda and lime.' He drew closer, and, gathering courage, traced his fingers down her arm until he reached her hand. Such a fine and delicate hand, and he was careful as he threaded his fingers through hers, stepped past her and tugged her gently towards the hallway. Touching Charlotte settled him in a way that he hadn't been settled all day.

'Where are we going?' asked Charlotte, but she followed willingly in his wake, and her fingers had curled around his, and that was something.

'Kitchen to get you a drink and something to eat.'

'You mean milk and cookies?'

'Do we have milk and cookies?' he asked, glancing back at her. He'd rummaged around in the commercial-sized kitchen at lunchtime. The cupboards had been mostly bare.

'No,' she said with the hint of a smile.

Something to do tomorrow, then. Shop.

'You were right about Aurora,' said Charlotte when they were halfway down the first-floor stairs. 'She could be a little eccentric. She never actually *did* any patchwork quilting that I recall. She just liked buying the materials. And I really don't know what to do with a lot of her collections. I was thinking of donating them to a university or a museum, although clearly not the university I no longer work for. Colour me a woman scorned.'

'Make them the property of the Greenstone Foundation, get a curator in to put together a touring collection, and send it around the galleries,' Grey offered by way of a solution. 'It'll promote your foundation, preserve Aurora's name, and get it out of your hair.'

'*Your* hair,' she said.

'That too.'

They'd reached the kitchen. Grey sat her on a stool and, reluctantly forgoing the touch of her hand, he set about fixing her a soda and lime, no apples. He served it with an unrepentant smile. 'You have to imagine the apples. I'm assuming this won't be too hard for you, given what you're *capable* of imagining.'

'Gil would have flung himself into the harbour and swum its length to get me apples for this juice,' Charlotte told him loftily.

'Yes, but then he'd have been hit by a paddle steamer on his way back and sliced up into apple-flavoured fish bait,' countered Grey. 'Gil had no sense of his own mortality.'

Charlotte allowed her smile to widen.

'So how much notice do you have to give the university that you're finishing up?' he asked, getting back to the issue at hand.

'Two weeks, one of which can be taken as leave. I'm tempted to take two of my colleagues with me. Millie, who you've met. And Derek, who you haven't met yet. I've a mind to make Derek the foundation's second in command and put him in charge of the digs. Derek's useful and he knows how to lead. He thought Gil was an idiot too.'

'Did he now?' said Grey darkly. 'Maybe we'll bond.'

'Of course, chances are Derek still thinks *you're* Gil,' murmured Charlotte. 'Unless Millie's told him otherwise.

Millie knows you're you. You being the stranger whose office she procured. I'm pretty sure she'd have mentioned you to Derek by now. Derek and Millie being an item. I'm assuming they talk between themselves.'

'Never assume,' said Grey. 'You wouldn't rather employ two people who *weren't* an item?'

'Don't know,' said Charlotte. 'Acquiring and managing employees will be a new experience for me. Any thoughts you have on that will be most appreciated. The plan is to catch on fast.'

'And not wear yourself out.'

'And work from home,' said Charlotte. 'This home. Which is why I'm thinking we should do a walk through now and make sure we're thinking similarly when it comes to which rooms to allocate to what.'

'Eyes off my sewing room,' said Grey.

'Keep your sewing room,' countered Charlotte. 'But I *am* thinking of turning over the ground-floor eastern wing of the house to foundation business. What do you think?'

'Tell me what you want shifted and I'll shift it,' said Grey.

'You *are* useful.'

'Never doubt it.'

They walked through the house, making plans and talking big until at last they reached the part of the house where all the bedrooms were and there they fell silent.

'You said you wanted to share a bedroom,' murmured Charlotte. 'And a bed.'

'Yep.' Grey shoved his hands in his pockets and stared into a massive bedroom with more floor space than the average house. The bed looked huge too, but there was only one of them, which was also what he'd intended, but the more he looked at it, the greater his apprehension about making love to a pregnant Charlotte grew. 'That's what I said.'

'Any further reflections on that?'

'Plenty.'

'Anything we need to discuss?'

'Probably.'

'You slept on the boat last night,' she said tentatively. 'Was it because you didn't want to sleep with me?'

'Charlotte—' How to explain his hesitation without sounding like an idiot? 'It's not you. It's just—' Apparently there was *no* way of saying this without sounding like an idiot. 'I've never made love to a pregnant woman before,' he admitted gruffly. 'I'm not a small man. You're pregnant. Fragile. What if I hurt you? What if I hurt the baby?'

'Is *that* what you're worried about?' Charlotte looked amused. Relieved.

'It's not all I'm worried about, no, but at the moment that's what tops the list. And don't look at me like that. It's a valid concern.'

Charlotte smiled. Charlotte walked his way until she stood directly in front of him. She took his hand and placed it on her still-flat belly, her hand atop his. Greyson's heart hammered once and settled to an unsteady rhythm. Impending fatherhood was going to take some getting used to.

'Our baby is well protected,' she murmured. 'Our baby's *mother* has no intention of spending another night like the last one. Worrying like crazy about all the things she's taken away from you, and wishing you were there beside her so she could at least give something back. Our baby's mother has no intention of denying herself the pleasure of your embrace. In point of fact, she's thinking she should probably address those concerns of yours right now.'

'How?'

'Directly.' Her hand atop his as she encouraged him to slide it higher, past her waist and on to the generous curve of her breast. 'She wants you to stop worrying about nothing. She needs to know she still pleases you in this regard.'

'Charlotte—'

'Greyson.'

One name a plea for mercy. The other full of rich amusement and gentle reassurance.

The future mother of Grey's child unbuttoned her blouse with her free hand. Slid it aside to reveal a lacy lavender half-cup bra. Beneath it lay flesh, warm and beckoning. Grey stroked the edge where lace met skin with his fingertips. He leaned forward and gently pressed a kiss to Charlotte's lips.

Charlotte responded as she'd always responded. Generously. Wantonly. Threatening his control and bringing him to instant aching arousal. Her next kiss slid deeper and promised all that he wanted and more.

'I should have known something was amiss when even the scrape of a bath towel made my breasts tighten and ache for your mouth on them,' she whispered. 'I thought I was just remembering you. Reliving the things you did to me and the things I did to you. Do you remember the things I did to you, Greyson?'

'Charlotte, have mercy,' he muttered, even as he slid her shirt from her shoulders. Her hair came down next and he slid his fingers through the tresses, glorying in its abundance and the silky-soft feel of it. Slow down, he wanted to say. Slow down so that I can too. So I can do this right and stay in control. But he didn't say any of that, just cupped her face in his hands and kissed her again and when she wound her arms around his neck, and when her eyes were suitably passion-glazed, he lifted her up and carried her to the bed.

'You'll have to stop that,' she murmured as he laid her gently on the bed and eased down beside her, careful where he put his weight, careful of everything.

'Stop what?'

'Thinking. Measuring. Assessing. I don't want careful from you, Greyson. Not in this.'

'Then what do you want?' he said as he lowered his head to her breast and pressed an open-mouth kiss to the curve of it. He tugged her bra aside and found her nipple next and this time the homage he paid her was a little more urgent. Charlotte strained against him, urging him to more so he gave her more and she whimpered her approval. 'Tell me what you want.'

'Everything.'

Sleeping arrangements sorted to mutual and blissful satisfaction, Charlotte turned her mind to turning part of Aurora's Double Bay home into Greenstone Foundation HQ. Millie accepted the admin position Charlotte offered her. Derek accepted the Project Manager's position. Generous wages plus voting positions for them both on the foundation's board of directors. The latter being Greyson's suggestion; his thoughts being that if she had to have a board of directors, better to have at least some people on it who were responsible for the work and who could speak for it.

Charlotte thought it a good idea. Greyson had a great many good ideas when it came to the running of the foundation. He could be very supportive, could Greyson.

And then, with his next breath he could hit her with a question she had no idea how to answer. Like, 'When do you want to tell my family that you're pregnant?' They were still in discussion over that one.

'Not yet,' she said, dreading the thought of sharing her baby news with Greyson's family and watching Olivia's eyes ice over.

'When?'

'After the first trimester. Wouldn't want them getting all joyous and then not have this baby come to pass.'

Grey looked at her with those eyes that sometimes saw clear through to her soul, ignoring her not-so-honest prediction of a joyful response and cutting straight to the heart of her fears.

'You think they won't be pleased.'

'I think they have a right to their opinions,' said Charlotte carefully. 'I think—under the circumstances—that they could probably be forgiven for wishing that you'd never set eyes on me.'

'They'll come round,' said Greyson firmly. 'Charlotte, give them a chance.'

'I will. And I know we have to tell them, and we will tell them. Soon. Just not yet.'

'Then how about we invite my mother to join us for lunch this week? Not here. Somewhere neutral. Just my mother. No baby talk. Just a straight letting her get to know you.'

He hadn't forgotten their conversation about how to introduce a woman to his family, bless him. But the thought of meeting Olivia again, and doing her best to impress, and potentially having Olivia remain singularly unimpressed, gave Charlotte pause.

'Where does she think you're living these days?' asked Charlotte, and this time it was Greyson's turn to look discomfited. 'She still thinks you're living on the cat, here in the harbour somewhere, doesn't she?'

'Probably.' Greyson eyed her steadily. 'I've no objection to telling her that we're living together. I can do it today.'

'Okay,' said Charlotte faintly. 'Maybe we should start with that.'

'And the invitation for her to join us for lunch?'

'Is a good idea.' The man was just full of good ideas. 'I know that. Olive branch and all that. Fresh start. No Sarah there to give your mother conflicting loyalties. Does your mother still see Sarah on occasion, do you think?'

'I believe they get together for coffee every now and again.'

Great. Just great.

'Charlotte, Sarah's out of the picture.'

'Because of the baby,' said Charlotte, feeling very, very small.

'Because of many things,' said Greyson gently. 'None of which are related to you.'

'She's still going to think I've trapped you when she finds out about the baby.'

'Charlotte, I'm not *trapped*.'

Yes, he was. He just didn't know it yet. Trapped into fatherhood, but at least she'd spared him from being bound to her by marriage. That much, she could give him and *would* give him if he didn't come to love her the way she was fast learning to love him. 'You're a rare and beautiful man, Greyson Tyler. I couldn't have wished for a better father for this child.'

'Marry me,' he said instantly.

'No.'

'Why not?'

'Because I'm not ready to take that step yet,' she said gently. 'And neither are you. First things first.'

Frustration rolled off Greyson in waves. Impatience.

Action man wanted action. He thrived on it and always would. Just one more very good reason for him to be perfectly sure of his feelings before buying into Charlotte's sedentary and peaceful life.

'All right. First things first,' Greyson said curtly. Not their first difference of opinion and it wouldn't be their last. 'Let's just meet my mother for lunch. See how it goes.'

'Okay,' Charlotte agreed, and fought to quell her instant and overwhelming apprehension. All her life she'd dreamed of having a family and this was her chance to secure Greyson's. Her child would have grandparents. Grandparents who loved and adored their grandchild, and that could happen, and probably *would* happen, provided Olivia's resistance towards Charlotte didn't get in the way.

'Okay,' she said again. 'Let's arrange to have lunch with your mother. I'm all for it. I am. But maybe next week rather than this week. This week's full.'

He gave her thirty days of household bliss. Thirty days and thirty nights of unstinting support and manly perfection, with nary a mother in sight, and on the thirty-first day a job offer came in for him and turned Charlotte's world upside down.

'I want you to read something,' he said on Charlotte's return from yet another meeting with her solicitors about the set-up of a Greenstone Foundation board of directors. He'd placed his laptop on the kitchen counter and opened up an email addressed to him. The email was titled Galapagos Project Leader Position and a little red exclamation mark next to it signalled the need for a prompt response.

'Who's Eleanor Stratten?' she asked, for that was who the email was from.

'She's a department head at CSIRO. Plant physiology. Bigwig. Very big wig.'

Charlotte scanned the first paragraph. Once-in-a-lifetime research opportunity, fully funded two-year project based around the Galapagos Islands. Project head needed, Eleanor had heard on the grapevine that Greyson was available. Details attached, was he interested?

Charlotte straightened. Greyson handed her a long tall glass of freshly squeezed apple juice and ginger beer with a twist of lime and a spoonful of mint. 'You haven't opened the attachment,' he murmured.

'I don't need to.'

'It's not based in the Galapagos,' he said. 'It can be run from here.'

Charlotte nodded and sipped her drink for good measure.

'There'd be travel, of course,' he said, not taking her entirely for a fool. 'A lot of back and forth. I'm not saying I wouldn't be away for weeks at a time, maybe longer.'

'You should do it,' she said. 'It's a once-in-a-lifetime opportunity.' Charlotte wanted to sound sincere but her voice came out all brittle and wrong. She'd known from the start that she'd never keep him anchored here, not without destroying everything he was and denying him all that he could be. 'When does it start?'

'Almost immediately. The team is already assembled and ready to go. They had a project leader sorted too. His wife had a stroke.'

'I'm sorry to hear that.' Charlotte set her drink on the counter and summoned up a smile. 'It really does sound like a wonderful opportunity for you.'

'Charlotte, it's the *Galapagos*.'

'I know.' No other place on earth could match it when it came to finding evidence for the evolution of the species. This job offer was the equivalent of someone walking up to an archaeologist and asking them if they wanted to be part of an expedition to the lost city of Atlantis. 'Holy Grail.'

'I'd still be based here. I'd do everything I could to ensure that I'd be here for you when the baby comes. I'd not miss that. I'd make it a contract condition.'

Charlotte looked away. It shamed her that her first response had not been happiness for Greyson but dismay for herself. It terrified her to reflect on just how much she'd come to rely on his company and his support.

'Charlotte, please. I can't do what I've been doing this past month on a permanent basis. I've enjoyed every minute of it and I'll do it again willingly, but not all the time,' he said. 'My work is part of who I am. I can't not do it.'

'I know,' she said softly. 'I think this position is perfect for you. You'd be mad not to apply for it, and I don't want you mad. I don't want you frustrated or feeling like you're just marking time here either. I'll be fine. I have everything I could possibly need right here, and as you say...you'll be back and forward. I'll probably hardly even notice you're gone.'

'This *will* work out for us. We'll *make* it work,' Greyson said huskily, as if by saying the words he could make them come true.

'Confident man.'

'No,' he said. 'Not confident, not always. Just determined.'

Grey got the job. He'd known when Ellie had emailed him that his chances were good. He'd tailored his entire working life towards this sort of project, building the skill set he needed to land just such a gem. Always taking the road less travelled. Never shying away from the difficult turns. He didn't shy away from them now.

All in.

It was the way he'd always lived his life and it remained to be seen if he could turn 'all in' into 'all in until Charlotte needed him', at which point he'd have to be all out and focusing on his life with her for a while. He'd need a good second in command. He'd already been in touch with Joey Tank, whose wife had had the stroke. She was home now and improving daily. Joey had high hopes that she'd be as good as new within a few months, or, more realistically, within half a dozen months. Joey had taken long service leave to be with his wife and he'd jumped at Grey's offer to keep him in the project loop, with a view to having him step in temporarily, later down the track, should family circumstances force Grey to step out. Now all Grey had to do was convince the powers that be that project sharing with Tank was an excellent outcome for all concerned. Do that, and the Galapagos project set-up would be as good as he could make it.

The only thing that wasn't going his way was the small matter of Charlotte's continued refusal to marry him.

'No,' she'd said when he'd broached the subject again.

No explanation, no tears or recriminations. Just a smiling, steadfast no.

The day of departure came around all too soon for Grey. He'd worked every day and long into each night for almost three weeks, planning the first Galapagos trip and co-ordinating team members and equipment, identifying priorities, sorting out glitches, and stamping his will on the way things would be done.

Charlotte came through in spades during this time, backburnering her own work in order to offer him the support that he'd hitherto offered her. Setting Millie—who now worked for the Greenstone Foundation—at his disposal when it came to admin tasks or tracking down certain pieces of equipment. She offered her own time when it came to prepping him for the trip and her extensive light-living and on-the-road expertise showed with every choice she made.

They ate together, laughed together, sailed together, and she slept in his arms, and on the day of Grey's departure Charlotte stood on the front steps of the house, beneath the portico, with Derek on one side of her and Millie on the other, and bade him farewell.

'You'll be calling me if you need me, day or night, it doesn't matter,' Grey told her firmly. 'I've left my mother's numbers on the fridge—home, work, and mobile. If you can't contact me, call her.'

'Absolutely.' If she was dismayed by his leaving, it didn't show.

'I *mean* it.'

'I know.' A crack, a tiny crack in her polished façade. A moment of desolation that she covered up with a bright bright smile.

'He's a little on the anxious side, isn't he?' Millie murmured.

That he was. 'And you...' Grey speared Millie with his sternest gaze. 'If something goes awry and Charlotte's not inclined to call me, *you* do it.'

'Of course,' said Millie soothingly.

'I won't be left out.'

'Not at all,' said Millie next.

'As for you,' he said to Derek—a grinning Derek whom he'd come to know and respect these past few weeks. 'You watch out for my future wife and the mother of my child. You do this from a respectable distance, you understand? Make sure she doesn't work herself too hard.'

'Not a problem,' said Derek cheerfully, and Grey scowled. It probably wouldn't do to beat the happy out of the man. Not if he wanted Derek to do his bidding while Grey was away.

Grey didn't linger long after that. He wasn't one for prolonged and tearful farewells. Neither, apparently, was Charlotte. She kissed him savouringly and told him to stay safe. She kissed him again and let the desperation creep in.

He told her he'd call her and she nodded and smiled and stepped back in place between Millie and Derek, and then he left before he changed his mind and stayed.

'Man's a goner,' said Derek.

'Well, he's gone, at any rate,' said Millie.

'He'll be back, and sooner than you think.' Derek tugged a lock of Charlotte's hastily tied ponytail and put his hands to her shoulders and turned her around to face the door.

'He's away for a month,' said Charlotte. She'd worn her favourite sundress for Greyson's departure, a high-waisted free-flowing floral silk that ended at her knees. Charlotte glowed these days, be it with happiness or with hormones. Skilful application of make-up had ensured that she glowed in particularly appealing fashion today. So that he wouldn't forget her. So that he'd think of her on his travels with pleasure and not dismay. Trying to make this farewell easy for him, and she *had* made it easy for him, hadn't she?

Over twenty years and a world's worth of practice had made perfect.

Farewells she could do.

Even when they broke her heart.

The Galapagos archipelago was everything Grey had hoped for and more. It appealed to the adventurer in him and more than satisfied the scientist. The other scientists working on the project were skilled, intrepid, and ready to work. The younger ones accepted his leadership without question because they knew how fortunate they were to be involved in the project. Some knew him and had worked with him before. The two grey-haired scientists—a biologist and an entomologist—knew the game of leadership and let him get on with it. They approved of Joey Tank's continued involvement—he won credit points with them for that. They wouldn't oppose him until something threatened their work. Grey intended to see that nothing did.

Communication was the only drawback. They had satellite phone, fax, and Internet but the service depended on the sending and receiving of strong signals, and that varied with movement. Boats moved. He sent messages to Charlotte when he could. He convinced himself it would be enough.

He found himself thinking about her at the oddest times. What she'd be doing, how the foundation was coming along. The university had really missed an opportunity to collaborate with Charlotte on that one, for the minute she'd set it up cheque books had opened and money had come pouring in. Declarations of faith in her abilities, Greyson had called them, and Charlotte had glowed, and worked twice as hard to prove herself worthy.

Charlotte wanted the foundation's first dig to be a triumph. Grey's hopes for her success were just as high. And everything—his work and hers—would be so much easier if only Charlotte would agree to travel.

Grey missed her. He wanted Charlotte's smiles when he woke up in the morning and he wanted her in his bed of a night. He wanted to watch her delighted responses to her changing shape and he desperately wanted to see her with his child in her arms—he didn't want to miss a thing.

He was the man who wanted it all.

Pining for Greyson wasn't part of Charlotte's plan. Greyson had his work and Charlotte had hers, and she made good headway with it. She met the neighbours, took exercise daily, ate nutritious food, and took better care of herself than she would have had she not been pregnant.

Charlotte emailed whenever Grey did, which was surprisingly often given the erratic communication services she knew to exist in the Galapagos. She appreciated his efforts to stay connected and smiled at the photos he emailed through and the comments that went with them. Her baby's father had a sense of humour. Good to know.

Day fourteen was a hard one. Loneliness stalked her these days, no matter how hard she tried to fill the hole Greyson had left with work. She hadn't heard from him in three days. Nothing to worry about, but worry she did.

Fretfully.

Needlessly—because he was probably simply out of communications range. It happened in such places. It happened a lot.

Two more days passed without word from Greyson.

Two more after that.

The emergency contact person on the card in her wallet had always been Aurora. It needed changing and on day nineteen of Greyson's first stint in the Galapagos Charlotte sat down and filled out a new emergency contact card for her wallet and put, not Greyson's phone number down, but his mother's. She hadn't forgotten the importance of having someone nearby, on the ground, when things went wrong. Someone who could be there in timely fashion to pick up the pieces of a child's life and wade through all the red tape. She needed to change her will as well, but to what? Leave all her worldly possessions to her next of kin? Was it too early to do that? Too morose? This baby hadn't even been born yet. Maybe until it was, the money should go to the Greenstone Foundation. Or Greyson. Or be put in trust, to be held by Greyson. Or something.

Aurora would have known what to do. Aurora, who'd been unafraid and full of affirmation. *Never be afraid to live, Charlotte.* How many times had Charlotte heard that? *Living,* not mourning or brooding or worrying about things that would probably never come to pass.

Only every now and then they did come to pass.

A trip to the solicitor's, then, to discuss futures and fortunes and hopefully set Charlotte's mind at ease. She made the appointment for four the following afternoon and vowed to sleep better that night because of it.

Maybe Charlotte's mind was just too full or too empty on her way to the solicitor's office. Maybe that was why she didn't see that the other driver had failed to stop at the Give Way. But her mind wasn't blank when she was sitting in the smoking car with the steering wheel jammed up against her solar plexus and the door caved into her side.

Her head… She could still move her head, that was good, right? And her arms, she could move them too. Stuck, just stuck, and something just stuck could be cut out of wreckage; all it took was a little patience and time.

Breathing took effort. Charlotte had read about how

when lungs were punctured they would fill up with blood. No blood here, not much anyway, except for the stuff trickling down from her forehead. Glass cut, most likely. Glass from the shattered windscreen.

Airbags were a bitch when they'd only half opened. Airbags came with white dust and the dust was everywhere. Airbags could be punctured too. Charlotte wondered hazily how much blood *they* could fit in them.

Charlotte's mind was far from empty in the moments after the crash and before oblivion claimed her.

She had plenty of time to ponder distance and travel time and come to the conclusion that the Galapagos Isles were a very long way away. She had time to think of Greyson and to apologise for what she'd done. She had time to construct a mantra, a silent outcry of fear and of pain. Over and over the same words repeated. Over again until darkness chased them away.

My baby.

Charlotte woke in a colourless hospital room.

A hospital room was good. Meant she was still here. That she was breathing without the assistance of tubes and masks meant even better things. She closed her eyes and concentrated on her body. Moving toes: check. Fingers: likewise. Baby:

Baby.

Charlotte forced her eyes open again and spotted a woman sitting by her bedside. She knew this face. Not well. Hardly at all. But she knew it and was grateful for its presence. A doctor. An experienced one.

Greyson's mother.

'Hello, Charlotte. Are you awake?'

Olivia had her doctor's voice on, soothing yet firm.

'Yes.'

'Do you know where you are?'

'Yes.'

'Who you are?'

'Yes.' Charlotte. But not just Charlotte. 'Is my baby okay?'

'There's been some spotting.' Olivia's voice had softened and her eyes were kind. 'A little more bleeding than we'd like. An ultrasound will tell us more. You have some chest trauma. Concussion. You're very lucky not to have displaced a rib or damaged your lungs.'

But Charlotte's attention had snagged on the only thing that mattered to her. *An ultrasound will tell us more...* 'Will I lose my baby?'

'It's too early to tell,' said Olivia gently and Charlotte looked away, for the 'no' she so desperately wanted to hear had not been forthcoming. 'You haven't yet.'

'That's good, right?' she said shakily, and, with her thoughts not really in gear yet, 'Are you my doctor?'

'No, but I've seen your charts.' Olivia looked supremely uncomfortable. 'Charlotte, I'm here because you had me down as your next of kin. The hospital contacted me when they brought you in.'

'Oh.' It seemed vitally important to Charlotte to explain the why of it. 'Not *my* next of kin. Greyson's. The baby's. I didn't know who else to put down. Greyson had left your numbers on the fridge...' Not exactly the most coherent explanation Charlotte had ever given. Uncomfortable words to have to say out loud. That she had no one. That she had too often had to rely on the generosity of strangers. 'I'm so sorry. My godmother died a few months back and I have no other family. There's no one, you see... No one left.'

Olivia went silent at that. Charlotte closed her eyes and

drifted away to where the grey places beckoned. When she returned, Olivia was still there.

'I took the liberty of going through your wallet to see what kind of medical insurance you had,' said the older woman. 'They'll be shifting you up to a private wing soon. They're going to want to keep you in bed for a while. You'll be more comfortable in a private room.'

'Is my baby still with me?'

'Yes.' Conflict ran deep in Olivia's brown eyes. 'Your baby's still with you. Your chest is still a problem. There's going to be pain. Treatment for that pain is going to be complicated because of the baby.'

'I can handle the pain,' said Charlotte, and Olivia smiled wryly.

'You haven't felt it yet.'

'I haven't?' So the excruciating pressure on her chest *was* the drugged-up version? 'Oh.'

'Charlotte, I haven't been able to get hold of Greyson.'

'Doesn't surprise me.' Weak tears stung the backs of Charlotte's eyes. 'He's been out of range for about a week now.'

'I've left messages at his workplace,' Olivia said grimly. 'They're tracking him down.'

'But—Olivia, no. There's really no need to concern him with this, is there? There's nothing he can do.'

'He can be here.' The ice in Olivia's voice put Charlotte in mind of Greyson at his most formidable. Clearly he hadn't learned the fine art of intimidation from a stranger. 'For you.'

'It's just… Greyson and I…we really don't have that kind of relationship.'

Olivia stiffened. Olivia glared. Not what she wanted to hear, never mind the truth of it.

'Why don't you let him be the judge of that?'

CHAPTER NINE

RECEIVING a problem notification call from the local marine authority was never a good start to a day. Grey and his team were bunked down on the *Cantilena*, the cruiser he'd hired to get them out to the experiment sites. They were eight days gone from the main island of San Cristobal. He'd been radioing in their location every day. Government bodies had an occupational health and safety obligation to know the whereabouts of their more intrepid employees and it never hurt for other boats in the area to know where they were either.

A pan-pan call wasn't as bad as an SOS or a mayday, but good news it wasn't. Greyson made contact, they changed channels. Standard operating procedure.

'CSIRO wants *Cantilena* back in sat-phone range,' said a gruff voice, chattier now that they'd changed channels. 'Got a message in for a Dr Greyson Tyler. There's been an accident. Charlotte's in hospital. Request he phones home.'

'Say again?'

The message was the same the second time round.

'Wilco.' Will comply.

'We'll tell them you've received the message and you're coming in. Station one out.'

And that was that.

Grey put the radio handpiece back in its cradle. He ducked his head, ran his hand through his hair. Heaven help him, he was in the middle of *nowhere*, with two scientists overnighting on the island nearby and scientific equipment scattered across four atolls. Leadership weighed heavily on his shoulders, *God*, it weighed a lot, for there'd be no leaving either people or equipment behind.

He rubbed his hands down his face, and turned to find at least half of the team standing on deck, watching him in silence. No one seemed keen to break that silence.

'So,' he said finally. 'Nothing maritime, just a message for me. Charlotte's my...' His *what*, exactly? She wouldn't even marry him. 'Significant other. We live together. She's pregnant.'

Silence followed his words. Silence and no little pity.

'Did a stint as a satellite engineer in my youth,' said grey-haired Ray into that heavy waiting silence. 'I reckon if we take the sat phone off the boat and onto the island and butcher up an antenna, we might just get a signal. I reckon it's worth a try.'

Grey ran his hands through his hair again, every instinct telling him not just to phone but to *go*. Back to San Cristobal and out of there on a plane. Ecuador, Hawaii, *Sydney*. But there were other people to be considered, experiments to consider, and he'd know better what course to take once he knew more about Charlotte's situation. 'Okay,' he said to Ray gruffly. 'Okay, do it.'

Grey arrived back in Sydney forty-seven hours and thirty-six minutes after talking to his mother on the jimmy-rigged phone. He'd travelled by boat and by bus and three different types of plane and by the time he hit the ground in Sydney he felt like hell and smelled worse. Early evening, Sydney time, and Olivia stood waiting for him at the arrival gates—mothers were like that. Sadly, they were also big on hygiene—particularly mothers who were doctors and who had filthy sons who wanted to be taken straight to the hospital. Olivia told him in no uncertain terms that he'd need a shave, a shower, and possibly fumigation before he went anywhere *near* Charlotte or a hospital.

Hard not to shoot the messenger, but he managed to nod and stay calm and direct her to the Double Bay house. He used his key to get in, left his mother in the kitchen and headed for the shower. By the time he was clean, clothed, and back in the kitchen, his mother was thin of lip and steely of eye. He knew that look. He didn't have time for it.

'This is where you live?' his mother wanted to know.

'Yes.'

'Who owns it?'

'Charlotte. She owns it outright. I dare say she owns plenty of things outright. Any more questions?'

'Yes. Is this baby yours?'

'Yes, the baby's *mine. Charlotte's* mine.' And he needed to see her. 'Where is she? Which hospital?' His Ducati was in the garage. Not that he wasn't grateful for his mother's support, but if she was more interested in chewing him out for his irresponsible actions than in taking a drive to the hospital, he'd get there under his own steam.

'Westmead,' she said. 'And why didn't you tell me Charlotte was pregnant?'

'Charlotte was still in her first trimester when I left. She didn't want it widely known. Not yet.'

'Greyson, I'm your *mother.*'

'Noted.'

'I'm also the person on Charlotte's emergency contact card,' Olivia said curtly. 'Why aren't you?'

* * *

Mothers were levelers; at least, Grey's mother was. She'd dropped him at the hospital and continued on her way, but her question gnawed at him all the way down the long corridors until he got to the ward Charlotte was in. Not visiting hours, but his mother had pre-empted an out-of-hours visit from him and the nurses had known who he was and how far he'd come and let him through.

'See if you can convince her to take some pain medication,' said the sister on the desk. 'Even paracetamol would be better than nothing, and it won't hurt the baby.'

His mother had explained Charlotte's chest trauma—muscle tear, cracked ribs, bruising, swelling. Pain. 'Where is it?' he said. 'The medication.'

'I'll be there in a few minutes and I'll bring it with me. Room 313, and don't wake her if she's asleep. She hasn't slept since she got here.'

Charlotte wasn't asleep. She was sitting up in the bed with a pile of pillows at her back. No television on, no lights on either, and she looked like a fey little wraith in a room full of shadows, with her ebony hair loosely plaited to one side of her face and trailing down over her shoulder. Her eyes widened when she saw him, and in their pain-glazed depths he saw dismay, mingled with relief.

She dragged up a smile from somewhere. She tried to sit up a little straighter and he saw what it cost her in the lines of pain on her pale, pale face. 'You didn't have to come,' she murmured as he entered and gently shut the door.

'My choice.'

'The baby's fine.'

'Good,' he said simply.

'Could have solved a lot of problems,' she said in a heartbreakingly ragged voice. 'Could have freed you up.'

She wouldn't look at him after that. She plucked at the lightly woven hospital blanket and wouldn't look at him.

He leaned forward and put his fingers beneath her chin to tilt her head. He wanted her eyes for these next few words and he would have them. 'No,' he said quietly. 'It wouldn't have. There'd still be you.'

He watched her eyes fill with tears that spilled onto her cheeks. He had no idea what came next. She wiped them away with shaking fingers. 'I'm feeling a little fragile at the moment,' she murmured, as if it was something to be ashamed of.

'You're entitled,' he said, and pressed a gentle kiss to the corner of her mouth before closing his eyes and resting his forehead against hers. He was feeling a little ragged around the edges himself. 'The nurses say you need to take your painkillers.'

'The baby—'

'Won't be affected.' He pulled back so he could see her eyes, but the need to soothe her was just too strong. He lifted his fingers to the curve of her face and tucked a stray strand of her hair behind her ear. 'They know what they're doing, Charlotte. Take the paracetamol, even if only for a few days. Give your body a break. Get some sleep. You'll feel better for it.'

'Yes, Doctor.'

'I mean it. We need to get you sleeping, then mobile and managing your pain before we can get you out of here.'

'Easy on the dancing, action man. The bed rest is helping the baby.'

'But you can still come home and rest there.'

Charlotte nodded. 'I got Millie to arrange for a nurse to live in for a week or so, starting from when I get home. It seemed prudent. No one would worry, then, about me being there by myself. Including me.'

Grey shook his head.

'What?' she said. 'Apparently it's a very reputable nursing service. Your mother recommended it.'

His *mother* could have offered up some hospitality of her own.

'She's been marvellous,' continued Charlotte awkwardly. 'Your mother. She just came in and...took charge. Organised the room and the doctors. Arranged for a specialist to see me. Apparently he doesn't come to this hospital. He did for me. Yesterday she arrived bearing a fresh berry yoghurt smoothie, stuffed with naturopathy's finest, and sat there until I drank it. She's worse than you.'

'I've always thought so,' said Grey. Maybe his mother wasn't so unfeeling after all. Maybe his mother had assessed the situation and decided that offering to care for Charlotte while she convalesced would have made everything just a little too convenient.

For him.

The nurse came in and stayed while Charlotte took her pills. 'They'll make you sleepy,' said the nurse. 'Don't fight it. You need the rest. And probably a few less pillows.'

'Not yet,' said Charlotte hastily and the nurse regarded her with knowing eyes.

'Sleep sitting up if you have to,' said the nurse. 'But I think you'll find it easier to lie back a little more once the meds kick in.'

'Looking forward to it,' said Charlotte.

'What do you want to do with him?' asked the nurse, shooting Grey a sideways glance.

'I'm not going anywhere,' said Grey grimly. 'If that helps the decision making process any.'

'He's one of them,' murmured Charlotte.

'So I see. Wish I had one,' murmured the nurse. 'I can't give him a bed, but the chair's not so bad. He can use one of the extra blankets if he gets cold, and you can give him some pillows. I'll leave it with you.'

The nurse left, shutting the door gently behind her.

'There's a twenty-minute wait on those pillows,' said Charlotte.

'Keep your pillows,' said Grey, and settled down into the chair with his legs stretched out before him. He closed his eyes. He let out the breath he'd taken approximately fifty-five hours ago, when the VHF call to the *Cantilena* had first come in. Three days to get here. Three days was too long.

'You look tired,' she said from the bed.

'So do you.' He opened his eyes a fraction and found her watching him.

'You should go home. Get some sleep. Really. What's there to gain by staying here?'

'Peace of mind.' Exhaustion sensed an opening and began to launch an attack. Wearily he tried to resist being dragged under. 'So this is where you invented Gil.'

'Pretty much. Except that I was the one in the chair.'

'Maybe I should invent something too.'

'Like what?' she said on a yawn. 'A fiancée?'

'No, I already have a significant other, which is a term I hate, by the way. I'd much rather have a wife.'

'Good luck with that,' murmured Charlotte, and after a pause, 'So what's she like? This wife?'

'Stubborn.'

'That's what I did too.' Charlotte's voice was growing sleepier. 'Went with what I knew. So much easier on the brain.'

'She's beautiful too.'

'Imaginary folk always are. Gil was dreadfully handsome.'

'In a tough and manly way, I hope,' murmured Grey.

The events of the last few days were finally catching up with him. Exhaustion was winning. Heaviness having its way.

'Yes. Very tough and manly, and with many fine qualities.'

'Like what?'

'Oh, the usual. Honesty. Loyalty. Fidelity. Handy. Gil was very useful.'

'My wife's not so much useful as essential,' murmured Grey. 'I thought one time, about a hundred years ago, that I could use her as an anchor. That I could go off and do my thing, and come back and there she'd be, perfectly willing to pick up where we'd left off. Didn't work.'

'Why not?' Charlotte's voice was nothing more than a sleepy whisper.

'I missed her too much. Nearly went insane when I couldn't get back to her in time when she needed me. If anything had happened to her...' He had a feeling that that particular game of *what if* would have him waking up in a cold sweat for years to come.

'What would you have done?'

'Blamed myself.'

'Dumb.'

'I needed to get back to her in time, you see. To tell her how much I loved her, because I never had. Not with words. Nothing mattered except telling her that.'

'Mh.' Hard to tell if that was a word or a snore. Grey forced his eyes open and hauled himself out of the chair. He went over to the bed and slipped first one pillow from the pile behind Charlotte's back, and then another. He didn't want them for himself; he just wanted to make Charlotte more comfortable.

'What's her name?' Charlotte snuggled down into the

remaining pillows as he drew the blanket gently over her. Moments later she was asleep.

'Charlotte,' he said huskily. 'Her name's Charlotte.'

CHAPTER TEN

HAVING Greyson home and taking care of her was the sweetest form of torture. The live-in nurse had not eventuated—Greyson had eventuated, and he hovered like a protective lover and father-to-be and he kissed and held her often. Long leisurely tastes of her and quick stolen kisses, he delighted in them both and Charlotte in turn delighted in him.

They slept in the same bed but they held off with the lovemaking. Two weeks, the specialist had said. Longer, if she felt uneasy about the notion or if she had any more spotting, but there'd been no more of that.

Almost all of Greyson's Galapagos project scientists were back in Australia now. Two team members had volunteered to stay behind and hold the fort. The group would rotate the stay-behind duty, but according to Greyson there were enough willing hands up for more than one stint at being left behind that the ones who had responsibilities back home wouldn't need to ante up if they didn't want to. He was more than happy with his team. There were some fantastic, experienced, and multi-skilled people on it. All this Charlotte gleaned from a relatively communicative Greyson.

What she *hadn't* managed to glean from him was

when *he'd* be heading out next and how long he planned to be away.

Truth be told, the man seemed to be having a wee bit of trouble leaving her side. A development that amused the hell out of Millie and Derek, and even Greyson's mother, the formidable Olivia, who'd taken to dropping by a few times a week to check on Charlotte's progress.

'How does it look?' asked Charlotte some three weeks after the accident, shirt off and bra on as she sat on the edge of the long narrow hallway sideboard that Olivia had deemed suitable as a makeshift examination table. Nothing like undressing in front of one's potential mother-in-law to break down a few barriers.

'Lie back,' said Olivia briskly, and Charlotte obliged and Olivia began to press down on Charlotte's ribs, one section at a time. 'Tell me when it hurts.'

But it didn't hurt and Charlotte sat up beaming. 'That's good, right?'

'Right,' said Olivia dryly. 'But no moving mountains just yet.'

'I don't want to move mountains.' Charlotte's words came out muffled courtesy of the shirt she was tugging over her head. 'Just Greyson.'

She pulled the shirt down and eased off the sideboard to find Olivia regarding her with guarded eyes. 'Olivia, may I ask you an awkward medical question?'

'If you must.' Olivia had a pained look on her face. Olivia had probably been a doctor long enough to know where this conversation was going.

'It's just that since the accident Greyson and I haven't— I mean, we don't—and I'd like to, and it's okay to now, right? The specialist said two weeks, and it's been three, so...'

'As long as you're careful.'

'Great. Thanks.' No need to dwell on the subject. No need to go anywhere near the subject with Greyson's mother ever, *ever*, again. Fortunately, Charlotte had another question lined up, which would steer the conversation elsewhere. 'Olivia, may I ask you advice on another issue? It's not medical. It's about Greyson.'

'That boy,' said Olivia. 'What's he done now?'

'Nothing,' said Charlotte defensively. And at the glimmer of amusement in Olivia's eye, 'Oh, I get it. Mothers are allowed to criticise their children. Just…no one else can.'

'Exactly.' Olivia offered up a smile, and Charlotte blinked. 'So, what's he done? Apart from nothing.'

'I'm worried that he's neglecting his work. Because of me. He won't say when he's going back to the Galapagos. I'm worried that he'll abandon this project altogether in favour of staying here in Sydney. With me.'

'Most pregnant women I know would want their partners at their side,' commented Olivia mildly.

'I do. But not at the expense of taking away everything Greyson's worked hard for. I know what your son is, Olivia. I know what he needs and it's freedom, and challenge, and the world at his fingertips. I won't trap him. I refuse to.'

'Then go with him,' said Olivia.

'I was thinking more along the lines of staying here and encouraging Greyson to come and go. That was the pre-accident agreement. It doesn't seem to be the post-accident one.'

'I should hope not,' said Olivia sternly. 'It's about time Greyson realised that he now has responsibilities beyond himself and his work. It won't break him to honour them.'

'But what if it does?' said Charlotte, and with those

words exposed her deepest fears. 'What if turning away from the work and the lifestyle he loves does break him?'

'Or you could go with him,' said Olivia. 'Given the extensive travelling you're accustomed to, I really don't see why that's out of the question. Good medical care can be found almost everywhere these days if money is no object, and in your case it doesn't seem to be. Come back for the birth of my grandchild. Compromise.'

Charlotte ran a hand through her hair, sorting through Olivia's words and her bone-deep resistance to them. 'I stopped travelling when my godmother retired,' she said hesitantly. 'I was ready to stop. I'd been ready for years. I wanted—needed—a place to belong. A home. I still want that.'

'Charlotte, do you love my son?'

'I do.' Charlotte eased off the sideboard and together she and Olivia walked back towards the kitchen where cups of tea beckoned and confidences were encouraged. 'He's everything I've ever dreamed of in a man. And so much more.'

'That's good,' said Olivia. 'Because if I'm any judge of my son, he certainly loves you. Enough to give up his Galapagos posting and stay by your side if that's what you want, and what you need from him.'

'But it's *not* what I want.' Charlotte felt the sting of tears behind her eyes. 'I don't *know* what I want.'

'I've never told you how I met Greyson's father, have I?' said Olivia conversationally, helping herself to the tea leaves and spooning them into Aurora's old tin pot. 'I was a very earnest young doctor interning at Randwick Hospital. Seth was a skipper on a forty-metre super yacht. He'd brought a crewman who'd dislocated his shoulder into Casualty. I had dinner with him when my shift finished.

Two months later I was sailing around the world with him. Greyson was born eight months later. We married six months after that, on a beach in Tahiti. Seth wasn't skippering super yachts any more, at this point. We had another yacht, a smaller one, and we were on our way back to Australia. It took us three more years to get there.'

'Really?' Charlotte's mind boggled at the carefree picture the immaculate Olivia Greenstone had painted. 'You raised Greyson on a boat?'

'Many ports. Many boats, some of which I loved more than others.' Olivia smiled at her memories, really smiled. 'There was this one yacht…ugh. I'll tell you about it some day.'

'Tell me now,' said Charlotte, but Olivia shook her head.

'No, let me make my point first. The point being that the one truth I learned during that time we were travelling around was that as long as Seth and Greyson were with me, I could turn anywhere into a home. *Our* home. As long as they were with me.'

'But you only did three years of it,' countered Charlotte. 'It gets harder.' So much harder with the years.

'And that's something Greyson would do well to take into account,' said Olivia. 'As his father did, when he brought us home.'

'How did it end?' asked Charlotte, totally fascinated. '*Why* did it end?'

'It ended back here in Sydney,' said Olivia. 'With a job in yacht design for Seth, a little boy who needed schooling and children his own age to play with, and a chance for me to return to the medical profession. Charlotte, I know I'm biased. I want what's best for my son and always will, but you're family now and I want what's best for you too. Take a chance on Greyson. Go with him the next time he goes to the Galapagos. Maybe the time after that, he'll feel happier about leaving you here. Maybe you'll happily go with him again. Things might get chaotic for a while, given the amount of work you both have on and the imminent arrival of my grandbaby, but I'm confident that if you could just bring yourself to *trust* your instincts and Greyson's...love will lead you home.'

Charlotte stewed over Olivia's words for two long days, turning them inside out and upside down looking for flaws, or dishonesty or hidden agendas. She didn't find any. She needed to know what Greyson was thinking when it came to the Galapagos project and going away. She needed to know these thoughts sooner rather than later.

By Charlotte's reckoning, today was the day.

A sweet autumn Saturday and they were cleaning out Aurora's study; a mammoth job that involved Greyson hefting and Charlotte directing from the comfort of Aurora's leather studded office chair that lived behind a vast mahogany desk. Such blatant displays of power and wealth didn't come cheap, and Charlotte planned to put them to good use for the foundation. This would be the shakedown room, the place where *her* will met the wills of influential investors and project partners.

Just as soon as they'd cleared the last of Aurora's things away, and sorted out exactly where their combined priorities lay.

Greyson had found one of her father's journals, half an hour or so ago, and Charlotte had settled back in the fancy chair to read it. The chair reclined in armchair fashion and the table had seemed as good a place for her feet as any. Greyson had sniggered when she'd made herself at home.

'If only your archaeology students could see you now,'

he murmured, between toting and hauling and proving himself a thoroughly useful individual. 'I knew that get-up that the good Professor Greenstone wore to work wasn't the real you.'

'Wait till you see what Director Greenstone of the Greenstone Foundation has in store for you,' she promised in dulcet tones. 'She's going to be channelling Katharine Hepburn. Besides, you can talk, Mr Eminent Botanist. Where's your tweed jacket with the elbow patches?'

'I don't own one.'

'Surely, though, you own a shirt?'

He grinned in thoroughly wicked fashion before turning his back on her and hauling down yet another stack of books from the highest row of bookshelves, giving her a stunning view of tanned skin and manly back muscles at play. 'I own several shirts,' he said loftily. 'But even in the field, the wearing of one is optional.'

As far as Charlotte was concerned, this was just one more reason to go with him next time he ventured forth.

'Greyson, when are you going to the Galapagos again?'

He shot her a lightning glance and kept right on toting.

'I'm not,' he offered finally. 'I'm off the project just as soon as they find a replacement.'

'Oh.' It was worse than she'd thought. Far, far worse. 'That's a pity. I was hoping to join you there this time. I wanted to see the tortoises.'

'Tortoises,' he echoed stupidly, box of books still in hand.

'And the iguanas.'

No repetition on the iguana statement.

'And I wanted to be with you.'

'You can be,' he said gruffly. 'Here.'

'Here's overrated,' she murmured. 'Especially when it comes at so high a cost.' Time to change tack. 'There's some interesting information in this diary. Very interesting, and very useful. For example, my father talks about a promising archaeological site that he wanted to go back to some day. In Ecuador. That's near the Galapagos.'

'I know where it is, Charlotte.' Grey dumped the books on the window seat and turned to face her, one deliciously dishevelled man with don't-mess-with-me in his eyes.

'I'm just saying,' she said mildly.

'*What* are you saying?' he snapped, not so mildly. Testy. Maybe their continued lack of sexual intimacy *was* getting to him more than he let on. Something else Charlotte planned to fix before this day was through.

'I'm just saying that you can't babysit me for the rest of your life, much as it seems to be your main goal at this particular point in time. You'd go mad. *I'd* go mad. And your career would go down the drain. That's not a scenario that appeals to me. Speaking of which, you should probably email bigwig Ellie and tell her you've changed your mind about giving up the Galapagos project leadership. I'd be inclined to tell her that, give or take a month either side of our baby's due delivery date, you'll stay on the job. As for your next trip, you can drop me in Ecuador on the way. We can meet up on some little island paradise on the weekends. You could bring a shirt. Or not.'

'Drop you in Ecua—' Greyson seemed to be have difficulty keeping up his end of the conversation. 'Are you *insane*?'

'Now is that any way to speak to your future wife?'

'*What?*'

'I forgive you, of course. I'll chalk it up to you being overwhelmed by my brilliant plan. As for getting married, it seems only prudent if we're going to be travelling together, especially with the baby. Authorities are very fond of minors travelling with natural parents of the same surname. It saves all sorts of lengthy explanations, and I should know. Having a different surname from Aurora's was the bane of our lives.'

But Greyson would not be sidetracked. 'We are *not* travelling to Ecuador with the baby.'

'I thought you said you *wanted* a wife and family who'd be open to travel,' argued Charlotte sweetly.

'That was before I *had* one!'

'Not that you do,' said Charlotte. 'Have one, that is. Strictly speaking, we'd have to be married for that particular statement to hold true.' She eyed the flint-eyed piece of steaming, stupendously muscled manhood standing before her with a thoughtful yet fully appreciative gaze. 'What are you doing next Wednesday?'

Dr Greyson Tyler, eminent botanist, expedition leader and all round useful guy, wasn't an unreasonable man. He tolerated insanity in others. He took his time and tried to work around it. He stayed calm and employed patience, secure in the knowledge that good sense and superior powers of reasoning would eventually hold sway. They had to, now more so than ever. This was his future wife and child they were talking about.

Unfortunately, all his fine qualities seemed to have temporarily deserted him.

'What kind of man drags his wife and newborn to the end of the earth and back?' he roared.

'So...you're opposed to the idea?' said Charlotte.

'*Yes*, I'm opposed to the idea! It's a very *bad* idea.'

'Even though I have a comprehensive knowledge of what's involved and you have a wonderfully protective streak that should stand us in good stead?'

Greyson glared at her.

Charlotte stifled a delighted grin. Olivia had been so right. There *was* compromise to be had here—in Greyson, and within herself. A commitment to family that would always bring them home. 'Okay,' she said. 'Let's assume that I *do* happen to agree with you when it comes to traipsing around Ecuador with a newborn. Let's assume that I want to give birth here in Sydney and get the hang of motherhood with grandparents in tow, and a doting Millie, and a long-suffering Derek, and most of all with you at my side. I'll give you that one.'

'Keep talking,' said Greyson, so she did.

'I'm talking about travelling with you to the Galapagos throughout my second trimester and maybe a little way into the third. I'm talking about finding me somewhere lovely to stay on San Cristobal, somewhere with good hospital facilities just in case, while you go do your work and Millie and Derek go looking for my father's site. I'm talking about not being emphatically opposed to travelling with you if future work opportunities demand it. We could choose our locations carefully. We could keep this as our home. We could have the best of both worlds.'

'Are you serious?'

'Very.' Time to get up and walk towards him, take his hands in hers, and make him see that when it came to their future together she was and would always be serious. 'I recently had a little epiphany.'

'That makes two of us,' he muttered.

'Mine was about belonging,' she said. 'I'd been working towards it for a while but you hastened it along, and a recent conversation with your mother simply clarified where I was headed. Having a permanent home has always been this shining dream for me, you see. Home was the place where nothing bad ever happened and I was always in control—my perfect world where parents never died and I was surrounded by a family who loved me. Thing is, that place was always just a dream. Make believe to keep the loneliness at bay. The same way Gil was make believe. None of it was ever real. You are.'

'That was your epiphany?' he said, and a smile tugged at the corners of his lips. 'That I'm real?'

'No, it's that being home isn't about staying put and living in the one place. It's about being with the man I love. Supporting him. Being there for him. And trusting him to know that when we do need to settle in one place for a time and raise our family, we will.'

'I need to think,' he muttered. 'My epiphany involved staying here because that was what you wanted. Safety. Security. Stability. You walked away from me once because I couldn't offer that to you—*wouldn't* offer it. I'm offering it to you now.'

'We *do* seem to be at cross purposes, don't we?' Charlotte sent him an encouraging smile. 'But never fear. You'll come round to my way of thinking eventually.'

But at this, he shook his head. 'I can't think here. I need to think.' He broke away from her and strode to the window, a man in need of clarity, a man at the end of his wits. 'I'm going for a swim.'

'Excellent idea,' murmured Charlotte. 'The pool's beautifully warm.' She'd already taken a dip in it to do the stretching exercises the physio had recommended for her ribs and chest. She stretched again now, drawing Greyson's gaze, deliberately adding physical desire to the cauldron and stirring gently. 'Are bathers optional?'

'Not in the pool,' he said darkly. 'In the harbour.'

'Oh.' Charlotte shuddered. 'You're on your own there.' She wasn't opposed to beach swimming or snorkelling around pristine island atolls; she loved the water.

But Sydney Harbour was different. 'Bring back some apples.'

'You have a distinct problem with reality,' he countered. 'You know that, don't you?'

'Hello-o.' Time to return to her chair and give her man the thinking time he'd demanded. Time to retreat behind the pages of her father's journal. 'Archaeologist.'

'Believe me, I hadn't forgotten,' he said grimly. 'Oh, and, Charlotte?'

'Hmm?' She peered over the top of the journal. 'You spoke, my love?'

'You mentioned marriage,' he said curtly.

'Yes. So I did.'

'Wednesday's fine.'

While Greyson cooled off in the water and planned his next move, Charlotte took advantage of his absence and planned hers. Sunset wasn't all that far away and one thing their bedroom did have was a spectacular viewing window to the west and a harbour view that had sold the house to Aurora in the first place.

Greyson didn't need candles but Charlotte lit some anyway. A man with a lot on his mind deserved as much. The nightgown she chose to wear was a wondrous piece of lavender silk and lace. The slave bracelets at her wrists added a nice hint of pagan. She shook out her hair and checked her ribs for tenderness. Feeling good. Still a little faded yellow bruising here and there, but the plan was to try and keep this nightgown *on* for the most part, and make Greyson forget her injuries and her recent brush with catastrophe. Life was for living, and live it she would.

Thank you, Aurora. You'd like him, I think. Greyson. My fiancé. He's useful, and honourable, and he helped me find my way home.

If wishes were wishes...
My wish has come true.

Greyson came back from the harbour all showered and
shaved and tidied up. He'd cleaned up on his boat, he'd put
a shirt on over the knee length canvas shorts he usually
reserved for sailing. It was a very nice shirt, collared, dove
grey, as soft and as warm as cotton could be—Charlotte
knew this from experience. He'd even buttoned it up.

Greyson's eyes gleamed when he saw her. He looked
like a man refreshed and ready for anything. Including
her.

'Feel better?' she asked, and crossed to the sideboard
where she'd set up a mini bar. Lime and soda for her,
smooth Scotch in a round glass for him and she handed it
to him with a smile and a challenge.

'Much better.'

'Decisive?'

'Very.' He eyed her nightgown with gratifying appreciation and her slave bracelets with sharp speculation. 'And
how is my fiancée feeling this fine, fine evening?'

'Obliging.'

'That's good.' Greyson's voice had deepened to a husky
rumble. 'That's very good.'

'I thought we might enjoy the sunset together.' Charlotte
sipped her soda and admired the view before her. So much
to admire about this man. The compromises he'd been
willing to make for her and their child. His fierce intel-
ligence and impressive focus. His strength of will and that
beautiful hard body that he'd kept on a leash of late, on
account of her injuries. She loved his protectiveness, for
it spoke of his love for her. She loved *him*, body and soul.
'If you wanted to, that is.'

'I do.'

'And then I thought you might want to enjoy me.'

'I do.' Greyson set his drink aside. 'Never doubt it.'

Charlotte gently set her drink next to his. She slid her hands up to his shoulders and around the back of his neck. Greyson's lips touched hers, gentle and worshipping. Not what she wanted from this man tonight. She deepened the kiss. Greyson's kisses grew fiercer and more passionate, but his arms did not come around her to gather her close.

'The doctor said—' he began, and she shushed him with gentle fingers.

'That was three weeks ago. The doctor says I'm fine and that our baby is fine and that there's absolutely no reason why I can't be making love to you if I'm careful.'

Charlotte freed the top few buttons on his shirt and pressed her lips to his collarbone. Greyson groaned again. Hard to say whether it was in dismay.

'Charlotte, we can't,' he said huskily. 'I can't. I'm too…'

'Protective?' she said helpfully. 'Stubborn?'

'Too afraid I'll hurt you,' he muttered and brought his hands up to her face and his lips to hers for a kiss that fed her soul. 'That I'll ask for too much and you'll give it and we'll both regret it.'

'That won't happen. I love you, Greyson Tyler. I love who you are and what you do. I'm in—all the way in—but there's balance here between us too. Can't you feel it?'

'I love you,' he murmured gruffly. 'There's nothing I want more than to share my life with you. Travel with you, stay here and raise a family with you, build a foundation, work on my own projects. I want it all.'

'I'm glad to hear it. Because I want it all too, including your lovemaking.' Charlotte stepped away from his touch, put her hand in his, and led him to the bed, urging him onto it, on his back, exactly where she wanted him. 'Starting from now.' She straddled him carefully, clothes and all. Plenty of time for the removal of clothes later. 'We can do this.' Leaning forward, she set her hands to Greyson's shoulders and watched with satisfaction as his eyes flared and darkened. 'We *are* doing this.' She kissed the edge of his lips and the line of his jaw until finally she reached his ear.

'What's more,' she whispered, 'we're going to love it.'

LOSING CONTROL

ROBYN GRADY

This book is dedicated to the friends I made during my own days working in the media. Never a dull moment!

With thanks to my editor, Shana Smith, for her support and work on this book and The Hunter Pact series.

Robyn Grady was first published by Mills & Boon in 2007. Her books have since featured regularly on bestseller lists and at award ceremonies, including The National Readers Choice Award, The Booksellers' Best Award, Cataromance Reviewers Choice Award and Australia's prestigious Romantic Book of the Year Award.

Robyn lives on Queensland's beautiful Sunshine Coast with her real-life hero husband and three daughters. When she can be dragged away from tapping out her next story, Robyn visits the theater, the beach and the mall (a lot!). To keep fit, she jogs (and shops) and dances with her youngest to Hannah Montana.

Robyn believes writing romance is the best job on the planet and she loves to hear from her readers. So drop by www.robyngrady.com and pass on your thoughts!

One

Eyes shot up and all conversation ceased as Cole Hunter burst in and let loose a growl. Cole wouldn't apologize. He abhorred being kept in the dark, particularly when the deception concerned the man he respected most in the world.

Once, Cole's father had been a corporate powerhouse, a leader to be admired and, frequently, feared. More recently, however, Guthrie Hunter had softened. The responsibility of running Hunter Enterprises had fallen largely upon Cole's shoulders. The eldest of four, he was the person family leaned upon in a crisis, whether the drama unfolded here in Sydney or at one of the other Hunter offices located in Los Angeles and New York City.

Cole didn't want to think about that ongoing drama in Seattle.

His father's personal receptionist flew to her feet. With a look, Cole set her back in her seat then strode toward colossal doors that displayed the flourishing Hunter Enterprises emblem. How the hell could he keep things well oiled and on track if he wasn't informed? *Dammit,* he couldn't fix what he didn't know.

Cole broke through the doors. Turning to close them again,

his gaze brushed over the three openmouthed guests waiting in the reception area, one being a woman with wide summer-blue eyes and flaxen hair that fell like tumbles of silk on either side of her curious face. His raging pulse skipped several beats before thumping back to life. Work in television production meant beautiful ladies day in and day out, but true star quality was one in a million and this woman had it in spades. She must be auditioning for a show, Cole surmised. A special project if Guthrie Hunter planned to conduct the interview himself.

Something else he knew zip about.

His jaw tight, Cole slammed the doors shut. Swinging around, he faced the polished hardwood desk, which had prefaced that wall of glittering awards for as long as Cole could remember. Unperturbed, a silver-haired man sat in a high-backed leather chair, receiver pressed to an ear. Cole's sources said three hours had passed since a second attempt had been made on his father's life. Guthrie had probably wondered what had kept his firstborn so long.

Stopping dead center of the enormous office suite, Cole set his fists on his hips. Despite broiling frustration, he kept his tone low and clear.

"Whoever's responsible won't see light outside of a prison cell before both poles have melted." When his throat uncharacteristically thickened, Cole's hands fell to his sides. "For God's sake, Dad, shots were fired. This guy's not about to stop."

Guthrie muttered a few parting words into the mouthpiece then set the receiver in its cradle. Surveying his son, he tipped his clean-shaven chin a notch higher.

"I have this under control."

"Like you had it under control a month ago when your car was run off the road?"

"The authorities concluded that was an accident."

Cole looked heavenward. *God, give me strength.* "The license plates belonged to a stolen vehicle."

"Doesn't mean the accident was an attempt on my life."

"I'll tell you what it does mean. Bodyguards until this is sorted. And I don't want to hear any argument."

When Cole went too far and shook his finger, Guthrie's smooth expression fell. Sixty-two-year-old palms pressed upon the desk and Guthrie pushed to his feet with the agility and posture of a man thirty years younger. Cole's jacketed shoulders rolled back. There wasn't a man alive who could intimidate him, although, even now, with an ax to grind, his father came close.

"You'll be happy to know I have organized a bodyguard," Guthrie said. "He's a private detective, as well."

Absorbing his father's words, Cole willed away the red haze rimming his vision. His temper dropped a degree and then two. Flexing his fingers at his sides, he blew out that pent-up breath.

"What were you thinking, keeping this from me?"

"Son, I've only just got in." Rounding the desk, the older man crossed over and set a bracing hand high on Cole's jacketed arm. "You have enough to worry about. Like I said… everything's under control."

Cole winced. Guthrie was kidding himself.

Four years ago, when his father was recovering from bypass surgery and Cole had turned thirty, the family empire had been sectioned up and each son designated an equal portion to manage. Here in Sydney, Cole manned the Australian television cable and free-air interests. When he wasn't chasing skirt, Dex, the middle son, looked after the motion picture end of business in L.A. The overindulged, overachiever and youngest of the Hunter boys from Guthrie's first marriage, Wynn took care of the print media slice of the company from New York. Cole's remaining full-blood sibling Teagan was off doing her own thing in Washington State.

Initially Cole had bristled at the idea of Daddy's Girl shunning her responsibilities and refusing to step up to help run the business. Hunter Enterprises had provided well for them all, Teagan's childhood operations and college designer gowns included…although, to be fair, with the top three jobs filled, her role would need to be a subordinate one. But given the time he spent watching and worrying over his brothers' business and personal decisions, Cole had to be grateful that the Hunter wild child had opted out. God knows he had enough to deal with.

Of course Cole still loved his brothers and sister. Nothing could ever change that. They'd shared a wonderful mother, a talented Georgian beauty who had beamed whenever she'd told a new acquaintance that both he and Wynn had been born in Atlanta. With only two years separating each, the Hunter children had grown up tight. But, thanks to gossip magazines and the Net, all the world knew about the rifts, which made the running of such a vast enterprise under separate helms even more of a challenge. Through Dex's overindulgence and Wynn's overzealousness, Hunter's reputation had taken some blows recently. For everyone's sake, Cole was determined to assume genuine leadership over every quadrant of Hunter Enterprises, or die trying.

Guthrie wanted his children to mend their fences, get along and continue to build together. With their father married a second time to a calculating woman, playing happy families—keeping it all together—was nigh on impossible.

Winding away from his father, Cole moved to an early-spring view of commuter ferries crisscrossing Sydney Harbour's vast blanket of blue.

"I'd be happier speaking to Brandon Powell about organizing full-time protection," he said.

"I know you and Brandon have been friends for years, and his security firm is one of the best. It's not that I didn't consider it… But, frankly, I need someone who's clear on who's paying the bill."

Cole pivoted around. "If you're suggesting Brandon would ever act unprofessionally—"

"I'm saying you'd be at him to divulge every detail of my every move, including what transpires beneath the sanctity of my family's roof, and that is not an option. I know you don't approve of Eloise, but—" Guthrie's furrowed brow eased and, weary of that particular fight, he exhaled. "Son, my wife makes me happy."

"As happy as my mother used to make you?"

"As happy as one day I hope you will be with someone you truly care for."

Cole refused to acknowledge the sheen in his father's eyes or the uncomfortable restriction in his own chest. Instead, he headed back to those massive double doors. Lust and love were two different states. A man his father's age should know better. His eldest son certainly did.

As if to highlight the point, the first thing to catch Cole's eye as he strode back into his father's reception lounge was that blonde and her star quality coaxing him into her long-legged, lush-lipped orbit. What red-blooded male would pass on the chance to bring those amazing curves close, to sample the soft press of that body and sweet scent of her skin? But that urge was sexual, only lust.

One day, Cole hoped to find the right woman. Someone he'd be proud to call the mother of his children. Someone he would respect and receive respect from in return. His step-mother didn't know the meaning of that word. In fact, he wouldn't be surprised if Eloise was behind those bullets for hire. Despite his father's edict just now, he had no qualms about finding out if Brandon Powell thought the same.

When his father's voice broke into his thoughts, Cole blinked his attention away from Ms. Summer-Blue Eyes.

Standing to Cole's left, Guthrie was studying him, salt-and-pepper brows hitched at a quizzical—or was that approving?—angle.

"I see you've met our new producer, Taryn Quinn."

Cole did a double take. Producer? As in *behind* the cameras as opposed to in front of them?

Again he examined the woman whose glittering gaze was pinned directly on him. Feeling his blood swell, Cole cleared his throat. Producer, talent…either way, it made no difference. If his father hadn't discussed this before now, anything other than a cursory introduction would have to wait. He had a meeting to attend, important documents to sort.

Cole muttered, "Good meeting you, Ms. Quinn," then prepared to shove off. But she'd already eased to her stiletto-heeled feet, and as she extended a slender hand, the light in her eyes seemed to intensify tenfold. Dazzling. Inviting. Cole couldn't deny he felt the warmth of that smile to his bones.

"You must be Cole," she said as, reaching out, his fingers curled around and held hers. A current—subtle yet electric—sizzled up his arm and, despite his ill humor, Cole found a small smile of his own.

Well, guess he could spare a moment or two.

"So, you're a producer, Ms. Quinn?" he asked.

"For a show I approved last week," his father interjected as Ms. Quinn's hand fell away. "Haven't had a chance to speak with you about it yet."

Cole asked, "What kind of show?"

"A holiday getaway program," Taryn Quinn said.

Out of the corner of his eye, Cole caught Guthrie fiddling with his platinum watchband the way he did whenever he felt uncomfortable. And rightly so. The last holiday series Hunter Broadcasting had piloted died a quick and deserved death. In these tough economic times, if viewers were to swallow yet another "best destinations" show, the promise would need to deliver fresh sparks week after week.

And what about the exorbitant budgets? Sponsors could pull down costs but, since the global financial crisis, any collaboration was a squeeze. Despite her obvious allure, if the decision had been his, Cole would've given Ms. Quinn's idea the thumbs-down before she'd cleared the gate.

Another mess he'd need to clean up.

From behind her desk, Guthrie's receptionist interrupted. "Mr. Hunter, you asked to know if Rod Walker from Hallowed Productions called."

Thoughtful, Guthrie stroked his chin before heading back toward his office. He paused beneath the lintel of that massive doorway.

"Taryn, I'll drop by and touch base soon. In the meantime…" His focus swung back to his son. "Cole, I've allocated Ms. Quinn the office next to Roman Lyons. Do me a favor."

Cole thrust both fists into his trouser pockets. He guessed the favor. No way would he raise his hand.

"I have a meeting—"

"First, see that Taryn's settled." Guthrie's light expression held while his voice lowered to a steely tone Cole knew well. "Your meeting will wait."

Taryn nodded her thanks to Guthrie Hunter then turned to his Hollywood-attractive son. Her jaw tightened even as her heart beat a thousand miles a minute. How women must melt at Cole Hunter's feet. How they must dream of his smile.

"Your father's a considerate man," she said as Guthrie's towering doors clicked shut, "but if you're busy, please don't let me keep you."

When she resumed her seat, crossed her legs and reached for a magazine, rather than run with the offer, Cole Hunter remained rooted to the spot, and for so long Taryn began to wonder whether he'd expected a curtsy before heading out.

Her gaze crept up from the fashion section.

In that rich graveled voice that made her stomach muscles flutter, he explained, "I can't put this meeting back."

"Oh, I understand."

She sent a quick smile he didn't return. Rather, the crease between the dark slashes of his brows deepened. "My father shouldn't be long. Rod Walker's a busy man, too."

Taryn nodded affably, recrossed her legs, and the magazine took her attention again. But as she flipped to the gossip pages, she was aware of the younger Mr. Hunter checking his wristwatch then shaking his jacket sleeve back down.

"My guest's flying back to Melbourne at midday," he went on. "We don't have much time."

Glancing back up, she cocked her head and blinked. "Then you'd best hurry."

Cole Hunter wasn't hard to work out. Foremost, he was get-out-of-my-way ambitious, which she understood. Nothing compared with the buzz of landing on top, achieving a true sense of financial and personal security. She'd grown up with an aunt. One of Vi's favorite sayings was, *At every turn, in every way, invest in yourself,* which meant achieving a good education, grabbing regular exercise, staying loyal to friends and, wherever possible, dodging "trouble." Which brought Taryn to Cole Hunter's *second* quality.

Clearly, he was an intensely sexual being and, for whatever reason, she had piqued his interest. The testosterone pumping through his veins, darkening those ocean-green eyes to a storm, was as tangible as the breadth of his chest or square set of his jaw. The man exuded a masculine energy that stroked Taryn's skin and stirred a delicious aching heat low in her belly.

Understanding these things about Cole Hunter was the reason for her reservation now. She didn't care who he was, what he thought of himself, how many women he'd bedded, with how much skill or how little effort. Certainly she wouldn't be rude, but *Guthrie* Hunter had hired her and no matter how knee-knockingly sexy, if the son was ambivalent, hell, she'd survive.

As she held her honest-you-can-leave look, Cole shifted his weight and those incredible eyes narrowed as if he were now seeing her in a somewhat different light.

"Actually," he finally said, "that office next to Roman's is on my way." When she opened her mouth to decline, he overrode her. "I insist."

He extended and continued to offer his hand until, knowing she was cornered, Taryn accepted. As expected, the same fiery trail that had flown up her arm the first time they'd touched sparked again—not that she let any hint of the rush dent her poise. She made certain her eyes didn't widen, that her breath didn't hitch. And yet the satisfied grin smoldering in Cole's eyes said that he knew what she felt because he felt it, too.

As they moved toward the building's main thoroughfare side by side, she imagined Aunt Vi holding up her hands in warning and shaking her head. Taryn agreed. Cole Hunter was one of those "trouble" spots. Hotheaded, superior, radiating sex appeal like a supernova gave off light and heat.

Thank God they wouldn't be working together.

Two

"Guthrie would've mentioned we'll be working together."

When his statement received no reply, Cole wasn't entirely surprised. Taryn Quinn was attractive and charming. She was also aloof. Mysterious. As they walked together down the eastern wing of the Hunter Broadcasting building, Cole admitted he was intrigued, as his father knew he would be.

Rod Walker's call was an excuse Guthrie had pounced upon to bring his son and new producer together, despite the fact that Cole was, one, hard-pressed for time and, two, obviously opposed to investing in Ms. Quinn's proposal. Money was too darn tight and Guthrie knew it. But when she'd seemed so indifferent toward him—sitting there demurely with those shapely legs crossed, engrossed in that glossy magazine— blast it, he'd been intrigued all the more. Against better judgment, he'd decided to escort Taryn to her office and see if he couldn't prick that haughty shell.

So far, no good.

Passing an interested group of employees, and still awaiting a response, Cole risked a glance. Taryn was staring at him as if he'd announced science had proven that the moon was indeed made of green cheese. Perhaps she was hard of hearing.

He spoke louder. "I said as long as you're with Hunter Broadcasting, you'll be working under me."

"I'm sorry." Shrugging back slender shoulders draped in an elegant black jacket, she looked dead ahead. "But you're wrong."

Cole's step faltered. Not deaf. Nor had she misunderstood. He threw a suspect glance around. Was there a hidden camera or was she purposely ruffling his feathers?

"You must be aware of my position here—CEO as well as Executive Producer—and that's for every show that comes out of Hunters. I give the nod on budgets, sponsor deals—" his gaze sharpened on her perfect profile "—as well as the overall vision of any given project."

The peaks of her dark blond brows arched as she met his gaze square on. "Guthrie and I have discussed all that. I'll be working directly beneath *him*."

Cole didn't hide his smirk. He disliked cruelty in any form but he might enjoy setting sassy Ms. Quinn back, flat on her pretty behind. Whatever Guthrie had said, he hadn't worked in that kind of hands-on capacity for years.

Or maybe he should look at this collusion from a different angle. What had Taryn Quinn said or done to get this close to his father? And exactly how close was that?

Suddenly a dozen other questions sprang to mind, like where did Taryn hail from? What was her personal background? Did she have a criminal record? Did she know anything about those murder attempts?

Up ahead, London-born Head of Comedy, Roman Lyons, was strolling out of his office, whistling that same Cockney tune that grated on Cole's nerves like nails down a chalkboard. When Roman first joined Hunters, the two had a disagreement over the direction of a series. Cole had terminated his contract. Guthrie, however, had persuaded Cole to give Lyons another chance. After two years, Cole would concede that Roman did a good job. He'd even stepped in to oversee things a few times when Cole had been called away. But they'd never be best buds.

Now as he and Taryn approached, Lyons issued a casual salute to Cole, but his focus was fixed on Taryn. From the awareness sparkling in Lyons's dark hooded gaze, anyone might think that he knew her.

"This must be the new girl. Taryn, is it?" Lyons offered a knowing wink as well as his hand. "Word gets around."

Cole's jaw jutted. Word hadn't gotten around to *him*.

"Thanks for the welcome," Taryn said as her hand dropped away. "And you are?"

"Name's Roman Lyons."

"Looks like we'll be neighbors, Mr. Lyons. I drew the office next to yours."

"I was about to grab a cuppa," Lyons went on. "Can I tempt you?"

Taryn's face lit. "I'd kill for coffee."

"Let me guess," Lyons said. "White, one sugar."

Cole growled. *Oh, give me a break.*

"I'll leave you two to get acquainted." He started off. "I have work to do."

"With Liam Finlay? I saw him headed toward your office a minute ago." Roman straightened the knot of his tie as if he were loosening a noose. "He didn't look happy, if you don't mind me saying."

Cole bit back a curse. Liam Finlay wasn't a man to keep waiting, particularly today. Finlay was CEO for Australia's most popular football league. Hunter Broadcasting had held the cable broadcast rights to the majority of that league's games until five years ago, when Guthrie and Finlay had suffered a major falling-out. This year those coveted rights were back up for grabs. Cole had had a hard time getting Finlay to even talk. At this juncture, he couldn't afford any perceived insults, like letting his guest sit around twiddling his thumbs.

In a near-sincere tone, Taryn said, "Thanks for taking the time, Mr. Hunter. I'm sure I'll be fine from here."

A pulse point in Cole's temple began to throb. He had to get to that meeting. But, dammit, he wasn't finished with Ms. Quinn just yet.

As Roman sauntered off, Taryn entered her new office, which was decked out with teak furniture and the latest tech equipment, including visual and audio state of the art. But she moved directly to the floor-to-ceiling windows. He imagined he heard her sigh as she drank in the billion-dollar harbor view, complete with iconic coat-hanger bridge and multistory-high Opera House shells.

Letting his gaze rake over the silken fall of her hair and the tantalizing curves concealed beneath that smart blue skirt, Cole leaned a shoulder against the doorjamb.

"You have qualifications other than in television production, Ms. Quinn?"

"I've worked in TV since attaining my Arts Business degree."

"Then you'd have experience—held positions—in other areas within the industry, correct?"

"I started out as a junior production assistant and worked up through the ranks."

"And my father was—" he scanned her skirt again "—suitably impressed by your credentials?"

When she angled around, her smile was lazy, assured. "As a matter of fact, Guthrie was more than impressed."

"I make a point of having all my employees' backgrounds screened, management particularly."

"Heavens, you must have skeletons jumping out of closets all over the place."

His mouth hooked up at one side. *Cute.*

He crossed his arms. "Any skeletons in your closet, Ms. Quinn?"

"We all have secrets, although they're rarely of interest to anyone else."

"I have a feeling I'd be interested in yours."

Those big blue eyes narrowed then she strolled up to him, the deliberate sway in her walk meant to challenge. When she was close enough for the scent of her perfume to tease his nostrils, she stopped and set her hands on her hips. Cole exhaled. Poor Ms. Quinn. Didn't she know he ate novices like her for breakfast?

"I've taken up enough of your time," she told him. "Don't keep your guest waiting. I'm sure your father will be along soon."

He grinned. Damn, he could play with her all day, if only he had the time—which he didn't. He pushed off the jamb.

"My father might have employed you, but I'm the one in charge of the books, and if your show doesn't perform, production stops. That is, if I allow it to get off the ground in the first place."

A shadow darkened her eyes. "My show will not only launch, it will be a new season smash. We're bringing in A-list guests."

"Been done."

"Choosing destinations that are considered rough as well as luxurious."

"Old."

"The host I have in mind is the most popular in the country. Voted Australia's most eligible with a string of hits under his belt."

Cole's gaze flicked to her naturally bee-stung lips. "That's the best you can offer?"

He imagined her quiver, as if a bolt of red-tipped annoyance had zapped straight up her spine. "I have a signed copy of the approved proposal as well as a contract setting my salary."

"A contract which will be paid out unless your pilot is fresher than tomorrow's headline news."

An emotion akin to hatred flashed in her eyes. "Perhaps I should put a call through to my lawyer."

"Perhaps you should."

Any space separating them seemed to shrink while the awareness simmering in that steamy void began to crackle and smoke. Taryn Quinn whipped up his baser instincts to a point where he could forget she was an employee. In fact, right now he was evaluating her through the crosshairs of a vastly different lens. She pretended to be cool, in control. Would she be so restrained in the bedroom? Instinct said she'd set the sheets on fire.

She was saying, "And if I were to come up with something you hadn't seen before?"

He gifted her with a slow smile. "Then, Ms. Quinn, I'd be happy to visit it."

He asked that she get the original and revised proposal to him as soon as she had something that would knock his socks off. But as Cole made his way down the corridor toward his office and Liam Finlay, he berated himself. Normally in these kinds of situations he wasn't distracted by sex appeal; that was playboy Dex's vice. But the challenging blue depths of Taryn Quinn's eyes, the impudent tilt of her slightly upturned nose, the fact he knew in his gut she was hiding something...

Thinking of those flaming sheets, Cole admitted, he was looking forward to prying open her closets.

"What do you think of the Commander?"

Familiarizing herself with her office LCD TV, Taryn glanced up. Roman Lyons had returned with two steaming cups in tow. Remote control in one hand, she accepted the coffee he offered while she grinned at Roman's nickname for Cole.

"Cole obviously likes to run a tight ship," she conceded.

"As much as he likes introducing newcomers to his infamous plank."

"Sounds as if you speak from experience."

"Cole has his fans—" bringing the cup to his mouth, Roman arched a brow "—as well as his foes."

"Which side do you fall on?"

"On the 'keeping my job' side. To survive in this industry, you need to roll with the punches. But you've been around. You'd know all that." He nodded at the static on the screen and gestured at the control. "This office was vacant for a while. I'll tweak the settings."

She handed over the control and watched as he concentrated to tune in channels, including internal feeds. Roman Lyons was good-looking in a saucy Hugh Grant kind of way. Certainly friendly, helpful and with a sense of humor, too. No wonder he rubbed "Trouble" the wrong way.

"Tell me how you came to be at Hunters," Roman said, as his thumb danced over the remote's keys.

"I had a long stint at the last network I worked for." She mentioned the name and recited a few of their shows. "Last year, one of the executive producers asked for ideas for new series. He was interested in a couple of mine but ultimately passed. In the meantime another network approached me."

"The industry does like to poach."

"I declined their offer of an interview. I was happy where I was. But management heard about the communication and when information about a new show was leaked, they questioned my loyalty." Remembering the scene when that EP had dressed her down, she shuddered and blew out a breath. Her direct boss was livid at his protégée's treatment, but he had a family to feed. She'd insisted he not get involved. "That afternoon, my desk was packed up and I was out on the curb."

Roman collected a second control off the stand. "TV is not for the faint of heart."

"I could have filed a suit for unfair dismissal. But I decided to rise above it, take the payout and move on."

"What happened to the network that wanted to poach you?"

"That position was already filled. But I knew my ideas would fly somewhere else. After wallowing for a couple of weeks, I plucked up the nerve to call here and speak to Guthrie directly."

As she took a sip from her cup, Roman handed back the first control. "Good for you."

"Frankly, I almost fell off my chair when he asked me to come in for an interview. I was even more blown away when he gave my show the green light straightaway." Thoughtful, she ran a thumb over the remote's keys. "I was on such a high, so convinced I'd do a great job, but after meeting Cole, I have to wonder if that green light is fast turning red." She set the remote down on the corner of her desk. "Roman, can you set me straight on something? Because I'm a little confused. Which Hunter is in charge here? I know control of the branches of the company was split a few years ago between the three sons, but I assumed Guthrie still pulled all the strings."

Beneath a flop of dark sandy hair, Roman's high brow creased. Then he held up a cautionary hand and, although they'd been speaking quietly, he crossed to close the door.

"Word is that after his wife's death," Roman said, moving back, "Guthrie lost all heart. No one knows for sure, but if you put it to a vote, most will say he gave up all control."

"You mean Guthrie has *no* say? What's he doing then, hiring me?"

"Guthrie was down for a while but when he married again, he got his wind back. Staff here were chuffed. It was as if he'd got another chance at life and he didn't intend to waste a minute. The wedding was big, expensive—" he hiked a brow "—and fast."

Of course Taryn remembered the publicity surrounding that big day, a huge celebrity bash with a bride who had looked thirty years the groom's junior—which was nobody's business but their own.

"At my interview, Guthrie seemed genuinely excited and behind my show," she said.

"Then he must believe in it."

"While his son's hand is twitching on the guillotine rope. He told me unless I can come up with an extraordinary twist, I'm out."

Roman thought for a long moment before giving a mischievous smile. He purposefully set down his empty cup. "Right-o. We need sketch pads. Markers. A plan."

She blinked and then brightened. "As in *you* and *me* 'we'?"

"Two heads, and all that. What say we come up with a twist that hits Cole right where he bloody well lives? He'll either love it or…"

"Or he'll love it." He *had to*. Taryn moved to scoop her laptop out from its bag. "Let's get started."

Three

When Cole stabbed the loudspeaker key and realized who was on the phone, he flung down his pen and grabbed the hand piece. It was past six—closer to seven. He'd been hanging out for this call all day.

"Brandon, thanks for getting back to me."

"Just got back into the country." Brandon Powell's familiar deep drawl echoed down the line. "What's up?"

Cole gave his friend a summary of events—the attempt to run his father's car off the road three weeks ago, the near miss with shots fired this morning, how Guthrie, to his mind, didn't appreciate the seriousness of the situation.

"You want to fix your father up with protection," Brandon surmised.

"He's already hired someone."

"Then I'm not sure what you want me to do."

"For starters, put a trace on Eloise."

"Your father's *wife?*"

"Second wife." Cole's lip all but curled. "I have a hunch she might be behind it all."

"You're accusing Eloise of attempted murder—based on what?"

"Based on the fact she's a—"

Cole let loose a few choice adjectives and nouns that had been building for years, starting when he'd first got wind that a much younger woman—a so-called family friend—was making a play on a man who'd recently lost a loving wife. None of the boys had thought Guthrie would be interested in her batting lashes and syrupy condolences. When it had become apparent the two were an item, their father was already hooked.

Brandon's reply was wry. "I take it you haven't warmed to your stepmother yet."

"I still can't believe he married her. My mother's best friend's gold-digging daughter."

Shame on Eloise but more shame on his father.

"I hate to mention this," Brandon said, "but Guthrie's an adult. He makes his own decisions."

"And I make mine. How soon can you organize a tail?"

"If you're sure—"

"I'm sure."

"Give me a few hours to track down the right guy and brief him. But I need to warn you. If your father has his own man on the job, there's a chance he'll find out you've done this behind his back. And if Eloise ultimately isn't implicated…"

Cole knew what his friend had left unsaid. Guthrie took the well-being and loyalty of his entire family seriously. His father had a five-year-old son with Eloise and another on the way. If he discovered his eldest had gone behind his back like this, he'd view it as a betrayal. Guthrie wouldn't disown a son, but he might kick Cole out of Hunter Enterprises for good.

Considering the options, Cole rapped his fingers on the desk before he drove down a breath and confirmed, "I'll take that chance."

He didn't want a rift to develop between two more members of the Hunter clan but, dammit, his father's safety came first.

After settling some details, he and Brandon caught up

briefly. Brandon was still enjoying his bachelorhood and was looking forward to a Navy Cadets reunion; they'd served in a unit together for three years rising up through the ranks from "dolphins" to petty officers. Brandon said he hoped to see Cole there, but he'd be in touch before then.

They signed off and, feeling worn out, Cole set his bristled jaw in the cup of his hand at the same time his empty stomach growled. He hadn't eaten since breakfast. There was still more he could do here tonight, but his brain needed fuel. Time to knock off.

While Cole shut down his laptop, a knickknack perched on his desk caught his eye. The winding steel-tube-and-rope puzzle had been a gift from Dex and was based on the Gordian Knot legend. Thousands of years ago, Alexander the Great had been asked to unravel that intricate knot, which everyone knew couldn't be done. But Alexander had thought outside of the box and found a simple solution. He sliced through the rope with his sword and, *hey presto!* With this gift, Dex was telling Cole to lighten up…life's problems didn't need to be so intense and all-consuming.

Cole would rather ignore advice from a playboy producer who was overdue a Hollywood hit. There *were* no shortcuts to success. No easy paths to victory. Cole kept the toy on his desk not as a reminder to take the low road as Dex was wont to do, but as a prompt to stay on course, even when he might rather say *to hell with it all*.

After shrugging into his jacket, Cole locked up his office, spun around and near jumped out of his skin. In the muted light, he'd almost run into something. Or rather, someone.

Taryn Quinn stood not a foot away, her scent still fresh, her eyes still bright. With her blond mane gleaming and plump lips bare of gloss, she looked like a vision. A drop-dead sexy vision, at that.

She inspected his briefcase, peered around his frame to the closed door and her eyes widened in alarm.

"You're leaving?"

He frowned. "Didn't realize I had to sign out."

"I thought that someone in your position would be here till all hours."

When Taryn lifted the open laptop she held, the penny dropped. She'd worked out a plan to spice up her proposal already?

"I was serious," he warned. "I don't want a Band-Aid. You need a highly polished knock-'em-dead new angle that I can't refuse."

"I've been at it all day. Didn't even stop to eat."

That made two of them. She must be as hungry as he was, and he was starved. After a day alternating between meetings and being glued to his desk, he felt restless, too. Itchy. *Hot.* When his gaze dropped to her lips again, he ran a finger inside his steamy collar. He ought to go.

Cole eased around her. "Now isn't a good time."

"Now is a *great* time."

"I'm late."

"What for this time?"

He rotated back. "I'm sure I don't have to answer that," he said. But when he saw the disappointment shining in her eyes, his gut kicked and, against his better judgment, he found himself giving in to this infernal woman for a second time that day.

"But, if you're that keen," he muttered, heading back, "I'll give you five minutes."

"Five minutes isn't nearly enough—"

"Five minutes." He set his case on his personal assistant's desk and flicked on the desk lamp. "Starting now."

Taryn froze for three beats before setting her laptop down. When she thumbed a button, an impressive spread—complete with feature banner—flashed on to the screen. Setting his hands on his hips, Cole slanted his head. Nice effect. Although he wasn't sold on the title.

"Hot Spots?"

"We thought it had more bite than the original name."

"We?"

"Roman and me. I know it sounds kind of provocative—"

"If you want to tape an endless stream of topless bars and nudist beaches," he cut in, "sorry, it ain't gonna fly."

The airwaves were clogged enough with that content.

"I was going to say that it's more a hook than anything erotic. Let me show you a preliminary list of locations that have shown interest *and,* as of today, have offered to cover all associated costs."

The screen page flipped over to reveal a slide show of a resort Cole knew—although not personally. Only a sheik could afford the prices. He could think of better ways to blow a million or two. Still, the cogs in his brain began to whir faster.

"That's Dubai."

When he named that country's most exclusive resort, Taryn nodded with a grin in her eyes. "All expenses paid there. *Everything.*"

"That's impressive. But that's *one* location. I imagine you'll do the grand tour of the resort and surrounds, which will make good footage, but what's the twist?"

Where's the something new?

Their shoulders all but touching, she angled in more and, in the soft shadows, those blue eyes were hypnotic. Then that natural warmth of hers reached out again. Sumptuous. Soothing. It was like being enveloped by the lure of a toasty fire after coming in from the cold. When his fingertips began to tingle where they lay splayed on the desk next to hers, he was struck by the urge to cover her hand, maybe tug her close and see if he couldn't experience some of that warmth head-on.

Sucking down a breath, he straightened.

Definitely time to go.

"I'll think it over."

"Will you?"

He arched a brow. "What's that supposed to mean?"

"You've already made up your mind."

"If you believe that, why are you here?" *Wasting my time.*

"Because I also believe in this show." Her chin lifted. "And that wasn't five minutes."

"It was long enough." Especially considering the way he was feeling.

"But I have more to show you, Cole. Lots more."

The tendons between his shoulders, up the length of his thighs, all hardened to steel and then locked. He should get this charade over with. Tell her now. Stay on course. But how was he supposed to deal with that dewy-eyed, indignant look without feeling like the world's biggest heel?

An image of Dex's puzzle flashed into his mind's eye and something he'd thought unbending inside of him grudgingly moved. Before he could talk himself out of it, he took a mental sword and cut them both some slack. Taryn had more to show him?

"Then get your gear." He grabbed his case and headed out. "You're coming with me."

Four

When Cole Hunter insisted she accompany him to dinner, Taryn's entire body flashed hot. Time alone in that kind of setting was a bad idea. The way he sometimes looked at her—with curiosity and hunger simmering in his eyes—he might want to consume a big juicy steak but in a deeper place, whether he admitted it or not, Cole was also flipping a coin, deciding whether he could afford a side order of her.

Sorry, but she wasn't on the menu.

Then again Guthrie Hunter's son was prickly enough. The edge she rode where he and her position at Hunters was concerned was already razor thin. If she refused this "invitation," Cole might close up completely and, like it or not, after listening to Roman's stories regarding the "Commander" all day, she'd come to the conclusion that she needed Cole on her side.

Plus, her brain and body were running on empty.

Although every instinct warned against leaving this building alone with Cole, she guessed they could talk business while they ate. The golden rule, however, still applied. She had no intention of getting too close to trouble.

So, with nerves jumping in her stomach, Taryn accompanied him out, collecting her bag on the way. They passed late-shift news employees with their noses to the grindstone. Cole sent a good-night to the uniformed security man, who stood watch near the giant glass autosliders, and a moment later he was opening the passenger-side door of a low-slung Italian sports car. Taryn's throat bobbed on an involuntary swallow. She had the weirdest feeling if she crawled inside that dark warm space, she might never come out.

Soon they were buckled up and weaving through Sydney's upper-end streets. In the near distance, arcing lights from the bridge spread shimmering silver ribbons over the harbor while beside her Cole changed gears with the intuitive grace of a professional. She couldn't ignore that subtle yet intoxicating masculine scent, the ease with which his large tanned hands gripped the leather of the wheel. In such close proximity, his legs seemed somehow too long, those shoulders almost too broad. Every available inch of this car seemed *filled* with the smoldering energy that was Cole Hunter.

Taryn pressed back into the molded bucket seat and clenched her hands in her lap. She'd never felt more unsettled. Never more female.

As they flew over a main arterial and the busy world whirred by, he said, "I'd kill for a good thick steak."

"I thought you'd be a steak man."

"You're not a steak woman?"

"Vegetarian."

"I'm sure my regular place caters for that."

"You mean caters for those of us who choose to live on the fringes."

In the rapid-fire shadows, his crooked grin flashed white. "No disrespect intended. I grew up in a male-dominated household. Tofu and soy weren't in our vocabulary."

Taryn peered out the window. She didn't care about Cole's eating habits. She cared only about getting this proposal through and at last moving forward with this show.

"Guess we're all products of our childhood," she offered absently.

"What about you?"

"What about me?"

"Lots of brothers and sisters?"

"I'm an only child."

His deep rich chuckle resonated around the car cabin, burrowing into her skin, seeping into her bones.

"You must have had a peaceful time growing up," he said.

Peaceful? "I guess you could call it that."

"What would you call it?"

That was easy.

"Lonely."

His hand on the gearshift, he hesitated changing down before he double-clutched then wove into the lit circular drive of an establishment that smacked of class and exorbitant prices. A uniformed man strode over to see to her door before a valet parked the car. They entered through open, white-paneled doors into an area decorated in swirls of bronze and planes of muted cherry-red. The large room's lighting was soft. Inviting.

Way too intimate.

While Taryn tried to concentrate on the weight of her laptop in her carryall over her shoulder rather than Cole's strong chiseled profile, from behind the front desk, the maître d' tipped his head.

"I'm afraid we weren't expecting you this evening, Mr. Hunter. Your regular table isn't available." The older man's attention slid to her and his helpful smile deepened. "We do, however, have a private balcony setting with a magnificent view of the harbor."

"Sounds good." Cole rapped his fingertips on the leather-bound menu lying on the counter. "And, er, Marco, you have vegetarian dishes here, right?"

Marco didn't blink. "We have a wide selection. Our chef will also be happy to accommodate any particular requests."

As Marco escorted them to that private balcony, Taryn swore she felt heat radiating from Cole's hand where she imagined it rested inches from the small of her back. Then, when they slipped through into a curtained-off area, her breath hitched in her throat. The mixture of lilting music and silver moonlight, along with her striking company for the evening…she felt as if she'd stepped into a dream. She'd been out to dinner with attractive men at fine restaurants before, but this scene—this surreal heady feeling—was something else.

Retracting an upholstered bergère chair for her, Marco asked, "A wine menu this evening, Mr. Hunter?"

Cole rattled off the name of a vintage that Marco's widening eyes hinted was exceptional. A moment later, the curtain was drawn and they were once again completely alone.

Enjoying the atmosphere despite herself, Taryn shifted in the chair, which was more comfortable than her sofa. "I wasn't expecting this."

"You'd prefer an all-you-can-eat salad bar?"

With delicious aromas filling the air, her taste buds had already decided. She opened the menu. "Here will do nicely."

And every one of those dishes listed without prices sounded divine. Still, she would keep in the forefront of her mind that this was not an occasion to forget herself. In fact, she might as well put this idle time to good use.

Having chosen her meal, she set her menu aside and extracted her laptop from her carryall. With a grunt of disapproval, Cole sat back.

"We won't do that now."

"I'd rather get to it before you have a drink or two."

"I can assure you a couple of glasses of wine won't affect my judgment." His lips twitched. "You, of course, may be a different matter."

"I'm not a giggler, Mr. Hunter."

His frown returned. "And ditch the Mr. this and manners that. My name's Cole. You call my father Guthrie, don't you?"

"That's different. We're on friendly terms."

"Really? Did *he* take you out to dinner?"

She almost gasped. She knew what he was implying. "Of course not."

"Maybe *you* took him."

She slanted her head. "You won't put me off—*Cole*. If you want me gone from Hunters, you'll have to drag me out, kicking and screaming."

"Is that what happened at your last job?"

On the tabletop her fists curled. What would she bet he already knew?

At that moment, Marco arrived to serve wine and take orders, giving Taryn time enough to sort out her answer—and her temper. With Marco having left through the curtains again, she admitted, "I was let go from my last position."

Wineglass midway to his mouth, Cole stopped. "Didn't get along with your boss?"

"We got along great."

"Ah." He sipped, swallowed. "I see."

She burned to set him straight, and in the bluntest of terms, but she wouldn't give him the satisfaction.

"Upper management made the decision," she said. "My direct boss was always good to me. Very much a father figure."

"Seems you're partial to them. Don't you have one of your own?"

"A father?" Taking a long cool sip of water, she swallowed past the pit in her throat. "As a matter of fact, I don't."

Cole's shoulders seemed to lock before he set down his wineglass and said in a lower tone, "We were talking about your previous employ."

She explained about ending up the scapegoat for leaked information regarding those series ideas. Her plan had been to keep her story brief but Cole had a question for everything. He was quite the interrogator. Thorough and emotionless, as Roman had warned. Finally satisfied on that particular subject, he nodded.

"But you've landed on your feet," he offered, finger-combing back a dark lock blown over his brow by a harbor breeze.

"Seems that will depend on you."

"Or, rather, what you've got for me."

At that moment, their meals arrived and Cole took the liberty of refilling her wineglass. She hadn't realized she'd almost drained it.

"But I'm too damn hungry to focus," he said, setting the wine back down. "Let's eat."

While they enjoyed their meals, small talk was difficult to avoid—general topics at first…the state of the industry, current affairs. When he asked, she let him know that Guthrie's personal assistant had rung to apologize that regrettably he wouldn't have time to welcome her into their fold properly that day. Then conversation swerved toward lighter subject matter about schools and interests growing up. Cole had served in the Navy Cadets with a friend who owned his own security firm now. He said that once he'd even wanted to become a high-seas officer. She'd grinned at that. Who would have guessed?

Cole changed the tone and the subject back to family. Almost finished with their meals, he spoke about his mother—just a few words, but they were said with such sincerity and affection, Taryn felt moved. More than instinct said that this was a side of Cole others would rarely see. His next question was obvious, and yet she'd been so caught up in ingesting this small taste of "human Cole" that she hadn't seen it coming.

"Most daughters are close to their mothers," he said. "Does yours live nearby? In town?"

Taryn's stomach jumped but she forced the emotion down. She'd lived with the reality all her life. Woke up to it every morning. And still that empty sick feeling rose in a surge whenever she needed to say the words aloud.

She set down her fork. "My mother's dead."

His brows nudged together and he took a moment before responding.

"I'm sorry."

Yeah. Where her mother was concerned, she was sorry about a lot of things.

But this wasn't a first date. They weren't here to analyze the past—how some were born to rule while others were left to build on crumbs. Still, the evening hadn't been the disaster she'd half expected, although now was the time to gently but firmly reset some boundaries.

"I'd rather not discuss my personal life."

"Sure." He nodded. "I understand. I was only making conversation—"

"I know, Cole. That's fine." She pushed down those rising levels again and pasted on a reasonable face. "But we're here because you wanted to eat. Let's get that out of the way so we can get back to work."

While Taryn set about consuming the remainder of her salad, Cole warred with himself. He understood this occasion was in no way a catch-up between friends or, God forbid, a night out for lovers. He had indeed been making polite conversation—and he'd ended up sticking his foot in his mouth once again. He knew about the pain of losing a parent, but how was he to know that Taryn had lost both a father *and* a mother?

Yes, best they keep any subsequent talk firmly centered on business, he decided, draining his glass. Definitely best they conduct future meetings in a work environment—*if* Taryn and her proposal made it past this evening.

One glass of wine, half a steak and no conversation later, Cole set his napkin firmly down on the table beside his plate.

"Okay. We're done. Let's talk." *And get back to our own lives.*

Finished, too, Taryn slid her plate aside, collected her laptop and scooted her chair slightly toward his, purely to offer a better view of the screen. Before the hard drive had finished booting up, she'd outlined logistics on travel points and was expounding on visions for the future. But he was done with being chatty. Now he wanted the heart of her revised idea, and he wanted it fast.

"What's the hook?" he asked. "The draw card that'll have everyone and their great-grandma tuning back in week after week and advertisers cuing up?"

A manicured fingertip brushed a key and an image flashed up on the screen…a rather uninspiring shot of a group of people standing in an ordinary suburban front yard. The way Taryn was beaming, you'd think she was about to Skype with the person at the top of her "must meet" list.

Cole loosened his tie. God, why had he bothered? Why was he bothering *still?*

"Rather than trained reporters," she said, moving to the next image—a handful of kids playing basketball in some run-down hall, "we'll use real-life couples or families or groups to check out each holiday hot spot. We'll ask viewers to email or text in reasons why they, or someone they know, ought to be the next to enjoy an all-expenses-paid trip to some amazing place, courtesy of Hunters."

He barely contained a groan. "This is another reality show idea, isn't it?"

"Reality shows are still extremely popular," she insisted, rolling through more similarly uninspiring images, "and with this formula—coupling luxury with underprivileged—we can truly tug at the heartstrings of our viewers." When he groaned aloud, she tipped toward him. "Open up your mind to the possibilities and all the people you could help make happy."

"I'm not here to organize charities. I'm here to make good television." Make money.

She blinked then returned her attention to the screen and went on.

"At the end of the season, the viewers get to vote on the number-one holiday couple, family, friends or whatever, and the main sponsor donates a potful of cash toward helping an associated community cause. The next season kicks off with a lucky draw winner from a list of all the voters."

She looked so animated—her big eyes twinkling and hands dancing—he practically saw sparks fly. But...

"It's not new enough," he said. When she looked at him, puzzled, he elaborated. "I need more. Maybe if you include some sort of elimination strategy—"

"*No.* I want everyone associated with my show to feel like winners."

He pinched the bridge of his nose. Great. He was dealing with an I-can-save-the-world type. Not that philanthropy wasn't admirable. In this instance, however, it simply wasn't feasible. He'd grown up living and breathing the culture of broadcasting. He'd learned from the best, and now, he delivered the same. Or wanted to. He didn't know why Guthrie had let this stunt get as far as it had, but in the morning he'd tell his father he should consider a vacation. In fact, a lengthy holiday away from business—and would-be assassins—sounded like a damn fine idea.

"This will be a feel-good program," she was saying. "Sure, along the way there'll be all sorts of trials and fears faced, but no one will be left feeling like a loser. This show could start a whole new genre."

"Taryn," he said gently but clearly, "there is no show unless I say so."

She tacked up her slipping smile. "Think of the sponsors."

"You can talk all you want about sponsor dollars, but in the end time is money. My time. The company's time. I won't put valuable people on a project I'm not convinced will succeed."

"Not convinced *yet*," she corrected.

Blast it all. She wasn't listening.

"You shouldn't have rushed this. You should have given yourself at *least* a couple of days to really think through every possible angle."

"My idea was good to begin with."

He sucked down a breath. Okay. Blunt ax time. "There's no room at Hunters for *good*. I'm after brilliant—or nothing."

"Brilliant?"

"That's right."

Her gaze hardened. Then it turned to stone. "Because you're so brilliant?"

"Because, I'm the *boss* and—" *dammit* "—no one gets to play in my sandbox unless I say so."

Her eyes filled with an emotion that glistened at the same time as it burned. Then her hands fisted an instant before she pushed out of her chair. On her way up, she bumped the table and her glass toppled toward him. Wine hurled through the air, ending up with a splash on his lap. His arms flew out; at the same time his temper spiked and he slid his chair back. Was that an accident or was she deliberately making matters worse?

Still in his seat, Cole gripped his napkin and pressed at the cool alcohol seeping into his trousers. Somehow he managed to keep his voice even.

"I'll assume that was an accident."

"It was." She leaned across the table and flung the wine from his glass, too. "That one, I *did* mean."

Five

She shouldn't have done it.

God knows, she ought to have kept her head and tried to contain the smoke rather than flinging more fuel on the fire. But as Taryn stormed out through the five-star restaurant, half-aware of curious patrons' heads turning, that more volatile side of her nature was glad she'd let Cole Hunter know precisely what she'd thought. Sandbox, indeed!

He was lucky a glass of wine was all she'd thrown.

Outside, the fresh air hit. Stopping at the bottom of the restaurant's half-dozen stone steps, she glanced around with stinging eyes before the realization struck. Cole had driven her here. To collect her sedan, she'd need to grab a cab back to Hunters.

And tomorrow? Cole had as good as said her idea sucked and she was through. Hopefully Guthrie would have something to say about that. But if she went to the senior Hunter about this situation, she'd feel like a tattletale whining to daddy about her bullying big brother. How she longed to circle her hands around Cole's big tanned neck and squeeze until he turned blue. Lord how she wished she'd never met the man.

She noticed a concerned-looking doorman crossing over at

the same time a low, smooth voice wrapped around to startle and disarm her from behind.

"Would you kindly tell me what that was about?"

She swung around and glared into Cole Hunter's flashing green eyes. She hated that her voice was shaky.

"Kindly leave me alone."

"You came with me—"

"And I'll leave without you." She directed her next words to the fidgety doorman. "Can you organize a cab, please?"

Waving a hand, Cole sent the poor doorman back to his corner. "I'll drive you to the station, or home, if you like."

"I'd prefer you didn't."

"I'd prefer that I did."

"So you can goad me into doing something else I might regret?"

He stepped closer until his shadow consumed her and his lidded gaze dropped to her lips. "And just what is it you're afraid you'll do?"

When his eyes met hers again, she felt the stakes between them change and swell. Was it her imagination or had he just propositioned her?

She ought to be outraged. She should want to slap his face. But the heat racing over her skin, snatching her breath and warming her insides, suddenly felt less like anger and a whole lot more like anticipation.

She croaked out, "I never asked to come here tonight."

"No. You were only jumping around like a Christmas puppy, wanting me to see your idea right away."

"You said you wanted to see it."

"When it was good and cooked."

She hitched her carryall strap higher on her shoulder. "Admit it. You never had any intention of giving me a chance."

"*Whoa.* Don't put this back on me."

"No. I should be overjoyed with needing to jump through your hoops after I've already landed the job."

He blinked at that then absently readjusted the platinum watchband on his wrist. "I'm yet to speak to my father about signing you without consulting me first."

"Perhaps you should have done that before putting me through that charade."

"Sorry for doing you a favor."

"Forgive me if I don't shower you with thanks."

A cab rolled up the lantern-lit drive while a valet brought Cole's car around at the same time. Shaking with rage—with hurt and frustration—she made a beeline for the cab with Cole hot on her tail.

That doorman came forward to open the passenger door. With one sharp look, Cole sent him packing again. Then, refocusing, he crossed his arms over that stained damp shirt.

"I'm sorry you can't handle the truth about the premise of your show."

"*Your* version of the truth," she pointed out.

"Like it or not, mine's the only version that counts."

She crossed her arms, too. "Has anyone ever suggested that your ego might be a trifle oversize?"

"My temper, too—particularly, but not excluding, when I'm soaked through and smelling like a barroom floor."

Her conscience pricked. She looked him up and down. Then, although it pained, she offered up what her aunt might consider polite and fair.

"I'll pay for dry cleaning."

"Shirt, trousers and tie." He pretended to wring the strip of royal-blue silk. "You didn't miss much."

"There's nothing wrong with my pitching arm. I was captain of my school softball team five years running."

"Remind me to stay out of your way if you try to swing a bat."

"Don't worry. I'll make sure none of my home runs land in your sandbox."

Cole looked at her harder, his gaze penetrating—judgmental—and yet she got the impression that a different, less hostile emotion churned just below his surface. Maybe a miniscule touch of grudging respect? She crossed her arms tighter. *Too little, too late.*

Finally he shrugged back both shoulders and tucked in his chin. "Maybe I was a little over-the-top with the sandbox line."

She pretended to tug her ear. "Was that Cole Hunter *apologizing?*"

"Merely an observation."

His brows lifted as if he were waiting for her to return the sentiment. No way would she give another inch.

Except…

She didn't need for Cole to walk away from this confrontation thinking he was the better man. She might be right, but she wasn't stupid.

With the cabbie and doorman hanging back, waiting, she eased out that pent-up breath and let her arms unravel.

"Well, maybe," she ground out, "I didn't need to toss that second drink over your lap."

The intensity of his gaze gradually lifted and, after another deliberative moment, he tilted his head at his car. "So you up for a lift back to the station?"

"Only if I choose the topic of conversation."

He clutched at his chest. "You'll even *talk* to me?"

"Not about anything personal. And I'd prefer not to discuss my project with you any more at this time."

"I'm sure that's wise." He started off then stopped, waiting for her to join him, which—after making him stand there wondering for another five full beats—she did.

"Maybe we could discuss vegetarian cuisine," she said as they reached his car.

He grunted. "What about sports?"

"I'm in charge, remember?"

After she'd slid in, but before he shut the door, she heard him mutter, "Enjoy it while it lasts."

Cole drove back to the station listening to Taryn share her secrets on the abundance of ways one could combine pumpkin with pine nuts. Fascinating.

But now, as he made his third stop for the evening—at his father's Pott's Point mansion—he could admit he'd almost enjoyed the final stint of his evening with this persistent producer. Even as the wine dried on his clothes, he surrendered a smile remembering the poised timbre of her voice and glorious lines of her legs as she'd chatted on.

One moment spitting fire, the next a consummate ice queen. He didn't know which intrigued him more. From the moment he'd laid eyes on her, sitting demurely in his father's reception lounge, he'd been struck by those lips, her hair, that barely subdued sexuality. After her spectacular meltdown at the restaurant tonight, perverse though it might sound, his attraction for her had only grown.

By the time he pulled up beneath his father's extravagant granite forecourt, Cole was trying to shake the image of Taryn twining her arms around his neck and searching out his kiss—not because he felt guilty necessarily, but because he didn't need any added aggravation when he visited this place. Guthrie he could handle. His father's wife, Cole didn't want to touch.

He'd fortified himself and was about to slip out of the car when his cell sounded. Two callers—Dex and Wynn combined. Cole connected and Wynn spoke first.

"How's Dad holding up?"

Then Dex. "Do the authorities have any clue who's behind it all?"

"We'll get the guy," Cole told them. "Don't worry."

Cole hadn't been able to get a hold of either brother this morning, or Teagan, for that matter. They had their differences but, beyond and above all else, they were a family. Cole wasn't certain which brother had organized this conference call, but he was grateful to have the opportunity to fill them in. Dex and Wynn had a right, an *obligation,* to know about this second attempt on their father's life, and Guthrie would never tell them. He wouldn't want any of his children to worry.

When Cole finished passing on the incident's details, Wynn cursed under his breath.

"Cole, what's the plan? You'll put some safety measures in place, right? Get a P.I. on board?"

Dex's deep laugh rumbled down the line. "As if Cole could stop himself from taking charge."

Cole huffed. "I don't hear either of you offering to fly back and help man the fort."

"As a matter of fact—" Wynn started at the same time Dex said, "I'll be right out—"

But Cole cut them both off. "Stay where you are." Wynn couldn't spare time away from his seat in New York and Dex's smugness would only drive his older brother nuts. "I can handle whatever has to be done."

Dex said, "Well, if you need anything…"

Flicking a glance toward the house, Cole thought of his stepmother. "Maybe a leash," he muttered.

Wynn asked, "What was that?"

"Nothing." Cole opened the car door. "I'll keep you guys in the loop." He hung up, and a moment later rang the bell. A woman he'd never seen before fanned open the tall timber door. His expression must have looked as confused as hers. Drab, overweight. Was that a mustache? Shrinking back, he thrust his hands into his pockets.

"Who the devil are you?"

"I work for the Hunters."

Cole examined the woman's garb: a dreary gray old-fashioned uniform. "What happened to Silvia?" And her vibrant colors and big friendly smile.

The woman shrugged a pair of round shoulders. "Think the madam said she'd been here too long."

He grunted. Obviously Silvia had become an annoyance for dear Eloise. He'd seen the calculating look in the younger woman's eye whenever the Hunters' much-loved housekeeper had entered a room or dared to have a laugh with Guthrie. Silvia knew this house, the history and its characters inside and out. And like the Hunter boys, Silvia hadn't approved of the master's new bride one scrap. Seemed it'd taken Eloise five years to weed their old friend out. So, who was next on the ambitious second Mrs. Hunter's hit list?

The new help wiped a worn hand down her starched apron and asked, "Who shall I say is calling?"

"Name's Cole."

Dull hazel eyes rounded. "Mr. Hunter's eldest?"

As she studied the wine drying on his shirt, he wove around her. "Where can I find him?"

In the cavernous double-story foyer, another voice joined in. One Cole recognized—and loathed.

"Cole, honey, come on through."

Decked out in a full-length silk robe the color of ripe strawberries, Eloise beckoned him from beneath the decorative arch that led into the front sitting room. He wondered if she were vain enough to wear all that makeup to bed. So different from his naturally beautiful mother. He wouldn't start on the difference between poise and class.

Dismissing the stirring in the pit of his gut, Cole strode forward. "I wanted to check in and see how he was doing."

"After that terrible business this morning, you mean."

Cole was already inside and glancing around that sitting

room. An *empty* room. He ran a hand through his hair. He really didn't have time for hide-and-seek.

"Where is he?"

He spun around. Eloise was standing so close behind, he almost knocked her over. Theatrical, as usual, she emitted a small cry of surprise and swayed, no doubt hoping he'd physically prevent her fall.

Cole only stepped well back then asked, "Is he in the study?"

Filing long graceful fingers back through her disrupted fire-red mane, Eloise pretended to gather herself before heading for the liquor cabinet and holding up a decanter.

"Can I tempt you?"

Cole shuddered. *Not on your life.*

He made a civil excuse. "I'm tight on time."

Examining his shirt, she set down the decanter and strolled back over. "Looks like you've already indulged."

"My father, Eloise. Where is he?"

"Your father's not here. He went out with that new bodyguard of his." Looking inward, she frowned. "Tall. Brooding. Not a friendly type at all."

Cole grinned. *Good.* Last thing Guthrie needed was the man meant to protect him succumbing to the mistress's so-called charm.

Retrieving his cell, Cole speed dialed his father. When Guthrie didn't pick up, Cole left a text message: Call CH ASAP. Then he headed for the door, muttering to Eloise on his way out, "I won't keep you."

But, in her sweeping strawberry robe, she was already scooting around him like her rear end was on fire. When she faced him again, a generous amount of cleavage was showing. Guthrie said she made him happy, and Cole could imagine Eloise doing just about anything to maintain her allowance.

Then again, if her older husband was out of the picture, she wouldn't have to please anyone but herself.

"Before you go, I was hoping you could help me out," she was saying. "Or rather help your little brother."

About to push on around her, Cole stopped. Dates indicated that Guthrie had married Eloise when she was already pregnant with a boy the whole family had instantly taken into their hearts. Whenever Cole visited, his little brother would talk about becoming a fireman, or, if he wasn't brave enough for that, one of Santa's elves. Oh, to be that innocent.

Cole asked, "What's Tate want?"

Eloise collected an electronic gadget off a nearby sideboard. "Tate was a horror this evening when he couldn't get this to work. I had to send him to bed early."

Cole almost reached for the children's e-tablet then thought better of it. He wanted to help, but it was wiser to leave.

"Dad can fix it when he gets home."

She laughed. "You're funny. Your father working something like this out."

Cole scowled. "He's an intelligent man."

"But, honey, he isn't a *young* man." Her gaze stroked the expanse of his chest. "What we need here is someone who's up-to-date with all the latest." She held the gadget out again. "Tate will be so proud when I tell him big brother Cole took the time to fix this."

Cole set his jaw. He had no time for Eloise, but he loved Tate. Cole pitied him too for having a mother who placed the importance of painting her nails above anything her son might like to share. Last Christmas, while Tate had ripped open his presents and pored over the bike and Rollerblades Santa had left, Eloise had been a big no-show. When she'd finally scraped herself out of bed around noon, bloodshot eyes told the story of a boozy Christmas Eve. At the time Cole had wondered with whom. His father had looked fit enough to run a marathon, even if he didn't quite meet his eldest son's unimpressed gaze.

Reminding himself to think only of Tate, Cole took the device and perused the program keys. When, pretending to be curious, Eloise and her claws tipped too close for comfort, Cole lifted his gaze and issued a pointed look. *Back off.* At the same time, he caught movement near the archway. That woman—the new housekeeper—stood halfway hidden behind the connecting wall. Eloise followed Cole's line of vision and, taken aback, drew her robe's opening shut.

"Nancy, you go on to your quarters," Eloise said. "I won't be needing you anymore tonight."

With a curt nod, Nancy and her mustache slunk away. If Eloise wanted female help that her husband would find not the least attractive, she'd creamed the top shelf. And Cole didn't restrict that to looks. Nancy was downright creepy.

Attention on the tablet again, Cole fiddled until the screen lit up. After making certain the applications worked, he slid the device back on the sideboard. As he headed out through the foyer, a disappointed Eloise called out in her annoying Southern drawl.

"Your daddy will be back soon. Sure you don't want to stay awhile?"

Cole opened the door and kept right on walking.

Taryn Quinn didn't like to discuss family. He didn't particularly like discussing his, either. An out-of-control playboy brother, a big bad stepmom and a father someone wanted dead.

As Cole slid back into his car then ignited the turbo engine, he wondered again who was the mastermind behind the bullets this morning. His father was absent tonight. Did that mean this bodyguard he'd hired was on someone's trail? When this ugly situation was done with and the perpetrator behind prison bars, he'd certainly sleep a lot better. But for now...

It was late and he was sticky.

Keeping the revs down so as not to wake Tate, he rolled down the drive as his thoughts swung again to Taryn Quinn. She'd denied any romantic connections with her former boss and he believed her. But a woman like Ms. Quinn wasn't long without an intimate relationship, and after witnessing the fiery side of her nature tonight, it'd be easier if the terms "Taryn Quinn" and "supersexy" weren't tangled up together in his head.

Accelerating, Cole swung onto the wide tree-lined Pott's Point road and wondered. Was Taryn "taken" or was she "taking a break"? Could be she was a new age woman who, too busy for connections, preferred the advantages of a friend with benefits. If he wasn't certain she'd hurl something heavy at his head, he'd set aside his business-only-with-employees rule and ask.

Giving in to a grin, he shot onto the expressway.

Hell, he just might ask anyway.

Six

"Thought I'd warn you. The boss is on the warpath."

Yanked from her thoughts by that familiar Brit voice, Taryn glanced up to find Roman Lyons poking his head into her office. She lowered her pen to her desk.

"Guthrie?"

"No. The *younger* Mr. Hunter. Grapevine says he's headed this way."

Sending a fortifying wink, Rowan bowed off for the relative safety of his own office while, holding her swooping stomach, Taryn siphoned down a breath.

Remarkably, after the wine incident last night, she and Cole had parted on amicable terms. Back here to collect her car, once again she'd offered to pay his laundry bill. Cole had declined then had said in a low sure voice that they'd talk more tomorrow. Well, tomorrow was here and, unlike her normal self, Taryn was positively shaky.

Discussing recipes on the drive back from the restaurant, she'd given the impression that she'd regained her customary cool, but remaining composed whenever Cole Hunter was around was more difficult than killing a blaze with a thimble of water. She'd barely slept for planning how best to handle this, their next meeting. Tossing and turning, she'd imagined a score of different scenarios, and each dreamed-up conversation had included her witty but also *upbeat* remarks. She'd decided. She wasn't throwing in the towel just yet.

Now every one of those let's-try-to-get-along phrases flew like buckshot from her mind as Cole's larger-than-life self strode into the room. This morning he looked broader, darker and, dammit, *hotter* than any man had a right…like an almighty tropical storm rolling in from the sea. Pressing back into her chair, Taryn quivered and spoke before she thought.

"You're always doing that."

"Doing what?"

"Thundering around."

The black slashes of his brows hiked up. "Well, good morning to you, too."

Taryn bit her lip to stop from telling him not to look at her that way—as if *she* was hard work when, in fact, she only wanted to get along and move forward. But, no matter how he pressed her buttons—and he seemed to press every one—her survival here at Hunters depended on making a monumental effort. Which meant reclaiming her biggest asset—her poise—and being hospitable as well as professional. In other words, she needed to present herself the way she would in any person's company other than the Commander's.

Willing her locked muscles to relax, Taryn resumed her calm and asked, "Have you had breakfast?" She reached for a food container, which waited strategically on her desk, and pried back the plastic lid. "Scones," she told him. "Homemade fresh this morning."

Curious, he craned to see. "Is there pumpkin involved?"

"But no pine nuts." She found her feet. "I was about to pour a coffee. Want one? I brought in my own percolator. I'm more your slow, full, satisfying type than an instant kind of girl."

"Slow and satisfying. Who'd have guessed?"

On her way to the percolator, she stopped and caught his look. But her comment wasn't meant to be provocative. She'd been talking about hot drinks, for God's sake, not sex. Before she could qualify or downplay her remark, Cole went on.

"So you've made yourself at home," he said, looking around.

She burned to say, *And why not?* This was her office until Guthrie said otherwise. Which reminded her.

She lifted the pot. "Have you spoken to your father yet?"

"I haven't been able to track him down this morning."

"He's off the station?"

"I have no idea where he is."

China cup full, she glanced over and was taken aback. Cole's assured expression had been replaced by a mask of worry. She hadn't thought he had any vulnerabilities, or none that he'd be prepared to show. Maybe it was inappropriate, but she wanted to ask him what was wrong.

But then that expression evaporated and, drawing himself up tall, he told her, "No coffee, thanks. And no scones."

Before he could say anything more—like, for instance, "I'm only here to tell you to pack your stuff and shove off"—Taryn revved her "perfect employee" enthusiasm back up to high.

"I've been going through my notes again, making phone calls. I'd like to do a full survey of *Hot Spots'* first destination."

"Why would I approve a survey when I haven't approved the show?"

"Because you have nothing to lose. I'll pay for airfares. Accommodation is sorted, no cost."

"And who do you propose to take along with you on this survey—*if* I approve?"

"I don't need anyone else. I know what to look for in locations and angles."

"Wouldn't it be prudent to take a cameraman so I could look over footage later? If—"

"If you approve," she finished before he could. She didn't need reminding again. "If it's a deal-breaker, I'll pay for a co-worker's fare, as well."

"Of course, it could save time and trouble if I simply came along and checked out the location for myself."

Taryn's heart jumped to her throat and then she remembered to breathe. But of course, with that menacing smile playing around the corners of his lips, Cole was only testing. Wanting her to rear up and give him a reason to be even more negative. He could toss on all the heat he could muster. She would neither wither into a quivering mess nor self-combust with indignation. She refused to let him get under her skin like he had last night.

Rather, she called his bluff.

"Sure." She wound her arms over her high-waisted black skirt and pegged out a leg. "If you want to come along, why not?"

His gaze sharpened. "You want me to go?"

"It was your suggestion."

Cole felt his grin grow. One thing he could say for Taryn Quinn—she wasn't a quitter. She had her teeth in here and she'd do anything not to let go. Of course, there would be no survey because, after her rushed effort last night, as soon as he got it straight with his father, Taryn's contract would be terminated and she'd be out the door. Business was business. His objective was to keep Hunter Broadcasting healthy—afloat and viable—even if he didn't always feel like a hero doing it.

His phone sounded with a message. Guthrie was in and wanted to see him straightaway. Cole wanted to see Guthrie, too, about Taryn but also for a catch-up regarding the most recent murder attempt. He'd been worried when Guthrie hadn't been home last night. More worried still when he hadn't been in the office this morning. He'd left messages but had gotten no reply.

He slotted his phone away and headed out. "We'll talk more about this later."

She sang back, "I'll be here."

Leaving Taryn, he headed for his father's office. Midway down that long connecting corridor, Cole noticed two assistant producers deep in conversation. He heard Taryn's name mentioned before they saw him. Talk ceased and they ducked off down an adjoining hall.

Everyone here knew belts were drawn tight. Most would also know about his lack of interest in certain types of shows and that the new kid on the block was touting just that kind of proposal. She might have gotten past Guthrie, but Cole wouldn't be surprised if bets were on, speculating on how soon her ax would fall. He hoped Taryn's ears weren't burning.

When he entered his father's office, Guthrie was sitting behind his desk, studying a spreadsheet. At the far end of the room, a tall, suited man Cole had never met before took in the harbor views. As the man turned to face him, Guthrie moved from behind his desk to the more casual area of his office. At a circle of tub chairs, Guthrie took a seat and introduced Cole to Jeremy Judge, his personal bodyguard.

Eyes on the stony-faced man, who was a private investigator as well, Cole folded down into the chair alongside his father's.

"Please take a seat, Mr. Judge."

Judge sent Cole a thin-lipped smile. "I spend too much time sitting around. In cars. Park benches. Surveillance work, you know. I prefer to stretch my back when I can."

No mistaking—Jeremy Judge had a vigilant air. Cole wasn't sure he'd blinked once.

Looking relieved but weary, Guthrie crossed his legs. "I'm

happy to say Jeremy has successfully tracked down the man responsible for the attempts on my life."

Cole sat straighter. Well, that was fast. "I hope he's under arrest."

"Last time I saw," Judge said, "he was under a car. While I was escorting your father home around seven, we were fired upon."

"I'd dropped in to see your uncle," Guthrie explained.

"Uncle Talbot?" His father's older brother? "I can't remember the last time you 'dropped in' on him."

The brothers hadn't spoken in years. Cole wasn't even sure what the problem was about anymore.

"We're different as chalk and cheese, but when we were younger, Talbot and I were close," Guthrie said. "I felt the need to catch up."

Cole absorbed his father's words. When someone's life was in danger, guess they'd feel compelled to sort out past differences with people who should matter...just in case.

"As Mr. Hunter moved to enter the car, two shots rang out," Judge said. "I pursued the gunman on foot. He panicked and ran in front of traffic."

Cole sized up Judge, and the situation. "A rather clumsy assassin, wouldn't you say?"

"Clearly," Judge said, "he didn't anticipate the chase."

"Which hospital was he taken to?" Cole asked.

"Head injuries were extensive," Judge said. "He died before paramedics got to the scene."

Cole cleared the sudden blockage in his throat. Had he heard right? Just like that, the guy had been creamed and this god-awful drama was over?

But of course this episode was far from finished. A stack of questions needed answers. The most obvious—why? Again Cole spoke to Judge.

"I suppose now your work truly begins."

"To dig into his background, the motives, whether he worked alone." Jeremy Judge nodded his long chin. "My first priority's to obtain the police report."

"We'll need a lawyer."

"It's cut-and-dried, son," Guthrie said.

Cole rapped his knuckles on the chair arm. He wanted to believe this problem was over. But this all seemed too quick. Too neat. And yet Judge looked so assured and his father so relieved. Hell, maybe he was too close to this situation to see this ending as the blessing it truly was. Still, he'd feel a whole lot better when this would-be killer's motives were revealed. No reason he shouldn't bring in the reserves.

Brandon was contacting him today regarding the Eloise tail, which he wouldn't call off just yet. And no reason Brandon shouldn't help Judge mop up.

"A good friend owns a security firm," Cole told Judge, reaching to find his wallet and a card. "I'll give him a call, you two can team up and—"

Guthrie cut in. "No need. Jeremy has this under control."

Judge's lips peeled back in a got-this-covered smile before he headed for the door. "I'll be in touch, sir. Good meeting you, Cole."

When Judge had left the room, Guthrie exhaled. "I can't describe the weight lifted. When you get to my age, you don't need those kinds of troubles."

Having someone hunting you down would not be pleasant. Thank God, he didn't know about his wife's antics. That'd kill him for sure.

Guthrie dabbed his forehead with a handkerchief. "Now on to more pleasant matters." He slotted the cloth away. "How are you and our new producer getting along? Moving forward?"

Cole hesitated. He wanted to give it to his father straight. He still wasn't good with Guthrie hiring Taryn Quinn without passing it by him first. Investment in any show was a huge commitment. Only surefire hits got the green light to go into production. Given the overseas hiccups—the strain on Hunter's reputation thanks to Dex's escapades and Wynn missing some plum opportunities—big brother had to watch the bottom line more closely than ever before.

But Cole swallowed the words. He imagined Taryn's big hopeful eyes then drank in his father's relaxed face again and his stomach muscles kicked.

"Taryn and I have been…talking," Cole finally said.

Leaning across, Guthrie clasped his son's forearm. "I should have consulted with you first. You know I value your opinion above all others. But I like this lady's style and I wanted to nab her before anyone else could. I have a good feeling about this." Guthrie pushed to his feet, looking taller—and stronger—than he had in weeks. "Keep me in the loop."

Cole left his father's office battling a mix of emotions. He was glad that murderous SOB who'd been trailing Guthrie was out of commission—if, indeed, that was the end of it. As far as Guthrie's opinion of Taryn Quinn and her show were concerned… Cole loved to see his father happy, but could he go against instinct and give Taryn's show a bit more rope? In the long run, cutting her free now would be kinder. He couldn't afford to spend good time and money on a project he didn't believe in, even if the producer herself intrigued him. It simply didn't make good business sense.

Down the corridor those assistant producers were back, clustered at the watercooler. Four others had joined them. They were so deep in conversation, no one saw him coming. Drawing closer, he overheard snippets:

"…haven't bothered to introduce myself."

"Bet she'll cry when he terminates…"

"…heard she's coming on to him now. Sucking up big-time."

There were few secrets in this building. Cole Hunter had

his hatchet out. Taryn Quinn's days were numbered. Logic said why waste time getting to know a newbie when she'd be history next week anyway?

That half dozen at the cooler spotted Taryn moving from her office down the corridor. She sent them a friendly smile. When all but two looked away, pretending not to see, Cole's chest squeezed and the back of his neck went hot. Then the mob saw the boss strolling toward them. Women's eyes rounded, men cleared their throats, and one or two muttered a hasty hello.

Cole strode right past and up to Taryn. Loud enough for all to hear, he asked, "When are you booking this location survey?"

Taryn looked sideways, as if he might be drunk or fevered. Then she shook herself and replied.

"I was thinking weekend after this."

Feeling six pairs of eyes and ears upon them, Cole nodded. "Sort out expenses with accounts."

Taryn took a few seconds to respond with a shaky smile. "Sure. I'll do it straightaway."

"That's expenses for *two*."

"A cameraman?"

"You and me."

Some of the color drained from her cheeks. "You really want to go?"

His reply was a curt nod. Then he headed off toward his office, but at a reduced pace. He wanted to hear the introductions as Taryn met with that watercooler crowd. There was even a smattering of laughter.

He wouldn't think about the potential mess he'd gotten himself into or the hope he'd given Taryn Quinn. He couldn't remember the last time he'd acted impulsively like that. If he didn't feel so good about it, if he couldn't imagine Taryn's smile right now, he'd be disappointed in himself.

Seven

"It's a mistake."

Leaning against the garage pylon, Cole crossed his arms and responded to Brandon's statement. "Duly noted."

And dismissed.

This morning, Cole had dropped in to this double-story bayside home to find his friend lavishing time and attention on his pride and joy—a vintage Harley-Davidson. He would have offered to help but Cole knew from old. Brandon didn't let anyone near his bike. That the showroom-quality cruiser ever made it out onto the street was a miracle. Guess everyone had their passions. Their weaknesses.

Cole's thoughts veered to Taryn Quinn and her exuberant expression the day he'd given the go-ahead for her location survey. He'd be a liar not to admit he was looking forward to spending time alone with her. And who knew? What she had organized might surprise him. If he'd planned to be away from the station longer, he'd have asked Roman Lyons to take the reins. But he'd only be gone from work Friday. Three days in all. And two nights. Brandon's conversation brought him back. He wanted out from Cole's request that he investigate Eloise.

"From what you tell me," Brandon said, polishing a handlebar as if it were a shapely female limb, "the guy responsible for the attempts on your father's life has gone to his maker."

"So it would seem."

"A death certificate's pretty final."

"What if this guy was a patsy?"

"It's possible. Has your father's man mentioned anything about inconsistencies with regard to Eloise's loyalties?"

"Not as yet."

"Like I said." In a white tee and faded jeans, Brandon straightened his linebacker shoulders and snapped the polishing rag at the air. "You want her tailed? Big mistake."

"That's my call." Cole wanted Eloise cleared of all suspicion, if only for his own peace of mind. "Tell me what you know so far."

Since their phone call five days ago, Brandon had dug around Eloise Hunter née Warren's background. Born in Atlanta. Current age, thirty-five. Father a political figure. Mother a close friend of Cole's mom. Busted for soft drugs in high school. No conviction.

Polishing the other handlebar now, Brandon confirmed that Guthrie had met Eloise when she was much younger. They caught up again when he flew out to visit his late wife's remaining relatives some months after her death. The subsequent contact between the two gave "consoling the bereaved" a whole new nauseating meaning.

Cole pushed off the pylon. "Stick with it. And can you look into my father's new housekeeper while you're at it? Nancy Someone-or-other. She's far too creepy to be actually guilty of anything. Still…"

Brandon chuckled. "Not your type?"

Remembering the mustache, Cole shuddered. "Not by any stretch."

Brandon ran a palm over the gleaming crimson fuel tank. "So what *is* happening with your love life?"

"What love life?"

"That's what I figured."

"I'm busy."

"Remember that sweet thing you dated in our Navy Cadet days? Don't think you've had a steady relationship since."

"A year-long crush on a lieutenant's daughter isn't a steady relationship."

"Dear, sweet Meredith McReedy. She broke your heart."

"Like an egg in a skillet," Cole confirmed with a grin, "and she didn't even know it."

"Selfish female, moving interstate and leaving you behind to pine."

"I got over it. Eventually."

"Wonder if she'll be at the reunion tonight." Brandon glanced up from tossing the cloth in his special blue bike-cleaning bucket. "You're going, right?"

"I received the invitation."

"Don't avoid my question."

Heading down the drive toward his car, Cole lowered the sunglasses perched on his crown onto his nose. "I'm beyond all that."

"Beyond catching up with friends?"

"Everyone's married now. I can do without the questions. *When are you settling down? Why haven't you got kids yet?* Last reunion, the woman I took along got it into her head I should fall down on one knee and propose."

Brandon's big hands found his jeans' waistband. "I'm sure you can come up with a few more excuses if you really try."

"You're taking someone?"

Brandon was never without a lady on his arm—a little like Dex, only his brother's affairs were usually plastered across the pages of numerous gossip magazines. Brandon was far more discreet.

"I've asked an interesting lady I met a few weeks ago."

"*Weeks,* did you say?" Cole's lips twitched as he opened the driver's side door. "Must be serious."

"Don't panic. No starry eyes on either side. We have more of a love/hate thing going on."

"Must be going around."

Leaning a forearm along the window edge, Cole spilled all about the delectable, infuriating Taryn Quinn—how he was attracted to her on a number of levels despite the fact that he'd soon need to terminate her contract.

Cole ended, "Then I'll be the one needing a bodyguard."

Brandon's eyebrows hitched. "Fiery, huh?"

"On occasion."

"Sounds interesting. Bring her along."

"She barely tolerates me."

"Oh, *and* she has brains."

Cole grinned. "As a matter of fact, she does."

"What's her story? Why isn't she attached?"

"That's a question I've asked myself."

Brandon's hands dropped to his sides. "You sound suspicious."

"No. Not anymore. Just curious."

The friends said goodbye. A moment later, hand on the ignition, Cole stopped to wonder. Should he invite Taryn to that reunion? Business issues aside, he did find her intriguing. Certainly she'd doused him in wine and had tried to put him in his place more than once. He'd responded by giving in to her—defending her—in ways that, frankly, astounded him.

Worried him.

Grunting, he kicked over the engine and shifted the gears into Reverse.

He didn't need more trouble. No way would he invite her to that reunion tonight. If the idea ever crossed his mind again, he'd make an appointment to have his head examined.

* * *

Taryn peered down at her cell's caller ID and froze.

She'd survived a whole five days at Hunter Broadcasting. Why was Cole calling her on a Saturday? Unless it was to tell her that the location survey scheduled for next weekend was off…that he'd only been teasing and of course he had no plans to consider her show.

She simply wouldn't pick up.

"Is that your phone ringing, sweetheart?" a voice called out from the kitchen.

Sitting on her modest home's back landing step, Taryn answered her aunt, who had dropped in as she did from time to time.

"Don't worry, Vi. I've got it."

She glared at the buzzing cell for a drawn-out moment and Vi's voice came again.

"Is something wrong?"

She didn't know. Didn't want to know. Then again, she'd go crazy waiting until Monday if she didn't find out.

Taryn braced herself. Stabbed the green key.

Cole Hunter's deep voice echoed down the line. "Sorry to disturb you out of work hours."

Taryn quivered at the same time she shrank into herself. She wanted to say, "Get it over with." Instead she said, "That's okay. I'm not doing anything special."

"It's Saturday."

She frowned. Waited. "Uh-huh."

A few seconds passed, long enough for Taryn to study the phone to make sure they were still connected.

"Thing is," Cole finally said, "I wondered if you were doing anything a bit later."

Slanting her head, Taryn cast a glance around the garden. *I'll probably still be sitting here trying to coax a frightened pregnant cat in for shelter before she gives birth.*

"No," she said. "Not especially. Did you want to go over my notes for the survey? I have a ton, although I want to keep the location a secret from you until the end."

She wanted Cole to absorb the undiluted impact when they arrived, which would hopefully inspire as well as challenge him.

When he said, "It's not about the survey," a sick withering feeling dropped through her center. Her mouth went slack. This was it. The "don't come back Monday" call. The end.

"You might remember that I mentioned many years ago I was a Navy Cadet. There's a reunion on tonight. I wondered if you might consider coming along."

She listened harder. There had to be more because this didn't make sense. A reunion? Had she missed something?

"Taryn? You there?"

"I'm not certain I understand."

"I'm inviting you out. Tonight. With me."

He meant on a *date?* Now she was *really* confused.

"If you're busy," he said, "of course I understand."

"I'm not busy."

"So you'll come?"

That voice from the kitchen again. "Any luck out there? Or is she still hiding?"

Her aunt was talking about the pregnant stray. No joy there. But maybe her luck was changing on another front. Taryn knew Cole was attracted to her, but she couldn't get her head around the idea of this suggestion to mix business with pleasure. Still, if he was in need of a date tonight, could she really refuse? She'd been taken aback when Cole had stopped her earlier this week and, in front of witnesses no less, had told her to go ahead and arrange the survey. And that he'd be going, too.

If he was willing to give an inch or two, shouldn't she reciprocate? She'd already vowed to be accommodating, no matter what. The upside was that she could always use the time tonight to bend his ear more about her show.

When she thought about it that way, she'd be mad to decline.

"What time and where?" she asked.

She heard his intake of air. Relief or disbelief?

"It's black tie. I'll collect you at—"

"No, I'll meet you." She'd find her own way there as well as back. She might want to take advantage of this opportunity, but she didn't need to dwell all night on how they would say good-night. A shake of hands in the car? A brush of lips against her cheek at the door?

Awkward.

Cole gave an address and a time. Taryn had ended the call and slumped back against the landing when her aunt appeared with a fresh bowl of cat biscuits. Vi studied her.

"You look like someone just handed you a million dollars."

"Even better. That was my boss."

"Guthrie Hunter. You told me about him. Nice man." Vi set the biscuits down. "*Smart* man."

"No. His son. Cole."

"Calling you on a weekend? Has something come up at the studio?"

Taryn had worked long enough in television for her aunt to know the lingo, the oftentimes crazy hours.

"It wasn't about work. Or not directly. He kind of, well, asked me out. A black-tie event tonight."

"And you said yes?" When Taryn nodded, Vi grinned from ear to ear. "You haven't gone out and enjoyed yourself in such a long time."

"It's not like that. I don't actually *like* him. Cole Hunter is arrogant. Ruthless…"

But her aunt was busy checking the ornate silver wristwatch she'd owned for decades. "If you want to get your hair done, it's already after eleven. Do you have something to wear?"

"A gown I bought for last year's awards ceremonies."

Full length. Sequined. Very Hollywood. Taryn cringed. Hopefully it wouldn't be over-the-top.

She caught her aunt smiling again and pursed her lips.

"Don't get all excited. Tonight isn't like that, okay? Even if I did want to settle down in a relationship—" and she didn't "—Cole's not that type." *Not my type.*

"How do you know?"

"Spend five minutes with the guy."

He had little time for anything other than work and bossing people around. She was amazed he had any personal life.

A noise filtered over from the garden...bushes rustling then a flash of yellow fur. That cat poked its whiskers out between some leaves but, in a heartbeat, vanished again. Taryn thumped a floorboard. She'd been trying to lure that poor cat out for weeks. She looked so mangy Taryn knew she must be without a home. And yet she resisted.

"Maybe she's happier that way," Taryn murmured, thinking aloud. "Maybe she's happier on her own."

Vi patted her niece's shoulder. "Don't give up. Everyone wants companionship. Someone to care for them. Even the most unlikely types."

Eight

He'd told Taryn 7:00 p.m. Black tie. When she'd insisted she find her own way, given the debacle that evening at Marco's when she'd wanted to escape but couldn't, he guessed he understood.

But as seven had wound on to half past, the shine on his understanding had begun to tarnish. At quarter to eight, he was debating whether to call to check up, stride into the party alone or forget about this reunion deal altogether. He had work he could be doing. Going over that football proposal, for one. Instead he was standing here, waiting, waiting. He must look like an overdressed idiot. He knew he felt like one.

Then a silver service cab swerved up. *She* got out. And Cole's chest expanded on a deep breath.

As usual, Taryn Quinn was all grace. Her evening gown—a silver sequined sheath—fit her body like a high-fashion glove. The neckline was a modest scoop, but as she turned to set her stilettos correctly on the pavement, he saw that the back was cut low enough to hover on the edge of X-rated. She spotted him standing alone at the entrance of the inner-city five-star establishment and sent a little wave. He waved back.

Her hair always looked great…a long bouncy blond river.

But tonight, beneath the city lights, it surrounded her face like a luxurious halo. And those lips, my God... Even from a distance, they looked tasty.

Cole met her at the bottom of the steps.

"Nice tux," she said.

"What? This old thing?"

She laughed and something new lifted up inside of him. "You said it was black tie. I took a chance and believed you."

"That's a stunning gown."

"Thank you."

"You look beautiful." Incredible.

Her brow pinched as if she wondered if he were only teasing, before her easy smile shone again. "Sorry I kept you waiting. The cab took forever."

He threaded his arm through hers. "Absolutely no need to apologize."

Inside the ballroom, soft music played while guests churned around, nibbling salmon and caviar canapés while reminiscing. Both he and Taryn accepted chilled flutes from a passing waiter. As she sipped, Cole noticed the flute hovered longer than necessary, covering her smile. Grinning, too, he let his gaze sweep over the glittering room.

"What's funny?"

"It's just since you mentioned the navy, I had visions of scores of officers dressed up in crisp white suits and matching gloves."

"You're partial to a man in uniform?"

Her eyes glistened beneath the lights. "Why? Do you have one hanging at the back of your wardrobe?"

"Hate to admit it but, as a cadet, I looked more like Popeye in my sailor's suit."

Her head went back and her hair bounced around her shoulders as she laughed. "Popeye? Well, at least you're honest. Was there a Brutus in your unit of cadets?"

"Sure. Big, burly, shaving daily by age ten. This guy's better looking than his cartoon counterpart, though."

Her gaze veered to the left. "Would that be him?"

Angling around, he spotted Brandon winding through the crowd. Cole grinned. "Guess the shoulders gave it away."

Brandon stopped before them, tipping his head at Taryn as he introduced himself. "And you must be the mysterious Taryn Quinn."

"Mysterious?" She smiled. "Maybe more your everyday working-class girl."

Brandon's expression said plainly not. And he was right. Taryn was a beauty wearing office garb. But in this glittering silver number, she could put a supermodel out of a job. Her aura was magnetic, her laugh, infectious. He couldn't remember feeling this proud standing beside a date in his life. Those old feelings for Meredith McReedy were left for dead in the shade.

Brandon must have been thinking the same. He was searching the room. When he beckoned someone over, Cole recognized the woman. Barely.

Meredith McReedy bounced straight up, then, on her toes, planted a smacking kiss on Cole's chin. Her lips were so rouged, he just knew she'd left a big red dot.

"Cole, we missed you at the last reunion." Meredith smiled at Taryn, an honest expression, which was nice given the difference in their appearance. While Taryn came off statuesque, poised and glamorous, Cole wasn't certain what had happened to his erstwhile love. Meredith filled them in.

"I'm married now. Three children under four. We're the happiest little family." Meredith spoke directly to Taryn. "You must be Cole's wife."

"Not wife," Cole cut in.

Meredith gave his lapel a playful slap. "You can't hide from responsibility forever."

Cole coughed. Him hiding from responsibility. That was a new one.

With a "We'll catch up later," Meredith disappeared into the tide.

Grinning, Brandon raised his beer. "Well, she looks happy."

Cole narrowed his eyes at his friend. If Brandon was thinking about blabbing, Taryn didn't need to know the background.

"Are you in the forces?" Taryn asked Brandon as the music changed and more couples headed for the dance floor.

"I own a security firm. I do some private investigating from time to time."

"Must be exciting."

"It can be," Brandon said, "when you're on to something with substance."

Her brow wrinkled. "What do you mean?"

"Sometimes a client gets it into his head to chase dead ends."

"No stone left unturned," Cole reasoned, then saw Taryn looking between the two, wondering. He changed the subject. She didn't need to know about Guthrie's recent woes, either.

He asked Brandon, "So, where's your date?"

"You know how I said we have a love/hate relationship? Right now, she's not feeling the love. In fact, I think it's fair to say the curtain has dropped on that particular union."

Taryn's shoulders fell. "I'm sorry to hear that."

Gaze on the filling dance floor, Brandon sipped his beer, swallowed. Exhaled. "Yeah, well, she's missing out. Marissa loves to dance."

"You do, too?" Taryn asked.

"With the right girl," Brandon said.

"You never know." Taryn's smile was encouraging. "Maybe you'll find someone nice to dance with tonight."

Brandon cocked his head then shifted his focus to Cole, arching a brow as if asking permission.

Setting both his and Taryn's flutes on a passing waiter's tray, Cole gave Brandon a "she's mine" look and led Taryn away for a dance of their own.

When they reached the floor, Cole half expected Taryn to kick up a fuss, maybe tell him that coming here was one thing, but dancing cheek to cheek was definitely another. Instead, in her glittering gown, which threw occasional sparks off beneath a slow spinning light, she stood calmly before him. Gaze fixed on his, she waited for his arm to wind around and tug her close.

He was happy to oblige.

Her dress rustled as his hand grazed over her waist then slid down until his palm rested on the bare small of her back. When he pressed enough to let her know she should come closer, she stepped into his space. He took her slim warm hand in his and her head tilted back as she drew in a long breath. Then her hand found his shoulder and, with other couples weaving around, they began to move.

"I like your friend," she said as her fingers on his shoulder scrunched a little then splayed.

"He's one of a kind."

"Good at his work, I assume."

"The best."

"A private investigator."

"That's right."

She looked down then back into his eyes. "Cole, you don't have him investigating me, do you?"

"No." He rotated her around. "I've decided I don't need to rattle your skeletons."

A smile touched her eyes but then she blinked. "He is working for you, though."

He exhaled. "There's been a couple of incidents."

"Concerning you?"

"My father."

Her expression fell and dancing stopped. "Is Guthrie in trouble?"

Peering down into those beautiful concerned eyes, Cole set his jaw. Why the media hadn't got ahold of the story was beyond him, but he didn't expect that to last. Someone somewhere only needed to slip a scrap of information and, next thing, this attempted-murder business would be all over the news. He'd already decided that he wouldn't share any of this with Taryn. Hell, he rarely shared *anything* personal with *anyone*.

But, for whatever reason, he wanted to tonight.

Cole retold the story surrounding the attempts on Guthrie's life, how Jeremy Judge had practically sewn up the case in a twenty-four-hour window and, finally, how he wasn't satisfied this was over.

Taryn shook her head in disbelief. "No wonder you're irritable."

Suppressing a grin, he moved her around in a tight circle. "I'm always irritable."

"I'm serious. I'd be frantic if Vi's life was in danger."

"Vi?"

"My aunt. She brought me up after…"

Her eyes glistened before her gaze skirted away. Obviously too personal. Cole got that.

He was about to say, "You don't have to talk about it," when she found his gaze again and explained.

"I didn't know either of my parents. I was too young to have any memories of that time, but I still wish things had been different. Normal."

The best he could offer was a supportive smile. She'd said so much with so few words. Now *he* couldn't find one.

"I grew up with my aunt," Taryn went on. "Vi's the best there is. She's crazy about cats. She was over today when you phoned. She likes to drop in, you know, but she doesn't smother me like I've heard some parents do." Her brow pinched and he felt her pull back an inch. "I'm boring you."

His gaze brushed her cheek, her lips. "I don't think that's possible."

Beneath the soft lights it was difficult to say, but he thought she might have blushed. Then he felt her draw away a little again. Put that wall back up between them.

"Do you miss the sea?" she asked, looking around at the other grown cadets.

"I'd mentioned there was a time I wanted to serve on a ship. I also thought I might buy a boat-building company and make my own. I imagined doing test runs all day long, standing bold and brave behind the wheel."

He was grinning, mocking himself, but Taryn's face was set.

"Why didn't you?"

He didn't have to think. "Obligation. Duty."

"To your family and Hunter Enterprises."

He nodded.

"So you enjoy what you do there?" she asked.

Searching her eyes, he gave a meaning-filled smile. "Some days are better than others."

"And some days you get lumbered with problems you could do without."

She was talking about her show, but her open look said she wasn't baiting him.

"There are positives to every situation."

"I agree." She seemed to gather herself, gather the words. "I haven't officially thanked you for approving my survey yet."

No, she hadn't. But...

His gaze dropped to her lips again when he said, "It's not too late."

When her head angled, questioning and understanding at

the same time, his pulse kicked, flames raced through his blood and impulse won out. His head lowered over hers.

Beneath his palm, he felt her quiver. Over the music's percussion beat, he heard her sigh. His lips parted slightly as her face tilted more, slanting at the perfect angle to greet him.

Then, as if someone had stuck her with a pin, her eyes rounded and, unraveling herself, she stepped well away.

"I'm not…" She brushed back a tumble of hair fallen over one eye then met his gaze again. "I wasn't expecting that."

"I should apologize." He chanced a smile. "But I'm not sorry."

In fact, truth be told, he wanted to bring her close and finish what he'd started.

Cole felt a tap on his shoulder and, realizing where he was—in a highly public setting—looked back. A man Cole remembered from his cadet days was straightening his bow tie, speaking to him but looking at Taryn.

"I wondered if I could beg a dance from the most beautiful woman in the room."

Without apology, Cole ground out, "Not now," then escorted her off the floor.

Keeping control was hard enough when they were in a room full of people. God help him when they were away on that survey. The way she'd almost surrendered just now, God help them both.

Nine

Throughout the evening, Taryn was introduced to some of Cole's friends from his youth. When they were alone, they talked about work, but neither broached the subject of that dance. Or of that near-miss kiss.

It was as if they'd both silently agreed never to mention it. Forget it had ever happened. Only Taryn doubted she could ever forget that swirling giddy feeling of surrender. The pull at her core was near impossible to resist. If she hadn't experienced the sensation for herself, she simply wouldn't have believed it existed.

But Cole was her *boss*. The future of her beloved project lay in his hands. Her physical side might have longed for his mouth to cover hers…for him to sweep her up and away somewhere ultraprivate. Her rational side, however, warned that clearly she was losing her mind. If they got involved, the lines would be forever blurred. It was bad enough fighting to keep him from tossing her out of Hunters on her ear. How much worse to be sacked and left to rot by someone who had held you? Kissed you?

Humiliating, to say the least.

* * *

The following week at work, although they were pleasant and spoke, neither she nor Cole discussed that evening. When Friday morning rolled around—the day they were scheduled to fly out—Taryn was excited. This was an important step toward seeing her show actually on the air. She was also near paralyzed with dread and fear. What if Cole got too close again? Forget that. Given her reaction when he'd held her on that dance floor, what if at some point she lost all reason and tried to kiss *him?*

By the time she'd finished packing, Taryn had come to a conclusion. One step at a time. If Cole tried to weave his magic over her—if she felt as if she wanted to be seduced—she would cross that burning bridge when she came to it.

At 9:00 a.m., Taryn answered a knock on her door.

Looking mouthwateringly sexy in a pair of dark blue jeans, Cole spotted her luggage waiting in the foyer.

"That's one serious-looking suitcase. We're only away for two days, right?"

Cole had insisted he drive them to the airport. He was here thirty minutes early, but she wasn't ready to leave just yet. She wasn't particularly comfortable with him watching her finish up here, either.

Dragging her gaze away from the V of bare chest visible above the opening of his shirt, she headed off with him following. "I have a few things to tidy up before we leave."

In the kitchen, she pulled a bag of cat biscuits from the pantry while Cole strolled over to her Formica counter.

"You have a cat?"

"She's not mine. Not really."

"Then why are you feeding it?" he asked as she set the food bowl down outside the back door and brought the water bowl in for a refill.

"*It* has a name. Muffin."

"Cats have name tags now?"

"She's a stray. But she's yellow and fluffy like a vanilla cake." Muffin just seemed to fit. She crossed back over to place the fresh water outside, too. "She's close to giving birth."

"Well, do you think you should encourage her?"

She sent him a look. "I can't just leave her and her kittens to starve, or be picked off by birds and snakes. I'd bundle her up and take her to the vet if I could get close enough. Even with her big belly, she's too quick to catch."

"Maybe she's a free spirit." He shrugged. "Maybe she doesn't want a home."

Taryn remembered saying the same thing to Vi last week. But her aunt was right. No one, and that included a cat, chose to be without someplace to feel safe and warm and wanted.

As she turned back from locking the door, Cole's cell phone beeped. He spoke for a couple of minutes then, thoughtful, slotted the phone away.

Moving to the sink, she asked, "Something up at the station?"

"No. That was Brandon checking in."

"More news on your father's situation?"

The sleeves of Cole's casual white button-down were rolled to below the elbow. Now he rested two bronzed forearms horizontal on the counter and absently rotated the platinum watchband circling one wrist, a habit that, she'd noticed, he'd inherited from his dad.

"Seems the man who Jeremy Judge chased in front of that car had a gripe with Hunter Enterprises News division. A year ago he spoke with one of our reporters about a financial institution moving to foreclose on his mortgage. The editor didn't pick up the story. When the man's home went under, he decided to blame us. Brandon hasn't been able to find anything else remotely criminal in his background." He rotated the watchband again. "His wife had left him. Kids are grown-up, moved away."

To Taryn's mind that made the situation all the worse. Sounded like that man had no one to turn to, no one to listen. Maybe he felt he had nothing to live for, which made the "falling under a car" part of the story more believable. All his problems were over now.

At the meals table, she collected a vase then crossed to drop dried blooms and brittle leaves into the trash. She adored choosing flowers for their perfume and color. It was her weekly indulgence. She only wished they lasted longer.

Cole had strolled over to a window. Drawing back the curtain, he scanned the scene outside. Was he looking for the cat, or something—someone—more sinister?

"The gunman didn't have a psychiatric history." He dropped the curtain. "Guess tough times can bring out the worst in us all."

Perhaps, but, "People have choices."

His smile was curious. Maybe admirable. "A woman of integrity."

"What are we without it?"

"Ask my siblings. Wait. I take that back. Wynn at least tries."

Filling the vase with water to soak, Taryn reminded herself, Wynn was the brother who looked after the magazine arm of Hunters in New York.

"He has good intentions," Cole said, checking his cell again. "But I'm afraid my younger brother has a tendency to think with his heart before his brain. Which is probably better than Dex's drawback."

Dex...Cole's movie-making brother in L.A., Taryn thought, checking the setting then clicking on the dishwasher.

"He's got it up here as far as business is concerned." Cole

tapped his temple. "Unfortunately he prefers to think with lower portions of his anatomy."

"I've read about his exploits," she said.

"I doubt he'd mind me saying that was skimming the surface."

"What do your brothers think about their father's situation?"

He followed as she moved around the house, making certain windows were locked.

"We shared a conference call," Cole said. "Wynn and Dex both want to fly out, give him some moral support. See if there's anything they can do."

"Your brothers aren't all bad, then."

She glanced over her shoulder. Cole's expression had turned wistful, as if he might be remembering happier times. Then his brows knitted again.

"I couldn't get in touch with Teagan."

"Your sister." She locked the last window. "She seems to keep a low profile. She's never mentioned in the gossip mags."

"When she was a kid, Teagan was a showstopper. Quickwitted, pretty as a bell, talented. She used to make us all sit down and watch her Spice Girls performances. Being the baby *and* the only girl, she got damn near everything she wanted."

Back in the foyer now, where her luggage waited, Taryn grinned. As if any Hunter child would have done without.

"What does she do in the company?"

"Teagan wants nothing to do with Hunter Enterprises. She calls her lack of interest 'independence.' I call it ingratitude. She runs her own fitness business out of Washington."

"You don't talk?"

"Not for a while."

"So Teagan's the stray who doesn't want a home?"

He did a double take then gifted her one of those sexy grins that secretly made her melt. "Guess she is."

Taryn caught the time on the wall clock. Her stomach jumped. Cole had arrived early, but now they were in danger of running late.

"We'd better go." She extended her bag's handle. "Don't want to miss the flight."

"Which is to where exactly?"

"Let's say a place where the sun and sea rule."

"And *that* narrows it down."

"All I can add is that I hope you packed sunscreen."

A thought exploded in Taryn's mind—a forgotten item—and she rushed into her bedroom with her bag rolling behind. She'd do her work, but she planned to have a window of time off, too. Her already stuffed bag could hold two more teeny-weeny can't-do-without pieces.

Ten

After six hours in the air, and within ten minutes of leaving the much smaller connecting flight, Cole decided that their destination should be named "Taryn Quinn has Rocks in her Head."

For some crazy reason, when Taryn had said she was surveying a location for her *Hot Spots* proposal, Cole had assumed luxury, first-class transportation and air-conditioned comfort at the very least. When she'd let on that they were ultimately destined to land somewhere in Polynesia, his assumptions seemed assured. Now, edging into the decrepit station wagon this island referred to as a taxi, Cole began to grasp the scope of his error.

Luckily the rust bucket was fitted with seat belts.

As the driver roared the gears into a crunching first and slammed his foot to the floor, Cole held on to the arm sling for grim life. He glanced over at Taryn, sitting beside him on the back-passenger seat, and growled. What the hell was she grinning at?

"Cole, you look surprised."

"What's the name of this place again?"

"Ulani. It means happy or gay."

They hit a massive pothole and Cole's head smacked the cab's sagging ceiling, while, bouncing around, Taryn actually laughed. Worse, she looked gorgeous doing it. Her face free of makeup, her hair loose and tousled, she was nothing short of radiant.

During the week, they'd chatted about this trip, and with such composure an outsider would never have guessed what had transpired on that dance floor almost a week ago. He'd thought about that close-proximity incident often since. If she'd leaned in another inch, it would have been on. Instead she'd pulled away at the last minute and he'd been given space to cool down, keep his head.

Only problem was that stir and urge hadn't left him. He might have behaved civilly this week, but underneath he'd wanted to lay this on the line and take what he believed she wanted to give. He should be dreading these next couple of days. But he was only glad this time had finally come. At last they were alone and this thing simmering between them could come to a head.

But he'd envisaged that would happen amid first-rate treatment and perhaps even satin sheets. Guess he'd get past this shock.

"Why did you choose this place?"

"I wanted different, out of the ordinary," Taryn said, gazing out over a landscape of vine-strangled palms backdropped by a sleeping monster of a volcano. "Anyone can go to Hawaii or Tonga."

"I take it the resort or hotel or wherever you're taking me isn't five-star."

"From the pictures and reviews, I'd give it six."

Another pothole sent him jolting and cringing in his seat again. "I'm thinking a remedial massage is a priority."

"I could always organize the next flight out for you," she offered.

"And miss all the fun?"

The taxi skidded to a stop. Cole shifted to inspect the building and his jaw dropped. This place wasn't much better than a shack.

He drawled, "You are kidding."

"Not even a little bit."

"Didn't you say that night at Marco's, and I quote, 'This program could start a whole new genre'?" He examined the gray-bearded dog asleep on its back in a most unflattering pose near the entrance. "Maybe we *should* head back," he muttered under his breath.

Did she really have no idea? More than ever before, after seeing this, chances were her show was dead in the water. Only a miracle could save it now.

The driver was lugging both her suitcase and his overnighter toward that reception shack. Above a barely hinged door rested a lopsided sign, which read in faded green paint, WEL OME.

"There's still time to escape," she told him slipping out of the taxi, whereupon Cole set his teeth, ran a hand through his hair then scraped himself out of the vehicle, too.

"I'll stay," he said, dragging his feet to follow, "if only to see what you think can possibly keep an audience glued to their seats."

As well as the promise of being alone with you.

In her tantalizing fitted blue wrap dress, she continued on with a laugh. Seeing those long tanned legs in that dress, that heavenly behind swaying as if to beckon him near...

Cole's pace picked up.

Sure. He could slum it for a couple of days.

From the moment they touched down, Taryn had fallen in love with this tropical oasis. As far as she was concerned, a weekend wasn't nearly long enough. Except, of course, she'd need to contend with the "Cole looking extra hot in casual wear" situation. But truth was she'd find him sexy even in his Popeye suit.

At a bamboo reception counter, a friendly middle-aged lady with oversize dentures and a gold-plated name tag that read Sonika checked their reservation, after which a man, naked from the waist up, collected their bags. Standing beside her, Taryn sensed Cole's masculine sensitivities prickle. Perhaps he was anticipating an equally stunning island girl to materialize and show off *her* assets. Best he didn't hold his breath. This island was particularly "woman user friendly."

Sonika's smile beamed brighter. "I'm sure you will be happy with your accommodation," she said in accented English. "Your bungalow has one of the best views on the island."

"How many guest bungalows do you have here?" Cole asked.

"Only six on the whole island. The other five are occupied," she said, closing her registry book. "But don't worry that you'll run into anyone if you don't want to. Privacy is our promise."

The man and his WrestleMania shoulders ushered them out a side door and down a long sandy path, which was bordered by lush ferns and palm trees on either side. Above them curious monkeys crouched on branches, a menagerie of birdlife hooted and cooed, heady combinations of floral scents filled the air and Taryn wanted to sigh. These surroundings would make for fabulous visuals and audio. All she needed was that final nod. She hoped Cole would be a good sport and admit this ultraexotic location and her idea were winners…that is, when he got over the next surprise.

A few minutes later, they arrived at their bungalow. While the porter continued on to drop their bags inside, a previously tetchy Cole seemed to enjoy a change of heart.

"I must say, I had my doubts." He scooped up a handful of powdery sand and let it filter through his fingers while surveying a bay that spread out before them like an endless throw of mirror-blue silk. "Not the Hilton but that *is* an exceptional view." He spotted a calico hammock waiting on the bungalow's porch and rubbed his shoulder. "I can picture myself swaying in that. In fact…"

But as he moved toward the steps and that hammock, Taryn crossed to block his path.

"I'm afraid you have a task or two to perform before you can lie back," she said.

"We'll take an hour to rest up before we start on your survey work."

"I'm not talking about that. When a person comes to this Polynesian island, there are certain…requirements. Duties."

"What do we have to do?"

"Not we. *You.*"

He threw another glance around and coughed out a laugh. "Like hunt down a wild boar? Descend into the fiery bowels of a live volcano?" When her expression held, his smirk died. "Please tell me that volcano isn't live."

"Remember I said that this island's name means *happy*. This place is also meant to be a sanctuary where individuals come to know and appreciate others and, more importantly, understand themselves."

He waited then finally shrugged. "And…?"

"Women here, Cole, are adored and revered. They're waited on hand and foot."

Trying to absorb the concept, he repeated her words. "Women are waited on here…"

"Yes. Hand and foot."

"So where's your slave?"

"Standing right there."

Cole actually looked over his shoulder. When he realized the joke was on him, he slowly turned back. She'd had fun imagining this moment. He'd invited himself along to see for himself. Like the emperor with his new clothes, Cole had gotten his wish. If he had half a funny bone, he'd take it on the chin. Hell, he might even laugh. But his expression fell flat.

"Other than the view and that hammock," he said, "you're not scoring too many points."

A bristle ran up the back of her neck. At times he could be so darn negative. "You don't have to stay if you can't handle it."

He challenged her gaze for a long moment then bent to slip off his loafers and wiggled his toes in the sand.

"But if I leave you here all alone," he said, "who will brush your hair? Peel your grapes?"

At that moment, that man with his amazing tan and billboard chest passed by. When he sent a dazzling helpful smile her way before leaving by the path again, Taryn sucked down a breath and gathered her thoughts.

Cole wanted to know who would peel her grapes?

Winding her arms over her waist, she angled her head and shrugged. "Oh, I'm sure I'll find someone."

From the way Cole's shoulders squared, he was back to unimpressed mode. "I thought you were selling this as a family show."

"I'm sure a lot of underappreciated mothers would love a slot."

"What's in it for the poor lugs who have to tag along?"

"Quality time to reflect?"

"While they're fanning the revered ones with palm fronds, I suppose."

"And all while enjoying that view." When his unimpressed look held, she spelled it out. "This island's magic lies in its reversal of social domestic norms. It encourages men to truly nurture their women, which will hopefully ultimately deepen and strengthen their relationships. You've heard of the saying, with sacrifice comes great reward? In the work comes the reward. The payoff."

"With sacrifice comes reward."

She nodded then headed toward the bungalow. "But, before you get busy peeling any fruit, we should unpack."

Cole massaged his brow. He was *her* boss. So why was he being bossed around? Oh, that's right. This "women are revered, men are slaves" twist. Novel. Cute.

Taryn was strong-willed. Even on her best behavior, she couldn't help but occasionally mock him. Over this past week, he'd almost gotten used to her particular brand of sass. She had a sharp wit. Sometimes *too* sharp. And he didn't enjoy being anyone's pincushion.

She'd told him that he needed to unpack.

He called out, "We're here two days."

"Clothes get rumpled."

"We're not dining with the queen."

On the bottom step, she rotated around. "If you want to live out of a bag, that's your business."

Darn right it was his business. This might be her location survey but, make no mistake, he was in charge regardless of this island's female bias. And as she continued up those steps in that hug-every-curve dress, a cog in his brain turned and clicked. When she reached the bungalow doorway, the ideal solution to this predicament lit his mind like the breaking of tomorrow's dawn.

Taryn wanted to explore the island's ethos. She expected him to serve. Get enlightened.

He called out again. "I might not need to unpack my bag but, if I have this setup right, while we're here—me being the male and you being the female—I'm supposed to revere you. Be your slave."

Pivoting again, she rested a hand on the bamboo doorjamb. "*Slave* was your term."

"But *Hot Spots* male guests here will be expected to look after any chores so their wife or girlfriend can lie back and soak up the atmosphere. That's the twist—the opportunity for confrontation and redemption—you want the contestants and viewers to experience, right?"

"Right."

"Which means, if we're really going to get a take on possible dynamics, while I might not want to unpack my bag, I should 'servant up' and unpack yours."

As he sauntered up the steps, she arched a brow. "We don't need to go to extremes."

"Do you want me to immerse myself in this project or don't you? Heaven forbid a rumor should spread that I didn't play by the rules and robbed you of a fair chance."

"I'm quite capable—"

"Then again if you don't want to give it your best shot..."

She seemed to hold her breath. As he imagined her heart pounding and thoughts racing, Cole contained his grin. She was embarrassed and uncertain and probably nudging toward really annoyed at this point. But she'd set the agenda and, as far as he could see, she'd left herself no room to back out.

"Just leave what's in the zipped pouch," she finally said.

"Sure. You go mix yourself a piña colada and leave all the work to me." He set a fingertip to his cheek. "Although shaking cocktails must be my job, too. Maybe wiggle your toes in the sand until I can be of further service."

Passing on his way inside the bungalow, Cole rolled a hand—a theatrical motion from forehead to waist—while, feeling robbed, Taryn moved down the steps and into the clearing.

Above her, palms fronds swayed and clacked in a gentle sea breeze. Like a balm, the sun's heat soaked into her skin. The salty scent drifting in from the Pacific was nothing short of drugging. Paradise. She'd promised herself, no matter what, she would find a little time to unwind.

But she'd been kidding herself. While Cole was around that would never happen. Yes, she'd planned to put him on the spot with that "women are revered" policy. She'd wanted him to squirm but more so think about setup in relation to ratings ramifications for her show. Not for one minute did she buy his spiel about being happy to serve. She had the biggest feeling he was up to something. Something that might leave her squirming instead of him.

A rustling in the brush drew her attention. From a mass of ferns, a boy aged six or seven appeared. He had the biggest, brownest eyes Taryn had ever seen. Wearing that blue-striped tee and toothy grin, he was positively disarming. Striding right up, he gestured toward her feet then indicated she should sit in a deck chair positioned to one side of the bungalow steps.

Wanting to ruffle his mop of clean dark hair, she laughed. "Thank you, but I'm not tired." She crouched to speak face-to-face. "What's your name?"

But the boy was already scurrying off back into the ferns. The next second, Cole's voice boomed out from the bungalow.

"Where do you want me to put these?"

She swung around. Cole stood in the doorway. He held her bikini top in one hand, her bottoms in the other.

After the blush had whooshed up from her toes to her crown, she got her mouth to work and very calmly asked, "What do you think you're doing?"

"Unpacking, as per instructions."

"I told you to stay away from the zip."

"These were right on top."

As he jiggled the top then the bottoms in turn, her thoughts rewound. Usually she put her delicates in a zipped compartment to keep them separate and easy to access. But when she'd remembered her bathing suit this morning at the last minute, she'd shoved it inside her case on top of everything else.

And, honestly—so what? They were two pieces of Lycra. Women had worn them for decades. And yet the way he was holding them, the ties twined loosely around those strong tanned fingers, she felt so suddenly flustered, as if he'd removed them not from her luggage but fresh off her body. His next comments made it all ten times worse.

"Interesting work attire, Miss Quinn." He pushed a sigh out over the hint of a grin. "And I thought you were serious about this weekend."

That flustered feeling stirring her insides swelled into something far more dangerous. She'd known he was hatching something he'd find amusing. Something to put her in her place. She strode up the steps and snatched both pieces from his grasp. Incredibly, he didn't laugh, didn't even smile. Rather he glanced away and rubbed the back of his neck, as if he felt uncomfortable, which, under the circumstances, she found difficult to believe.

She narrowed her eyes at him. "What's that look?"

"I thought I'd better mention now…"

"Mention what?"

"There's only one bed?"

After a moment of numb shock, she hacked out a laugh. *Ridiculous.* "Of course there's more than *one bed.*"

When she'd received her reservation details, she'd been assured of two bedrooms. And on opposite sides of the hut.

"Maybe you should have booked separate bungalows," he said, "just to be sure."

"You heard the woman at the desk. There are only five other bungalows and they're all taken."

Her words trailed as reality tunneled in and set like reinforced concrete. There'd been a terrible mix-up, and even if she had any hope another guest might consider swapping for a single-bedroom bungalow, she wouldn't put Sonika to the embarrassment and trouble. A weekend's accommodation here cost an arm and a leg and they were staying for free. There must be another way. She might find Cole attractive. She might have wondered how these two days would pan out. But she didn't want him to think she'd actually planned it this way.

After running the problem around in her head a few more times, she offered a weak smile. "You did say you liked the hammock."

"You want me to be sucked dry and eaten by mosquitoes?"

"There must be a couch?"

"It's been a while since I slept on a sofa."

"Then *I'll* take the couch."

"If you don't mind the lack of privacy, I won't complain."

Taryn's temper began to boil. Hopefully, she would come away from these two days with that contract for *Hot Spots* finally secured. There was also a chance that before this time was through, she'd regress, give in to temptation and show Cole Hunter again just how much he irritated her.

Right now, he irritated her a lot.

Cole's expression changed; he stiffened then he peered off into the brush. She followed his line of vision. Among the ferns, blue stripes of a tee flashed before all was quiet again.

She explained, "It's a boy. He was here earlier, wanting me to sit down and rest."

"I thought I was in charge of your pampering."

She headed inside to inspect the bedroom situation. "Maybe you've been assigned a helper."

"You think I need help?"

She rolled her eyes. *Let me count the ways.*

In the casual main room, she turned. Cole was standing right behind her. As his gaze intensified and stroked her lips, her breathing came a little quicker and her chin reflexively raised a notch. When his head slanted and deliberately lowered closer to hers, for one horrifying moment, she thought that force urging her to lean in would win.

And maybe she shouldn't fight it. Maybe she should let her defenses down, throw up her hands and finally give in. Because truth was she wanted to kiss Cole Hunter harder than she'd kissed any man.

His hands found hers and their fingers tangled together among those bikini strings. Her eyes drifted shut and, in a heartbeat, that tingling burn grew into a storm where a thousand shooting flames combined to ignite and consume every inch of her soul. Suddenly, she felt so dizzy she couldn't think straight, unless it was to wonder if his mouth was even half as confident and skilled as instinct said it must be.

Her heavy eyelids dragged opened.

His gaze still on her lips, he lifted her clasped hands to his hard chest and after a few mind-numbing moments, he smiled slowly and said, "Know what I'm thinking?"

Her chest rose on a deep breath. "Tell me."

"I'm thinking one bedroom's probably enough."

Eleven

As all the world funneled back and left just the two of them, Cole wondered how he might handle the situation should Taryn suffer a sudden change of heart and, at this last possible moment, step away like she had that night on the dance floor.

But when his arms wove around and gathered her close, she didn't struggle, didn't regroup or seem to rethink. Rather, when he finally claimed that long-anticipated scorching kiss, she melted like warm butter, her lips parting on a sigh that both fed his growing hunger and invited him in. He knew as well as she did—this kiss had always been in the cards. This embrace was only their first.

At the same time as he moved to cradle her nape and slant back her head, his other hand scooped lower...over the slope of her hip then around the tight high curve of her behind. She responded by quivering while her palms cupped his jaw then ironed higher up through his hair. She arched in until they were glued together, front to front.

When their kiss shifted, deepened, nearly every drop of blood he owned flooded and filled his loins. The physical longing gripping every one of his senses was unprecedented. Off the chart. But he needed more. He had to get rid of her dress, his clothes, splay her out on that bed and push up inside of her until she lost her breath and sobbed out his name.

His touch wandered farther, sliding up under the back of her skirt, beneath her panties then down over that sumptuous curve and between her thighs. When he found her so warm and well on the road to ready, his burgeoning erection jerked, demanding to be freed. Scooping her that much closer, his chest rumbled as he thought of the pleasure that lay ahead. As she arched and began to move around his touch, he slid farther in between her thighs until he discovered that tiny ultrasensitive treasure at her rainbow's end.

With a soft groan, she wound her lips away from his, even as her body nudged down against him. He grazed his lips over hers. "The bed's just over there."

Her eyes closed, her brow pinched a little and then she reached behind and gripped his wrist.

"I'm sorry, Cole. We can't do this."

"Of course we can. This has been brewing since the day we met."

"We've known each other two weeks."

He nipped her lower lip. "Now we'll know each other better."

Her eyes dragged open. "Cole, this is a bad idea."

"Does this feel bad to you?"

He claimed her mouth again, and again she dissolved, this time to the point where her knees must have turned to jelly. When she sagged against him, he shifted to sweep her up into his arms. As she pulled herself higher and her breasts ground against his chest, he didn't lighten the kiss. Rather, relying on instinct, he navigated his way toward that bedroom door. But as he made it through, she stiffened and dragged her mouth from his again. Her eyes were glistening, pleading.

"Cole, will we regret this?"

"Trust me." He smiled gently. "We won't."

"You don't want to feel as if you gave me the okay on my show simply because we slept together."

"Don't worry." He lifted her in his arms and nuzzled her sweet-scented neck. "I wouldn't do that."

"You wouldn't?"

She smelled like flowers mixed with sunshine. Her skin was so smooth, he couldn't imagine she'd ever owned a blemish. She murmured his name and Cole remembered her question. Would this sway his decision regarding her show? If anything he was impartial.

He nuzzled more.

Or tried his best to be.

"Business is business," he murmured against her cheek.

"So you could kiss me, make love to me, then change back to being the boss? Being *you*?"

He shifted to look into her eyes. "What's so wrong with being me?"

"Nothing. Usually." She shrugged. "I suppose."

His head went back. "You sure know how to destroy a beautiful moment."

"I was about to say the same."

While his chest tightened, her eyes darkened and the focus of their intensity shifted then changed course. They peered into each other's eyes. Taryn's vision seemed to have gotten clearer.

"I think you should put me down," she said then proceeded to wiggle like a cat getting free from a bag.

His brain said to set her down. This union wasn't happening, or not happening now. But his arms were having a hard time understanding.

She stopped struggling and a shudder of something like panic filtered over her face. "Cole? Please…"

He set her down on both feet and she straightened her dress then her hair.

"I don't think we should do that again," she said.

"You're the one pushing up against me. I was only following orders."

"Don't use that excuse."

"I didn't pack a miniscule bikini."

"And that gives you the right to pounce on me?"

"Look, I put you down. But don't try to tell me that you didn't want that to happen."

"You didn't give me a choice."

"I think you're confused."

"Maybe I am. I know I need some time alone. Some space." Her cheeks flushed, and she nodded at the doorway.

"You want me to leave?"

"In the next five seconds would be good."

Cole dragged a hand down his face. She might not have meant for the situation to get out of hand so quickly, but he'd seen what she'd packed by way of a nightdress and, in his books, baby-doll white lace didn't say "not interested." If she wanted him to go now, he'd go.

But he'd be damned if he'd apologize.

And double damned if this was over.

Hearing Cole thump away across the wood floor, out onto the verandah and hopefully farther into the deep dark never-to-be-seen-again jungle, Taryn bit her lip. What rankled most was the fact he was right. She *had* wanted that kiss. She'd wanted his strong, steady arms around her. At one crazy point, she'd even wanted to fall into bed with him then and there. She examined the rattan ceiling fan, colorful shaggy rug, spray of side-table flowers and a frangipani-print quilt with a mountain of matching pillows. If she'd gone ahead, she and Cole would be on that bed right now, prying off clothes, rejoicing in the hot slick slide of each other's skin....

Taryn hauled herself back.

No matter how strong the attraction, obviously a coming

together with Cole in a sexual sense would be way too complicated. Too much was at stake. Her show. Her job. Her self-respect, as well as other emotions.

But she couldn't change what had happened. She could, however, carry on with her plans for this survey. Cole had admitted that he wouldn't automatically approve her proposal if they'd made love. Which on the flip side meant he shouldn't hold yet another heated episode against her, either. Hell, she'd tossed a glass of wine at him and he hadn't thrown her out.

But there was a part of her that wanted to let Cole know she hadn't forgiven him for teasing her, handling her bikini the way he had. He'd looked so amused by her reaction.

She tugged the tie at the side of her wrap dress.

Well, maybe it was her turn to be amused.

Needing to cool off fast, Cole took a long swim in his Calvin Kleins. When he finally wandered out from the bay, shaking water from his hair, he wished he'd thought to bring a towel. But rather than go inside and meet up with that woman whose mission was to drive him crazy, he'd lie out here on the warm sand. Hopefully, the way his luck was going, a coconut wouldn't fall and crack open his head.

He'd dropped to his knees and was leveling out a piece of sand with a palm while admiring a flock of lorikeets squawking across the flawless blue sky, when Taryn sauntered out from the bungalow and down those steps. As his focus zeroed in, the ground slanted, his heart jumped and Cole had to lean against a nearby boulder to keep from tipping over.

He would have growled. In fact, he did. But the sound he made didn't come from a place of residual annoyance. The vibration rumbling around in his chest, leaking from his throat, was a reaction to the clothes Taryn was wearing. Make that *wasn't* wearing. He couldn't believe she'd actually gone and slipped into that bikini.

He'd imagined the next time they met, Taryn would have resumed her cool. He was right about that. Standing at the bottom of the steps, face tilted upward and enjoying the sunshine, she was as relaxed as they come. She hadn't even draped one of those poolside skirts around her hips in a token show of modesty. If she'd meant to disarm him—show him that this was, in fact, her gig and she'd do as she pleased—well, it had worked.

Glancing around, she caught sight of him. She didn't wave but she did smile, a lazy grin that relayed remarkable confidence. Then she walked straight up to him, heavenly hips swaying as her feet dug in and out of the soft sand. When her knees were at eye level, she stopped. What option did he have but to take a deep breath and look up?

In the direct light, her skin glowed with a natural cinnamon tone. Her legs looked smoother and longer than he'd even imagined. Manicured fingers sat splayed on two mouthwatering hips. She looked down at him as if he were a lost dog she might want to pat, if he behaved.

"How's the water?" she asked, looking out over the bay while her toe absently cut a line in the sand under his nose.

Cole toppled forward but recovered quickly, angling up to sit with one leg bent and a crooked arm resting on that knee. Getting his head back together, he purposely ran an interested eye over her attire.

"You look as if you're about to find out for yourself."

She glanced down as if only noticing she was pretty much naked. "Oh, I slipped these on under some dungarees. I wanted to be comfortable doing an initial scout of the surrounds. I've marked a couple of great spots I'd like to utilize." She reached to lift the hair off the back of her neck. "I'm glad to be out of those work clothes. I've really worked up a sweat."

He stopped staring and clapped shut his mouth. His throat felt thick, his body hard. "You deserve a break."

"I was thinking the same."

He thought a moment, wondering if he should play this aloof like her, but, frankly, he was suffering a twinge of guilt. Why not get it out in the open? Be a man.

"If you wanted to make a point," he said, "consider it made."

"What point would that be?"

"That this is your survey, your time to manage, and maybe I shouldn't have tried to embarrass you earlier by showing off what was obviously private." That being the bikini she didn't seem the least embarrassed about now.

She blinked twice, as if she were surprised by his honesty, then her unaffected air returned. "Is that an apology?"

"With a caveat. By setting me up with this island's 'men are servants' slant, you asked for it."

"The way you provoked me, you deserved it."

He looked heavenward. Blew out a breath. "Fine. Just show a little mercy and go cover up."

Victory sparkled in her eyes, but she kept up the pain and suffering by walking past him to provide an incredible rear view. "It's not as if you haven't seen a woman in a bathing suit before."

"Right now, I can't remember a one."

When she angled around, a frown knotted her brow. Surprise again? Hell, in that swimsuit, she was stunning and she knew it. In fact, Taryn was stunning no matter what she wore. No matter what she did or said or thought.

Out of the corner of his eye, Cole spotted movement: that blue-striped tee he'd seen earlier. The boy Taryn had told him about.

When Taryn spotted the boy, too, her thoughtful look evaporated on a quick smile.

"Hey, you're back," she was saying, but, as quick as a rabbit, the boy already had her hand and was urging her back toward the bungalow. Cole pushed to his feet and, dry enough, stepped into the jeans he'd cast off earlier.

He called after them, "What's the problem?"

The boy didn't acknowledge the question. Rather he kept leading Taryn to the deck chairs.

"He wants me to sit and relax," she said.

Before one of the chairs, the boy set down a tray he'd been carrying. Then he shot off around the corner of the bungalow. In a heartbeat, he'd returned with an old wooden bucket.

Cole moved forward. "What's he up to?"

Taryn was looking at the boy as if he were the most adorable entity on the planet. "I think he's preparing me a footbath."

Cole mentally took a long step back. Wonderful. But he wouldn't get involved in that particular discussion again. If the males here wanted to wait on their women, that was better than great. Junior could slave over footbaths all he pleased. But from now on Cole Hunter was nothing more than a bystander. It was past time he found a cool drink and chilled out in that hammock.

But the boy had skipped up to *him* now and, having grabbed his hand, was pointing at the foliage. Cole gently wound his arm free.

"Sorry, kid. I'm off duty."

Taryn opened her mouth then, sitting down in the chair, shut it tight. As she glared at him, Cole pinned her with a look of his own.

"What?"

"It's just I can't understand how you can ignore that face. Those big brown eyes." Sitting back, she rapped fingertips on the chair arms. "Guess big TV executives don't have time for children."

"As a matter of fact I have a kid brother about his age. Stepmom, remember?"

"Oh." She recovered. "See him much?"

"As much as circumstances allow."

"That often, huh?"

Cole set his jaw. He wouldn't bother to explain.

But now that he looked closer, this boy did share similarities with Tate. Same innocence shining like Christmas lights in his eyes. Same eager look, wanting to hang out.

Cole let the air out of his lungs then surrendered.

"Okay. Where do you want to take me?"

The boy presented his bucket.

"You want this filled?" Cole examined the area, saw an outside faucet and moved to collect the bucket. But the boy shook his head and stabbed a finger toward a track that disappeared in the tropical wild.

Taryn crossed those luxurious long legs. "He wants you to go with him."

When the boy flashed that smile again, Cole scratched his head and muttered, "It's a good thing you're cute." He took the bucket and told Taryn as they headed off, "Try not to miss me."

"How will I cope?"

Cole walked away, a grin tugging one corner of his mouth. Probably best that he remove himself from the scene in any case. Taryn was obviously intent on showing him that she wasn't the least bit fazed by his dangling of that bikini or by that explosive kiss. He wondered if she'd heard the saying: trying a little too hard.

Ten minutes later, he and Junior were weaving through layers of ferns and other undergrowth, which rested beneath a dense canopy of vegetation. As birds whistled and insects clicked, Cole got to wondering how this boy and Tate might get along. Tate could show him how to use his most recent gadget—the one Cole had reset the other night—and this little guy could demonstrate how to catch fish in a handmade net or canoe. Hell, *he'd* even like to try that. Maybe one day he could come back and bring Tate along. He hadn't liked Taryn's remark, but they really didn't spend enough time together.

Eventually they stopped at a freshwater spring surrounded by mossy boulders. Watching a line of small snails slither over a leaf the size of a pizza, Cole hunkered down. It was muggy under the canopy and he'd worked up a sweat. First he splashed water over his head. Then, enjoying the icy trickles trailing down his back, he scooped up a handful and drank. He groaned aloud. It tasted so good and clean. Cole drank his fill then dragged the bucket through the pool.

Heaving the bucket out, he spotted a large red flower fallen to the ground…some kind of hibiscus hybrid. Only the petals were closed up tight, like it was asleep in the middle of the day. Noticing his interest, the boy carefully gathered the flower up. Perhaps he meant to make a gift of it to Taryn. Cole smiled. Nice kid. Obviously brought up the right way.

When the boy looked at him again, Cole asked, "Where are your mother and father?"

Immediately the boy set off along that path again but veered down a different track that was crisscrossed with pygmy palm fronds and littered with color-filled butterflies. After several minutes' journey, a clearing came into view. Pulling up, the boy nodded toward a clutch of bungalows. A score of people in casual Western dress were making meals, crafting woods. Kids laughed as they chased each other around buildings and other structures. When a woman carrying a baby in a sling strolled into view, the boy pointed.

"Your mother?" Cole asked.

The boy spoke a word in his language and nodded. Then, thoughtful, he lowered his gaze to the bloom.

Cole remembered giving garden flowers to his mother when he was around that age. He recalled her loving smiles and warm hugs those times she'd held him close and said, "You're a special boy, Cole."

Nowadays, when he was dating a woman and a birthday or some other occasion came around, he'd choose a nice pendant or bracelet. Might be more the norm, but, to his mind, the giving of flowers in new relationships was too personal. And his relationships rarely lasted past "new." What female would choose a floral arrangement over gold or gems, anyway?

The boy was heading off again with that sleeping flower still protected in the cup of his hands. Cole shifted the bucket to his other hand and followed.

Back at the bungalow, Taryn had indeed shown mercy. A light dress now covering that bikini, she was taking shots of the bay where a pod of dolphins played. Closing his eyes, Cole lifted his nose to the air. God, he loved the smell of the ocean. Taryn had once asked and it was true. If he hadn't been bequeathed a career in television, he'd have found a vocation that took him offshore. He'd sometimes wondered if some sailor or pirate ancestor had passed down the seawater that seemed to flow through his veins.

Her shoulders glowing from their time in the sun, Taryn angled around. "You're back."

"And bearing gifts." Cole presented his bucket.

Lowering her camera, Taryn watched Cole move forward with his bucket and pint-size companion.

"This water is guaranteed to leave your soles feeling like silk," he said as she snapped the cap over her camera lens.

"That good, huh?"

"Just ask the man." Cole glanced down but the boy was already disappearing back into the trees. Grinning, he shrugged. "Busy man."

He moved toward the chairs, obviously preparing to fill that tray.

Taryn wanted to tell him, don't bother. She wasn't taking a footbath. The game of "on this island, men must serve" was over, at least between the two of them. But, caught up in admiring that vision of masculine perfection—all those rippling muscles in Cole's arms and chest as he'd moved toward her—Taryn's thoughts got waylaid. She had appreciated the physique of the man who'd brought down their luggage but, to her mind, Cole's proportions were far more appealing.

His shoulders, she already knew, were delectably broad. The muscles that sloped from the sides of his neck to each shoulder were stacked and those pecs were pure power. Dark crisp hair covered his chest, disappearing where the definition of his abs began and starting again where a trail snaked from below his navel. As he moved past with that bucket, she imagined sliding a hand from his taut belly all the way up to the beating hollow of his throat and quietly sighed.

She had indeed meant to tease him with her bikini show earlier. She'd wanted to leave him gobsmacked and sorry that he'd ever thought to provoke her. But where her state of half undress had been calculated, Cole's current condition was not. He was perfectly comfortable in his body, even if the sight was making *her* mouth water.

Finished filling the tray, he straightened and faced her, gifting her a glorious square-on chest view. Wetting suddenly dry lips, she shrugged and made light.

"You didn't have to do that."

He was running a hand back through hair flopped over his brow. She couldn't resist drinking in the way that biceps hardened and bulged before his arm lowered again.

"Couldn't disappoint our friend, now, could I?" He headed for the steps. "I'm off to check out the drink situation."

"Liqueurs are in the cabinet," she said. "Mixers and wine in the fridge." But she'd spoken before she'd thought. After their passionate embrace earlier, she probably shouldn't be offering alcohol.

But he only said, "A beer'll hit the spot. Can I get you anything?"

When he stopped at the top of the landing and glanced back, looking like a bronzed god from on high, her insides tightened and that pleasant tingling burn began to filter through her veins again. Feeling light-headed, she waved him on.

"I'll grab something with dinner."

Before she'd finished her sentence, his focus shifted and he nudged his chin toward the clearing. "Which, if I'm not mistaken, seems to have arrived."

Three men and two women appeared, carrying in with them enough supplies to feed a king and his court. Good news because Cole was famished. He never found lunch on aircraft particularly satisfying.

While the guys set up a table close to the shoreline, the ladies covered a separate serving table with chowder, shellfish and juicy fingers of papaya. Around thatched food containers sat cracked coconuts filled with salads, tomato flowerets and frangipani leis.

He sauntered down to where Taryn stood watching, too, as their ultraprivate and—dare he say—romantic dinner was arranged.

The sun had begun to slip behind the island's western dome. Shadows cast by the surrounding palm trees had grown a little darker and longer. As a lone petrel flew low over the water, the tip of its wing slicing the glassy surface, the men wedged torches into the sand and, a moment later, mellow flames licked at the coming dusk. After a glass carafe filled with a pale pink drink was set at the center of the meals table, with customary wide smiles, the wait team bowed off.

Stomach growling, Cole rubbed a hand over his chest. "Well, this is special."

"I was emailed images and menus but, yeah..." Taryn moved forward. "This is pretty amazing."

Alone again, Cole retracted the chair placed on her side of the table and Taryn took her seat.

"This kind of scene will make for amazing footage," she said, sweeping a gaze over the tables, the bay and a sapphire sky pinpricked with the earliest awakening of stars.

"I wonder if the natives eat like this every night." Cole pulled in his chair, too. "On our way back from that spring today, our little friend showed me his village. Not a cell phone or laptop anywhere to be seen."

"It's good to turn off the outside world." She flicked out her napkin. "When was your last vacation?"

"I don't have time for vacations."

"You never take time off?"

"Not since my father semiretired." He filled her glass from the carafe then took care of his own. "Can't let the ship go under, remember?"

"You can delegate. Roman could take care of some things."

Cole conceded. "He's come on board, for as long as a week at a time when I've needed him to."

"Then why not take a break? Refill your well?"

"I'm here now, aren't I?" He raised his glass. *Cheers.*

"This isn't supposed to be a vacation." She sipped and sighed at the cool fruity blend he'd already tasted and fallen in love with. "Besides—" she set down her glass "—it's only a couple of days."

"Which I'm rather enjoying." Despite their spat earlier.

"Only goes to show. You should do it more often."

"Guess we should."

Midway through setting down his glass, Cole hesitated. He hadn't meant to respond to her suggestion in the plural. But Taryn didn't bat an eye at his *we* rather than *I*. Instead she reached for a coconut to spoon salad onto her plate, and Cole eased out the breath he'd held.

He didn't intimidate her. Or not for long. In fact, he'd never felt so challenged yet strangely at ease in a woman's company before. She made every other person he'd dated seem staid.

Not that this was a date, Cole reminded himself, spooning salad out for himself…even if, with Taryn's eyes sparkling in the torchlight, nature's music playing a lazy tune, an open-ended evening ahead of them and a bold afternoon behind, it sure was beginning to feel like one.

Twelve

When they'd finished the last of that tasty pink nectar, out of nowhere one of the women who'd set up earlier appeared with a fresh batch. Taryn thought she'd make an inquiry.

"Can you tell me the best direction for a walk along the beach tonight?" She explained to Cole, "I want to take some night shots."

"A full moon will be out," the woman said, refilling their glasses. "Either stretch is free from outcrops. There are more turtle nests down that way." She slanted her head toward their right. "You might even see a batch hatching."

Taryn sat straighter. "Really?"

She'd seen a turtle nest hatching on YouTube. The sand had bubbled then a circle overflowed with tiny flippers and shells pushing themselves out into the world. A nest was supposed to contain from fifty to over two hundred eggs. Now *that* was a big family.

"Throw a blanket out high on the beach and you might get lucky," the woman said, setting down the carafe. "But don't use a torch or flashlight. That confuses hatchlings." Swinging back her heavy fall of brunette hair, she again gestured down the beach. "You'll see the nests. The children mark them off."

Cole seemed interested, too. "You really think we might see some hatch?"

"Female turtles like to return to the same nesting ground, and that section is popular." After the woman had replaced used plates for clean, she ended, "Don't forget a blanket. Sea breezes can be cool at night."

As the woman headed off, Taryn sized Cole up. "So you like turtles, huh?"

"Tate's grade is signed up in some conservation program about them."

"Hopefully we'll get lucky and snap some close-up shots he can take to class." She pushed back her chair. "Think I might take the opportunity to catch up with that woman and get her ideas on other spots to check out while we're here."

"You'll find me on hammock duty."

As he got to his feet, too, and stretched those magnificent arms at angles above his head, Taryn pressed her lips together then said it anyway. He looked so striking yet relaxed. So unlike his usual blustering self.

"Maybe you shouldn't take a real vacation. It might feel so good, you'd never want to come back."

"Leave someone else in charge permanently?" Intentional or not, his fingers brushed hers as he passed. "Dream on."

"I've got blankets."

Cole glanced over from where he lay, swaying, half-asleep. Taryn stood a few feet away on the verandah, a stack of blankets in her arms. Rousing himself, he rocked out of the hammock onto his feet.

"Was that an invitation?" he asked.

"You said you liked turtles."

"I said Tate liked them." But, seriously, who didn't like turtles? He moved closer. "You won't be disappointed if nothing happens?"

"But something *might* happen."

Taking in the confident curve of her grin and—in that pink cotton slip of a dress—her other curves, too, he had to agree. *Something might happen,* and not just on the turtle front. But did he really want to put them both in that situation…alone on a secluded beach for an undefined amount of time, and with bedcoverings to boot?

Taking the blankets, Cole supposed the answer was an unconditional yes.

A few moments later, they were wandering down the beach with a full moon hanging high in its starry night sky.

"That woman was telling me how well this island does through visitors like us," she said. "They have a joint council and apparently invest the revenue wisely."

"Maybe they should spend some on decent public transportation and fixing up that welcome sign."

"Oh, Cole, it's all part of the charm. If you've stayed at one five-star, you've stayed at them all. But you'll never forget that taxi ride."

He winced. "Neither will my shoulder."

They came across a spot where a number of thigh-high stakes were erected and red tape wound around the wood. Protected areas for turtle nests.

Cole surveyed the surrounds—gently sloping dunes, soft sand, idyllic view. He laid out one of the blankets. "Looks like this is our base."

The blanket-covered dune made for one very comfortable backrest. Reclined side by side, he cast the other blanket over Taryn's bare legs. That woman was right. He found the breeze off the water refreshing, but Taryn might think it cool.

After several minutes of listening to water wash on the shore and foliage clattering behind them, he asked, "What do you think would be their favorite time to break out? Don't babies usually come around two in the morning?"

The breeze caught her soft laugh and carried it away. "Can you imagine them all asleep safe in their shells waiting for the right moment? And so many of them." She frowned. "Do you think mother turtles ever wonder how their babies make out?"

He grinned to assure her. "No, I don't."

Her gaze dropped and grew distant, then she said, "I wonder how Muffin and her big belly are holding up."

In the mix of moonlight and shadows, Taryn looked so thoughtful, he wanted to reach over and squeeze her hand for support, even if her concern was only over a cat.

"She'll be okay." Remembering her philosophy on strays wanting a home, he asked, "Have you got families picked out for the litter?"

"Are you interested?" She gave a playful smirk. "Oh, that's right. Real men don't own cats."

"I do like the fact they can look after themselves. Independent characters."

"There's no better feeling than knowing you can make your own way in life."

"So you don't dream of marrying a rich man who'll shower you with every luxury for the rest of your decadent life?"

"Guess you've met a few women who want to settle down with a wealthy tycoon slash tyrant."

He pretended to preen a tie. "Gee, you make me sound like such a catch."

She surrendered to a smile. "To answer your question, no. I've never wanted to marry for money."

"Me, either," he quipped.

"*If* you ever had the time to marry."

"Perhaps I'd make time if the right person came along."

When her eyes widened and suddenly neither of them had anything to say, Cole wished he'd thought before he'd come out with something that had sounded like a bad pickup line. He didn't use pickup lines—good, bad or anything in-between.

She jerked upright and looked ahead. "Was that some movement?"

He glanced around. "Not that I saw."

She reclined back, pulling the blanket extra high on her neck.

Cole exhaled. He really had made her uncomfortable. Best to let that thread drop and talk about something else. Something nonpersonal. But, truth was, he *wanted* to get personal. Whether it was the moon or the water or maybe even that delicious pink nectar, another twenty-four-plus hours alone with Taryn didn't seem long enough.

He picked up grains of sand and, in their silence, let them fall.

"I've made you anxious."

Still looking dead ahead, she shrugged. "Why would I be anxious?"

Oh, maybe because you're alone on a secluded beach with a man you want to kiss and who also wants to kiss you. Because earlier you'd gotten away with convincing yourself that you shouldn't—we shouldn't—when you know deep in your blood that we should.

"I'm not anxious," she went on. "I'm not…anything."

He mulled for a moment. Studied her profile.

"You're not."

She was winding her fingers deeper into the blanket, lifting the cover higher still around her neck. "Not in the least."

"And if I were to do this?"

He leaned toward her but stopped a heartbeat before his mouth met the sweep of her neck…when she'd be able to feel the warmth of his breath on her skin. "Are you anxious now?"

He heard her swallow. "That's not the word that springs to mind."

"Maybe we shouldn't worry about words." Giving in to the tide, he breathed in her intoxicating scent then brushed his lips over a pulse that beat erratically at the side of her throat. He felt her quiver, almost heard her questioning her own resolve. But she didn't bawl him out. Didn't move away.

Rather, still looking ahead, she lifted her chin and said, "I think we should go back."

"Anything you want." His lips brushed a line up to her lobe. *Anything at all.*

Her neck rocked slowly back. He imagined her eyes drifting shut...the hormones in her system heating and sparking just like his own.

Gently he turned her head until they were gazing into each other's eyes, noses touching. She quivered, but not from the cold.

"Would it surprise you to know," he said, "that I've always wanted to make love on a beach under a full moon with a batch of turtles ready to hatch?"

A smile touched her eyes. "What a coincidence."

He twirled his nose around hers, stole a featherlight kiss from one side of her mouth.

"Cole, when I said something might happen, I didn't mean this."

His hand on her arm, he brought her closer.

"I did."

Thirteen

Cole had said they shouldn't worry about words. As he drew her close and his mouth took hers, Taryn couldn't help but agree. The time for talk and gibes and delays was over. When she'd said she hadn't thought this would happen, she'd lied, and not only to Cole. She'd lied to herself.

All barriers needed to be lifted. No matter the reason for them being here, neither of them was able to escape the fact that they were attracted to each other—sexually, intellectually. On every level she could think of, she found Cole…intriguing.

Make that irresistible.

And as she pressed into his heat and accepted his kiss, that was all her mind could grasp and hold on to. He may be mulish; there were times she'd like to grab his shoulders and shake. He could irritate her. Goad her. At the same time, he stimulated her so often and so deeply, there was a part of her that had begun to crave the sound of his laugh, the slant of his smile. The incredible way he made her feel inside and out.

She drove her hands up through his hair, letting him know he didn't have to stop. He could kiss her harder, if he wanted. The physical flesh-on-flesh pleasure he stirred up within her… the heady, almost desperate feelings that followed… People may have been making love since the dawn of time, but never like this. If the world were to end in an hour, she wouldn't care, as long as she spent these last moments here, with Cole, like this.

Cole had flicked open his shirt buttons and was rolling out one shoulder and then angling while he shucked out of the other. When the rock-hard breadth of his chest brushed her bodice, her body instantly responded, her breasts swelling and nipples hardening to tight aching points.

Running out of air, she broke their kiss long enough to suck down a breath then clutch the hem of her dress. His gaze dark and hungry, Cole reached to help. While he grabbed the fabric rumpled around her thighs, she lifted up and raised both arms. She wiggled, he wrenched, and a moment later she was naked from her panties up.

His gaze filling hers, he crowded her back until she lay against the blanket-covered dune again. Then his head lowered, his mouth covered the peak of one breast and his tongue began to twirl. When his teeth nipped twice quickly, a bolt of shimmering lightning ripped through her veins.

Groaning in her throat, she held on to his head as her own rocked to one side and she arched up to soak in as much of this heaven as she could. His palm had molded over her other exposed breast, tracing and tickling the bead in an expert, mind-bending way. As her hands knotted in his hair then trailed to knead either side of his broad steamy back, she trembled with an overwhelming carnal need. She had to discover *all* of him. Every inch. Every shape and line.

He was kissing her again, his palm ironing down her belly, in beneath the elastic of her panties. When he reached the feminine crease between her legs, he sighed into her mouth. It felt as if his every muscle relaxed and then contracted extra tight. As he murmured something against her lips, a phrase about how beautiful she was—how much he'd looked forward to this moment—a more cynical Taryn might think that those were the kinds of things men said when they made love to a woman. But in a place she trusted more, she knew that he meant it. And right now she felt beautiful. Beautiful and about to go up in flames!

She fumbled to grip the waistband of his jeans. Grinning against her mouth, he let her struggle while his fingertip rose up and down her swollen cleft. The crotch of her panties was soaked and he seemed intent on only making her wetter. Dabbing soft moist kisses on her chin, her cheek, on each side of her mouth, he drove a slow, burning circle around and over her clit. She couldn't contain the tremors…the soul-deep sighs. She wanted that smoldering bliss to go on and on, but she also wanted to feel and experience him.

"Take off your jeans," she told him.

He stole another penetrating kiss then assured her, "Soon, sweetheart, soon."

He shifted down, his lips trailing the slope of her neck, the aching mounds of her breasts then over her ribs and her ticklish belly. When he reached her navel, his tongue rode the same captivating circle his finger now drew. In her mind's eye, she saw his head working in a tight deliberate ring while the circling down below grew tighter, too.

Her shoulders hunching up, she reflexively pushed his head down. The next moment, the pressure of his finger was replaced by the adoring swirl of his tongue. Taryn gasped back a breath and when the precursor rain of stars settled, she began to move, her hips coaxed by his rhythm, her heart pounding in time to that constant pulsing beat.

Bit by bit, the factions of light building in every quadrant of her body began to glow brighter, and the heat condensing at her core smoldered to a point where any moment, she would catch on fire. Absorbing it all, she pressed down and into herself, her eyes clamped shut, her breathing labored. She thought he might back off a little, stop and start as a way of drawing her out. One half of her wanted him to do precisely that, while the other half dug in her claws and worked harder to find release.

Her hips moved faster. Biting her lip, she willed the looming orgasm to peak and break. Then, at the same time his mouth covered her completely and he began to lightly suck, she felt her lips eased apart and a long strong finger slip inside of her. When he applied the right amount of pressure to precisely the right place, a whirlpool of sensations flew together and magically fused. For a heartbeat, all feeling and thought were suspended, hovering in some far-off twilight universe. Then the explosion hit, shards flew out and a series of high fierce waves rocked every cell in her body.

Cole wasn't surprised her climax had come so quickly, that it was so intense. As much as he'd been driven by pure instinct these past few minutes, so had she, and the reward was complete immersion. Total release.

He'd loved the feel of his lips covering hers. He'd hardened to a brick when he'd tasted her breasts. But when his tongue had come in contact with this private slice of heaven, he hadn't known if he'd be able to hold off from ripping her panties completely off and, without patience or apology, driving his erection home. Given all the signals, she had wanted him inside of her that way, too.

But he'd held off, enjoying beyond belief giving her this pleasure. Now that it had come, he wanted to prolong her peak as long as possible. If his shaft hadn't been pounding away, he'd have happily stayed here all night doing only this. And as he withdrew his finger and felt just how intense her orgasm must have been, it was natural that he'd want to enjoy that, too. He nudged her thighs wider apart and settled his lips an inch or so lower. Her scent, mixed with that flavor, was wonderfully earthy yet intoxicatingly sweet.

Enjoying her this way, he felt the last of her contractions squeeze and pulse until, reaching to rub her fingers through his hair, Taryn hummed in her throat and urged him up.

Face-to-face again, she looked into his eyes and her slumberous gaze said it all. His lips wet with the taste of her, he traced them over hers then kissed her, at first very softly then more and more deeply. At the same time, he maneuvered until he was free of the rest of his clothes.

He always carried his wallet in his back pocket. Now he broke the kiss only long enough to find one of the foil wraps he kept inside the zipped section.

Spread out on their blanket, she reached her arms to him at the same time he moved to position himself. As her thighs wrapped around the back of his, he kissed her again and the engorged head of his erection pierced and at last entered her. Her head went back as she sucked in a breath while he clenched his jaw and every tendon in his body locked tight.

When he had the pressure under control, he began to move, his mind drifting, floating, as he filled more and more of her and his own sensations climbed.

He pushed up onto elbows and, eyes closed, drilled ever deeper while Taryn's fingers fanned over his chest and the bulging cords in his neck. Even though he knew there would definitely be a next time, and soon, he wanted this to last… the throbbing, pushing burn, the heavenly slide of her body beneath his. But the fire was too hot. His need for release too great. As he craned his neck toward the moon, she held on to his arms and he pumped a final mind-blowing time.

Fourteen

"Doesn't Australia seem a long way away?"

Taryn and Cole were lying together under the stars. The moon had dropped halfway into the ocean and everything was spookily quiet—as if the whole world were asleep.

Except for them.

Cuddling closer into the heat of his hard chest, she replied, "Doesn't sound as if you're in a hurry to get back."

"I feel strangely at ease." His lips nuzzled her hair. "Wonder why."

Because they'd just made love. But even in her mind, that sounded way too simple. Yes, their bodies had joined, but she felt as if their spirits had met, too. This was what being with someone was supposed to feel like. Totally absorbing. Completely fulfilling. Wondering how she'd ever find the wherewithal to move from this divine spot and leave this time behind, she snuggled in more.

Whether Cole felt as moved by the experience as she did, Taryn couldn't say. Nor would she ask. She might be feeling all wistful and in love with the universe. But more than instinct said Cole, or any man for that matter, didn't want to come over all marshmallow, dissecting feelings composed mainly of postcoital buzz…with feeling unbelievably fulfilled on every level. Rather he might like to broaden the discussion. Probably not such a bad idea.

"There's another reason you'd feel more relaxed. Your father's troubles are sorted."

He was quiet for a long time, simply stroking her arm with two fingers.

"I was thinking about my mother earlier today," he finally said. "Do you know she used to call me special?"

Taryn smiled. "I'm sure you were."

"She said I was so brave and clever, I was bound to grow into a man everyone could rely on."

"And you're living up to her prediction."

"Yeah. I'm the fix-it guy."

"What do you think would happen if you didn't run yourself ragged trying to fix everything all the time?"

Now that she'd seen him a league away from the office, unburdened like this, she couldn't help but wonder.

"If I didn't keep an eye on Hunter's dealings in the States as well as back home, frankly, I'd run the risk of seeing it all fall apart."

"Is it really that bad?"

"Let's just say, it's a full-time job."

"And the price you pay is a coronary."

"I got the impression you were a 'dot every i' type, too. I'm still not convinced you didn't order one bedroom, even subconsciously."

She knuckled his ribs. "You're not that good."

"Aren't I?"

He drew her up so that she lay on top of him. Then he kissed her, tenderly and with infinite meaning…in a way he hadn't kissed her before. And all the problems and doubts in the world faded clean away.

When they came up for air, she breathed out a long sigh then lay her cheek on his shoulder.

"Well, on second thought," she said, "maybe you are that good."

When Taryn woke in bed the next morning, the sun had just peeked over the horizon and the sheet-rumpled space beside her was empty.

Sitting up with a start, she pushed back hair fallen over her brow then relaxed, remembering how her evening with Cole had ended. The most romantic night of her life.

After making love again on the beach and coming to terms with the fact that no baby turtles were likely to hatch, they'd meandered back to the bungalow. Sandy and sticky, they'd showered together—soaping each other up then taking their sweet time to wash each other down. After drying off, they'd jumped into this bed and, with that rattan fan beating warm air over their heads, had continued to talk and kiss and more.

What time had she fallen asleep? Didn't matter. She'd never felt more refreshed. And disappointed. She'd imagined cuddling up with Cole this morning and repeating what had unfolded atop that blanket the night before, and possibly exploring other pleasure points, too…finding more ways to please. Then again, she couldn't envision feeling any more satisfied. The problem was she wanted more.

Wanted *now*.

So much it frightened her a little.

As she found her negligee wrap, Taryn wondered. Perhaps she would live to regret this coming together. Cole Hunter was first and foremost her boss, after all. Carrying on from that, he was committed to his company—to his family—and had no room for anything or anyone else in his life. Any woman foolish enough to entertain flowery notions about a lasting relationship with a man like that was headed for trouble.

Thoughtful, she knotted her wrap's sash and wandered out to the main room.

Trouble. Yes, Cole was certainly that. But he was also exciting and sexy and, dammit, she was going to take this unexpected, wonderful moment in time for what it was. A thrilling, soul-lifting one-off. Once they were back home, the involvement no doubt would end. Because nothing screwed with a girl's career more than trying to negotiate an office affair.

A good friend had walked down that long dark road and had come out losing everything on the other side—job, self-respect, pretty much her sanity. Taryn had quietly deemed herself too smart to fall into that trap.

But this slip with Cole didn't need to be fatal. It was like having one bad day on a diet. Come day after tomorrow, she'd simply correct her course, get back on the bike and wean herself off him. Difficult, but doable.

From a bowl on the coffee table, she grabbed a banana and, peeling the skin, made her way toward the larger entrance of the bungalow, which invited in a panoramic view of the bay. Biting into the fruit, she surveyed the near surrounds but Cole was nowhere to be seen. Perhaps he'd hooked up with that sweet boy.

She crossed over to the kitchenette. While pouring some chilled nectar, she eyed her laptop sitting on the counter. Those pictures and videos she shot yesterday were waiting to be downloaded. Roman had made her promise she'd take loads. He wanted to see them all.

Roman was an intuitive type, Taryn decided. Would he pick up on the changed vibe between her and Cole? What would he think of the situation—of her—if he discovered she'd slept with the one man who decided whether her show made the cut?

A flash of guilt gripped her stomach, but right now Taryn only wanted to embrace feeling good. She wanted to remember the way Cole's mouth and hands had moved over her body like an artist's, creating sensations and bringing out emotions she hadn't thought existed.... Standing here alone, naked beneath this filmy wrap, she felt helpless not to close her eyes and conjure up more memories, more bone-melting must-have-again moments.

When Taryn opened her eyes, her gaze landed on an item lying on the main table—a flower. Massive and scarlet in color, it looked so perfect, Taryn wondered if it were fake. Crossing over, she ran two fingertips across a satin-soft petal. She could check on the video she'd taken of this room not long after they'd arrived, but she was certain it hadn't been here then. And no one else had been inside this room since that man had dropped off their luggage.

Had Cole brought this flower home for her this morning? Beneath it all, was he that romantic?

She'd assumed Cole would want this interlude to be short and sweet. He was an astute businessman with little time for R & R, not a man to be led by his heart. But did she have it wrong? He had dropped a hint once, hadn't he? Was Cole Hunter truly looking for the right person? The right woman?

Not that she wanted to be that woman necessarily. She was a career person. Foremost, at this time in her life, she wanted her show to air and succeed.

But maybe this island truly could work miracles. Make people rethink who they were and why they were here on this earth.

Outside, footfalls sounded on the steps. The next minute, Cole's masculine frame filled the doorway. He was wet, rubbing a towel down his face, over his slick dark hair. His bare chest pumping after what Taryn guessed had been a jog up from the beach, he saw her and broke into a smile that left her heart thudding all the more. Would he present her with the gorgeous flower now?

Moving forward, he brushed a cool kiss across her cheek

and stayed close to drawl, "I was hoping you'd still be in bed."
He drew back a little. "I couldn't resist the idea of a swim."

"I can't resist you."

Bouncing up on her toes, she snatched a kiss a moment before a hungry smile swam up in his gorgeous green eyes. Dropping the towel, he wound his big cool arms around her.

"That felt like an invitation."

"I figure it's too early for work."

His focus had dropped to her neck, to the slope of flesh that led to one shoulder. The cold tip of his index finger eased her wrap away from the spot before his head lowered. She sighed as his mouth lightly sucked then nibbled then sucked again.

He murmured against her skin, "You taste good."

"And I have it on good authority that's not the best part."

She tugged the tie at her waist, shucked back her shoulders and the wrap joined his towel on the floor.

With firm intent, his hands slid lower, over her backside, as his wet shorts pressed unashamedly against her belly. He was already hard and she was keen to make him harder.

"I'd better warn you," he said. "I'm ravenous in the morning."

She coiled her arms around his neck. "You're always hungry."

His playful gaze darkened to a more serious hue as he concentrated on her lips. "So feed me."

He carried her back to that bed where they stayed, and played, until well after ten when his cell on the dresser beeped. He hesitated, clearly wondering who was after him now, before he resumed tickling her nipple with the tip of his very skilled tongue.

Bodily exhausted, but passions still switched on to high, she ran a hand over the back of his head, through his tousled dark hair.

"You don't want to see who that is?"

He switched to her other breast. "Nope."

Sighing, she arched up as his tongue twirled one way around the peak then the other.

"It might not be work related," she said dreamily.

"It's work related."

"Might be family."

"Like I said…"

"Might be Tate."

She felt him smile. "Tate isn't allowed to use the phone."

"Guess he is a little young."

"But smart. He knows his own home number. Mine, too."

Moving up, he curled an arm around her head and asked, "When did your aunt trust you with a phone of your own?"

"I got one when I started a part-time job during senior year in high school. It was the first thing I bought with a wage. No. Second. I'd had my eye on a cream silk dress for weeks."

"What was the third thing?"

"I saved up and gave some money to an agency to help find someone from my past."

Tipping on his side, he rested his weight on his elbow. Finally he asked, "Your father?"

"Mother. My father abandoned us before I was born. My mother bowed out later when I was a tot. If it hadn't been for Vi, I wouldn't have had an opinion on family worth voicing. She's supportive and understanding, and she saved me from feeling worse about my childhood than I should.

"I remember," she went on, "when I was maybe only five or six, Vi dated a man with kind smiling eyes and a belly laugh that filled the house. I thought they'd be together forever and I'd get the mob of brothers and sisters I wanted. But they broke up. I remember finding my aunt sometimes trying to cover her tears." Taryn had spilled a few tears of her own.

Cole seemed to take that all in before he asked, "Did the agency find her?"

"Yep. I even went to see her. She was living with a bunch of people on the coast of Northern New South Wales. My aunt said she'd come with me, but I wanted to do it on my own."

"Was it a happy reunion?"

"Actually it was a huge letdown. She tried to make out like she was glad to see me, then she came up with a ton of excuses why she'd needed to leave me behind. She never stopped fidgeting, acting cornered. Just one of those women who should never have had children, I guess. But I'm glad I went. We even swapped emails for a time. When she died a few years later, I went to the funeral. Paid for a headstone. Would you believe she wanted to be buried with a bottle of rum?"

He drew in closer and held her gaze with his. "She missed out."

"I've thought about organizing to have flowers put on her grave each anniversary of her death, but I can't bear to think of them sitting there, week after week, all withered and brown. I should probably go plant a rosebush or something. Not sure if that's allowed."

But she'd talked enough about the past. She wanted to get back those other, happy feelings.

Winding a finger through a lock of hair that had fallen over his brow, she said, "By the way, I like the flower you brought back for me this morning."

"Flower?"

"The red hibiscus. It's as big as a plate." When he frowned, she went on. "You left it on the table, remember?"

"Oh, that. No. That boy with the bucket brought it back from the spring yesterday. He must have ducked in to leave it there for you. It was closed up, asleep, when we found it."

Taryn blinked then said, "Oh," and forced an easy smile. "I just assumed it was you. Doesn't matter."

But deep down, it stung a little. Made her feel foolish for thinking he'd gone to the trouble.

Which meant she was getting way too caught up here. Yes, they'd slept together—a number of times in only a few hours. The day they'd met, Cole had suggested she may have had an affair with her former boss, which she'd denied, and she felt he'd believed her. But did he wonder about that now? Or did he see this experience for what it was? A once-in-a-lifetime fling between two consenting adults who happened to work together. It wasn't ideal but it happened. It had happened to *them*.

And thinking of it that way only reinforced that she had no reason to come over all adolescent now. He didn't give her that flower. Didn't matter. No big deal.

He was studying her neck, sliding a fingertip around the décolletage.

"You don't wear a chain," he said.

"I have a pile of costume jewelry," she said, her thoughts preoccupied now.

"But nothing that says Tiffany?"

"Their pieces are beautiful, but I'm not a jewelry kind of girl." She was a *flower* kind of girl.

He looked at her for a long moment as if debating something in his head…like maybe how he would handle this situation when they got back? How he would go about closing the door. Perhaps with a parting gift. A piece of jewelry. She'd already accepted that what had happened between them was never meant to last. And yet as that feeling of preoccupation turned into unease, suddenly she knew they'd spent enough time in bed. They needed to start moving. Get back to reality. To work. She'd mentioned it earlier so Cole knew that her video camera was charged, ready for a shoot involving that volcano.

He must have sensed or seen her change in mood because, tipping back, he said the words for her.

"Perhaps we should get on with our day."

"I think that's a good call."

Without another word, he slid out from beneath the sheets and, naked, headed for the adjoining bathroom. But Taryn lay there a moment longer, going over in her mind the past few minutes. She didn't accept expensive gifts. She didn't want them. But believing that he'd brought a flower back here for her...

A simple thought like that would have meant so much.

When he came out from the shower, into the main room, Taryn was moving away from the table. He saw that flower lying there. She'd said it had been as large as a plate, but now, again, all the petals were closed.

"Did you get your message?" she asked, moving to her laptop, which sat on the kitchen counter.

"Message?" he asked.

"Your phone beeped again. Twice."

He rubbed his brow, dragging his hand down his face. It was a gorgeous Saturday morning. He was on a picturesque Pacific isle with a woman who made love like a goddess and, ten minutes ago, had again put up her wall. Because he'd hinted at giving her a gift? Well, that was one for the books. Or was there something he wasn't seeing?

He returned to the bedroom and slid his cell off the dresser. Three recent messages. All from his father.

After he'd listened to the first, he didn't need to hear the rest. Didn't need to feel any sicker. Angrier. When he got hold of Jeremy Judge, by God, he'd throw him down on the ground and—

"Business?"

He glanced up. Taryn stood at the doorway, her long fair

hair loose and hanging over bare shoulders. She wore a strappy lime-green dress that complemented her skin tone. Her gaze was bright but also very much back to reserved. He stabbed the redial key. He didn't have time for holding hands now.

"There's been another attempt on my father's life."

Her breath caught. "That can't be."

"I'll get Brandon front and center on the case straightaway," he said to himself, fast dialing then grabbing his bag off the floor, dumping it on rumpled sheets then striding into the bathroom to collect his gear, all with the cell pressed to his ear.

For God's sake, pick up!

"Does that mean that other man, the man who died, wasn't responsible?" she asked. "Or that he wasn't working—"

"How the hell should I know?"

Storming out from the bathroom, he was confronted by Taryn's wounded gaze. Oh, hell. He so didn't need this right now. Neither did he want to act like a brute.

He left a quick urgent message for Brandon then took one step toward her. "Look, I'm sorry. It's just…" He shut his eyes and cursed at himself. "I should *never* have left."

"What could you have done?"

"What I should have done from the start. Taken charge. And to hell if someone didn't like it."

"Meaning your father."

"Meaning anyone on God's green earth."

He shoved his toothbrush and aftershave in his bag then drove a hand in to drag out a clean pair of trousers.

"You're leaving?" she asked.

"Soon as I can."

"There's no connecting flight out until this afternoon."

"Then I'll organize a private flight."

He stepped into his chinos. Pulled out a tee. He heard her question as if from afar.

"Cole, what happened?"

"Two men clubbed my father. When a bystander rushed up to help, they almost managed to shove Tate into their van. I would never have forgiven myself if…"

His stomach pitched. Dammit, he wanted to hit something. Break it in two and hit it again.

"Cole, this isn't your fault."

"Someone else started this, but, by God, I'll finish it."

Driving the shirt on over his head, he noticed Taryn at the wardrobe, dragging out her own bag. He frowned.

"What are you doing?"

"I'm going with you."

"This isn't your fight."

"You need someone with you."

"I've never needed anyone."

"Everyone needs someone, Cole."

Something shifted deep inside of him, but he pushed it aside and reminded her, "That volcano's expecting you and your camera."

"Guess the volcano will have to wait."

"But this survey, your show—"

"Are important. But this takes priority."

He held her gaze then, remembering the clock was ticking, he turned to find his shoes.

She went over and held his hand. When he met her gaze again, she asked, "Is your dad okay?"

After a tense moment, he blew out a breath.

"He's at home, resting."

"And Tate?"

With his free hand, Cole held his throbbing head. "There are some crazy sons of bitches out there. People who don't have a moment's hesitation in hurting someone who can't defend themselves. Tate's all right. I'm going to make sure he stays that way."

"What is it you think they want?"

"Always comes down to money, doesn't it?"

"A ransom. But I thought these were attempts on your father's life. A ransom demand's no good if you don't have a bargaining chip."

His stomach tightened before it rolled over twice. He murmured, "I have this horrible feeling…"

"What?"

"That Eloise is connected to this in some way."

"Guthrie's wife? Trying to kill him? Why on earth would she want to do that? He must treat her like a queen."

"Women like Eloise are never satisfied." He remembered the way she'd come on to him—Guthrie's oldest son—whenever they were alone, and the sick feeling in his stomach grew ten times worse. He grabbed his cell again.

"I need to make a couple of phone calls. To organize that private flight first off…"

"And the second call?"

"Jeremy Judge." He scowled. "I'm looking forward to firing his ass."

Fifteen

What had gotten into her?

How had she ever summoned the nerve to tell Cole that not only was she leaving on that private flight off the island with him, but she was also tagging along when he confronted his family about these ongoing attempts on his father's life?

Now, hours later, Cole pulled his car up in front of the Hunter mansion. Taryn told herself again: there was no reason for her being here, other than the one she'd already given. After the intimate time they'd shared, brief though it had been, she cared about him. She cared about Guthrie and little Tate, too. She wanted to help if she could, even if help only meant offering her support.

Call her curious, but she also wanted to meet Eloise Hunter.

Cole hadn't elaborated on his suspicions—that he believed his father's second wife was involved in these assassination attempts against Guthrie. But there must be some good reason for Eloise to have created such a big blip on his radar. Taryn assumed no one else knew of his concerns, least of all Guthrie. How would his father react if his would-be killer turned out to be the woman who had pledged to love him till death us do part?

But Taryn knew better than most. Some people didn't give a rat's behind about the people they should care most about.

Taryn sympathized with Cole. The Hunter family was indeed a tangled web. How must he feel being the "special one," feeling responsible for trying to keep all the spiders out?

Cole opened her passenger-side door and she followed as he strode up a half dozen wide granite steps to the massive front doors. Before she'd caught up, he'd rung the bell twice. Now he was thumping the panels with the side of one fist. When a woman—obviously staff—responded to the ruckus, Cole seemed less impressed than he had been all day.

The woman said, "Are Mr. and Mrs. Hunter expecting you?"

Cole all but pushed the woman out of his way. He was halfway across the huge shining foyer when he stopped, turned and held out his hand, waiting for her before he charged on.

Absorbing her surrounds, Taryn took his hand and followed. The grounds of the estate were impressive enough. Pristine manicured lawns with soaring pines delineating an endless paved drive. Inside, however, Taryn was left near speechless. Everything screamed wealth. Extravagant embroidered furnishings. Magnificent art hanging from towering walls. The room they'd entered was larger than a regular-sized city apartment. The cost of maintaining this grandeur must be exorbitant.

Guthrie was resting on a couch, gazing out a window that took in a one-eighty-degree view of a back lawn that presented more like a state garden. Guthrie looked over as they entered but he didn't get to his feet. One leg rested on cushions on the couch and a square bandage sat high on the right side of his forehead.

Cole came straight to the point. "I fired your wonder P.I."

"Jeremy told me that you called." Guthrie swiveled a little

and spotted his other guest. "Taryn, sorry to call you away early from your work."

Feeling horrible for the whole situation, she edged forward. "Are you all right?"

Guthrie touched his head. "A bruise here and there. My pride's wounded the most. If not for that man who'd been walking his dog, I can't say where we'd be now."

Cole asked, "Where's Tate?"

"In the media room with a policeman standing guard. Son, I wonder whether we should put Tate somewhere safe until this is over."

"Safe like where?"

"Perhaps with one of your brothers. Whatever madman we're dealing with here, hopefully he won't have connections that far abroad."

"Let's get Brandon in on this first," Cole said, "then we can nut out what needs to be done."

At that moment, a fourth person entered the room. Taryn recognized the face from media shots and the photo Guthrie kept on his desk. Eloise Hunter was of medium height and svelte, other than a baby bump. Wearing a black silk-and-chiffon pantsuit straight out of the pages of Vogue, she looked as if she were attending a celebrity wake. Only no one was dead. God willing, it would stay that way.

Taryn expected the mistress of the house to be either overly gracious to her or serve up a cursory glance; she was, after all, no one of consequence. But on seeing Taryn, Eloise stopped in her tracks and, without regard to social etiquette, eyed her up and down as if *she* might have been a person who intended her family harm.

Taryn bristled. Within five seconds of meeting Mrs. Hunter, she understood Cole's disapproval. What happened next made her hackles rise more. Eloise's focus slid away from her and settled upon the younger of the Hunter men present. The glimmer in those amber eyes was unmistakable. Eloise found her stepson physically attractive. She might be running her fingers up and down the side of the water glass she held but in her mind, her hand was stroking something far more personal.

Apparently unaware, Guthrie took care of introductions. "Darling, this is Taryn Quinn, a producer we've put on."

Eloise's gaze flicked back and a meaningless smile curved her lips. But then a wiser glint shone in her eyes and she focused again on Cole. It took all Taryn's restraint not to save Eloise the trouble of guessing and admit out loud that, yes, she and Cole were lovers. And that was the *second* reason Eloise needed to keep those restless paws to herself.

Another guest entered the room. Beside her, Cole stiffened and braced. She heard him mutter, *"Judge.*

"What are you doing here?" Cole spoke to the man. "I said we were done."

"I take my orders from the elder Mr. Hunter," the man—Judge—said, lacing his hands before him. "And unless he's changed his mind in the past five minutes, I'm still on the payroll."

Cole growled. "How did you get things so wrong? Where were you when my father was bashed and my brother nearly kidnapped?"

"I understand you're upset—"

"You know nothing about me."

"I have a father, too," Judge pressed on. "A man I respect and would give my life for. Instead of locking horns, Cole, let's work together to put the people responsible away."

Cole looked set to pounce when Guthrie cut in.

"Cole, you have my blessing to bring Brandon in. Tell him he can have anything he needs. But on one condition. He works with Jeremy. He did, after all, save my life that night."

As if she were oblivious to it all, Eloise sidled up closer to Cole. "It's been a long day. Need a drink?"

Cole grunted, "What I need is a club."

Regardless of injury, Guthrie got to his feet. "That's enough, son. Nothing more can be done here today. Go home. We'll talk again tomorrow."

Cole lifted his chin. "I'm seeing Tate before I go."

He took Taryn's hand and, plowing on past Judge, led her through that room, down a long corridor and up a level where they finally entered a room without knocking.

A uniformed man stood inside the door. Now one hand flew to his holster. Taryn covered her mouth to smother the gasp while, at the center of the room, a young fair-haired boy turned his head. Tate's face burst into a deep-dimpled smile. He threw down his game controller and ran full speed up to them. He flung out his arms at the same time Cole scooped him up and held him tight. Taryn thought she saw moisture at the corners of Cole's closed-tight eyes while the policeman answered a call on his two-way: Judge passing on to expect the eldest of the Hunter boys soon.

Still hugging Tate close, Cole's voice was thick when he asked, "How you doing, kiddo?"

"I got a scratch on my knee, Cole, but it doesn't hurt." Tate wound back and looked over. "Who are you?"

"I'm Taryn. It's good to meet you."

Tate spoke again to his big brother. "She's pretty. Are you staying for dinner?"

"Not tonight, chum." Cole set Tate down but stayed crouched so they could talk eye to eye. "There's no need to be scared, okay?"

"I'm not scared. Not anymore. But I still wish you could stay." Tate's mouth swung to one side then he leaned closer and whispered, "Daddy says I might get to fly over to see Dex or Wynn for a while."

"How do you feel about that?"

"Good, so long as it's Dex."

"Why Dex?"

"Coz he lives right near Disneyland and he's always saying on the phone he wants to take me."

Cole chuckled and in that moment Taryn felt a large measure of his tension drain away. Her aunt said that blood was always thicker than water. He might grumble about his brothers in California and New York, but Cole would trust them to look after the person he loved perhaps more than anyone in the world. That said a lot.

Cole ruffled Tate's hair. "Go finish your game."

"I'd better go wash up for dinner."

"You hungry?"

Tate beamed up. "I'm always hungry."

Laughing, Cole stooped to give Tate another bear hug then, together, she and Cole walked down that hall. But he didn't take the turn that led back to the sitting room they'd left. Instead they found their way out via another route. A couple of minutes later they were buckled up in his car, leaving the estate and its majesty behind.

His gaze on the road and mouth drawn tight, Cole said, "Thanks."

"What for?"

"For leaving the island to be here with me today. I know how much getting the most out of that survey meant to you."

Taryn was taken aback by the sincerity in his voice, by the vulnerability in his face. To save herself from sounding too moved, she almost quipped, *Sure. You owe me one.*

But she was happy she'd come and had witnessed firsthand the pressure Cole was under. She'd come out with an even broader understanding of his ingrained sense of commitment. To everyone.

As far as her being here for him was concerned, he didn't owe her a thing.

* * *

When Cole pulled up in her drive, Taryn didn't have to ask ask him inside. He must know that she wanted him to spend the night and although he was understandably on edge, she knew he wanted to be with her, too.

He carried her bag into the bedroom then, standing in the early evening's misty shadows, he turned to face her. For a moment, a flicker of some emotion she couldn't name shuttered over his expression before a fated smile lifted one corner of his mouth. Without a word, he reached for her and she came.

They didn't kiss. Not at first. He found the zip at the side of her summer dress and eased it down at the same time as she unbuttoned his shirt. After he'd slipped the dress off over her head, she tipped forward and, breathing in his musky scent, let her fingers roam over his pecs then higher to skim his powerful shoulders. She slid the sleeves off his strong long arms while he gazed down into her eyes, searching deeper than he ever had before.

When she caught the button at his trouser's waistband, he held her hand back then carefully dropped his head into the sweep of her neck. As his teeth slow danced over the skin, her every fiber ignited with a desire so pure, the sensations stole her breath. His warm, slightly roughed palms drew arcs over her bare back, up under her hair, and he murmured at her ear.

"I like when you don't wear a bra."

She quivered and sighed, pressing herself closer as pulsing heat drifted to converge in the lowest point in her belly. His mouth was moving lower, too, tenderly drinking its way across the curve of her collarbone as one hand moved to cup and measure the weight of one breast.

"Don't wear them anymore," he said, obviously meaning bras. "Not when you're with me."

The tip of his tongue slid up her neck, ran a line over her parted lips, and as his fingers swooped around then lightly pinched and rolled one burning nipple, she opened up more and welcomed him into her mouth.

Although she adored his foreplay, she was near desperate to have him on top, pushing inside of her. She needed that connection. She knew he needed it, too. She wanted to tell him just that, and in words that shouldn't be uttered in public. She needed him naked and she didn't care if it was on the bed, on the floor, pressed up hard against that dark cupboard wall. The time they'd already spent together making love had been intoxicating, but this minute she was fevered, burning up. That he'd begun to slide down against her body to his knees didn't help. These past hours had been so filled with concern. She'd missed the intimate feel of him, his scent, the thrill.

With his tongue trailing lower past her navel and a set of fingers hooking down into her panties' front, she let her neck rock back and the conflagration take over.

He parted her folds and kissed her with his lips then with his tongue. All the while he stayed with her nipple, rolling and gently extending the peak while his mouth circled that other ultrasensitive bead. His teeth nipped and tugged at the same time as she heard his deep groan of pleasure. He felt so strong whereas she was trembling, every thought she'd ever owned set aside to concentrate on the growing fire, the rhythmic rub of his jaw against her inner thighs.

Mind-blowing sparks began shooting through her blood. Her legs started to shake and nothing in the world mattered other than the fact that she hovered above and all around this excruciatingly sweet crescendo. She needed the release so badly, but she was already half out of her mind, and she wanted to do something new for them both.

She tried to shift away from his mouth, but the hand on her behind held her firm while his rhythm didn't miss a beat. Again she let herself be drawn toward that throbbing light before, grinning, she wedged a palm between his mouth and her mound and pried herself away.

In patches of thin light, she saw him glance up, his brow furrowed.

"But you like that," he said.

"I do."

"Well, I like it, too." He grinned. "In the work comes the reward."

She laughed but when his head went forward again, she wound away and climbed up onto the bed. His teeth flashed white on a smile. With a couple of deft moves, his trousers were down and kicked aside. He set something—she guessed a condom—on the bedside table and then he came to her, ready to resume where they'd left off. Instead of letting him take the lead, she pounced and drove him onto his back.

Craning up, he laughed. "Hey, you play rough."

"Is that a complaint?"

His back met the mattress again. "No, ma'am."

Leaving her panties on, she came closer and feathered her lips over his small flat nipples, down over his ribs. She dotted hungry openmouthed kisses in four spots around his navel. Then her head went down.

Grazing her nails over his scrotum, she held his shaft in her other hand and rolled the full length of her tongue around that hot rounded tip. Beside her head, his hand fisted into the coverlet as his hips arched up. Smiling to herself, she circumnavigated a few more times before, squeezing lightly, she slid farther down.

He throbbed in her mouth, and at the back of her throat she tasted a little of him…a tease of what was yet to come. His palm slid up over her shoulder to knead her nape as she moved and stroked, and his erection hardened more. Deep, maddeningly sexy sounds rumbled through his chest and body, vibrating over her lips and lower. He began to move and his strokes on the back of her head became more instinctive. Immersing herself in all her senses, she shifted until she was embedded between the V of his legs and he couldn't escape. She doubted he wanted to.

She'd thought she could handle him, but the width and thrust soon became too much. A moment before she could slide her lips away, perhaps reading the signs, he reached down to ease her up. He didn't roll her over but rather held her on top by gripping her high on the back of one thigh. Grabbing the condom, he rolled on protection then expertly pushed up and in. A rush of euphoria doused her inside and out. So many endorphins, she felt intoxicated...floating on a slipstream that was about to take her unbelievably high.

Her lips ran over the damp slide of his brow before she came away to look into his eyes as he smiled softly, moving and coaxing her sizzling fuse closer to that beautiful big bang. She was balanced, on the verge, when he held her cheek and whispered her name.

A heartbeat later, his erection drove in to the hilt, hitting that single perfect spot. As the orgasm took him, he squeezed her thigh, she let out a gasp and the universe contracted before blowing wide apart.

Sixteen

They spent Sunday together at her place, not working, not stressing. Just unwinding, her reading a novel, him watching sports on TV. Cole didn't think he'd ever enjoyed an entire day of doing nothing before. He felt guilty. Rested. A small part of him even felt at peace.

For the most part, however, he was thinking about Guthrie and Tate—how bad that day when Tate had almost been abducted could have turned out. Brandon had been brought into the loop. His father insisted that he keep Judge on the case, too. Nothing Cole could do about that. But he wanted those animals, and whoever was behind this whole sordid mess, found and appropriately dealt with. *Fast.*

The next day, Cole visited Taryn in her office. She said she'd get together what she could from the survey, given they'd been called away early. He said he needed a more definite budget projection. Then she asked whether she ought to start organizing host auditions. Between leaving her office and stealing a drugging hot kiss, Cole told her to hang off for now.

Tuesday night he spent over at her place. He watched on while she called for that cat to come in from the cold. Later they'd had pizza and watched a movie neither of them saw much of. Wednesday night Taryn stayed at his place. Thursday, he was back at hers and she was still calling in that stubborn pregnant cat. They'd had Chinese and he'd told her about the time the boys had built a cubby house in the backyard and it had collapsed with him inside. She'd been impressed by the scar on his shin caused during the cave-in by a dislodged dartboard.

By Friday, he was prickly over the fact Brandon and Judge had nothing new to report. However, Brandon passed on in private that, despite her many vices, Eloise was clear of any suspicion. That spooky maid was cleared, too. Come lunchtime, Cole was settled behind his desk, working on more tweaks to that massive, frustrating, football league contract, when Taryn swept into his office and put a pamphlet on his desk.

Grinning, Cole sat back. She was a cross between angelic and sexy in that crisp white linen dress that, to his mind, could have benefitted from an inch or two less length around the hem. Calculating back how many hours it had been since they'd last kissed—last made love—he collected the pamphlet and looked it over.

"What's this?" he asked.

"A new park opened not far from here." She came around to his side of the desk. Her perfume teasing his nostrils and testing his resistance in a work setting, she tapped a picture on the sheet. "There are paddleboats."

He nodded. "Okay."

Her blue eyes flashed and a big smile spread. "Then you'll come?"

"Come where? When?"

"To paddle with me. Now." She checked her wristwatch. "It's lunchtime. I vote foot-long hot dogs."

Shunting the pamphlet aside, he chuckled. Taryn was a mile away from the aloof woman he'd met three weeks ago. Of course, she would never lose that poise; a person either had class or she didn't. And, God knows, he would love to ditch and go play for a couple of hours. But he'd been slack all week. He'd even slid across some duties for Roman to take on full-time. But he couldn't hide forever from his responsibilities. He had an example to set.

"Sounds tempting," he said, "but I ought to get this contract sorted."

She leaned back against his desk's edge. Her palms set flat behind her, shoulders raised, her skirt lifted that ideal inch or two.

"The work will still be here when you get back," she reasoned with a silky tone, and he flicked a glance at the open office door. Maybe they could enjoy some hands-on time now without needing to leave the building.

After easing out of his chair, he stood before her then leaned in until his hard thighs pinned hers. His palms anchored on either side of hers on the desk, he closed his eyes, grazed his chin lightly up her cheek then murmured in her ear.

"I think we should lock the door."

When her hand came up and fingers twined through his hair, every pulse point in his body started to tick and, soon, throb.

"You spend too much time indoors," she told him while he tasted the satin curve of her neck. "Let's get some sunshine. It's a gorgeous day."

"And later?"

"Later you can finish with that contract."

He pressed in more. "What contract?"

She laughed. "You have some casual clothes here, don't you?"

As his hand slid over and scooped around her back, the best he could do was grunt his affirmative.

"I do, too," she said, then sighed. "We'll change, go paddle some boats and then…"

He drew back slightly. "Couldn't we do the 'and then' part first?"

She pushed against his chest and he let her shift him away. "I'll meet you in the lobby."

He took from those hypnotic lips a lingering kiss. "I'll be there in five."

They drove to the park. For a Friday—a workday—it was packed. Guess it was a combination of the good weather, he mused, a novel array of food vendors and the curiosity of a new place to take the kids. Or your lover.

He paid for thirty minutes in a paddleboat, but, willing to pay more and give their legs a fine workout, they spent an hour on the lake. If ever he thought about that contract, or his father, Cole told himself to chill. They were headed back to her place for the "and then" part, after which he'd get back on top of things, but when they were almost at her address, he decided to check his cell for messages. Just to be safe.

He had parked in her drive, which was looking quite familiar these days, and Taryn was already out and scooting up to open the front door. Cole opened his messages and was bombarded by a stream of recent texts and voice mail. As he went through, his gut sank lower and the sense of dread swelled until he wasn't certain he could breathe.

Liam had been trying to get him. He'd been offered a better deal with a rival network. He needed to make a decision. What could Cole do for him? He needed to know *now*. Cole dragged a hand over his damp brow. This deal was major, major. If this didn't happen, Hunter Broadcasting was in deep trouble.

Feeling that cold sweat break behind his neck now, Cole stabbed a few keys. He was talking, trying to mend a critical situation, when Taryn wandered back and peered in at him, questioning, through the window. Needing to talk to Liam— with no distractions—Cole angled away.

Even as they spoke, Cole's brain was shouting at him. *Why*

did you let down your guard? If he cruised for long enough, of course something bad would happen. And as the negotiations deteriorated, and Taryn, worried and disappointed, moved inside her house, Cole made a vow. If only this worked out, if he didn't lose this deal and have to put off workers, need to shut down shows, he would never take his position for granted again.

Not for any reason.

Not for anyone.

"I'm ba-ack!"

With his usual cheery smile, Roman Lyons moved into Taryn's office at Hunter Broadcasting and, at her desk, set a big "friends only" kiss upon her cheek.

Genuinely happy to see him, trying to tack up a smile, Taryn set down her pen. "How was the script-writing junket?"

"Junket?" Roman swung a leg over the corner of her desk. "I'll have you know that my colleagues and I worked bloody hard on sorting out angles and zingers for our next and biggest season yet. Did you miss me?"

"Terribly."

"Good job I was only gone a week then." Roman leaned closer. "So, tell me. Has the Commander finally given your show the nod? You've been back from that survey two weeks. The budget's been worked over a thousand times. Surely he's made a decision."

When her insides ached, she could only look away.

While they hadn't discussed it, Taryn guessed Roman knew she and Cole were lovers. Or *had* been. Frankly, she was confused at how things had turned out, although she guessed she shouldn't be surprised. Since that Friday, just over a week ago, when Cole had needed to perform circus tricks to keep that football contract from going down in a landslide, things had changed between them. For the worse.

Although they saw each other at work and a couple of times had gone out to lunch, Cole had distanced himself. He hadn't come over to her place, hadn't invited her to his. Whenever she suggested they do something fun, he said he was far too busy. If she brought up her show, he told her he'd get back to her soon.

Of course, Cole blamed himself for the panic that had ensued when that man, Liam Finlay, had been unable to get in contact the afternoon they'd played hooky in the park. And, although he would never admit it, or accuse her, she was certain Cole blamed her, too, for tempting him outside of his usual dutiful boundaries.

She'd never been a party girl, but that week with Cole had been the best of her life. More than that, she'd reevaluated. Thought about priorities. She still wanted her show to go into production, but she'd come to see that in recent years she hadn't laughed enough. She'd usually taken herself so seriously. Last week, Vi had said she was a different woman. Hell, Taryn had thought Cole had become a different man.

Apparently not.

Taryn answered Roman's question. "Cole put through word today. *Hot Spots* has his approval."

Roman's expression exploded. Giving a hoot, he swung an arm through the air.

"That, my lovely, deserves a celebration. Cups of tea all around." Jumping off the desk, he eyed her percolator. "Although coffee will more than suffice."

The news had come via email and was signed, Best, Cole Hunter, Executive Producer In Charge. Certainly everyone had a template, but couldn't he have given her this news in person?

While Roman moved over to that counter, Taryn sucked down a fortifying breath. She didn't have to confess anything to this man. Except, firstly she trusted him. And secondly she'd felt so isolated, so alone here since Cole had bit by bit shut her out. She needed catharsis. To purge her doubts. Clear her conscience.

"I suppose you figured it out," she began.

Roman was lumping sugar into his cup. "Figured out what?"

"That we…that Cole and I have been, well, *together*."

Roman hesitated only a second before pouring the coffee. "Totally your business."

"I didn't do it to gain the advantage," she said. "I didn't sell myself to get my show through. It happened and now *Hot Spots* will go into production…"

Roman returned with two cups. "And that is top news."

She shut her eyes but those doubts wouldn't leave her. "I can't stop wondering if Cole finally slid it through because he felt obligated. He never approved of the idea. He never stopped telling me he thought it would fail."

"Here's a big tip." Roman pulled in a chair. "Don't torture yourself. Just run with it and give those ratings a jolly good jolt."

She half smiled but had to ask. "Has this ever happened before? Cole getting involved with a colleague, I mean."

"Cole's not the blast-his-own-horn kind of guy. Or, rather, not with regard to love affairs. Low-key. As far as I know, no one from here. And never anything serious."

"Guess that hasn't changed."

Roman heaved out a breath and gave her a comforting smile. "It's not your fault. You know what they say about a leopard and his spots."

Around ten, Roman said *cheerio*. At the exact moment he left, Cole strode by her office without slowing down.

A hollow gutted feeling gripped her and wouldn't let go. The walls seemed to fade back at the same time they pressed in. She set her face in her palms and tried to fathom this out.

From the moment they'd first kissed, she'd known what she was getting into. Trouble. But there'd been a time when she'd thought she'd meant something more than a convenience to him. Another element in his world to be manipulated. Eliminated.

Seems she'd been wrong.

An urge overwhelmed her. An impulse greater than she'd ever known. Taryn pushed back her chair and, needing answers or closure or *something,* she caught up with him outside of the accounts department. Cole obviously hadn't thought she'd put on a chase. He jumped when he saw her appear beside him.

A little out of breath, she asked, "Any more word?"

His Adam's apple bobbed above his tie's Windsor knot then control returned to his face.

"Word on what?"

"Your father's situation."

"No breakthroughs yet although I have every confidence Brandon will come through. If you'll excuse me, I have a meeting. I'm already late."

He headed off, but she wasn't finished.

"Still thinking about sending Tate to your brother's?" she asked, catching up again.

"That's one plan."

Not willing to talk about it? *Okay. Next.*

"I finally got Muffin inside. She's had her kittens. Four in all."

"I hope they find good homes."

Still walking, she said, "I thought you might want to see the rundown for the first show. It's in draft form—"

"Leave it with my PA. You know Leslie."

His personal assistant was a nice lady with the patience of a saint. She'd need to be, working with Cole.

"Any special requests to be included in the draft?"

"Just slot out your expanded ideas for the six locations—"

She didn't hear the rest. She slapped a hand on his arm to try to pull him up.

"What do you mean *six?* A season is thirteen episodes."

"We'll see about that after initial ratings come in."

"I'm not happy with six shows, Cole. You're not giving it a chance."

He was checking his watch, edging away up the hall. "Like I said…"

She growled. If he said just one more time he was late…

She blurted it out. "Why are you treating me like this?"

Darren from the Sport department was walking by, slowing down to take a good long look. Cole took her arm and led her into a nearby unused office.

After shutting the door, he set his hands low on his hips. "You want to cause a scene?"

"I want some answers."

"Six shows is my limit, Taryn." His chin notched up. "I don't recall promising you anything."

So she should be grateful?

"I don't recall asking for anything other than you meeting the terms of my contract."

He folded his arms, cocked his head. "Are you done?"

"No. I'm not done. I want to say you don't have to go around hiding from me anymore."

"I don't hide from anyone."

"If you regret that time away, that week when we came back and were happy, it's not half as much as I do."

She'd said the words. How much easier her life would be if she believed them.

"You're jumping to conclusions," he said.

"I'm inventing the fact that you're avoiding me?"

His eyes slowly narrowed.

"Do you want to know how I've been filling in my time

these past days? Not only have I got that murder mystery hanging over my head, my brother Dex has managed to get himself tangled up in some blackmail scheme."

"Since when?"

"Dex mentioned it last night when he called. He clammed up when I asked questions. But that's not enough. He's kindly informed me that the finances over there are dangling by a bare-assed thread."

"He actually said that?"

Cole's jaw shifted. "Well, no. Not in so many words. But I can hear in his voice that he's worried." His chin went up. "Add to that the fact Liam Finlay informed me that he's still an inch away from accepting another network's deal. That's where I'm headed now, if you care to know. To try to avoid that last looming disaster from falling on our heads."

Not only were his irises dangerously dark, the half-moons underneath his eyes were dark, too. Not nearly enough sleep. Taryn knew what that was like. But she didn't have the weight of the future of at least two multimillion-dollar enterprises riding on her back. She was simply trying to survive an ill-fated love affair. Get her show the time on air she believed it deserved.

"I didn't know," she muttered. "You didn't say."

His tone dropped. "I could have come to you and whined and moaned, but that's not what I do. I fix things. I take responsibility."

All the emotions she carried around trapped deep inside of her these past days began to bubble up and spill over. If he'd made her feel insignificant before, now she felt as inconsequential as a gnat. Her gaze dropped to her shoes. Her vision blurred. God, she wanted to die.

She heard him exhale and a moment later two fingers were under her chin, lifting her face until, her throat thick, she was peering into his eyes.

"I'm sorry I haven't had two minutes to spare lately," he said. "That doesn't mean I didn't enjoy our time together. But pizza and rerelease DVDs are out of the question right now." His fingers slid down her arm until he was holding her hand. "You understand, don't you?"

Taryn sagged into herself. She'd started out wanting to corner him and yet she'd been the one who was crowded back and bombarded until her head was left spinning. But at least now she had an explanation for his lack of interest. If she looked at it logically rather than emotionally, he had a good reason. She supposed.

She found the wherewithal to nod.

"I guess I understand."

"Will you be all right getting back to your office?" She nodded again. "Okay." He pressed a lingering kiss on her cheek. "I really have to go."

He strode away, leaving her alone, numb, and the door wide-open for everyone to see.

Seventeen

Taryn usually enjoyed seeing her aunt. But tonight's visit she could have done without. Not because Vi had done anything disagreeable. They hadn't had an argument since high school when Taryn had decided she had more important things to do than keep her room halfway clean and suffer regular homework.

But when Vi had rung and invited herself over for dinner, Taryn wanted to postpone. She wouldn't make good company. She only wanted to sit around alone and keep rehashing in her mind whether or not she ought to have forgiven Cole for his recent behavior.

Her stronger self wanted to tell him to take a hike. Who needed to feel like a convenience? She also wanted to give Cole the benefit of the doubt. Maybe when this particularly tough time in his life was over, he would miraculously revert to the charming, at times sensitive man she'd discovered on that island.

Passion. Desire. A constant need to be close. Until now she'd never been able to comprehend how a woman could get so caught up in those kinds of emotions that she could act in ways that would normally make her retch. She understood better now. It was as if she were *infected* by him. Her blood, her heart, her mind.

When she'd confronted him yesterday, she'd held out hope that he would at least make a small effort and drop by her office today. He hadn't. And tomorrow…? Hell, he had to talk to her *sometime*. They worked together, for Pete's sake.

As Taryn sat with her aunt in her living room, with Vi nattering on about how gorgeous the new kittens were, she realized her aunt had asked a question. Realigning her thoughts, Taryn smiled over.

"Sorry. What was that?"

"I was asking if that man at your work had gotten any closer to letting you know whether your show will go ahead."

"He made his decision yesterday. We start production next week."

Vi jumped in her seat then grabbed her niece to give her a big hug.

"I'm so proud of you. Not that I ever had a doubt. That other lot was mad to let you go. But, see, it's all worked out for the best. You're with a company who respect who you are and what you can give." Reaching down, Vi preened Muffin's head where the mother cat lay in her big open box by their feet. "I must say, I was beginning to wonder when your boss would get around to making it official. It's been over two weeks since you got back from that survey. Was he very difficult while you were away? You'd told me he was a bit of a tyrant at the office."

"We…came to an understanding."

Vi stopped stroking and tilted her head. "An understanding, darling?"

"Or I thought we had."

"I'm not sure I understand."

"I'm not sure I understand, either."

Vi's voice and shoulders dropped. "He took advantage of you, didn't he?"

As that sick ache spread in her chest, Taryn shut her eyes. She could say that she had no idea what her aunt was talking about. She could tell Vi that she wasn't in high school anymore. She didn't have to clean her room if she didn't want to, and she could sleep with a man—this man—if she chose. But Vi wasn't attacking her. Her aunt loved her, had always taken care of her and never failed to give the best advice.

"He didn't take advantage of me," Taryn finally said. "I wanted it to happen. He's an extremely charismatic man."

Vi's brows sloped as if she'd figured that out.

"From the moment we met," Taryn went on, "there's been a thing between us. You know. A connection."

"An attraction."

"It would have happened eventually whether we went away together or not."

"So you don't regret it?"

"I didn't *think* I would."

Taryn explained about the attempt on Guthrie Hunter's life. She told Vi how much Cole seemed to have appreciated her support when they'd called into the Hunter home that night. She also told her about all the trouble at Hunters in L.A. and of Cole's concerns regarding that big sporting contract.

While she talked on, Vi listened, nodding at certain points, scowling when it was appropriate. Taryn ended by saying that over the past week, Cole's affections and attention toward her had cooled. Actually, other than that token brush of his lips over her cheek yesterday before leaving her alone in that empty office, his dealings with her verged on chilly.

"But when he explained what was behind his being so distant, I understood. Or I tried to." When her aunt remained quiet, Taryn asked, "Don't you have any advice?"

"I'm not sure you want to hear it."

"Other than suggesting I should lower my hem or not leave assignments till the last minute, I can't remember a time I didn't take your advice."

Vi's attention dropped again to Muffin and her week-old litter of three.

"You'd spoken about this cat for months," she said. "How you'd call to her, lay food trails for her, how you'd even tried to pounce on her a couple of times. You figured that once you got her inside, she'd want to stay."

Taryn wasn't certain where this was headed. "She looks happy enough now she's here."

"Do you think she would have been if you'd caught her and locked her up in this house?"

Taryn blinked. "I was trying to help."

"You wanted to give her a home here with you. But if you'd forced her, chances are she'd only want to escape."

"You're saying I should let Cole do what he wants—let him go—and maybe, one day, he'll come back to me." Taryn shrank back. "I can't do that."

"You can't force someone to act a certain way, either."

"Like be halfway decent?"

Why should Cole have it all his way? By nature, she was a reserved person who tolerated much, but she did not like to be used—taken for granted—and Vi's advice seemed to insinuate that she do and accept just that.

Vi stood. "I'll get dinner on. I brought blueberry pastries for a treat afterward."

Vi was heading toward the kitchen when Taryn said, "I remember when I was very young, you dated a man. He was nice from what I recall. You were happy. But one night I heard a disagreement and we never saw him again."

Vi nodded as if she remembered it well. "That was a long time ago."

"I'd hoped that you two would get married," Taryn confessed.

"I'd hoped for that, too. Marty was a wonderful man, married before with three children all around your age."

"What went wrong, Vi? What was the argument about?"

"Marty was a family man. He would've liked nothing more than to have made his family with us."

"And he loved you."

"I believe he did. I most certainly loved him."

Taryn held her swooping stomach. "It wasn't because of me, was it? The reason you broke up."

Vi laughed and crossed back over. "You were an angel. Still are. Marty said often what a good girl you were. That you and I were lucky to have each other. It tore him up that he could only see his own children every other weekend."

"So his wife hadn't passed away."

"They were divorced. He said it was the hardest thing in the world to pack his bags and know that from that moment on his family would be forever fractured. We'd been seeing each other for six months when he asked his children if they'd like to meet a special lady and her niece. They'd innocently told their mother. Suddenly she wanted him back."

"So no one else could have him."

"He didn't contact me for a few days after that. Then, that night you remember, he tried to explain how cornered he felt. I didn't understand. Or didn't want to. If he loved me, he wouldn't consider going back to live with another woman, even the mother of his children." Vi's eyes began to glisten. "I couldn't bear the thought of his sleeping in the same bed with her, of her kissing him good-night when I was the one who loved him, not her."

Feeling sick for her all these years later, Taryn reached up to hold her aunt's hands. "But you said you'd wait for him, right?"

"I told him that if he was even considering that, he could go now. Or he could do the decent thing and tell me, then and there, that he was staying where he was, with us." She sighed. "He left. I was so upset. As far as I could see, he mustn't have loved me. Or, at least, not enough."

"Maybe you did the right thing."

Vi's resigned look returned. "Three months later, his ex kicked him out again. I saw his photo in the back pages of a paper three years later. He'd married a woman with a big bright smile. I wondered if they'd be happy together. I wondered if she loved him as much as I still did."

Taryn slowly got to her feet. "I never knew."

Never had any idea. Vi was a person who rolled up her sleeves and got on with things. But she was also a woman, with emotions, passions, like everyone else.

When her aunt inhaled deeply, Taryn knew she was willing back tears.

"So, you see," Vi said, "you can't force someone to stay. You have to let them make up their own mind. And there are no rules to say that decisions that might seem easy for one aren't incredibly difficult for another. When I look back now, if I'd been him, I would have gone back to her, too."

Taryn thought about that, but it was obvious. "Because of the children."

Muffin let out a loud *meow* and Vi brought herself back. "I think she's telling us dinner is long overdue."

Wanting to cry for her, Taryn wrapped her arms around her aunt. "I'm so glad you came today. So thankful you've always been there for me."

Vi hugged her back, stroked her hair. "I wouldn't have had it any other way."

Cole glanced at the time on his laptop screen then rubbed a hand over his stinging eyes. He was beat. Time to knock off.

Time he ate. But he still had so much to do trying to figure out how to shuffle the figures in L.A. so Hunter Productions could enter the next season as strongly as possible.

What he'd much rather do is drop by Taryn's place and take her out to dinner. Only, like the rest of the East Coast, given the time, she would already have eaten. And, besides, he wasn't good for her right now. Or was that she wasn't good for him? Either way, a man could only have one mistress, and his was Hunter Enterprises. He couldn't let the company—his family and mother's memory—down again. Not for a woman. Even a woman like Taryn.

His cell phone buzzed. Cole read the ID. A rush of heat filled his neck, his head, his chest. Two deep breaths and he connected. His brother's smooth baritone echoed down the line.

"Hope I didn't wake you," Dex said.

"I don't get the luxury of much sleep these days."

"In a happy mood as usual, I see."

Cole bit down. What must it be like to go through life pretending you had nothing more to worry about than which starlet you were going to sleep with next?

He ground out, "What do you want?"

"To brighten your day. The revenue figures are in on our latest release. After a huge opening weekend, we're solid, sitting well on top of the black."

Cole let the line hang.

"Cole, you there?"

"Uh-huh."

"Aren't you even slightly pleased?"

"I'm waiting."

"What for?"

"The bad news."

Dex laughed, a deep and carefree sound. He'd been the same since they were kids. Dex was the charmer, who man-

aged to wiggle in and out of trouble without getting so much
as a scratch, while Cole was busy learning the business, making sure someone of integrity would one day take over what
their grandfather and father had worked so hard to build. Dex
didn't seem to worry too much about any of that.

Eyeing Brandon and Jeremy Judge's latest report lying read
twice on his desk, Cole asked, "Want the latest on Dad?"

"What's happening there? Tate all right now?"

"He's fine."

Cole gave a rundown on security measures and the fact
Brandon was working hard with Judge to uncover new leads.

Dex got back to Tate. "Well, if the little guy wants to come
over for a visit…"

"That's funny. Take a five-year-old away from kidnapping
troubles to put him with a man who is the target of a blackmail campaign."

"I told you not to worry about that." Dex grunted. "I must
have been raving mad letting that slip in the first place."

"If I don't worry, who will?"

Dex pushed out a breath. "All I'm saying is that Tate is
welcome anytime."

"Who have you got lined up to babysit? Some Hollywood
starlet you're screwing?"

The line went deathly quiet. "Be careful, bro. You might
find reward in your near monklike lifestyle, the fact you get
off on telling everyone how hard you work and how no one
appreciates what you do, but I intend to go on enjoying what
a man is meant to enjoy."

"That would be an endless string of empty affairs."

"You're a sanctimonious son of a—"

The conversation went downhill from there.

Cole was still fuming when he left the building an hour
later. How could two brothers be so different? Birth order? A
swap at the hospital the day Dex was born? Although, Cole

could admit, Dex had got the tail end of his latest foul mood. At least that new release was doing well. There was still the problem of Tate. Hopefully his little brother wouldn't be involved in any future incidents, but should Tate happen to get hurt in any way because of this murder attempt mess, Cole would feel directly responsible. He didn't want Tate to get mixed up in Dex's blackmail business, if it came to anything. Then again, what could be worse than living with Eloise as a mother? The answer was the possibility of being shoved in a van never to be seen or heard from again.

Cole was driving on autopilot when he noticed the sign announcing the arterial route to Taryn's neighborhood. She might think he hadn't thought much about her lately. Truth was he'd thought about her a great deal. Way too much. Another reason he wasn't getting much sleep.

This past week he'd had to put up a barrier between them. Not that he'd wanted to, but, frankly, she'd been interfering with his responsibilities. And, to be fair, he'd let himself get sidetracked. Taryn's company was always preferable to flogging himself with budget and technical reports, proposals and financial crises. But if *he* didn't cover all the bases, who would? Admittedly, Roman Lyons was proving to be a big ongoing help. His father, however, barely came into the office anymore, which, Cole supposed, meant less likelihood of decisions needing to be reversed.

That brought him back to Taryn.

He couldn't risk distractions. While she was employed by Hunter Broadcasting, he would know little relief. He'd okayed her show out of obligation more than anything. A sense of loyalty, or maybe expectation. And while that may be understandable, given the nature of the time they'd spent together, he wasn't looking forward to the anticipated hit to the company. Hell, he'd just chastised Dex for not thinking with his head. Recently, had he been any better?

Setting his jaw, Cole stepped on the gas and drove past that turnoff.

Grandpa Hunter used to say, *There's no better time for change than the present.*

No smarter time than now to move on.

Eighteen

Taryn took her aunt's advice. She would never again consider hounding Cole, like she had that day a week ago when he'd informed her that her show would record six episodes rather than a full season's complement of thirteen. Now she didn't seek out his company and most certainly he didn't seek out hers.

As the days had gone by, she'd kept herself busy with one of two occupations. She was either immersed in her show's preparation—organizing crew, sponsors, studio time—or sourcing people who would love to adopt a kitten.

She did little socially, although when Roman had asked, she'd gone to a movie. They'd grabbed a bite beforehand, had enjoyed buttered popcorn throughout the show and had said goodbye in the complex's parking lot.

Given he knew about the Cole situation, Taryn guessed Roman felt sorry for her. Which was thoughtful. Nice. But she was done with feeling sorry for herself.

Over the past couple of days, her hope to stay with Hunter Broadcasting had dimmed. She'd swallowed the six-show deal. But then Cole had cut her budget in half. Had told her that he could not agree to sign the host she liked. Today he'd put the nail in her coffin. His PA had passed on the news that rather

than five people helping to put the show together, she'd have
two, one being a seventeen-year-old graduate. No experience
equaled cheap labor.

Technically, Cole might have approved her show but,
clearly, he still wanted her gone. She hoped he slept well at
night.

Earlier today, Taryn had learned Guthrie was in, which
happened less and less. When Taryn had phoned through, his
personal assistant had said he'd see her straightaway.

Walking down that long corridor, Taryn guessed she ought
to feel nervous, one of the reasons being that she didn't normally do snap decisions. Usually she formulated a plan, studied all the angles then pursued her goal until said goal was
attained. Whereas the action she'd decided upon this morning
had seemed to come to her out of the blue. Kind of the way
she'd handled her conflagration of an affair with Cole. Only,
no matter how much this might hurt, she was certain this decision was the right one.

She entered Guthrie's office. He stood by that long stretch
of window, studying that panoramic view of Sydney and its
harbor, his fingers loosely thatched at his back. Hearing her,
he turned, smiled and asked, "What can I do for you, Taryn?"

They took seats and suddenly Taryn couldn't find the right
words. While the son might be difficult, Guthrie had only
ever been supportive. But, whether he knew it or not, Guthrie
wasn't in charge here. If he were, she wouldn't need to jump
through Cole's endless hoops.

Taryn looked Guthrie in the eye. "I have to leave Hunter
Broadcasting."

His eyebrows snapped together. "Trouble with staff?"

"With management." She swallowed. "With Cole."

Guthrie studied her for a long queasy moment. Then he
pushed to his feet and, with a slight limp leftover from that
last assault, crossed to his desk.

"I'll have a word with him," he said, stabbing a button. "Stay put. We'll sort this out."

"That won't do any good." Having found her feet, too, she moved closer.

Guthrie had the receiver to his ear. "He has his own mind, but Cole listens when he knows I'm serious."

She was serious, too. "He doesn't believe in my project. I won't put my all into doing my best when Cole is doing everything in his power to cut me off at the knees."

Guthrie tried again. "My son's motives can seem harsh at times, but underneath all the woo-hah, he's only trying to take care of things."

"I believe you. I do. But it doesn't work in this situation." *Doesn't work for me.*

"Taryn, are you certain there's nothing more behind this? I was preoccupied that afternoon you both flew back from that survey, but…"

"Whatever happened between the two of us doesn't change his work attitude, then or now. I'm unhappy here." Not appreciated or respected. Cole had seduced her and, yes, she'd wanted to be seduced. He liked to be in charge, but in this final stretch, she was taking the reins.

"I wish it were different," she said, "but I don't ever see that changing. I'll leave Hunters today."

Despite today's heavy rain, Taryn had ventured out to collect some cat milk for Muffin and a bunch of roses from the corner store. She was arranging the flowers in her favorite vase, thinking about dicing some vitamin-rich food for the lactating mother, when a knock sounded on the door. She glanced up. She wasn't expecting her aunt. Her friends all had jobs during the week. Perhaps it was a delivery, only she wasn't expecting an order.

As she passed by Muffin and her litter, who were snuggled

and asleep in a large bed-box in the living room, Taryn had a flash but quickly pushed the thought aside. Guthrie had accepted her resignation and she didn't regret the move. The CEO slash Executive Producer of Hunter Broadcasting had never liked her show's premise. Had never approved of her being hired without being consulted first. No doubt, when all was said and done, Cole would be grateful to be rid of that headache. She was relieved to have gotten rid of hers. She was more calm. Her usual cool self again.

Then Taryn fanned back the door and her heart leaped so high, she had to swallow to push the lump halfway back down. Cole stood on her porch, looking unhappy about being drenched because of the rain and, she supposed, being here. Well, he could simply turn around, jump in his sports car and go back to the office. She certainly hadn't invited him.

Cole set his monster black umbrella down, tapping the steel spike against the timber floorboards twice—to help shake off the water or make certain she was paying attention?

"What's this about you quitting?"

She feigned surprise. "You're only finding out now? I gave Guthrie my resignation two days ago."

"Did you think to consult me?"

"Consider yourself consulted." Her hand still on the door-knob, she stepped back. "Hope I don't sound rude, but I was in the middle of something important."

"Finding another job?"

"Feeding the cat."

Her face and neck hot, she moved to shut the door. One big black leather lace-up slid out, acting as a stop.

He said, "You don't have to leave."

"It was a choice, Cole. I don't have to go. I *want* to go." She slanted her head. "Why are you here? You never liked my idea. You've done everything you could to have me land flat on my backside." *You've ignored me day after day.*

"I'll come in and we'll discuss it."

"I'm not letting you in." Not ever again. "Give yourself until next week. You'll have forgotten all about this by then."

Setting his umbrella up against the outside wall, he dragged a hand down his face as if this were all too hard.

"Look, I'm sorry I had to make all those cuts."

"That's fine. All forgotten. Now please leave."

He cast an exasperated look back at the rain teeming down beyond her porch and exhaled.

"I can't help the way things are," he said. "You knew what my life was from the start."

When heat from frustration and anger threatened to overtake her, she closed her eyes and shook her head. If he felt guilty about the way he'd treated her, that was his bad luck. She only wanted him to vanish so she could go back to arranging flowers and forgetting that man ever existed.

"Let me in. We'll talk—"

As he moved forward, finished with games, she moved, too. And shut the door.

But Cole's barrier now was a thousand times more effective than the one he'd used earlier. He reached out and, without apology, hooked one arm around her waist then hauled her close until her breasts were pressed against his shirt and she felt the booming of his heartbeat too near her own.

She opened her mouth to tear him down. After what he'd done, how dare he handle her this way. But in one blinding heartbeat, his mouth had taken hers. With one palm supporting the small of her back, he kissed her long and hard and shockingly deep. Flames swirled through her blood, instantly melting her bones, causing her to become a rag doll in his arms.

But when his palm scooped lower and she felt him harden against her belly, her strength returned. Making fists, she pushed with both barrels against his chest. She might as well have tried to shift a mountain. He was on a mission. And, damn the man, he was winning.

As his head angled more and the rough of his beard rubbed a path against her cheek, gradually, bit by bit, her fight drained away. He was so determined, so *hot,* what hope did she have? But she wasn't beaten so much as temporarily tamed. If he'd only quit with the caveman act—if he'd stop kissing her long enough for her to get her thoughts together—she'd tell him this kind of treatment wouldn't change her mind...

never...

ever.

By the time his mouth eventually left hers, the world was spinning twice as fast. Not only were her breasts aching, begging for his touch, the throbbing at the apex of her thighs told her that past indiscretions were forgiven. Forgotten.

As his lidded eyes searched hers, Taryn couldn't bring herself to move away. She could only remember the heaven she'd experienced on that island when he'd coaxed and adored her body, teasing her nipples, stroking her curves, loving her to the point where nothing and no one else had existed.

Then, over the pounding rain, she heard another noise. His cell phone sounding. Rather than take the call, he pressed soft moist kisses at one corner of her mouth while two hot fingers rode a drugging circle low on her back. But his cell beeped again, and again. Giddy with want, she felt his hesitation and forced herself to focus. The sound of the rain drifted back in. Behind her, Muffin mewed twice. When Cole carefully released her, the firm set of his jaw said he wasn't finished sorting this out but he also needed to read that text.

Crawling out from the fog, Taryn remembered Aunt Vi's advice. Keep the door open because once it's shut, there's no going back. But when Cole held up one finger to ask her to hold on a minute, Taryn touched her still-burning lips and a good measure of the stardust faded and fell away. She watched him check the cell, dial into his voice mail, then press a finger to an ear, shutting out a roll of thunder while he turned his back to concentrate fully on business.

Taryn blinked and thought, but when she'd made up her mind, she didn't bother to interrupt. She simply shut the door, bolted the lock and didn't open it again, no matter how hard he knocked.

With two chilled beers in hand, Cole sidled up to the chair next to Brandon's. Talking above the din of the local club, he handed one over and asked, "So, anything to report?"

"Judge and I have exhausted every lead from the guy who threw himself under that car. If he was connected to those earlier incidents and this latest one, whoever's pulling the strings has done a fine job of camouflaging their trail. I've assigned a private detail for Guthrie's and Tate's protection. I also suggested one for your stepmother, but she declined."

Cole nodded then downed a mouthful of beer.

Brandon went on to describe in detail the areas he would sweep next: again questioning neighbors and also employees, setting up surveillance cameras that reached outside of normal parameters. Cole absorbed it all at the same time as his brain switched to a different box in his head. Lately, more and more, he found his thoughts drifting there and wanting to stay.

He thought he knew himself pretty well and yet he was stumped figuring out why he'd bothered showing up on Taryn's doorstep the other day. She was right. Although he'd enjoyed their time together, he'd never gone for her show's concept. Obligation had caused him to okay it. Duty had compelled him to sabotage it. Guilt had sent him knocking on her door to… Apologize? Make amends?

Hell, he was a fool and he knew it.

"Any questions?"

Cole blinked back. "About what?"

"You didn't hear anything I just said, did you?"

"Of course I did. This is my father's life we're talking about."

"Which means whatever it is eating you must be important."

Cole swirled his bottle. No reason he couldn't share with his best friend. If anyone would understand, it was Brandon.

"It's a woman. Taryn Quinn."

Brandon sat slowly back. "You blew it?"

"I let it go."

He explained the story from go to woe.

"Holy crap," Brandon said when Cole had finished. "No wonder she's pissed at you. You sleep with her like there's no tomorrow then barely acknowledge her because of a contract. To add insult to injury, you set her show up for a slide into the mud."

Cole cocked an eyebrow, swallowed beer. "That's pretty much it."

"You might be company obsessed, but you've never treated a woman like that before."

Gazing at his beer, Cole confessed, "Taryn's special."

"God help the ones who aren't."

"I have too much on my plate, too much to keep in order, to have to worry about a relationship."

"Like Meredith said at the reunion, you can't run forever."

"I can try."

"You need to ease up on yourself. Quit taking all the responsibility for Hunters. That's too much for anyone."

"You say that as if I have a choice."

"Oh, it's a choice, all right. Don't try to say you don't *like* being 'the man.' At school, if you didn't get 'school captain this' or 'regional champion that,' you dragged your feet for days."

"It's healthy to be competitive. It's natural."

"Until it starts to screw with your life."

"Work *is* my life. With all my family tangled up in it, it has to be."

"I'll give you my take. I think this woman's in love with you. And my bet is you're in love with her, too."

After the moment of shock had passed, Cole barked out a laugh. "Remember who you're talking to? I've *never* been in love." He held up a warning finger. "Meredith McReedy doesn't count. Hell, I've only known Taryn a few weeks."

"Sometimes it happens that way. Fast and deadly, like a snake bite."

"I'm not looking to get hitched."

"All I've heard about this lady is how strong and beautiful and perfect she is. But you're not really seeing it."

Cole drained the rest of his beer then set the bottle down on the table hard. "I don't see any ring on your fat finger."

"Maybe that's because I haven't found the right person."

Cole's thoughts skidded to a halt as those words echoed through his brain.

Was that it? Why he couldn't for the life of him shake her from his mind. And the fascination was growing worse every day. Love? It was great his mother and father had shared it. He'd always thought that *someday* he'd settle down, too.

Question was, if Brandon was right—if this was it and she was the one—given that she hated his guts…

What did he do now?

The next day was Saturday. At home, Cole was about to settle down with that pain-in-the-butt Liam Finlay contract yet again. He got this was an important deal with a *huge* amount of money hanging in the balance, but he was beginning to wonder if Finlay was playing games, stretching this out, making him suffer because of his past unsatisfactory dealings with Guthrie. Still, what could he do? Hunter Broadcasting needed this deal. Therefore Cole couldn't slack off. Or, rather, not again.

His home phone extension rang. Business calls came through on his cell. Majority of his personal calls, too. Probably some poor sales sap doing another cold call. Or…

Tate knew that number. He'd learned it off by heart. When the phone stopped then rang again, a shiver ran through Cole's blood and he picked up. Sure enough, that familiar sweet voice filtered down the line.

"Daddy's not home and Mommy says I'm too noisy," Tate said. "She's tired."

"Where your dad?"

It was the weekend and Guthrie had been spending most of his time at home lately. Where else might he be?

"Don't know." Cole imagined Tate's little shoulders shrugging. "Can you come and play with me?"

Cole recalled that tome of a contract sitting on his home desk. There was loads of other work he could catch up on, too. But then he thought of Tate, what a bum deal he'd gotten having a mother like Eloise, feeling as if he had to get around like a mouse when he was a robust five-year-old boy who should be out kicking a ball, not stuck inside playing with electronic games.

Cole scrubbed his jaw, made his decision.

"Are you watching TV, kiddo?"

"Uh-huh. *SpongeBob*'s just started." Tate laughed. "He's funny."

"Grab a hat. By the time your show's over, I'll be there."

Cole arrived bang on time and let Creepy Nancy know that he was taking Tate out for the day. Eloise didn't bother to come downstairs to say have a nice time. Wearing a bright red tee, Tate sat like an angel in the passenger-side seat while they drove to a park, the one Cole and Taryn had paddled those boats in, not that he'd intentionally planned his and Tate's time together today that way.

Cole parked and grabbed the football he'd brought along. They filled their stomachs with hot dogs and Coke first. Watched the ducks on the lake while the food settled. When Cole couldn't control Tate's fidgets any longer, they kicked and tossed the pigskin back and forth. Cole showed his brother techniques required for a handball, a pass famous in Aussie Rules Football. Tate was doing well, stepping into the action, getting his punching fist almost right. They'd been out an hour. Given Tate wasn't nearly tired yet, Cole was thinking about teaching him a torpedo punt kick when his cell phone buzzed.

"This might be your dad," he called out to Tate, who was perhaps twenty yards away. But when Cole answered without checking the ID, the voice on the other end wasn't the one he'd expected.

"Liam Finlay here."

Cole's every sense zoomed in to concentrate fully on this conversation. "What's up?"

"My lawyers are with me. There's another conflict, page 103, item 24."

Cole's mind flew back, trying to identify the passage.

Liam went on to inform him that now the Players Association weren't happy with their cut, given the exclusivity clause relating to live games televised. Cole replied they'd been through this just last week. He'd already bumped his offer up. Liam said the dotted line was still blank. Now was the time to iron these creases out. Cole said he didn't want to increase his offer. He didn't believe anyone would. Liam said that was up to him. He could give him an answer now or come to the headquarters and talk it through.

A red soccer ball shot up and hit Cole in the shin, on the same leg that bore that old cubby house scar. In that instant, Cole remembered his brothers, Dex, Wynn, Tate—

His head snapped up. He looked left, right. Then the panic, cold and creeping, began to seep into his bones.

Cole spun a three-sixty. Looked down low. Up high. Behind benches and trees. His world shrank then funneled out fast. That tiny five-year-old was nowhere to be seen.

He held his stomach as it pitched and pitched again. He didn't often pray but now he looked to heaven and, as the strength seemed to drain from his body and his brain began to tingle, he vowed he would give anything—*everything*—if he was only overreacting and Tate would magically reappear.

On the ground, a toss away, Cole spotted his cell. His scattered thoughts pieced together. If Tate was indeed missing—and given recent history, that idea couldn't be discounted—there was a logical step he must take. Sending another swift glance around, he scooped up the phone where he'd dropped it then frowned at the noise coming out. Finlay was still bleating on the other end?

Cole didn't think twice.

He ended that call.

While he strode around, asking the ice-cream vendor then a man walking his dog if they'd seen a little boy in a bright red tee, he dialed the three-digit number to connect to emergency services. As he spoke to the representative on the other end of the line, sickening panic crushed in again, but this time it was peppered with resolve. If Tate was lost, if he'd been taken, he *would* find his brother. If he had to ask every person in this park, cut down every tree, check on each—

Cole's tracking gaze stopped and he froze.

In the parking lot some fifty yards away, a big black van was reversing out. The windows tinted an impenetrable shade, Cole couldn't make out the plates but, through the windshield, he saw the shaggy-haired driver wore dark glasses that covered half his face. His father had said one of the men who'd tried to abduct Tate had shaggy hair, big black glasses. Cole also knew those men had driven a black van.

Cole belted off. He heard Tate's name called out. Twice. Three times. Limbs pumping, he realized that voice was his own.

He slammed into the van before it could leave, thumped on the sliding door and didn't stop. The driver, an angry weedy man, soon appeared.

"What the hell you doing to my vehicle?"

Cole grabbed him by the scruff of his shirt and pulled him up so he could talk to his weasel face. "Open that door. Do it now. *Now!*"

If he was right, if Tate was in there, he'd deal with weasel-man after his brother was out in the light again. But when he flung aside the door, peered inside, the space was empty other than an old washing machine dumped in one corner.

Cole stormed over, his footfalls echoing through the metal cage. He flung open the lid of the machine and then—

His heart dropped to the ground. He staggered back. *Empty.*

Cole wandered out into the sunshine feeling sucker punched. He was the son who always had things under control. He couldn't stand to have surprises sneak up and bite him in the rear. He complained about Dex, about Wynn. Huffed at memories of a grown woman like Teagan having her own life. He'd thought he was so much better, responsible, worthier than any of them.

And here he'd failed in the most devastating way possible.

How would he ever tell his father?

People were milling around him. Cole knew he must look like a madman. On a different level, he understood he needed to get himself together. He couldn't help Tate if he disintegrated into a mute, dazed mess.

Cole cast another look around. Curious faces peered back. Old, young, different colors and heights and—

Cole's head went back. He rubbed his stinging eyes and then focused hard. A little boy in a red tee was walking toward him, a football slotted under his arm, looking for all the world as if nothing had happened, nothing was wrong.

A rush of adrenaline propelled him forward at the same time a cry broke from his lips. Then he was on his knees, hugging his brother so tight that, if it had been anyone else, Cole would have told them to back the hell off.

"Cole? You okay?"

Both cheeks damp, Cole forced himself to draw back. He inhaled through his nose, smelled that peanut-butter smell that was Tate and almost lost the battle not to hug him extra tight again. Was the nightmare truly over?

His throat and voice were thick as molasses. "I lost you for a minute, kiddo."

"I went to see the paddleboats." Tate turned and pointed to the lake and the oblivious couples peddling around. "Wanna try it with me? Looks really fun."

Chest aching, Cole laughed. He thought he might never stop. "It *is* fun. But give me a minute to catch my breath. I was worried."

"Coz you were alone?"

Suddenly exhausted, Cole grinned. "Uh-huh."

His small smile comforting, Tate brought his big brother close again. Patting his back, he said, "Don't worry, Cole. I'll never leave you. I love you. You know that."

"I do. I know." Cole's throat closed more. "But I'm just not around enough to hear it, am I?"

"You can come around more. Lots more. Daddy's not spending so much time at Hunners now. You shouldn't, too."

"You'd look after me?"

Giving a big sigh, Tate held his brother's hand. "And you can make all the noise you want."

That's when Cole's dam cracked wide-open and, in front of a crowd, on his knees in his little brother's arms, the CEO of Hunter Broadcasting surrendered and broke down.

Nineteen

"Thanks for coming with me, sweetie. I know you're busy polishing up your résumé."

Parking her car, Taryn glanced across at her aunt, who was sitting with her best handbag on her lap in the passenger seat.

"Spending the morning with you is tons more fun than sorting out job history and qualifications." *Everything that reminds me how I quit a job I thought I'd love. That I will never again see the man I stupidly fell in love with.*

Taryn switched off the ignition, opened her door and got her thoughts on track. "I'm just wondering when you got interested in nautical themes."

"It's time for a change. I'm over polished oak and tapestry upholstery. When I saw that flyer earlier this week, the stock and colors leaped out and grabbed me."

Taryn checked out the run of storefronts, which paralleled a busy marina. Shielding her eyes from the sun, she inhaled the scent drifting in on a gentle saltwater breeze. Sydney was interlaced with so many gorgeous bays, but this morning, all that clear blue water stretching out toward the "great beyond" made her heart squeeze tight in her chest.

Each day she told herself to focus on tomorrow not on yesterday. Having left Hunter Broadcasting for good, the world was her oyster. She could pursue her dream of producing; she still believed *Hot Spots* would appeal to a wide audience. On the other hand, just because she'd worked in TV all her adult life didn't mean she wouldn't enjoy a different vocation. A job that would suit her a hundred times more, maybe.

In a place that didn't remind her of Cole.

As they crossed the parking lot, Vi examined that flyer again.

"According to this, the store's way down the other end. I only want a quick look, first up. No deposits until I've chewed over all the options."

They were passing a café, its display cabinet filled with rows of scrumptious-looking cakes. Taryn wasn't surprised when Vi's step slowed and she asked, "Want to stop for a coffee before tackling the shops?"

"Sure. I missed my caffeine hit this morning."

"And that torte is calling me. I'll go on ahead for a preliminary once-over of that floor stock, you order us something nice and I'll meet you back here in ten."

"Take your time."

Taryn headed for an outside table while Vi, in her denim pedal pushers, hurried away.

After consulting the menu, Taryn passed on her orders to a waitress: latte and torte for Vi, fresh seasonal berries with a Muscat cream and a flat white for her. As she sat back and drank in a view crammed with boats, of course she thought of Cole again, and of how close she'd come to crumpling and inviting him back into her life.

Even now when she thought of the way he'd held her that rainy day at her door—the determination of that sizzling kiss—she suffered the same doubts. What if Vi were right in her advice? If she hadn't pushed Cole away that final time, perhaps that path might have somehow opened for them again.

At some stage Cole must realize he couldn't battle everyone's storms all of the time. Couldn't he cut himself some slack?

Didn't he want his own life?

But as Roman had said, a leopard doesn't change its spots. Cole blustered around, letting all and sundry know how indispensible he was. The kicker was, as far as she was concerned, he *was* special. Incredibly so.

No one else would ever make her pulse race the way he did. When they made love, every move was perfect. Every stroke sublime. This constant gnawing she felt must fade with time but, sitting here now, remembering their amazing night on that quiet moonlit beach, she simply couldn't see it.

Guess there was the possibility she would never fall in love again. Hadn't that been true for Vi? Some people's hearts could only be given away once. With only passersby and squawking gulls for company, Taryn couldn't help imagining going through life alone...with no partner, no children.

No family of her own.

Taryn gazed blindly at her sandals and forced herself to be positive. Common sense said she'd feel so much better in three months. Probably her old self again in six. If only she could stop thinking about how wonderful his mouth had felt grazing over hers. How alive she'd been when they'd laughed together and had opened up. It had felt so...*real*.

A flower blew under the next table—a large red bloom that looked much like the one she admired on that island. Angling, Taryn focused on the petals, the soft scarlet plains. Was everything today meant to remind her of Cole?

About to lean over and collect that flower, Taryn tipped back as cake and berries arrived. But when the plates slid onto the tabletop, she noticed the hands that served her were male. Not uncommon. Except she recognized those hands, the bronzed corded forearms. Oh, God, she knew that watch.

From head to toe she began to tingle. But it couldn't be.

This had to be her imagination running wild. Too much mulling had short-circuited her brain. But then that voice resonated out, drifting like a warm welcome veil over her senses and denial was simply no use.

He asked, "Is there anything else I can do for you?"

As time seemed to slow, Taryn clamped shut her eyes. In a heartbeat, the island and those bittersweet memories were back. A stinging pain penetrated her ribs. How would she ever move on if he kept showing up like this?

When she opened her eyes, that flower was sitting on the table in front of her as if placed there by magic. The impulse to either sweep the bloom aside or hug it close was overwhelming. Her fingers itched to stroke the velvet petals, place them against her cheek and wish them all back to that time.

Instead, she pushed her back into the chair and bit down as a man rounded the table. When their eyes met, Taryn's stomach looped and her head began to prickle with heat, just like the tips of her breasts. In casual white trousers, rubber-soled shoes and a black short-sleeved shirt, Cole gazed down at her as his dark hair rippled in a stiffening breeze.

"Nice view," he said.

She crossed her arms. Found her voice. "I'm waiting for my aunt. She'll be back any moment."

He nodded as if it were of little consequence. "You're looking well."

Taryn didn't feel well, but she noticed that his eyes were clearer than the last time they'd spoken...the last time they'd kissed. And the smudges underneath had faded, too. The strong angle of his jaw was clean-shaven and his expression reflected a completely relaxed air she hadn't seen since their time in the Pacific. Just how had he come to be here this morning, serving her cake when surely he had business to sort?

As if reading her mind, he explained, "I bought a boat."

She'd bite. "Plan to do some cruising around the harbor?"

"Actually, I was planning to set sail for far deeper waters."

"Such as?"

"Ulani."

Taryn blinked. Her *Hot Spots* destination?

"Why there?"

"I have a yearning to see if those turtles hatched and broke out on their own. Must be hell sharing that kind of space with so many siblings."

She looked at him sideways. *Really?* "What happened to all your responsibilities? Has your dad's assailant been caught?"

"Not yet, but I have every faith in Brandon."

"You're not worried something might happen while you're gone?"

"I'll worry. But no more than my brothers and sister. Teagan says she wants to come out."

Taryn started. "You talked to your *sister?*"

He grinned. "It was really good to catch up."

"And what's happening with Tate?"

"He's safe and well. All set to fly over to stay with Dex. I'll stay and keep him company until he does. He hasn't stopped talking about Disneyland."

"But what about your work commitments? The way you spoke, your L.A. section's a hairbreadth away from closing its doors?"

"Yes, well," Cole tugged his ear, "I may have overreacted. I was wrong not to give Dex more credit. Wynn, too. Truth is they're doing their best in hard times."

Taryn couldn't believe she was hearing it. "What brought you to that conclusion?"

"A great big dose of 'appreciate what you have because it could be gone tomorrow.'" He searched her eyes. "Taryn, I need to apologize. You were right. I'd already made my mind up about your show and nothing could change it. But I should have taken a chance. I should have taken a chance on, and believed in, a lot of things."

When his gaze intensified, Taryn's stomach muscles kicked. Pressing a palm against the spot, she switched the focus back onto Cole and this left-field decision to sail off into the sunset.

"And your football contract?" she asked. That was supposed to be critical.

"I finally told Finlay he could jam it," he said. "We signed the next day. We're set there for the next five years."

Taryn was slowly shaking her head. Cole was walking away, just like that? It couldn't be true.

"But you have the everyday running of the place. So many things to oversee—"

"Roman's been given a permanent promotion. He has enough experience in the role. I'm sure he'll do a great job as Hunter Broadcasting's CEO."

Now Taryn was holding her brow. She was happy for Roman but she felt positively dizzy at the news. "I can't believe that you're…that you'll—"

"Leave on a long overdue vacation." Looking so tall and commanding, he cocked his head toward the berths. "Come and take a look at my baby."

For a moment, Taryn felt lost for words. Someone was playing a joke. "You've been brainwashed. Or you fell and hit your head."

"I haven't thought this clearly in years. Come have a look. You don't have to go inside. Just admire her from the jetty."

Her gaze dropping to that flower, Taryn felt her thoughts begin to spin. Cole seemed like a different person. But that wasn't quite right. The man who was smiling and looking so laid-back before her now was the same man she'd fallen for on that island. The person she'd been so drawn to. Was drawn to still.

She schooled her face and her feelings. "Thanks for the invitation, but I'll stay where I am."

Where it's safe.

She collected her spoon and tasted her berries, but Cole didn't take the hint. He didn't leave.

On her second mouthful, he said, "Taryn, I won't blame you if you don't come, but I'm asking you…please. Two minutes, that's all."

Taryn set down her spoon. She knew she ought to stick with no. He couldn't make her go.

Still, what harm could come from taking a quick look?

Besides she was curious.

But when he offered his hand as she moved to stand, she merely got to her feet and walked with him down a pier until they reached a berth that housed an impressive powered catamaran. Her lines were all glossy white, the trimmings gleaming chrome. She was long and the towered flybridge seemed to touch the clouds. Taryn could imagine Cole standing up there, facing the wind and the sea, enjoying the sunshine and battling ocean storms. The name on the boat's side was written in bold blue letters—*BREAK OUT*.

"I thought it was appropriate," he said. Setting his fists low on his hips, he studied his boat from bow to stern. "So, what do you think?"

"She's beautiful."

"*You're* beautiful."

Taryn met his gaze. He was smiling softly, seductively, with that I'm-going-to-kiss-you-soon look sparkling in his eyes.

So not happening.

"I'm sure you'll enjoy many pleasant voyages together," she said, edging away, feeling a smoldering quiver build in her stomach. "I really should get back."

"Want to come along?"

Her mouth dropped open. Cole meant on his trip? He *had* gone mad.

"No," she told him. "I do not want to come along."

"I had the carpenters build a mini quarters for the cats inside."

She blinked several times, let out a short sharp laugh. "Cole, firstly I don't think you could take cats on a boat. They'd jump off and drown." Surely.

"Then I'll take them."

At the sound of that third voice, Taryn pivoted around.

Vi stood close enough to have heard the conversation. Her aunt shrugged. "You know how I love cats."

Taryn could only stare. Was this some kind of conspiracy?

When she got her breath back, Taryn asked her aunt, "You knew about this, didn't you? You purposely led me down here so that Cole could run into me."

Cole intervened. "I contacted Vi and asked for her help."

Taryn couldn't remember an occasion when Vi had lied to her before. Honesty had always been the best policy in their house. But on a deeper level, looking into Vi's apologetic yet hopeful face now, she believed her aunt was sincerely doing what she thought was best. She didn't want her niece to throw away what might prove to be her only chance of real happiness. But Taryn had already made up her own mind about that, and she intended to stick with it.

She headed off. "I'm done."

But before she reached Vi, she ran into a man—a delivery guy by his uniform.

The man asked, "Are you Taryn Quinn?"

She frowned then nodded. "Who wants to know?"

He simply handed over his delivery—an enormous, fragrant bouquet. And not just any bunch of flowers. They were big bright scarlet blooms, like the one that boy had given her on the island, like the one she'd found under that café table moments ago.

A jet of emotion filled her chest, her throat. Then her eyes were stinging with the threat of real tears. This was not fair. Was Cole this desperate to get her back into his bed? To snag a sleeping buddy on his Pacific voyage? She wasn't that easily bought, no matter what he might think.

She was ready to swing around and hand these flowers back to the person who had obviously arranged for them to arrive, when another deliveryman strode up, and another. Both were holding similar bouquets. And the men and flowers kept coming. When she couldn't possibly hold any more, Cole directed the men to arrange them on the deck of his boat.

Gobsmacked, Taryn inspected the end of the pier. There must have been ten florist vans lined up. Deliverymen were still traveling down the pier, conveying her very own private world full of petals.

While she choked back emotion, Cole took the bouquets from her arms and handed them over to be laid out with the rest. Then he found her hands and, lifting one at a time, tenderly kissed the back of each wrist.

"Other than my mother, I've never so much as given a daisy to a woman before."

A hot tear slipped from the corner of her eye. She remembered. "You give jewelry."

"I want to give you a piece now."

She stepped back. "But I don't want anything from you."

He closed the space separating them. "This isn't a trick, Taryn. There's no need to be afraid." He smiled. "I'm not."

From a back trouser pocket, he withdrew a small velvet-covered box. He opened the lid then angled the box around for her to see what lay inside.

A large diamond sat at the heart of the ring's setting. Two

Ceylon sapphires, the color of their island's bay, hugged the main stone on either side.

"You're that one special person I've been waiting for," Cole told her. "The woman I want to have as my wife. To bear my children." He grinned. "When we're not sailing the high seas, that is."

"B-but your work," she stammered. "Your family commitments." She knew what he'd told her, but she couldn't believe it.

"From this day forward, I intend to take on board and cherish life's biggest responsibility. To love and care for the woman I adore." One hand took hers. "Taryn, I can't sleep, can't eat, can barely think when you're not around. I need you in my life. As my partner. As my friend."

He slipped the ring on her finger then set that palm against the sandpaper rough of his jaw as his eyes searched hers and he waited for her response.

Taryn was drawn by the steam of his body, the determination of his will. Then she glanced back. Vi's gaze was upon her, her hands and bag clasped at her breasts while she obviously wished only the best for the grown woman who would always be her child. Behind her aunt, all those deliverymen were waiting, leaning on rails or against their vans. And a curious crowd had gathered, too, shoppers she'd watched pass by, the waitress who had taken her order. All were hanging out for her reply. Yes. Or no. Taryn swallowed deeply then slowly turned back.

She thought of her torment these past days then she thought of how bright and clear the future suddenly looked. As Cole's brow pinched a little and more of his heart shone in his eyes, she took a breath and confessed....

"I'm in love with you." Her sigh came out half sob, half laugh of sheer joy. "I can't believe this is happening."

He didn't waste a second. In a heartbeat, she was wrapped

up in his arms and he was telling her, "This is only the start. Our beginning." He pulled away enough to see her face, the tears of joy running down her cheeks. "I was thinking maybe a ceremony at sea. But it's your call." He grinned. "You're in charge."

"With a honeymoon on *Break Out?*" Salty trails curled under her chin. Given all those flowers, she warned him, "I don't think there's any room on that boat left for us."

"I gave the florist explicit instructions to leave the bunk free."

"That's where we sleep?"

His mouth brushed and tickled her ear. "Besides other things."

Cole swept her up into his arms. With the marina filled with vocal cheering well-wishers, he carried her aboard. Standing on the deck with her still in the cradle of his arms, he told her, "There's a tradition for future newlyweds."

Running an adoring hand over the square of his jaw, she murmured, "Give me a hint."

"I'll give you more than that."

With a wicked smile, he lifted her higher and then his mouth claimed hers. She was aware of hoots and cheers going up from the pier. But she was more aware of the promise of the future in her fiancé's kiss. Their life together would never be dull. Could never come second. All their tomorrows would only ever feel warm and safe and loved.

Epilogue

Later in Los Angeles...

Dex Hunter pushed aside his cheeseburger and fries to check out an alert on his phone. When he opened the text, he nearly choked on his food. Receiving a message to say expect a wedding invitation wasn't anything out of the ordinary, and he could've understood if this was news from his *younger* brother. Wynn had been seeing someone steadily for a couple of years now.

But if a woman had convinced *Cole,* the eldest, to walk down the aisle, she must be a special lady, indeed. Dex looked forward to meeting—

He flicked to the top of the message for a name.

Taryn Quinn.

And it looked as if the *youngest* of the Hunter clan—five-year-old Tate—was about to pay that visit, which meant finally making good on that promise to do Disneyland. Tate was expected in L.A. a week from today.

Dex's face fell and he spluttered on a mouthful of coffee.

One week!

He brought up his calendar, starting this Sunday. A premiere he couldn't miss, a couple of charity events, meetings with financial directors... *Oh, joy.* He'd just need to rearrange some things, was all. *And* hire a babysitter for Tate, Dex thought as he lifted his cup again. Didn't matter what she looked like, as long as she was maternal and tuned in to his little brother's whirlwind personality. Hell, she could be old and toothless for all he cared. Hairy and bowlegged, made no difference to him.

A thump on his back sent Dex's espresso splashing over the tablecloth. The dropped cup clattered into its saucer as Dex shook out his scorched wet hand and a concerned voice came from behind.

"Oh, no. Oh, God, are you all right?"

A waitress with luxurious hair, the color of polished mahogany and set in pigtails, skirted around to stand before him. Wearing white flats and a uniform that offered little justice to her obvious curves, she dragged a cloth from her apron's pouch and dabbed at his hand and his sleeve.

"Please don't tell anyone," she whispered, darting a nervous glance around. Her eyes were green, bright and fringed with naturally thick lashes. "I've already dropped a plate of tacos today."

Dex didn't fall back on his obvious and, in his case, warranted, line too often. However, now he couldn't help but ask.

"Have you ever considered a career in movies?"

She kept dabbing. "I couldn't act my way out of a paper bag. I didn't come to L.A. for that. Although I have put my name down at a couple of agencies."

Dex cocked a brow. So she was new to town? When she straightened, he took in her height, those cheekbones—that aura—and surmised. "Modeling."

"*Nannying.* I want to work with kids." She flashed a big white smile. "Children like me. I like them, too."

Smiling back, already making plans, Dex pulled out a business card. Someone was watching over him today. Clearly this union was meant to be.

* * * * *

THE GIRL HE NEVER NOTICED

LINDSAY ARMSTRONG

Lindsay Armstrong was born in South Africa, but now lives in Australia with her New Zealand-born husband and their five children. They have lived in nearly every state of Australia, and have tried their hand at some unusual—for them—occupations, such as farming and horse-training—all grist to the mill for a writer! Lindsay started writing romances when their youngest child began school and she was left feeling at a loose end. She is still doing it and loving it.

CHAPTER ONE

'MISS MONTROSE,' Cameron Hillier said, 'where the hell is my date?'

Liz Montrose raised her eyebrows. 'I have no idea, Mr Hillier. How should I?'

'Because it's your job—you're my diary secretary, aren't you?'

Liz stared at Cam Hillier, as he was known, with her nostrils slightly pinched. She didn't know him well. She'd only been in this position for a week and a half, and only because an agency had supplied her to fill the gap created by his regular diary secretary's illness. But even that short time had been long enough to discover that he could be difficult, demanding and arrogant.

What was she supposed to do about the apparent non-appearance of his date, though?

She looked around a little wildly. They were in the outer office—his secretary Molly Swanson's domain—and Molly, heaven bless her, Liz thought, was holding a phone receiver out to her and making gestures behind his back.

'Uh, I'll just check,' Liz said to her boss.

He shrugged and walked back into his office.

'What's her name?' Liz whispered to Molly as she took the phone.

'Portia Pengelly.'

Liz grimaced, then frowned. 'Not the model and TV star?'

Molly nodded at the same time as someone answered the phone.

'Uh—Miss Pengelly?' Liz said down the line and, on receiving confirmation, went on, 'Miss Pengelly, I'm calling on behalf of Mr Hillier, Mr Cameron Hillier…'

Two minutes later she handed the receiver back to Molly, her face a study of someone caught between laughter and disaster.

'What?' Molly queried.

'She'd rather go out with a two-timing snake! How can I tell him that?'

Cam Hillier's office was minimalist: a thick green carpet, ivory slatted blinds at the windows, a broad oak desk with a green leather chair behind it and two smaller ones in front of it. Liz thought it was uncluttered and restful, although the art on the walls reflected two of the very different and not necessarily restful enterprises that had made him a multi-millionaire—horses and a fishing fleet.

There were silver-framed paintings of stallions, mares and foals. There were seascapes with trawlers in them—trawlers with their nets out and flocks of seagulls around them.

Liz had studied these pictures in her boss's absence and

discovered a curious and common theme: Shakespeare. The three stallions portrayed were called Hamlet, Prospero and Othello. The trawlers were named *Miss Miranda*, *Juliet's Joy*, *As You Like It*, *Cordelia's Catch* and so on.

She would, she felt, like to know where the Shakespeare theme came from. But the thing was you did not take Cam Hillier lightly or engage in idle chit-chat with him. She'd been made aware of this before she'd laid eyes on him. The employment agency she worked for had warned her that he was an extremely high-powered businessman and not easy to handle, so if she had any reservations about how to cope with a man like that she should not even consider the position. They'd also warned her that 'diary secretary' could cover a multitude of sins.

But she'd coped with a variety of high-powered businessmen before; in fact she seemed to have a gift for it. Though, it crossed her mind that she'd never had to tell any of those men that the woman in their life would rather consort with a snake...

And there was another difference with Cam Hillier. He was young—early thirties at the most—he was extremely fit, and he was—well, she'd heard it said by his female accountant: 'In an indefinable way he's as sexy as hell.'

What was so indefinable about it? she'd wondered at the time. He was tall, lean and rangy, with broad shoulders. He had thick dark hair, and deep, brooding blue eyes in not a precisely handsome face, true, but those eyes alone could send a shiver down your spine as they summed you up.

In fact, to her annoyance, Liz had to admit that she was not immune to Cam Hillier's powerfully masculine presence. Nor could she persuade her mind to discard the cameo-like memory that had brought this home to her…

It was a hot Sydney day as they walked side by side down a crowded pavement to a meeting. They were walking because it was only two blocks from his offices to their destination. The traffic was roaring past, the tall buildings of the CBD were creating a canyon-like effect and the sidewalk was crowded when Liz caught her heel on an uneven paver.

She staggered, and would have fallen, but he grabbed her and held her with his hands on her shoulders until she regained her balance.

'Th-thanks,' she stammered.

'OK?' He looked down at her with an eyebrow lifted.

'Fine,' she lied. Because she was anything but fine. Out of nowhere she was deeply affected by the feel of his hands on her, deeply affected by his closeness, by how tall he was, how wide his shoulders were, how thick his dark hair was.

Above all, she was stunned by the unfurling sensations that ran through her body under the impact of being so close to Cam Hillier.

She did have the presence of mind to lower her lashes swiftly so he couldn't read her eyes; she would have been mortified if she'd blushed or given any other in-dication of her disarray.

He dropped his hands and they walked on.

Since that day Liz had been particularly careful in her boss's presence not to trip or do anything that could trigger those sensations again. If Cam Hillier had noticed anything he'd given no sign of it—which, of course, had been helpful. Not so helpful was the tiny voice from somewhere inside her that didn't appreciate her having the status of a robot where he was concerned.

She'd been shocked when that thought had surfaced. She'd told herself she'd have hated him if he'd acted in any way outside the employer/employee range; she couldn't believe she was even thinking it!

And finally she'd filed the incident away under the label of 'momentary aberration', even though she couldn't quite command herself to banish it entirely.

But somewhat to her surprise—considering the conflicting emotions she was subject to, considering the fact that although Cam Hillier could be a maddening boss he had a crooked grin that was quite a revelation—she'd managed to cope with the job with her usual savoir-faire for the most part.

He wasn't smiling now as he looked up from the papers he was studying and raised an eyebrow at her.

'Miss Pengelly...' Liz began, and swallowed. *Miss Pengelly regrets?* In all honesty she couldn't say that. *Miss Pengelly sends her regards?* Portia certainly hadn't done that! 'Uh—she's not coming. Miss Pengelly isn't,' she added, in case there was any misunderstanding.

Cam Hillier twitched his eyebrows together and swore under his breath. 'Just like that?' he shot at Liz.

'Er—more or less.' Liz felt her cheeks warm a little.

Cam studied her keenly, then that crooked grin played across his lips and was gone almost before it had begun. 'I see,' he said gravely. 'I'm sorry if you were embarrassed, but the thing is—you'll have to come in her place.'

'I certainly will not!' It was out before Liz could stop herself.

'Why not? It's only a cocktail party.'

Liz breathed unevenly. 'Precisely. Why can't you go on your own?'

'I don't like going to parties on my own. I tend to get mobbed. Portia,' he said with some exasperation, 'was brilliant at deflecting unwanted advances. They took one look at her and I guess—' he shrugged '—felt the competition was just too great.'

Liz blinked. 'Is that all she was…?' She tailed off and gestured, as if to say *strike that…* 'Look here, Mr Hillier,' she said instead, 'if your diary secretary—the one I'm replacing—were here, you wouldn't be able to take *him* along to ward off the…unwanted advances.'

'True,' he agreed. 'But Roger would have been able to find me someone.'

Liz compressed her lips as she thought with distaste, *rent-an-escort*? 'Well, I can't do that either,' she said tartly, and was struck by another line of defence. 'And I certainly don't have Portia Pengelly's…er…powers of repelling boarders.'

Cam Hillier got up and strolled round his desk. 'Oh, I

don't know about that.' He sat on the corner of the desk and studied her—particularly her scraped-back hair and her horn-rimmed glasses. 'You're very fair, aren't you?' he murmured.

'What's that got to do with it?' Liz enquired tartly, and added as she looked down at her elegant but essentially plain ivory linen dress, 'Anyway, I'm not dressed for a party!'

He shrugged. 'You'll do. In fact, those light blue eyes, that fair hair and the severe outfit give you quite an "Ice Queen" aura. Just as effective in its own way as Portia, I'd say.'

Liz felt herself literally swell with anger, and had to take some deep breaths. But almost immediately her desire to slap his face and walk out was tempered by the thought that she was to be very well paid for the month she'd agreed to work for him. And also tempered by the thought that walking out—not to mention striking him—would place a question mark if not a huge black mark against her record with the employment agency...

He watched and waited attentively.

She muttered something under her breath and said audibly, but coolly, 'I'll come. But purely on an employer/employee basis—and I'll need a few minutes to freshen up.'

What she saw in his eyes then—a wicked little glint of amusement—did not improve her mood, but he stood up and said only, 'Thank you, Miss Montrose. I appreciate this gesture. I'll meet you in the foyer in fifteen minutes.'

* * *

Liz washed her face and hands in the staff bathroom—a symphony of mottled black marble and wide, well-lit mirrors. She was still simmering with annoyance, and not only that. She was seriously offended, she discovered—and dying to bite back!

She stared at herself in the mirror. It was on purpose that she dressed formally but plainly for work, but it was not how she always dressed. She happened to have a mother who was a brilliant dressmaker. And the little ivory dress she wore happened to have a silk jacket that went with it. Moreover, she'd picked up the jacket from the dry cleaner's during her lunch hour, and it had been hanging since then, in its plastic shroud, on the back of her office door. It was now hanging on the back of the bathroom door.

She stared at it, then lifted it down, pulled off the plastic and slipped it on. It had wide shoulders, a round neck, a narrow waist and flared slightly over her hips. She pushed the long fitted sleeves up, as the fashion of the moment dictated, but the impact of it came as much from the material as the style—a shadowy leopard skin pattern in blue, black and silver. It was unusual and stunning.

She smiled faintly at the difference it made to her—a bit like Joseph's amazing coloured coat, she thought wryly. Because her image now was much closer to that of a cocktail-party-goer rather than an office girl. Well, almost, she temporised, and slipped the jacket off—only to hesitate for another moment as she hung it up carefully.

Then she made up her mind.

She reached up and pulled the pins out of hair. It tumbled to just above her shoulders in a fair, blunt-cut curtain. She took off her glasses and reached into her purse for her contact lenses. She applied them delicately from the pad of her forefinger. Then she got out her little make-up purse and inspected the contents—she only used the minimum during the day, so she didn't have a lot to work with, but there was eyeshadow and mascara and some lip gloss.

She went to work on her eyes and again, as she stood back to study her image, the difference was quite startling. She sprayed on some perfume, brushed her hair, then tossed her head to give it a slightly tousled look and slipped the jacket on again, doing it up with its concealed hooks and eyes. Her shoes, fortunately, were pewter-grey suede and went with the jacket perfectly.

She stood back one last time and was pleased with what she saw. But she stopped and frowned suddenly.

Did she look like an ice queen? If only he knew...

Cam Hillier was in the foyer talking to Molly when Liz walked in. He had his back to her, but he saw Molly's eyes widen as she looked past him and he swung round.

For a moment he didn't recognise Liz. Then she saw him do a double-take and he whistled softly. It was something she would have found extremely satisfying except for one thing. He also allowed his blue gaze to drift down her body, to linger on her legs, and then he looked back into her eyes in the way that men let women know they were being summed up as bed partners.

To her annoyance that pointed, slow drift of assessment up and down her body reignited those sensations she'd experienced when she'd tripped on the pavement: accelerated breathing, a rush through her senses, an awareness of how tall and beautifully made he was.

Only thanks to her lingering resentment did she manage not to blush. She even tilted her chin at him instead.

'I see,' he said gravely. He shoved his hands in his trouser pockets before adding equally gravely, although she didn't for a moment imagine it was genuine. 'I'm sorry if I offended you, Miss Montrose. I was not to know you could look like this—stunning, in other words. Nor was I to know that you could conjure *haute couture* clothes out of thin air.' He studied her jacket for a moment, then looked into her eyes. 'OK. Let's go.'

They reached the cocktail party venue in record time. This was partly due to the power and manoeuvrability of his car, a graphite-blue Aston Martin, and partly due to his skill as a driver and his knowledge of the back streets so he'd been able to avoid the after-work Sydney traffic.

Liz had refused to clutch the armrest, or demonstrate any form of nerves, but she did say when they pulled up and he killed the motor, 'I think you missed your calling, Mr Hillier. You should be driving Formula One cars.'

'I did. In my misspent youth,' he replied easily. 'It got a bit boring.'

'Well, I couldn't call that drive boring. But you can't park here, can you?'

He'd pulled up in the driveway of the house next door to what she could see was a mansion behind a high wall that was lit up like a birthday cake and obviously the party venue.

'It's not a problem,' he murmured.

'But what if the owner wants to get in or out?' she queried.

'The owner is out,' he replied.

Liz shrugged and surveyed the scene again.

She knew they were in Bellevue Hill, one of Sydney's classiest suburbs, and she knew she was in for a classy event. None of it appealed to her in the slightest.

'All right.' She reached for the door handle. 'Shall we get this over and done with?'

'Just a moment,' Cam Hillier said dryly. 'I've acknowledged that I may have offended you—I've apologised. And you, with this stunning metamorphosis, have clearly had the last laugh. Is there any reason, therefore, for you to look so disapproving? Like a minder—or a governess.'

Liz flushed faintly and was struck speechless.

'What exactly do you disapprove of?' he queried.

Liz found her tongue. 'If you really want to know—'

'I do,' he broke in to assure her.

She opened her mouth, then bit her lip. 'Nothing. It's not my place to approve or otherwise. There.' She widened her eyes, straightened her spine and squared her shoulders, slipping her hair delicately behind her ears. Lastly she did some facial gymnastics, and then turned to him. 'How's that?'

Cam Hillier stared at her expressionlessly for a long moment and a curious thing happened. In the close confines of the car it wasn't disapproval that threaded through the air between them, but an awareness of each other.

Liz found herself conscious again of the width of his shoulders beneath the jacket of his charcoal suit, worn with a green shirt and a darker green tie. She was aware of the little lines beside his mouth and that clever, brooding dark blue gaze.

Not only that, but she seemed to be more sensitive to textures—such as the beautiful quality fabric of his suit and the rich leather of the car's upholstery.

And she was very aware of the way he was watching her… A physical summing up again, that brought her out in little goosebumps—because they were so close it was impossible, she suddenly found, not to imagine his arms around her, his hand in her hair, his mouth on hers.

She turned away abruptly.

He said nothing but opened his door. Liz did the same and got out without his assistance.

Although Liz had been fully aware she was in for a classy event, what she saw as she stepped through the front door of the Bellevue Hill home almost took her breath away. A broad stone-flagged passage led to the first of three descending terraces and a magnificent view of Sydney Harbour in the last of the daylight. Flaming braziers lit the terraces, pottery urns were laden with exotic flowering shrubs, and on the third and lowest terrace an aquamarine pool appeared to flow over the edge.

There were a lot of guests already assembled—an animated throng—the women making a bouquet of colours as well. In a corner of the middle terrace an energetic band was making African music with a mesmerising rhythm and the soft but fascinating throb of drums.

A dinner-suited waiter wearing white gloves was at their side immediately, offering champagne.

Liz was about to decline, but Cam simply put a glass in her hand. No sooner had he done so than their hostess descended on them.

She was a tall, striking woman, wearing a rose-pink caftan and a quantity of gold and diamond jewellery. Her silver hair was streaked with pink.

'My dear Cam,' she enthused as she came up to them, 'I thought you weren't coming!' She turned to Liz and her eyebrows shot up. 'But who is this?'

'This, Narelle, is Liz Montrose. Liz, may I introduce you to Narelle Hastings?'

Liz extended her hand and murmured, 'How do you do?'

'Very well, my dear, very well,' Narelle Hastings replied as she summed Liz up speedily and expertly, taking in not only her fair looks but her stylish outfit. 'So you've supplanted Portia?'

'Not at all,' Cam Hillier responded. 'Portia has had second thoughts about me, and since Liz is replacing

Roger who is off sick at the moment, I press-ganged her into coming rather than being partnerless. That's all.'

'Darling,' Narelle said fondly to him, 'call it what you will, but don't expect me to believe it gospel and verse.' She turned to Liz. 'You're far too lovely to be just a secretary, my dear, and in his own way Cam's not bad either. It is what makes the world go round. But anyway—' she turned back to Cam '—how's Archie?'

'A nervous wreck. Wenonah's puppies are due any day.'

Narelle Hastings chuckled. 'Give him my love. Oh! Excuse me! Some more latecomers. And don't forget,' she said to Liz, 'life wasn't meant to be all work and no play, so enjoy yourself with Cam while you can!' And she wandered off.

'Don't tell me how to look,' Liz warned him.

'Wouldn't dream of it. Uh—Narelle can be a little eccentric.'

'Even so, I knew this wasn't a good idea,' she added darkly.

He studied her, then shrugged. 'I don't see it as a matter of great importance.'

Liz glanced sideways at him, as if to say *you wouldn't*! But that was a mistake, because she was suddenly conscious again of just how dangerously attractive Cameron Hillier was. Tall and dark, with that fine-tuned physique, he effortlessly drew the eyes of many of the women around them. Was it so far off the mark to imagine him being mobbed? No, that was ridiculous...

'It's not your reputation that's at stake,' she retorted finally. 'That was probably...' She paused.

'Ruined years ago?' he suggested.

Liz grimaced and looked away, thinking again, be-latedly, of black marks on her record. *Did not actually come to blows with temporary employer, but did insult him by suggesting he had a questionable reputation...*

'This place is quite amazing,' she said, switching to a conversational tone, and she took a sip of champagne. 'Is the party in aid of any special event?'

Cam Hillier raised his eyebrows in some surprise at this change of pace on her part, then looked amused. 'Uh—probably not. Narelle never needs an excuse to throw a party. She's a pillar of the social scene.'

'How...interesting,' Liz said politely.

'You don't agree with holding a party just for the sake of it?' he queried.

'Did I say that? If you can afford it—' She broke off and shrugged.

'You didn't say it, but I got the feeling you were think-ing it. By the way, she happens to be my great-aunt.'

Liz looked rueful and took another sip of champagne. 'Thanks.'

He looked a question at her.

'For telling me that. I...sometimes I have a problem with...with speaking my mind,' she admitted. 'But I would never say anything less than complimentary about someone's great-aunt.'

This time Cam Hillier did more than flash that crooked grin; he laughed.

'What's funny about that?'

'I'm not sure,' he returned, still looking amused. 'Confirmation of what I suspected? That you can be outspoken to a fault. Or the fact that you regard great-aunts as somehow sacred?'

Liz grimaced. 'I guess it did sound a bit odd, but you know what I mean. In general I don't like to get personal.'

He looked sceptical, but chose not to explain why. He said, 'Narelle can look after herself better than most. But how come you appear to handle a position that requires great diplomacy with ease when you have a problem with outspokenness?'

'Yes, well, it's been a bit of a mystery to me at times,' she conceded. 'Although I have been told it can be quite refreshing. But of course I do try to rein it in.'

'Not with me, though?' he suggested.

Liz studied her glass and took another sip. 'To be honest, Mr Hillier, I've never before been told to pass on the message that my employer's…um…date would rather consort with a two-timing snake than go to a party with him.'

Cam Hillier whistled softly. 'She must have been steamed up about something!'

'Yes—*you*. Then there was your own assertion that to go to a party alone would leave you open to being mobbed by women—I had a bit of difficulty with that—'

'It's my money,' he broke in.

'Uh-huh? Like your great-aunt, I won't take that one as gospel and verse either,' Liz said with considerable irony, and flinched as a flashlight went off. 'Add to that the distinct possibility that we could be now tagged as an item, and throw into the mix that death-defying drive through the back streets of Sydney, is it any wonder I'm having trouble holding my tongue?'

'Probably not,' he conceded. 'Would you like to leave the job forthwith?'

'Ah,' Liz said, and studied her glass, a little surprised to see that it was half empty, before raising her blue eyes to his. 'Actually, no. I need the money. So if we could just get back to office hours, and the more usual kind of insanity that goes with a diary secretary's position, I'd appreciate it.'

He considered for a moment. 'How old are you, and how did you get this job—with the agency, I mean?'

'I'm twenty-four, and I have a degree in Business Management. I topped the class, which you may find hard to believe—but it's true.'

He narrowed his gaze. 'I don't. I realised you were as bright as a tack from the way you handled yourself in the first few hours of our relationship—our *working* relationship,' he said as she looked set to take issue with him.

'Oh?' Liz looked surprised. 'How so?'

'Remember the Fortune proposal—the seafood marketing one? I virtually tossed it in your lap the first day, because it was incomplete, and told you to fix it?'

Liz nodded. 'I do,' she said dryly.

He smiled. 'Throwing you in at the deep end and not what you were employed for anyway? Possibly. But I saw you study it, and then I happened to hear you on the phone to Fortune with your summation of it and what needed to be done to fix it. I was impressed.'

Liz took another sip of champagne. 'Well, thanks.'

'And Molly tells me you're a bit of an IT whiz.'

'Not really—but I do like computers and software,' she responded.

'It does lead me to wonder why you're temping rather than carving out a career for yourself,' he said meditatively.

Liz looked around.

A few couples had started to dance, and she was suddenly consumed by a desire to be free to do what she liked—which at this moment was to surrender herself to the African beat, the call of the drums and the wild. To be free of problems... To have a partner to dance with, to talk to, to share things with. Someone to help her lighten the load she was carrying.

Someone to help her live a bit. It was so long since she'd danced—so long since she'd let her hair down, so to speak—she'd forgotten what it was like...

As if drawn by a magnet her gaze came back to her escort, to find him looking down at her with a faint frown in his eyes and also an unspoken question. For one amazed moment she thought he was going to ask her to dance with him. That was followed by another amazed moment as she pictured herself moving into his arms and letting her body sway to the music.

Had he guessed which way her thoughts were heading? And if so, how? she wondered. Had there been a link forged between them now that he'd noticed her as a woman and not a robot—a mental link as well as a physical one?

She looked away as a tremor of alarm ran through her. She didn't want to be linked to a man, did she? She didn't want to go through that again. She was mad to have allowed Cam Hillier to taunt her into showing him she wasn't just a stick of office furniture...

She said the first thing that came to mind to break any mental link... 'Who's Archie?'

'My nephew.'

'He sounds like an animal lover.'

'He is.'

Liz waited for a moment, but it became obvious Cam Hillier was not prepared to be more forthcoming on the subject of his nephew.

Liz lifted her shoulders and looked out over the crowd.

Then her gaze sharpened, and widened, as she focused on a tall figure across the terrace. A man—a man who had once meant the world to her.

She turned away abruptly and handed her glass to her boss. 'Forgive me,' she said hurriedly, 'but I need—I need to find the powder room.' And she turned on her heel and walked inside.

How she came to get lost in Narelle Hastings' mansion she was never quite sure. She did find a powder room, and spent a useless ten minutes trying to calm herself down, but for the rest of it her inner turmoil must have been so great she'd been unable to think straight.

She came out of the powder room determined to make a discreet exit from the house, the party, Cam Hillier, the lot—only to see Narelle farewelling several guests. She did a quick about-turn and went through several doorways to find herself in the kitchen. Fortunately it was empty of staff, but she knew that could only be a very temporary state of affairs.

Never mind, she told herself. She'd leave by the back door!

The back door at first yielded a promising prospect— a service courtyard, a high wall with a gate in it.

Excellent! Except when she got to it, it was to find the gate locked.

She drew a frustrated, trembling breath as it occurred to her how acutely embarrassing this could turn out to be. How on earth would she explain it to Cameron Hillier—not to mention his great-aunt, whose house she appeared to be wandering through at will?

She gazed at the back door, and as she did so she heard voices coming from within. She doubted she had the nerve to brave the kitchen again. She turned away and studied her options. No good trying to get over the wall that fronted the street—she'd be bound to bump into someone. But the house next door, also behind the wall, was the one whose driveway Cam had parked in—the one whose owner was out, according to him. He must know them and know they were away to make that assertion, she reasoned. It certainly made that wall a better bet.

She dredged her memory and recalled that the driveway had gates that could possibly be locked too—and this adjacent wall was inside those gates. But hang on! Further along the pavement, hadn't there been a pedestrian gate? No—just a gateway. Yes! So all she had to do was climb over the wall...How the hell was she going to do that, though?

She tensed as the back door opened, and slipped into some shadows as a kitchen hand emerged and deposited a load of garbage into a green wheelie bin and slammed it shut. He didn't see her and went back inside, closing the door, but his use of the wheelie bin gave her an idea. She could push it against the wall, hoist herself onto it and slip over it to the house next door.

As with just about everything that had happened to her on this never-ending day, it wasn't a perfect plan.

Firstly, just as she was about to emerge from the shadows and move the bin to the wall, more kitchen hands emerged with loads of garbage. This led her to reconsider things.

What if she did manage to get over the wall and someone came out to find the bin in a different position? But she couldn't skulk around this service courtyard for much longer. A glance at her watch told her she'd already been there for twenty minutes.

She was biting her lip and clenching her fists in a bid to keep calm, almost certain she would have to go through the kitchen again, when something decided the matter for her.

She heard a male voice from the kitchen, calling out that he was locking the back door. She even heard the key turn.

She closed her eyes briefly, then sprinted to the bin, shoved it up against the wall, took her shoes off and threw them over. She looped her purse over her shoulder and, hitching up her dress, climbed onto the bin. Going over from Narelle's side was easy, thanks to the height of the wheelie bin. Getting down the other side was not so easy. She had to hang onto the coping and try to guess what the shortfall was.

It was only about a foot, but she lost her balance as she dropped to the ground, and fell over. She was picking herself up and examining her torn tights and a graze on her knee when the driveway gates, with the sound of a car motor behind them, began to open inwards.

She straightened up and stared with fatal fascination at a pair of headlights as a long, low, sleek car nosed through the gates and stopped abreast of her.

The driver's window was on her side, and it lowered soundlessly. She bent her head, and as her gaze clashed with the man behind the wheel things clicked into place for her…

'Oh, I see,' she said bitterly. '*You* own this place. That's how you knew it was safe to park in the driveway!'

'Got it in two, Liz,' Cam Hillier agreed from inside his graphite-blue Aston Martin. 'But what the devil *you* think you're doing is a mystery to me.'

CHAPTER TWO

'WHO IS HE?'

The question hung in the air as Liz looked around.

She was ensconced on a comfortable cinnamon velvet-covered settee. Across a broad wooden coffee table with a priceless-looking jade bonsai tree on it was a fireplace flanked by wooden-framed French doors. Above the fireplace hung what she suspected was an original Heidelberg School painting, a lovely impressionist pastoral scene that was unmistakably Australian. Tom Roberts? she wondered.

There were two matching armchairs, and some lovely pieces of furniture scattered on the polished wooden floors. The windows looked out over a floodlit scene—an elegant pool with a fountain, tall cypress pines, and beyond the lights of Sydney Harbour.

Not as spectacular as his great-aunt's residence, Cam Hillier's house was nevertheless stylish and very expensive—worth how many millions Liz couldn't even begin to think.

Its owner was seated in an armchair across from her.

He'd shrugged off his jacket, pulled off his tie and

opened the top buttons of his shirt. He'd also poured them each a brandy.

As for Liz, she'd cleaned herself up as best she could in a guest bathroom. She'd removed her torn tights, bathed her knee and applied a plaster to it. She'd washed her face and hands but not reapplied any make-up. It had hardly seemed appropriate when she had a rip in her dress, a streak of dirt on her jacket and was shoeless.

She'd been unable to find one shoe in the driveway— until they'd discovered it in a tub of water the gardener was apparently soaking a root-bound plant in.

So far, the only explanation she'd offered was that she'd seen someone at the party she'd had no desire to meet, so she'd tried to make a quick getaway that had gone horribly wrong.

She took a sip of her brandy, and felt a little better as its warmth slipped down.

She eyed Cameron Hillier and had to acknowledge that he was equally impressive lying back in an arm-chair, in his shirtsleeves and with his thick dark hair ruffled, as he'd been at his great-aunt's party. On top of that those fascinating, brooding blue eyes appeared to be looking right through her…

'He?' she answered at last. 'What makes you think—?'

'Come on, Liz,' he said roughly. 'If this story is true at all, I can't imagine a woman provoking that kind of reaction! Anyway, I saw you fix your gaze on some guy, then go quite pale and still before you…decamped. Causing *me* no little discomfort, incidentally,' he added dryly.

Her eyes widened. 'Did you get mobbed?'

He looked daggers at her for a moment. 'No. But I did get Narelle to search the powder rooms when I realised how long you'd been gone. She was,' he said bitterly, 'riveted.'

'And then?'

He shrugged. 'There seemed to be no sign of you, so we finally assumed you'd called a taxi and left.'

'Meanwhile I was lurking around in the service courtyard,' Liz said with a sigh. 'All right, it *was* a he. We...we were an item once, but it didn't work out and I just—I just didn't want to have to—to face him,' she said rather jaggedly.

Cam Hillier frowned. 'Fair enough,' he said slowly. 'But why not tell me and simply walk out through the front door?'

Liz bit her lip and took another sip of brandy. 'I got a bit of a shock—I felt a little overwrought,' she confessed.

'A little?' he marvelled. 'I would say more like hysterical—and that doesn't make sense. You laid yourself open to Narelle suspecting you of casing the joint. So could I, come to that. One or the other or both of us might have called the police. Plus,' he added pithily, 'I wouldn't have taken you for a hysterical type.'

Ah, but you don't know the circumstances, Liz thought, and took another fortifying sip of brandy.

'Affairs of the heart are...can be different,' she said quietly. 'You can be the essence of calm at other times, but—' She stopped and gestured, but she didn't look at him because she sounded lame even to her own ears.

He surprised her. 'So,' he said slowly, and with a considering look, 'not such an Ice Queen after all, Ms Montrose?'

Liz didn't reply.

He frowned. 'I've just remembered something. You're a single mother, aren't you?'

Liz looked up at that, her eyes suddenly as cool as ice.

He waved an impatient hand. 'I'm not being critical, but it's just occurred to me that's why you're temping.'

'Yes,' she said, and relaxed a little.

'Tell me about it.'

She cradled her glass in both hands for a moment, and, as always happened to her when she thought of the miracle in her life, some warmth flowed through her. 'She's nearly four, her name's Scout, and she's a—a living doll.' She couldn't help the smile in her voice.

'Who looks after her when you're working?'

'My mother. We live together. My father's dead.'

'It works well?' He raised an eyebrow.

'It works well,' Liz agreed. 'Scout loves my mother, and Mum...' She looked rueful. 'Well, she sometimes needs looking after, too. She can be a touch eccentric.' She sobered. 'It can be a bit of a battle at times, but we get by.'

'And Scout's father?'

Liz was jolted out of her warm place. Her expression tightened as she swallowed and took hold of herself. 'Mr Hillier, that's really none of your business.'

He studied her thoughtfully, thinking that the change

in her was quite remarkable. Obviously Scout's father was a sore point.

He grimaced, but said, 'Miss Montrose, the way you were climbing over my wall, the way you apparently roamed around my great-aunt's house *is* my business. There are a lot of valuables in both.' His blue eyes were narrowed and sharp as he stared at her. 'And I don't think I'm getting a good enough explanation for it.'

'I—I don't understand what you mean. I had no idea this was your house. I had no idea I'd be going to your great-aunt's house this evening,' she said with growing passion. 'Only an idiot would on the spur of the moment decide to rob you both!'

'Or a single mother in financial difficulties?'

He waited, then said when she didn't seem able to frame a response, 'A single mother with a very expensive taste in clothes, by the look of it.'

Liz closed her eyes and berated herself inwardly for having been such a fool. 'They aren't expensive. My mother makes them. All right!' she said suddenly, and tossed her head as she saw the disbelief in his eyes. 'It was Scout's father I saw at the party. That's what threw me into such a state. I haven't spoken to him or laid eyes on him for years.'

'Have you tried to?'

She shook her head. 'I knew it was well and truly finished between us. I came to see he'd been on the rebound and—' her voice shook a little '—it was only a fling for him. I had no choice but to—' She broke off to smile bleakly. 'No choice but take it on the chin and retire. The only thing was—'

'You didn't know you were pregnant?' Cam Hillier said with some cynicism.

She ignored the cynicism. 'Oh, yes, I did.' She took a sip of brandy and prayed she wouldn't cry. She sniffed and patted her face to deflect any tears.

'You didn't tell him?' Cam queried with a frown.

'I did tell him. He said the only thing to do in the circumstances was have an abortion. He—he did offer to help me through it, but he also revealed that he was not only making a fresh start with this other woman, he was moving interstate and taking up a new position. He—I got the impression he even thought I may have tried to trap him into marriage. So...' She shrugged. 'I refused. I said, Don't worry! I can cope! And I walked out. That was the last time I saw him.'

Cam Hillier was silent.

'Although,' Liz said, 'I did go away for a month, and then I changed campuses and became an external student, so I have no idea if he tried to contact me again before he moved.'

'He still doesn't know you had the baby?'

'No.'

'Do you want to keep it from him for ever?'

'Yes!' Liz moved restlessly and stared down at her glass, then put it on the coffee table. 'When Scout was born all I could think was that she was *mine*. He'd never even wanted her to see the light of day, so why should he share her?' She gestured. 'I still feel that way, but...' She paused painfully. 'One day I'm going to have to think of it from Scout's point of view. When she's older and can understand things, she may want to know about her father.'

'But you don't want him to know in the meantime? That's why you took such astonishingly evasive measures tonight.' Cam Hillier rested his jaw on his fist. 'Do you think he'd react any differently?'

Liz heaved a sigh. 'I don't know, but it's hard to imagine anyone resisting Scout. She—she looks like him sometimes. And I did read an article about him fairly recently. He's beginning to make a name for himself in his chosen field. He and his wife have been married for four years. They have no children. There may be a dozen reasons for that, and I may be paranoid, but I can't help it—I'm scared stiff they'll somehow lure Scout away from me.'

'Liz.' He sat forward. 'You're her mother. They can't—unless you can't provide for her.'

'Maybe not legally, but there could be other ways. As she grows up she might find she prefers what they have to offer. They have a settled home. He has growing prestige. Whereas I am...I'm just getting by.' The raw, stark emotion was plain to see in her eyes.

'Have you got over him, Liz?'

A complete silence blanketed the room until the hoot from a harbour ferry broke it.

'I haven't forgotten or forgiven.' She stared out at the pool. 'Not that I was—not that I *wasn't* incredibly naïve and foolish. I haven't forgiven myself for that.'

'You should. These things happen. Not always with such consequences, but life has its lessons along the way.'

And, to her surprise, there was something like understanding in his eyes.

She moistened her lips and took several breaths to steady herself, because his lack of judgement of her was nearly her undoing. She gazed down at her bare feet and fought to control her tears.

Then she bit her lip as where she was, who *he* was, and how she'd poured all her troubles out to a virtual stranger with the added complication of him being her employer hit her.

Her eyes dilated and she took a ragged breath and straightened. 'I'm sorry,' she said huskily. 'If you want to sack me I'd understand, but do you believe me now?'

'Yes.' Cam Hillier didn't hesitate. 'Uh—no, I don't want to sack you. But I'll take you home now.' He drained the last of his brandy and stood up.

'Oh, I can get a taxi,' she assured him hastily, and followed suit.

He raised an eyebrow. 'With only one shoe? Your other one is ruined.'

'I—'

'Don't argue,' he recommended. He shrugged into his jacket, but didn't bother with his tie. Then he glanced at his watch. At the same time his mobile rang. He got it out of his pocket and looked at the screen.

'Ah, Portia,' he murmured. 'Wanting to berate me or make disparaging comparisons, do you think?' He clicked the phone off and shoved it into his pocket.

Liz took a guilty breath. 'I shouldn't have told you that. And—and she might want to explain. I think you should talk to her.'

He looked down at her, his deep blue eyes alight with mocking amusement. 'Your concern for my love-life is touching, Miss Montrose, but Portia and I have come to the end of the road. After you.' He gestured for her to precede him.

Liz clicked her tongue exasperatedly and tried to walk out as regally as was possible with no shoes on.

Cam Hillier dropped her off at her apartment building, and waited and watched as she crossed the pavement towards the entrance.

She'd insisted on putting on both shoes, although one still squelched a bit. He drummed his fingers on the steering wheel as it occurred to him that her long legs were just as good as Portia's. In fact, he thought, her figure might not be as voluptuous as Portia's but she was quite tall, with straight shoulders, a long, narrow waist. And the whole was slim and elegant—how had he not noticed it before?

Because he'd been put off by her glasses, her scraped-back hair, an unspoken but slightly militant air—or all three?

He grimaced, because he couldn't doubt now that under that composed, touch-me-not Ice Queen there existed real heartbreak. He'd seen that kind of heart-break before. The other thing he couldn't doubt was that she'd sparked his interest. Was it the challenge, though? Of breaking through the ice until he created a warm, loving woman? Was it because he sensed a response in her whether she liked it or not?

Whatever, he reflected, in a little over two weeks she was destined to walk out of his life. Unless…

He didn't articulate the thought as he finally drove off.

The next morning Liz placed a boiled egg with a face drawn on it in front of her daughter. Scout clapped her hands delightedly.

At the same time Mary Montrose said, 'You must have been late last night, Liz? I didn't even hear you come in.'

Yes, thank heavens, Liz thought. She'd been curiously unwilling to share the events of the evening with her mother—not to mention to expose the mess she'd been in, ripped, torn and with one soaked shoe.

Now, though, she gave Mary a much abridged version of the evening.

Mary sat up excitedly. 'I once designed an outfit for Narelle Hastings. Did you say she's Cameron Hillier's great-aunt?'

'So he said.' Liz smiled inwardly as she decapitated Scout's egg and spread the contents on toast soldiers. Her mother was an avid follower of the social scene.

'Let's see…' Mary meditated for a moment. 'I believe Narelle was his mother's aunt—that *would* make her his great-aunt. Well! There you go! Of course there've been a couple of tragedies for the Hastings/Hillier clan.'

Liz wiped some egg from Scout's little face and dropped a kiss on her nose. 'Good girl, you made short work of that! Like what?' she asked her mother.

'Cameron's parents were killed in an aircraft accident,

and his sister in an avalanche of all things. What's he like?'

Liz hesitated as she realised she wasn't at all sure what to make of Cameron Hillier. 'He's OK,' she said slowly, and looked at her watch. 'I'll have to make tracks shortly. So! What have you two girls got on today?'

'Koalas,' Scout said. She was as fair as Liz, with round blue eyes. Her hair was a cloud of curls and she glowed with health.

Liz pretended surprise. 'You're going to buy a koala?'

'No, Mummy,' Scout corrected lovingly. 'We're going to see them at the zoo! Aren't we, Nanna?'

'As well as all sorts of other animals, sweetheart,' her grandmother confirmed fondly. 'I'm looking forward to it myself!'

Liz took a breath as she thought of the sunny day outside, the ferry-ride across the harbour to Taronga Zoo, and how she'd love to be going with them. She bit her lip, then glanced gratefully at her mother. 'There are times when I don't know how to thank you,' she murmured.

'You don't have to,' Mary answered. 'You know that.'

Liz blinked, then got up to get ready for work.

The flat she and Scout shared with her mother was in an inner Sydney suburb. It was comfortable—her mother had seen to that—but the neighbourhood couldn't be described as classy...something Mary often lamented. But it was handy for the suburb of Paddington, for Oxford

Street and its trendy shopping and vibrant cafés. There were also markets, and history that included the Victoria Army Barracks and fine old terrace houses. If you were a sports fan, the iconic Sydney Cricket Ground was handy, as well as Centennial and Moore Parks. They often took picnics to the park.

The flat had three bedrooms and a small study. They'd converted the study into a bedroom for Scout, and the third bedroom into a workroom for Mary. It resembled an Aladdin's cave, Liz sometimes thought. There were racks of clothes in a mouth-watering selection of colours and fabrics. There was a rainbow selection of buttons, beads, sequins, the feathers Mary fashioned into fascinators, ribbons and motifs.

Mary had a small band of customers she 'created' for, as she preferred to put it. Gone were the heady days after Liz's father's death, when Mary had followed a life-long dream and invested in her own boutique. It hadn't prospered—not because the clothes weren't exquisite, but because, as her father had known, Mary had no business sense at all. Not only hadn't it prospered, it had all but destroyed Mary's resources.

But the two people Mary Montrose loved creating for above all were her daughter and granddaughter.

So it was that, although Liz operated on a fairly tight budget, no one would have guessed it from her clothes. And she went to work the day after the distressing scenario that had played out between two harbourside mansions looking the essence of chic, having decided it was a bit foolish to play down the originality of her clothes now.

She wore slim black pants to hide the graze on her knee, and a black and white blouson top with three-quarter sleeves, belted at the waist. Her shoes were black patent wedges with high cork soles—shoes she adored—and she wore a black and white, silver and bead Pandora-style bracelet.

As she finished dressing, she went to pin back her hair—then thought better of that too. There seemed to be no point now. She also put in her contact lenses.

But as she rode the bus to work she was thinking not of how she looked but other things. Cam Hillier in particular.

She'd tossed and turned quite a lot last night, as her overburdened mind had replayed the whole dismal event several times.

She had to acknowledge that he'd been... He hadn't been critical, had he? She couldn't deny she'd got herself into a mess—not only last night, of course, but in her life, and Scout's—which could easily invite criticism...

What did he really think? she wondered, and immediately wondered why it should concern her. After her disastrous liaison with Scout's father she'd not only been too preoccupied with her first priority—Scout, and building a life for both of them—but she'd had no interest in men. Once bitten twice shy, had been her motto. She'd even perfected a technique that had become, without her realising it until yesterday, she thought ironically, patently successful—Ice Queen armour.

It had all taken its toll, however, despite her joy in Scout. Not only in the battle to keep afloat economically, but also with her guilt at having to rely on her mother for help, therefore restricting her mother's life too. She had the feeling that she was growing old before her time, that she would never be able to let her hair down and enjoy herself in mixed company because of the cloud of bitterness that lay on her soul towards men.

So why was she now thinking about a man as she hadn't for years?

Why was she now suddenly physically vulnerable to a man she didn't really approve of, to make matters worse?

She paused her thoughts as a mental image of Cam Hillier came to her, and she had to acknowledge on a suddenly indrawn breath that he fascinated her in a curious sort of love/hate way—although of course it couldn't be love… But just when she wanted to hurl a brick at him for his sheer bloody-minded arrogance he did something, as he had last night, that changed a person's opinion of him. He hadn't been judgemental. He'd even made it possible for her spill her heart to him.

It was more too, she reflected. Not only his compelling looks and physique, but a vigorous mind that worked at the speed of lightning, an intellect you longed to have the freedom to match. Something about him that made you feel alive even if you were furious.

She gazed unseeingly out of the window and thought, what did it matter? She'd shortly be gone from his life. And even if she stayed within his orbit there was always the thorny question of Portia Pengelly—or if not Portia whoever her replacement would be.

She smiled a wintry little smile and shrugged, with not the slightest inkling of what awaited her shortly.

Ten minutes later she buzzed for a lift on the ground floor of the tower that contained the offices of the Hillier Corporation. One came almost immediately from the basement car park, and she stepped into it to find herself alone with her boss as the doors closed smoothly.

'Miss Montrose,' he said.

'Mr Hillier,' she responded.

He looked her up and down, taking in her stylish outfit, the sheen of her hair and her glossy mouth. And his lips quirked as he said, 'Hard to connect you with the wall-climbing cat burglar of last night.'

Liz directed him a tart little look before lowering her carefully darkened lashes, and said nothing.

'So I take it you're quite restored, Liz?'

'Yes,' she said coolly, and wasn't going to elaborate, but then thought better of it. 'Thank you. You were...' She couldn't think of the right word. 'Thank you.'

'That's all right.'

The lift slid to a stop and the doors opened, revealing the Hillier foyer, but for some strange reason neither of them made a move immediately. Not so strange, though, Liz thought suddenly. In the sense that it had happened to her before, in his car last evening, when she'd been trapped in a bubble of acute awareness of Cameron Hillier.

His suit was different today—slate-grey, worn with a pale blue shirt and a navy and silver tie—but it was just as beautifully tailored and moulded his broad shoulders just as effectively. There was a narrow black leather belt around his lean waist, and his black shoes shone and looked to be handmade.

But it wasn't a case of clothes making the man, Liz thought. It was the other way around. Add to that the tingling fresh aura of a man who'd showered and shaved recently, the comb lines in his thick hair, those intriguing blue eyes and his long-fingered hands... Her eyes widened as she realised even his hands impressed her. All of him stirred her senses in a way that made her long to have some physical contact with him—a touch, a mingling of their breath as they kissed...

Then their gazes lifted to each other's and she could see a nerve flickering in his jaw—a nerve that told her he was battling a similar compulsion. She'd known from the way he'd looked at her last night that he was no longer seeing her as a stick of furniture, but to think that he wanted her as she seemed to want him was electrifying.

It was as the lift doors started to close that they came out of their long moment of immobility. He pressed a button and the doors reversed their motion. He gestured for her to step out ahead of him.

She did so with a murmured thank-you, and headed for her small office. They both greeted Molly Swanson.

'Uh—give me ten minutes, then bring the diary in, Liz. And coffee, please, Molly.' He strode through into his office.

'How did it go? Last night?' Molly enquired. 'By the way, I've already had three calls from Miss Pengelly!'

'Oh, dear.' Liz grimaced. 'I'm afraid it might be over.'

'Probably just as well,' Molly said with a wise little look in her eyes. 'What he needs is a proper wife, not these film star types—I never thought she could act her way out of a paper bag, anyway!'

Liz blinked, but fortunately Molly was diverted by the discreet buzzing of her phone.

Eight minutes later, Liz gathered herself in readiness to present herself to her employer with the diary.

She'd poured herself a cup of cold water from the cooler, but instead of drinking it she'd dipped her hanky into it and splashed her wrists and patted her forehead.

I must be mad, she'd thought. *He* must be mad even to contemplate getting involved with me. Or is all he has in mind a replacement for Portia? Someone to deflect all the women he attracts—and I refuse to believe it's only because of his money.

Things were back to thoroughly businesslike as they went through his engagements for the day one by one, and he sipped strong black aromatic coffee from a Lalique glass in a silver holder.

'All right,' he said. 'Have you got the briefs for the Fortune conference?'

She nodded.

'I'll want you there. There's quite a bit of paper-work to be passed around and collected, et cetera. And I'll need you to drive me to and pick me up from the

Bromwich lunch. There's no damn parking to be found for miles.'

'Fine,' she murmured, then hesitated.

He looked up. 'A problem?'

'You want me to drive your car?'

'Why not?'

'To be honest—' Liz bit her lip '—I'd be petrified of putting a scratch on it.'

He sat back. 'Hadn't thought of that. So would I—to be honest.' He looked wry. 'Uh—get a car from the car pool.'

Liz relaxed. 'I think that's a much better idea.'

His lips twitched, and she thought he was going to say something humorous, but the moment passed and he looked at her in the completely deadpan way he had that had a built-in annoyance factor for anyone on the receiving end of it.

Liz was not immune to the annoyance as she found herself reduced to the status of a slightly troublesome employee. Then, if anything, she got more annoyed— but with herself. She had been distinctly frosty in the lift before they'd found themselves trapped in that curious moment of physical awareness, hadn't she?

She had told herself they would both be mad even to contemplate anything like a relationship—and she believed that. But some little part of her was obviously hankering to be treated... How? As a friend?

If I were out on a beach I'd believe I'd got a touch of the sun, she thought grimly. This man doesn't work that way, and there's no reason why he should.

She cleared her throat and said politely, 'What time would you like to leave?'

'Twelve-thirty.' He turned away.

The Fortune conference was scheduled for nine-thirty, and Liz and Molly worked together to prepare the conference room.

It got underway on time and went relatively smoothly. Liz did her bit, distributing and retrieving documents, providing water and coffee—and coping with the over-effusive thanks she got from the short, dumpy, middle-aged vice-President of the Fortune Seafood Group.

She only smiled coolly in return, but something—some prickling of her nervous system—caused her to look in Cam Hillier's direction, to find his gaze on her, steadfast and disapproving. Until a faint tide of colour rose in her cheeks, and he looked away at last.

Surely he couldn't think she was courting masculine approval or something stupid like that?

On the other hand, she reminded herself, she might find it stupid, but it could be an occupational hazard of being a single mother—men wondering if you were promiscuous...

It became further apparent that her boss was not in a good mood when she drove him to the Bromwich lunch in a company Mercedes. The reasons for this were two-fold.

'Hmm...' he said. 'You're a very cautious driver, Ms Montrose.'

Liz looked left and right and left again, and drove

across an intersection. 'It's not my car, your life is in my hands, Mr Hillier, and I have a certain respect for my own.'

'Undue caution can be its own hazard,' he commented. 'Roger is a better driver.'

Liz could feel her temper rising, but she held on to it. She said nothing.

He went on, 'Come to think of it, I don't have to worry about Roger receiving indecent proposals from visiting old-enough-to-know-better seafood purveyors either. Uh—you could have driven a bus through that gap, Liz.'

She lost it without any outward sign. She nosed the Mercedes carefully into the kerb, reversed it to a better angle, then switched off and handed him the keys.

She didn't shout, she didn't bang anything, but she did say, 'If you want to get to the Bromwich lunch in one piece, *you* drive. And don't ever ask me to drive you anywhere again. Furthermore, I can handle indecent proposals—any kind of proposals!—so you don't have a thing to worry about. As for the aspersions you cast on my driving, I happen to think *you're* a menace on the road.'

'Liz—'

But she ignored him as she opened her door and stepped out of the car.

CHAPTER THREE

TWO MINUTES LATER he was in the driver's seat, she was in the passenger seat, and she had no idea if he was fighting mad or laughing at her—although she suspected the latter.

'Right,' he said as he eased the car back into the traffic. 'Get onto Bromwich and tell them I'm not coming.'

Liz gasped. 'Why not? You can't—'

'I can. I never did want to go to their damn lunch anyway.'

'But you agreed!' she reminded him.

'All the same, they'll be fine without me. It is a lunch for two hundred people. I could quite easily have got lost in the crowd,' he said broodingly.

Liz thought, with irony, that it was highly unlikely, but she said tautly, 'And what will I tell them?'

'Tell them…' he paused, 'I've had a row with my diary secretary, during which she not only threatened to take me apart but I got told I was a *menace*, and that I'm feeling somewhat diminished and unable to contemplate socialising on a large scale as a result.'

Liz looked at him with extreme frustration. 'Apart

from anything else, that has *got* to be so untrue!' she said through her teeth.

He grimaced. 'You could also tell them,' he added, 'that since it's a nice day I've decided the beach is a better place for lunch. We'll go and have some fish and chips. Like fish and chips?'

She lifted her hands in a gesture of despair. 'I suppose nothing will persuade you this is a very bad idea?'

'Nothing,' he agreed, then grinned that lightning crooked grin. 'Maybe you should have thought of that before you had a hissy fit and handed over the car.'

'You were being enough to—you were impossible!'

'Mmm...' He said it meditatively, and with a faint frown. 'I seem to be slightly off-key today. Do you have the same problem? After what happened in the lift?' he added softly.

Liz studied the road ahead, and wondered what would happen if she admitted to him that she had no idea how to cope with the attraction that had sprung up between them. Yes, it might have happened to her for the first time in a long time, but did that mean she wasn't scared stiff of it? Of course she was. She knew it. She clenched her hands briefly in her lap. Besides, what could come of it?

An affair at the most, she reasoned. Cameron Hillier was not going to marry a single mother who sometimes struggled to pay her bills. Marry! Dear heaven, what was she thinking? Even with the best intentions and no impediments they had to be a long way from *that*.

And, having thought of her bills, she couldn't stop

herself from thinking of them again—that and the fact that she had no other job lined up yet.

Just get yourself out of this without losing your job if you can, Liz, she recommended to herself.

'I apologise for losing my temper,' she said at last. 'I—I'm probably not a very good driver. I haven't had a lot of experience, but I was doing my best.' She looked ruefully heavenwards.

Cam Hillier cast her a swift glance that was laced with mockery. 'That's all?'

She swallowed, fully understanding the mockery—she was dodging the issue of what had happened between them in the lift and he knew it.

She twisted her hands together, but said quite evenly, 'I'm afraid so.'

There was silence in the car until he said, 'That has a ring of finality to it. In other words we're never destined to be more than we are, Ms Montrose?'

Liz pushed her hair behind her ears. 'We're not,' she agreed barely audibly. 'Oh.' She reached for her purse—anything to break the tension of the moment. 'I'll ring Bromwich—although I may not get anyone at this late stage.'

'So be it,' he said, and she knew he wasn't talking about the lunch he was going to miss.

She hesitated, but decided she might as well cement her stance on the matter—in a manner of speaking... 'You don't have to take me to lunch, Mr Hillier. I'd quite understand.'

'Not at all, Ms Montrose,' he drawled. 'For one thing, I'm starving. And, since Roger and I often have lunch when we're on the road together, you don't need to view it with any suspicion.'

'Suspicion?'

This time he looked at her with satirical amusement glinting in his blue eyes. 'Suspicion that I might try to chat you up or—break down your icy ramparts.'

Liz knew—she could feel what was happening to her—and this time nothing in the world could have stopped her from blushing brightly. She took refuge from the embarrassment of it by contacting the Bromwich lunch venue.

The restaurant he took her to had an open area on a boardwalk above the beach. They found a table shaded by a canvas umbrella, ordered, and looked out over the sparkling waters of Sydney Harbour. They could see the Opera House and the Harbour Bridge.

And he was as good as his word. He didn't try to chat her up or break her down, but somehow made it possible for them to be companionable as they ate their fish and chips.

He was so different, Liz thought, from how he could be at other times. Not only had he left the arrogant multi-millionaire of the office behind, but also the moody persona he'd been in the car. He even looked younger, and she found herself catching her breath once or twice—once when an errant breeze lifted his dark hair, and once when he played absently with the salt cellar in his long fingers.

'Well…' He consulted his watch finally. 'Let's get back to work.'

'Thanks for that.' She stood up.

He followed suit, and for one brief moment they looked into each other's eyes—a searching, perfectly sober exchange—before they both looked away again, and started to walk to the car.

Liz knew she was to suffer the consequences of that pleasant lunch in the form of a yet another restless night.

Not so Scout, though. She was still bubbling with excitement at what she'd seen at the zoo, and she fell asleep almost as soon as her head touched the pillow.

Liz dropped a kiss on her curls and tiptoed out. But when she went to bed she tossed and turned for ages as flashes of what had been an extraordinary day came back to haunt her.

Such as when that light breeze had ruffled his hair and it had affected her so curiously—given her goose-bumps, to be precise. Such as when he'd played absently with the salt cellar and she'd suffered a mental flash of having his hands on her naked body.

I've got to deal with this, she told herself, going hot and cold again. I don't think I can get out of this job without affecting my rating with the agency, and without having to take less money—which would play havoc with my budget. I've got to think of Scout and what's best for her. A brief affair with a man who, if you go on his present track record, doesn't appear to be able to commit? Not to Portia Pengelly, anyway, and that means he was using her—he more or less admitted that.

I've got to remember what it felt like to find out

I'd been used, and to be told an abortion was the only course of action in the circumstances...

She stared into the darkness, then closed her eyes on the tears that came.

She resumed her monologue when her tears subsided. So, Liz, even if you are no longer the Ice Queen you were, you've got to get through this. Don't let another man bring you down.

She was helped by the fact that Cam Hillier was away for the next couple of days, but when he came back she still had two weeks left to work for him.

He seemed to be in a different mood, though. Less abrasive—with her, anyway—and there were no *double entendres*, no signs that they'd ever stood in a lift absolutely mesmerised by each other.

Had he made it up with Portia? she wondered. Did that account for his better mood? Or had he found a replacement for Portia?

Whatever it was, Liz relaxed a bit, and she did not take exception when they got caught in a traffic jam on the way to a meeting, and to kill the time he asked her about her earlier life.

It was a dull day and had rained overnight. There was an accident up ahead and the traffic was hopelessly gridlocked. There was a helicopter flying overhead.

'It must be a serious accident,' Liz murmured. 'We could be late.'

He switched off the motor and shrugged. 'Nothing we can do,' he said, with uncharacteristic patience. 'Tell me how you grew up?'

Liz pleated the skirt of the red dress she wore with a light black jacket, and thought, Why not?

'Uh...let's see,' she said reflectively. 'My father was a teacher and very academic, whilst my mother...' She paused, because sometimes it was hard to sum up her mother. 'She's this intensely creative person—*so* good with her hands but not terribly practical.'

She smiled. 'You wouldn't have thought it could work between them, but it did. She could always liven him up, and he could always deflect her from her madder schemes. As a teacher, of course, he was really keen on education, and he coached me a lot. That's how I came to go to a private school on a scholarship. I also went to uni on scholarships. He—' She stopped.

'Go on,' Cam murmured after a few moments.

She cast him an oblique little glance, wondering at the same time why he was interested in this—why she was even humouring him...

'I used to think I took more after him—we read to-gether and studied things together—but lately some of Mum has started to shine through. She's an inspired cook, and I'm interested in it now—although I'll never be the seamstress she is.'

'So how did you cope with getting your degree and being a single mum?' he queried. 'Simple arithmetic suggests Scout must have intervened somewhere along the line.'

Liz looked at his hands on the steering wheel and switched her gaze away immediately. Was this just plain curiosity, or...? But was there any reason not to give him the bare bones of it anyway?

'It was hard work, but in some ways it kept me sane. It was a goal I could still achieve, I guess—although I had to work part-time.' She paused and looked rueful. 'At all sorts of crazy jobs at the same time.'

'Such as?'

'I was a receptionist in a tattoo parlour once.' She looked nostalgic for a moment. 'I actually got a bunch of flowers from a group of bikies I came to know there when Scout was born. Uh—I worked in a bottle shop, a supermarket. I did some nanny work, house cleaning.'

She stopped and gestured. 'My father had died by then—he never knew Scout—but I was determined to get my degree because I knew how disappointed he would have been if I hadn't.'

'How did you get into this kind of work?'

Liz smiled. 'I had a lucky break. One of my lecturers had contacts with the agency, and a good idea of the kind of replacement staff they supplied. She schooled me on most aspects of a diary secretary's duties, my mother set me up with a suitable wardrobe, and *voilà!*—as they say.'

'Helped along by being as bright as a tack.' He said it almost to himself. 'I gather you take time off between assignments?'

She nodded. 'I always try for a couple of weeks—not only to give my mother a break, but to be able to spend more time with Scout myself.'

'So she still makes your clothes? Your mother?'

'Yes. She made that jacket.' Liz explained how she'd come to have it with her on the day of the cocktail party. 'She actually made it for the part-time weekend job I have as cashier at a very upmarket restaurant.'

'Your father would be proud of you.'

'I don't know about that.'

'And Scout's father? Any more sightings?'

Liz shook her head but looked uneasy. 'I'm wondering if he's moved back to Sydney and that's why he was at your great-aunt's party.'

'I can find out, if you like. But even if he has Sydney's a big city.' He flicked her an interrogative look.

'No. No, thanks. I think I'll just let sleeping dogs lie. Oh, look—they're diverting the traffic. We could be just in time.'

He seemed about to say something, then he shrugged and switched on the motor.

As often happened when something came up out of the blue, things came in pairs, Liz discovered that same evening. She heard a radio interview with Scout's father in which he talked mainly about the economy—he was an economist—but also about his move back to his hometown from Perth. And the fact that he had no children as yet, but he and his wife were still hoping for some.

She'd flicked the radio off and tried to concentrate on the fact that her only emotion towards Scout's father was now distaste—tried to concentrate on it in order to disguise the cold little bubble of fear the rest of it had brought her.

The next morning her boss made an unusual request.

She was tidying away the clutter on his desk, prior to a meeting with his chief of Human Resources, when he took a phone call that didn't seem to be business-orientated.

'Broke the window?' he said down the line, with a surprised lift of his eyebrows. 'I wouldn't have thought he was strong enough to— Well, never mind. Tell him not to try it again until I'm there.' He put down the phone and watched Liz abstractedly for a few minutes, and then with a frown of concentration.

Liz, becoming aware of this, looked down at her exemplary outfit—a summer suit. Matching jacket and A-line skirt. There didn't seem to be anything wrong with it—no buttons undone, no bra strap showing or anything like that. So she looked back at him with a query in her eyes.

He drummed his fingers on the desk. 'Do you remember a song about a boomerang that wouldn't come back?'

She blinked and thought for a moment, then shook her head. 'No.'

'I seem to,' he said slowly. 'See if you can find it, please.'

Liz opened her mouth, but she was forestalled by the arrival of his chief of Human Resources.

Later that day she was able to tell him she'd found the boomerang song, and was rather charmed by it. 'It's a golden oldie. Charlie Drake was the artist,' she said. 'Not only wouldn't his boomerang come back, but he hit the Flying Doctor.'

'Excellent,' Cam Hillier said. But that was all he said, leaving Liz completely mystified.

* * *

Some days later he surprised her again.

She was a bit preoccupied, because just before she'd left for work and had been checking her purse she'd found she'd inadvertently picked up a note meant for her mother. It was from an old friend of her mother's who ran a dancing school, and it concerned the school's annual concert. Would Mary be interested in designing the costumes for the concert? It would mean about three months' work, it said.

But Mary Montrose had penned a reply on the back of it.

So sorry. Would have loved to but I just don't have the time these days. All good wishes…

She hadn't posted it yet.

Only because of looking after Scout could she not do it, Liz thought to herself, and flinched. But what to do? Scout spent two mornings a week at a daycare centre; more Liz could not afford. And those two free mornings a week would not be enough to allow Mary to take on a job she would have loved.

Liz had replaced the note on the hall table, feeling jolted and miserable, and came to work.

It was after she'd gone through the day's schedule with her boss that he asked to see the next day's schedule.

Liz handed the diary over.

He scanned it in silence for a minute or two, then said decisively, 'Reschedule the lot.' He handed the book back to her.

Liz actually felt herself go pale. 'The lot?'

'That's what I said.' He sat back in his chair.

'But…' Liz stopped and bit her lip. There were at least ten appointments in one form or another to be re-scheduled. There were at least five major appointments amongst them, involving third, fourth and even fifth parties, so cancellation would produce a ripple effect of chaos down the line.

She swallowed. 'All right. Uh—what will you being doing tomorrow? I mean, what would you like me to say? Mr Hillier has been called away urgently? Or…' She paused and gazed at him.

That crooked grin chased across Cam Hillier's lips, but he said gravely, 'Yep. Especially said in those cool, well-bred tones. It should do the trick admirably.'

Liz frowned. 'I don't sound—are you saying I sound snooty?'

'Yes, you do.' He raised an eyebrow at her. 'Probably your private school.'

She grimaced, and after a moment deliberately changed the subject. 'Should I know what you *are* doing tomorrow, Mr Hillier, or would you rather I remained in ignorance?'

He noted the change of subject with a twist of his lips. 'That would be hard, because you'll be with me. I'm going up to Yewarra and I need your help, I'll be engaging staff.'

'Yewarra?' she repeated, somewhat dazedly.

'It's an estate I have in the Blue Mountains.'

'The Blue…' Liz caught herself sounding like a parrot and changed tack. 'I mean—how long will it take?'

'Just a day—just working hours,' he replied smoothly, and shrugged. 'Let's leave here at eight a.m.—then we *will* be back in working hours. And come casual.'

'You're planning to drive up there?' she queried.

'Uh-huh. Why not?'

Liz moved uneasily. 'I prefer not to feel as if I'm low-flying when I'm in a car.'

He grinned. 'I promise to obey the speed limits tomorrow. Anyway, it's a very good car and I'm a very good driver.'

Liz opened her mouth to say his modesty was amazing but she changed her mind. As she knew to her cost, you could never quite tell how Cam Hillier was going to react in a confrontation...

'So,' he said, lying back in his chair with his hands behind his head, 'only three more days before Roger is restored to our midst—completely recovered from his glandular fever, so he assures me.'

'Yes,' she said quietly.

'And you head off into the sunset, Liz.'

'That too,' she agreed.

'But we've worked well together. Oh—' he sat up and gestured widely '—apart from the couple of times you've narrowly restrained yourself from slapping my face, and the day you threatened me with worse.' His blue eyes were alive with satanic amusement.

'I get the feeling you're never going to let me forget that, so it's just as well I *am* riding off into the sunset or something like that.'

She was destined not to know what his response

would have been, because the door of his office burst open and Portia Pengelly swept in.

'Cam, I have to speak to you—*oh*!' Portia stopped dead, then advanced slowly and ominously with that knee-in-front-of-knee model's walk. She wore a simple black silk shift dress splashed with vibrant colours. She had a bright watermelon cardigan draped over her shoulders, and carried a large tote in the same colour. Her famous straw-coloured locks were gorgeously dishevelled and her long legs were bare.

'Who is *this*?' she demanded as she gazed at Liz.

Liz got up and took up the diary. 'I work here. Uh—if that'll be all, Mr Hillier, I'll get back to work. Excuse me,' she said to Portia, and left the room—but not quite quickly enough to miss Portia Pengelly uttering Cam Hillier's Christian name in what sounded like an impassioned plea.

They set off on the dot of eight the next morning.

Liz had taken her boss's advice to 'come casual' to heart. She wore a short-sleeved pale grey jumper with a black and white bow pattern on the front, and slimline jeans with a broad cuff that came, fashionably, to just above her ankles. She had a cardigan to match the jumper, a black leather bag, and pale grey leather flatties.

He also wore jeans, with a denim shirt, and he slung a leather jacket into the back of the Aston Martin.

They didn't say much as he negotiated the traffic out of Sydney—with decorum, she noted, and relaxed somewhat—and headed west. Once they were beyond Penrith the road started to climb—and the Blue Mountains started to live up to their name.

Liz had read somewhere that their distinctive blue haze was the result of the release of oils into the air from the forests of eucalypts that cloaked their slopes. She'd further read, though, that they were not so much mountains but the rugged ramparts, scored and slashed with gullies and ravines, of a vast plateau.

Whatever, she thought, as the powerful vehicle chewed up the kilometres effortlessly and the road got steeper, they were awe-inspiring and yet somehow secretive at the same time, cloaked in their blue haze. And indeed they had proved to be. Until 1994 they'd kept in their remote and isolated valleys the secret of the Wollemi pine—a living fossil said to date back to Gondwana and the time of the dinosaur.

It was when they'd almost reached their destination that he said out of the blue, 'What's your next assignment, Liz?'

She grimaced. 'I don't have one yet. But I'm sure something will come up,' she added. 'It's just hard to predict at times.'

'How will you manage if something doesn't come up for some time?'

Liz moved restlessly. 'I'll be fine.' She paused, then cast him a cool little look. 'Please, I do appreciate your concern, but I think it's best left alone. I'll be gone in a couple of days and it's difficult for me—for both of us, probably—to remain professional if this keeps cropping up between us.'

'Professional?' He drove for a mile or so. 'That flew

out of the window, in a manner of speaking, before any of *this* "cropped up".'

Liz frowned. 'What do you mean?'

He took his eyes off the road to look at her just long enough for her to see the irony in his eyes. 'Narelle was right. We're not cut out to be only employer and employee. There is, Ms Montrose, not to put too fine a point on it, a kind of electricity between us that started to sizzle right here in this car outside my house almost two weeks ago. Or perhaps even earlier—that day in the office when you put on your magic coat and let down your hair.'

CHAPTER FOUR

LIZ'S MOUTH fell open.

'And it continued the next morning in the lift,' he added, as he changed gear and they swept round a corner. 'In fact it's never gone away—despite your best efforts to kill it stone-dead.'

It struck Liz that they had driven through the pretty village of Leura with her barely noticing it, and were now on a country road. It also struck her that it was impossible to refute his claim.

She stared down at her hands. 'Look,' she said, barely audibly, 'you'd be mad to want to get involved with me. And vice versa.'

Out of the corner of her eye she saw that crooked grin come and go before he said, 'It doesn't work that way.'

'If we're two sane adults, it should,' she replied coolly. 'You can make choices, can't you?'

He changed gear again and slowed down. 'On the virtually nothing we have to go on? It'd be like a stab in the dark.' He turned the wheel and they coasted into a driveway barred by a pair of tall wrought-iron gates.

'Is this it?' Liz asked.

'This is it.' He pressed a buzzer mounted on the dashboard and the gates started to open. 'Welcome to Yewarra, Liz.'

For a moment Liz felt like escaping—escaping his car, his estate and Cam Hillier himself. She fleetingly felt overburdened, and as if she were entering a zone she had no control over.

Moments later, however, she was enchanted as he drove slowly up the gravelled driveway.

Beneath majestic trees there were beds of white and blue agapanthus. There was flowering jasmine and honeysuckle climbing up jacarandas bursting into pale violet bloom. There were gardenias and roses. It was a glorious riot of colour and perfume.

She turned to him, her face alight with appreciation. 'This is just—beautiful.'

He grimaced. 'Thanks. In a way it's a tribute to my mother. A tribute to her love of gardens and her innate sense of refined living that somehow survived the often harsh life she shared with my father.'

He pulled up beside a fountain. The house beyond it was two-storeyed and built of warm, earthy stone with a shingle roof. The windows were framed in timber and had wrought-iron security grids. The front door—a double door—was beautifully carved with a dolphin motif and had curved brass handles.

'The house isn't bad either,' she commented with a wry little smile. 'Did you build it?'

'No. And I've hardly done anything to it. Well, I changed that,' he amended, and gestured to the fountain.

'It was this rather nauseating circle of coy naked ladies clutching plump cherubs.'

What stood there now couldn't have been more different. A bronze dolphin leapt out of the water, cascading sparkling droplets.

Liz stared at it. 'Do dolphins have any special significance?'

He considered. 'It's not inappropriate for someone whose roots go back to a seafaring life, I guess.'

Liz thought of the paintings in his office in Sydney. 'But you've come a long way since then,' she offered quietly.

'A long way,' he agreed. But, although he said it easily enough, she thought she detected the faintest echo of a grim undertone.

At that moment the front doors flew open and a small boy of about five stood on the doorstep, waving excitedly at the same time as he was restrained by a nanny.

Liz's eyes widened. 'Who…?' she began, and bit her lip, not wanting to sound nosy.

'That's Archie,' Cam Hillier said. 'He's my sister's orphaned son. I've adopted him.'

He opened his door and got out, and Archie escaped his nanny's restraining hand and flew over the gravel, calling, 'Cam! Cam—am I glad to see you! Wenonah has had *six* puppies but they only want to let me keep one!'

Cam Hillier picked his nephew up and hugged him. 'But just think,' he said, 'of the five other kids who'd love to have a puppy but couldn't if you kept them all.'

Liz blinked. She'd assumed his nephew Archie would

be older. She certainly hadn't expected to see Cameron Hillier so at home with a five-year-old...

'I suppose that's true,' Archie said slowly. 'Oh, well, maybe I won't mind.' He hugged Cam. 'Are you staying?'

'Not tonight,' Cam said, but added as Archie's face fell, 'I'll be up for the weekend.' He put the little boy down. 'Archie, meet Liz—she works for me.'

'How do you do, Liz?' Archie said with impeccable manners. 'Would you like to see my menagerie?'

Both Cam and the nanny, still standing on the doorstep, opened their mouths to intervene, but Liz got in first. 'How do you do, Archie? I would indeed.'

Archie slid his hand into hers. 'It's down this path. I'll show you.'

'Not too long, Archie,' Cam said. 'Liz and I have work to do.'

Archie's menagerie was in a fenced-off compound not far from the house. There was netting stretched over the top, and there were shrubs growing within and without to shade it. Old hollow tree trunks lay inside. The paths were gravel. He had rabbits in hutches, and a family of guinea pigs in a marvellous cage fashioned like a castle, with climbing wheels and slides and bells. He had a white cockatoo with a sulphur crest and a limited vocabulary— 'Hello, cocky!' and 'Oh, golly gosh!' He had a pond with a small waterfall and slippery stones, with greenery growing through it all and six frogs enjoying it. In another pond he had goldfish.

'Did you do all this?' Liz asked, rather enchanted,

surveying the menagerie and thinking how much Scout would love it.

'No, silly. I'm only five,' Archie replied. 'Cam did most if it. But I helped. Here.' He handed Liz a guinea pig. 'That's Golly, and this one—' he drew another one out of the castle-like cage '—is Ginny. She's his wife and they're all the kids.' Archie pointed into the cage.

'I see,' Liz replied gravely as she stroked Golly. 'So where is Wenonah? And her puppies?'

'Down at the stables. Wenonah can be a bit naughty about rabbits and things. She likes to chase them. But I'm going to train the puppy I get not to. Thing is—' his brow creased '—I don't know whether to get a boy or a girl.'

'Perhaps Cam can help you there? He might have an idea on the subject.'

Archie brightened. 'He usually does. Now, this is something special—my blue-tongue lizard!'

'Oh, wow!' Liz carefully put Golly back and sank down on her knees. 'Oh, my!'

That was how Cam found them some time later, both Liz and Archie on their knees and laughing together as they tried to entice Wally the blue-tongue lizard out of his cave.

Liz looked up and got up, brushing her knees. 'Sorry, but this is fascinating. I was just thinking how much Scout would enjoy it.'

'Who's Scout?' Archie enquired. 'Does he like animals?'

'*She*—she's my little girl, and she adores animals at the moment.'

'You should bring her over to play with me,' Archie said.

'Oh—'

Cam intervened. 'We'll see, Archie. Can I have Liz now?'

Archie agreed, but grudgingly.

'You made a hit there,' Cam commented as they walked back to the house.

'You get into "little kid mode" if you're around them long enough,' Liz said humorously, and stepped through the dolphin doors—only to stop with a gasp.

The entrance hall was a gallery that led to a lounge below. It had a vast stone fireplace and some priceless-looking rugs scattered about the stone-flagged floor. It was furnished with sumptuously comfortable settees and just a few equally priceless-looking ornaments and paintings. The overall colour scheme was warm and inviting—cream and terracotta with dashes of mint-green. But it was the wall of ceiling-high windows overlooking the most stunning view that had made Liz gasp.

A valley dropped precipitously below that wall of windows and fled away into the morning sunlight in all its wild splendour.

'It's—amazing. Do you ever get used to it?' she asked.

'Not really. It changes—different lights, different times of day, different weather. Uh—the study is down those stairs.'

The study came as another surprise to Liz. It presented

quite a different view—a sunlit, peaceful view—across a formal garden to grassy paddocks with wooden fences and horses grazing, lazily switching their tails. Beyond the paddocks she could see a shingle-roofed building with two wings and a clock tower in the middle—obviously the stables.

She turned back from the windows and surveyed the study. It was wood-panelled and lined with books on two sides. On the other walls there were very similar paintings to those in his office in Sydney: horses and trawlers. Her lips twitched.

The carpet was Ming blue, and the chairs on either side of the desk were covered in navy leather.

She sat down as directed, and he took his place behind the desk.

'I don't know how you manage to tear yourself away from the place,' she commented, as he poured coffee from a pewter flask. She cocked her head to one side as she accepted her cup. 'Was the menagerie your idea?'

'More or less.' He stirred his coffee. 'Archie's always been interested in animals, so I thought instead of mice in shoeboxes we might as well do it properly.' He looked down at his mug, 'It has also, I think, helped him get over the loss of his mother.'

Liz hesitated, then decided not to pursue that. 'Well, I *am* here to work, so—' She broke off when she noticed an ironic little glint in his eye as he crossed his arms and simply watched her.

And it all came flooding back—what had been said in the car before her enchantment with his gardens and his nephew's menagerie had claimed her.

She closed her eyes as she felt the colour that flooded her cheeks. As her lashes fluttered up, she said with effort, 'Let's not go there, Mr Hillier. In fact I refuse to discuss it.'

He lay back in his chair, dangling a silver pen in his long fingers. 'Why? It *did* happen.'

'It was an aberration,' Liz said coolly, reverting to her Ice Queen role.

He grinned—a full version of that crooked but utterly charismatic smile this time. 'Just a bit of naughtiness between two people for reasons unknown?'

'Well,' Liz said, thinking fast, 'you *had* been stood up out of the blue. Could that have been at the back of your mind?'

'Portia couldn't have been further from my mind.' He drummed his fingers on the desk and shrugged. 'That may sound—'

'It sounds pretty cold-blooded,' she broke in.

He looked at her. 'Portia thought that in exchange for her—charms—she could persuade me to back a clothing range. Swimsuits, in fact. She had her heart set on designing and no doubt modelling them,' he said dryly. 'When I looked into it I found it was an overcrowded market and a poor investment. Despite the fact that I'd never made any promises of any kind, she took the view that I had—uh—two-timed her.'

Liz blinked. 'Oh?'

He raised an eyebrow at her. 'You sound surprised.'

'I am,' Liz confessed.

'You assumed it was all over another woman?'

he suggested, with a glint of wicked amusement in his eyes.

Liz bit her lip and looked annoyed, because she knew she was being mocked. All the same it *was* what she'd automatically assumed. 'Well…yes. But did you honestly expect her still to want to go out with you?' she added. 'I would have thought not.'

Cam Hillier dragged his hand through his hair with a rueful look. 'Yep—got that bit wrong,' he confessed. 'I thought she'd at least trust my judgement.' He shrugged. 'Where money's concerned anyway.'

'I see,' Liz said—quite inadequately, she felt. But what else could she say?

He sat back with a faint smile. 'And it is over between us.'

'But only yesterday it didn't sound as if it was over for her!' Liz protested.

'Look, it is now,' he said dryly. 'Believe me.'

Liz shivered suddenly as she watched his mouth set, and knew she couldn't disbelieve him.

'But don't for one minute imagine that Portia won't find someone else.' He paused and looked at her penetratingly. 'Probably a lot sooner than I will, since you're so hell-bent on being the Ice Queen.'

Liz's lips parted in sheer shock. 'How did you…?'

He shrugged. 'We've known each other for nearly a month now. Quite long enough for me to detect when you're in chilly mode.'

Liz blinked helplessly several times and opened her mouth—but he spoke first. 'Never mind, we'll leave all that aside. How are you with horses?'

She opened her mouth again—to repeat bewilderedly *Horses?*—but just stopped herself in time. 'I have no idea why you want to know,' she said, 'but I like horses. I rode as a kid. If, though, you're going to ask me about trawlers, I've never been on one and have no desire to do so!'

His eyebrows shot up. 'Why would I?'

Liz gestured to the walls. 'They seem to go together for you. Horses and trawlers. And, probably because I don't understand any of this, in a fog of bewilderment I thought they might come next.'

He looked quizzical. 'No, but I suppose they *do* go together for me. I inherited a trawler fleet from my father, which eventually made the horses possible.'

Liz gazed at him. 'Why Shakespeare, though?'

He looked surprised. 'You noticed?'

She nodded.

'My mother again,' he said. 'She was hot on Shakespeare.'

'I see.' Liz was silent for a moment, then, 'Do you want to tell me why it matters whether I like horses? Come to that, why you've pretty thoroughly gone through my background with a toothcomb—and why I have the feeling I'm up here under false pretences?' she added, as she was gripped by the sensation that all was not what it seemed.

'Well, it *is* about engaging staff, Liz. I'd like to offer you the position of managing this place.'

This time Liz was struck seriously speechless.

'It's not a domestic position, it's a logistic one,' he went on. 'I do quite a lot of entertaining up here, and we often have house parties. I have good household staff, but I need someone to co-ordinate things both here and in the stables.'

'How...how so?' she asked, her voice breaking and husky with surprise. 'I'm not that good with horses.'

'It's not to do with the horses *per se*. We stand three stallions, we have twenty of our own mares, and we agist outside mares in foal and with foals at foot. The paperwork to keep track of it all alone is a big job. Checking the pedigrees of prospective mares for our stallions—it goes on. I need someone who can organise all that on a computer program.'

Liz breathed deeply but said nothing.

'I need to free up my stud master and the people who actually work with the horses from the paperwork—and incidentally free them up from all the people who stream in and out of the place.'

'Ah.' It was all Liz could think of to say.

He cast her an ironic little look, but continued. 'There's a comfortable staff cottage that would go with the position—big enough for you and Scout, as well as your mother. There's even a ready-made friend for Scout in Archie,' he said, and gazed at her steadily.

'But—' She stopped to clear her throat. 'Why me?'

'You've impressed me,' he said, and shrugged. 'You're as good as Roger—if not better in some areas. I think you're wasted as a diary secretary. I think you have the organisational skills as well as the people skills to do the job justice.'

'I...' Liz pressed her hands together and took another

deep breath. 'I don't know what to say,' she confessed. 'It's the last thing I was expecting.'

'Let's talk remuneration, then.' And for the next few minutes he outlined a package that was generous. So much so that to knock it back would be not so much looking a gift horse in the mouth but kicking it in the teeth…

'We'd have a three-month trial period,' he said, and grinned. 'Just in case you hanker for the bright lights or whatever.'

'If I didn't bring my mother—' Liz heard herself say cautiously, then couldn't go on.

He eyed her narrowly. 'Why wouldn't you?'

She gestured, then told him about the note she'd intercepted. 'She's been so wonderful, but I know it's something she'd love to do—I just haven't been able to work out how.' She shook her head. 'It wouldn't work up here, either.'

'You could share Archie's nanny for the times when you couldn't be with Scout.'

Liz stared at him, her eyes suddenly dark and uncertain. 'Why are you doing this—really? Are there any strings attached?'

'Such as?' He said it barely audibly.

'Such as going down a slippery slope into your bed?'

They stared at each other and she saw his eyes harden, but he answered in a drawl, 'My dear Liz, if you imagine I'd need to go to all these lengths to do that, you're wrong.'

'What's that supposed to mean?'

'You know as well as I do that if we gave each other just the smallest leeway we wouldn't be able to help ourselves. *But*—and I emphasise this—' his voice hardened this time '—if you prefer to go on your solitary way, so be it.'

'You were the one who brought it up,' Liz said hotly, then looked uncomfortable.

'At least I'm honest,' he countered.

'I haven't been dishonest.'

'Not precisely,' he agreed, and simply waited for her reply.

Liz ground her teeth. 'What you may not know is that being a single mother lays you open to...to certain men thinking you're...promiscuous.'

She wasn't expecting any more surprises at this point, but she got one when Cameron Hillier leant forward suddenly, his blue eyes intent. 'I know quite a bit about single mothers. My sister was one—and that, I guess, even while I'm not prepared to be dishonest, is why I have some sympathy for you, Liz Montrose.'

Her mouth fell open. She snapped it shut. So that explained the understanding she thought she'd seen in his eyes when she'd told him her story!

'And, further towards complete honesty,' he went on, 'I need the right influence in Archie's life at the moment—which I think you could be. I can't be with him nearly as much as I should. He starts school next year, so that will distance us even more. I want this last year of his before school to be memorable for him. And safe. And happy.'

'You don't know—how do you know I could do that?'

He sat back. 'I saw you with him just now. I've seen, from the moment you first mentioned her, how much your daughter means to you. How it lights you up just to say her name.'

'I still…' She paused helplessly. 'It's come up so fast!'

'It's part of my success—the ability to sum things up and make quick decisions.'

Liz looked at him askance. 'Your modesty is amazing at times.'

'I know,' he agreed seriously, but she could suddenly see the glimmer of laughter in his eyes.

'Well—'

'Er…excuse me?' a strange voice said, and they both swung round to see a woman standing in the doorway. 'Lunch is ready, Mr Hillier. I've served it in the kitchen if that's all right with you?'

Cam Hillier rose. 'That's fine, Mrs Preston. Thank you.'

It was a huge kitchen—brick-walled, with a tiled floor and rich woodwork. Herbs grew in pots along the windowsills, a vast antique dresser displayed a lovely array of china, but all the appliances were modern and stainless steel.

There was a long refectory table at one end that seated six in ladder-back chairs with raffia seats.

The lady who answered to 'Mrs Preston', grey-haired, pink-cheeked and of comfortable girth, was dishing up steaks, Liz saw, and baked Idaho potatoes topped with sour cream and chives. A bowl brimming with salad—cos lettuce, tomatoes, cucumber, capsicum and shallots—was also set out, and there was a bread basket laden with fresh warm rolls.

The steaks, she realised from their tantalising aroma, had been marinated and grilled along with button mushrooms.

A bottle of red wine was breathing in a pottery container.

'Hungry?' Cam asked as they sat down.

'I've suddenly realised I'm starving,' she confessed and looked around. 'Where's Archie?'

'At the dentist in Leura—just for a check-up. Mrs Preston,' Cam added, 'may I tell Miss Montrose what you told me on the phone a couple of days ago?'

Mrs Preston blinked at Liz, then said, 'Of course.'

Cam reached for the bottle of wine and poured them each a glass. 'For quite some years now Mrs Preston has been housekeeper and most inspired chef all rolled into one.' He lifted his glass in a silent toast and went on, 'Well, maybe *you'd* like to tell it, Mrs Preston?'

The housekeeper clasped her hands together and faced Liz. 'I did ring Mr Hillier a couple of days ago because I knew he'd understand.' She stopped to cast her boss an affectionate glance. 'I'm getting on a bit now,' she went on to Liz, 'and I'd really like to concentrate on my cooking. I've always liked to choose my own fresh ingredients, but for the rest of the provisioning of a household this size, and with the amount of entertaining we do, I'd like just to be able to write a list and hand it over to someone.'

She paused to draw several breaths and then continued, 'I don't want to have to worry any more about the state of the linen closet or whether we need new napkins. I don't want to have to worry about the hiring and firing of the cleaning staff, or counting the silver in case any of them are light-fingered, or wondering if I gave the same set of guests the same meals the last time they were here because I forgot to make a note of it. I'd rather there was someone who could co-ordinate it all,' she said a little wistfully.

Cam looked at Liz with a question in his eyes, and she registered the fleeting thought that he hadn't conjured up this job he'd offered her out of the blue—for whatever reason. It *did* exist. What also existed, she found herself thinking, was the fact that Cameron Hillier was well-loved by his staff. Not only Mrs Preston but Molly Swanson—and a few others she had met…

She swallowed a piece of melt-in-the-mouth steak and said, 'I think, whatever the outcome—my outcome, I mean—it would be criminal to burden you with all those other things any longer, Mrs Preston. This meal is one of the most delicious I've ever had.'

'Thank you, Miss Montrose.' Mrs Preston looked set to turn away, but she hesitated and added, 'Archie really took to you. He said you've got a little girl?'

'I do,' Liz confirmed. 'She's nearly four.'

'It's a wonderful place for kids up here.'

* * *

'So far, what do you think?' Cam Hillier queried as they walked side-by-side down to the stables after lunch.

There was a light breeze to temper the bite of the sun and to stir her hair, and the summery smell of grass and horses was all around as the path wound through the paddocks.

'I—I still don't know what to say,' Liz confessed.

He looked down at her. 'In case you're worried it's a glorified housekeeper position, I can tell you that you'd not only be in charge of the inner workings of the house but also the gardens—the whole damn lot,' he said, with a wave of his hand.

'Surely you'd be better off with a man?' she countered. 'I mean a man who could…well…' She looked around a little helplessly. 'Mend fences and so on.'

'A man who could mend fences in all likelihood couldn't run the house. A woman, on the other hand, with a sharp eye and the ability to hire the help she needs when she needs it, should be able to do both.' He paused and looked down at her. 'A woman, furthermore, who stands no nonsense from anyone has to be an asset.'

Liz released a long slow breath. 'You make me feel like a sergeant-major. I'm sorry I once threatened you, but you did ask for it.'

'Apology accepted,' he said gravely. 'Where were we? Yes. The house does need some upgrading. I've noticed it lately. Also there's the stable computer program.'

Liz was silent.

'It would look good on your résumé,' he said.

'Manager of the Yewarra Estate. It would look better than Temporary Diary Secretary.'

'Assuming I agreed, when would you expect me to start?'

He looked down at her wryly. 'Not before Roger comes back and you hand over to him. And you might need a few days off to get organised. Here we are.'

The stables were picturesque, with tubs of petunias dotted about, swept walkways and the earthy smell of manure combined with the sweet smell of hay on the air. They were also a hive of activity—and Liz saw what Cam Hillier had meant when he'd mentioned all the people who streamed in and out of the place. The stables had a separate entrance from the house.

The office yielded another scene. A giant of a man in his forties, with sandy hair and freckles, and 'outdoor type' written all over him, was sitting in front of a computer almost literally tearing his hair out.

He was Bob Collins, stud master, and he greeted Cam and Liz distractedly. 'I've lost it again,' he divulged as the cause of his distraction. 'The whole darn program seems to have disappeared down some bloody cyber black hole!'

Cam glanced at Liz. She grimaced, but pulled up a chair next to Bob and, after a few questions, began tapping the computer keys. Within a few minutes she'd restored his program.

Bob looked at her properly for the first time, clapped her on the back, and swung round to Cam. 'I don't know where you got her from, but can I have her? Please?'

Cam grinned. 'Maybe. She has to make up her mind.'

* * *

They were walking back to the house, not talking, both lost in their own thoughts, when his phone rang.

'Yep. Uh-huh… This afternoon? Well, OK, but tell Jim he'll have to fly straight back to Sydney.'

He clicked the phone off and turned to Liz. 'Change of plan. Our legal adviser needs to see me urgently. He's flying up in the company helicopter and staying the night. I—'

'How will I get home?' Liz interrupted with some agitation.

'I wasn't planning to keep you here against your will,' he said dryly. 'You're going back to Sydney on the chopper.'

Liz went red. 'Sorry,' she mumbled.

He stopped and rested his hand on her shoulder, swinging her round to face him. 'If,' he said, 'you really don't trust me, Liz, we might as well call the whole thing off here and now.'

She drew a deep breath and called on all her composure. 'I haven't had time to wonder about that—whether I trust you or not,' she said. 'I was thinking of Scout and my mother. I've never been away from them overnight before.'

His hand on her shoulder fell away, and she thought he was going to say something more, but he started to walk towards the house.

She hesitated, then followed suit.

The helicopter was blue and white, and the legal adviser looked harassed as he climbed out of it. The helicopter pad was on the other side of the house from the menagerie.

Liz felt harassed as she waited to board, but hoped she didn't look it. It was now late afternoon. She'd spent the rest of the afternoon in Mrs Preston's company, being shown over the house. It was impossible not to be impressed—especially with the nursery wing. There was a playroom that would be any kid's dream. All sorts of wonderful characters in large cut-outs lined the walls—characters out of *Peter Pan*, *Alice in Wonderland* and more—and many toys. There was a small kitchenette and three bedrooms…

On the other hand Cam Hillier, waiting with her beside the helipad, looked casual and relaxed. He had Archie with him, and it was obvious the little boy was delighted at this unscheduled change of plan.

'Can I think this over?' Liz said.

'Sure,' he agreed easily, and advanced towards the legal adviser. 'Good day, Pete. This is Liz, but she's on her way out. In you get, Liz.'

Is that all? Liz found herself wondering as she climbed into the chopper and started to belt herself up. Then she stopped abruptly.

'Uh—hang on a moment,' she said to the pilot. 'I forgot to ask him—can we just hang on a moment?'

The pilot shrugged rather boredly. 'Whatever you like.'

So Liz unbuckled herself and climbed out, and the two men on the pad turned back to her, looking surprised.

'Uh—Mr Hillier, I forgot to ask you if you'll be in the office tomorrow and at what time?'

'Not sure at this stage, Liz.'

Liz paled. 'But I've rescheduled some of today's appointments for tomorrow!'

'Then you may have to reschedule them again.'

She planted her hands on her hips. 'And what will I tell them this time?'

He shrugged. 'It's up to you.'

Liz took an angry breath, but forced herself to calm down. 'OK,' she said with an airy shrug. 'I'll tell them you've *gone fishing*!'

And with that she swung on her heel and climbed back into the chopper. 'You can go now,' she informed the pilot, her eyes the only giveaway of her true mental state. They were sparkling with anger.

He looked at her, this time with a grin tugging at his lips. 'That was telling him—good on you!'

'You—you find him hard to work for?'

The pilot inclined his head as he fired up the motor and the rotors started to turn. 'At times. But on the whole he's best bloke I've ever worked for. I guess we all think the same.'

'And that,' Liz said to her mother later that evening, having summed up the salient points of her day, 'is a sentiment shared by I would say his housekeeper, his stud master, and his secretary Molly Swanson. He can be difficult, but they really admire and respect him. His nephew adores him.' She shook her head in some confusion. 'I really didn't believe he had that side to him. Not that I'd actually thought about it.'

'Take it,' Mary said impulsively. 'Take the job. I say that because I see it as a career move for you. I see it as a way that may open all sorts of opportunities for you. If it doesn't, you can always come back to this. Anyway, the money alone will take a lot of the stress and strain from you. And I'll come with you!'

'Mum, no,' Liz said, and explained about the note she'd read. 'If I take it, one of the reasons I'll do it is so that you can have more of a life of your own, doing what you love and are so good at.'

Mary looked stubborn, and the argument went backwards and forwards until Liz said frustratedly, 'He may even have changed his mind by tomorrow—he can be annoying at times, and I more or less told him so today. He can certainly be an arrogant multi-millionaire.'

But when she went to bed she was thinking of Archie, and that brought his uncle into a different light for her. Arrogant Cam Hillier could certainly be—but when you saw him with his nephew he was a different man. Different and appealing…

Unaware that he'd just been categorised as an arrogant multi-millionaire, Cam Hillier nevertheless found himself thinking of Liz as he poured himself a nightcap and took it to his study. His legal adviser had gone to bed and so had Archie—a lot earlier.

She was a strange mixture, he decided, and grinned suddenly as he recalled her parting jibe on the helipad. So bright and capable, so attractive… He thought of her slim, elegant figure today, beneath her jumper and jeans, and the easy, fluid way she walked. He thought of the way she could look right through you out of those chilly blue eyes, but on the other hand how she could light up as she had over his gardens and with Archie.

He sobered, though, as he thought that there was no doubt she had a tortured soul.

No wonder, he reflected as he stared into the amber depths of his drink, and remembered with the stabbing sense of loss it always brought his sister Amelia, Archie's mother, and what single motherhood had done to her...

He sighed and transferred his attention to the paintings on his study walls—horses and trawlers and Shakespeare. And one trawler in particular, *Miss Miranda*, because it had been the first trawler his parents had bought. There was a new Miranda now, *Miss Miranda II*, much larger than her predecessor, and yet to be immortalised in paint.

He shrugged as he strolled back to his desk and sank down into his swivel chair. He found himself thinking back to his parents' early days.

They must have made an unlikely couple when they'd first married: the girl from an impoverished but blue-blooded background, and the tall, laconic bushman who'd grown up in Cooktown in Far North Queensland on a cattle station, with the sea in his veins and a dream of owning a prawning fleet.

In fact they'd made such an unlikely couple to his mother's family, the Hastings clan, they'd virtually cast her off—apart from Narelle, his great-aunt. Yet his parents had been deeply in love until the day they'd died—together. It had been a love that had carried them through all their trials and tribulations—all their hard days at sea on boats that smelt of fish and diesel and often broke down. Through days of tropical heat in Cooktown, when the boats had been laid up in the off-season, and through nights when the catch had been small enough to break your heart.

Somehow, though, his mother had managed to make wherever they were a home—even if only via a hibiscus bloom in a glass, or a little decoupage of shells, and her warm smile. And she'd been able to do that even when she must have been longing for more temperate climates, a gracious home and great gardens such as she'd known as a child. And his father, even when he'd been bone-tired and looking every year of his age and more, had always seemed to know when that shadow was not far from his mother. He'd always been able to make the sun shine for her again—sometimes just with a touch of a hand on her hair.

Cam drained his glass and twirled it in his fingers.

Why did thinking of his parents so often make him feel—what? As if he was playing his life like a discordant piece of music?

Was it because, although he'd taken the strands of all their hard work and pulled them together, and gone on to make a huge fortune from them, he didn't have what they'd had?

On the other side of the scale, though, was the memory of his sister Amelia, who'd loved unwisely and been dumped, never to be the same girl again. And now there was Archie—both motherless and fatherless because Amelia had taken the secret of who his father was to her grave.

If that wasn't enough to make one cynical about love and its disastrous consequences, what was?

He grimaced. Hot on the heels of that had to come all the women who pursued him for his money.

Funny, really, he mused, but in his heart of hearts was he as cynical about love as Liz Montrose?

He stretched and linked his hands behind his head, and wondered if the fault was with him—this feeling of discord with his life. Were his expectations of women way too high? Was that why he'd stopped even looking for his ideal woman? Was it all underpinned by the tragedy of his sister?

And in a more general sense was he frustrated because he felt he wasn't doing the right thing by Archie? Yes, he could give him everything that opened and shut—yes, he could come up with ideas like the menagerie—but his time was another matter.

He unlinked his hands and sat up abruptly as it came to him that it wasn't only Archie who needed more of his time. He himself had got onto a treadmill of work and the acquisition of more power that at times felt like a strait-jacket, but he didn't seem to be able to get himself off it.

He took up his glass and stared unseeingly across the room.

Was it all bound up with not having a permanent woman in his life or a proper family? he wondered. He set his glass down with a sudden thump at the thought.

Was that why he was making sure Liz Montrose couldn't ride off into the sunset? Because of more than a physical attraction he couldn't seem to eradicate? Did he have at the back of his mind the prospect of creating a family unit with her and her daughter and Archie? Was that why he'd broken the unspoken truce between them just before offering her a job?

He hadn't planned to do that. He'd been needled into doing it because she could be so damn cool—and he not only wanted her body, he wanted *her*.

But what if a tortured Ice Queen turned out to be the one he really wanted and couldn't have? he asked himself.

CHAPTER FIVE

LIZ WAS LATE for work the next morning—thanks to an uncharacteristic tantrum from Scout. She hadn't wanted to get dressed, she hadn't wanted breakfast, she hadn't wanted to do anything she usually did.

Since she wasn't running a temperature, and had no other symptoms, Liz had concluded that her daughter had picked up her own uneasy vibes after another restless night.

'Go,' Mary had said. 'Well, finish getting dressed first. She'll be fine with me. And remember what I said,' she'd added pointedly.

So Liz had hurriedly finished dressing, thanking heaven she'd chosen a simple outfit—the ultimate little black dress, with a square neck, cap sleeves, a belted waistline and a short skirt. She'd slipped on high-heeled taupe shoes, dragged on two broad colourful bangles, grabbed her purse and run for the bus.

She was only fifteen minutes late now, after a lightning call into the staff powder room to put on some make-up and check her hair. Therefore it was a rather nasty surprise to be told as she greeted Molly that her boss was waiting for her.

'W-waiting?' she stammered. 'I didn't think he'd be in today—well, not this morning anyway.'

'He's been here over an hour. Grab the diary,' Molly recommended.

Liz did as she was told, and, after taking several deep breaths, knocked and let herself into Cam Hillier's office.

He was on the phone and gestured for her to sit down.

She put the diary on the desk and not only sat down but tried to regroup as best she could, while he talked on the phone, lying back in his chair, half turned away from her.

She pushed her hair behind her ears, smoothed her skirt and crossed her ankles. She did some discreet facial exercises, then squared her shoulders and folded her hands in her lap and studied them.

'Ready?'

Her lashes flew up and to her consternation she realised that she hadn't noticed him finish his call. 'Uh—yes. I'm sorry I'm late.'

'But you weren't expecting me to be in?' he suggested.

'It wasn't that. Scout was a little off-colour. Mind you,' she added honestly, 'I *wasn't* expecting you to be in.'

He watched her for a long moment, his dense blue eyes entirely enigmatic. 'I decided,' he said at last, 'that my reputation might not stand a "gone fishing" tag.'

Liz coloured faintly. 'I wouldn't have done that,' she murmured.

'Yesterday afternoon you would have,' he countered gravely.

Liz moved a little uneasily and said nothing.

He got up and walked over to the wide windows that overlooked the city. Gone was the informality, clothes-wise, of yesterday. Today he wore a navy suit, with a grey and white pinstriped shirt and a midnight-blue tie. Today he looked every inch the successful businessman who'd diversified from a fishing fleet into many other enterprises.

He turned to look at her. 'So? Any decision?'

Liz licked her lips. 'Well, I've discussed it with my mother, and she—' She broke off and cleared her throat. 'No,' she amended. '*I'd* like to take the position—if you haven't changed your mind?'

He shoved his hands into his pockets. 'Why would I?'

Liz grimaced. 'Because of the "gone fishing" tag?'

He smiled briefly. 'I was being bloody-minded. I probably deserved it. No, I haven't changed my mind. Go on? I take it you'd like me to believe you and not your mother made the decision?'

'Yes,' she admitted, and smoothed her skirt again. 'To be honest, I couldn't in all conscience turn it down. Financially it would put me in a much better place. It would be like working from home, and it would mean I don't have to take part-time weekend work. Career-wise—as you said—it would look much better on my résumé. It would give me so much more time with Scout, and...' She paused and swallowed. 'Overall, I think it would make me look like a much more suitable mother—able to offer Scout much more, sort of thing.'

'If Scout's father decided to contest your suitability, do you mean?'

She nodded.

'So you're going to tell him?'

'No. But...' Liz hesitated. 'He has moved back to Sydney.' She explained how she'd come to know this. 'So that's another reason I'd be happier somewhere else.'

'You can't keep running away from him, Liz.'

She spread her hands. 'I know that. Still, I would be happier. And I think a better job like this would make me feel I had more...stature—would make me feel a lot better about myself, my life, et cetera.'

He brooded over this for a moment, then, 'And your mother? What's her opinion?'

'She's all for it—although it took a bit of persuading to get her to agree to stay in Sydney and take up the costume design job. But I pointed out that she's only fifty and she needs a life of her own. Of course she'll come up and spend time with us—if that's OK?'

'Fine.' His lips twisted. 'Are you looking forward to it, though? All the pragmatism in the world isn't going be much good to you if you hate it up there. If you feel it's beneath your skills or whatever.'

'*Hate* it up there?' Liz repeated wryly. 'That would be hard to do.'

'Or if you feel lonely.'

Their gazes caught as he said it, and Liz found she

couldn't look away. Something in the way he said it, and the way he was looking at her, held her trapped.

She moistened her lips. 'I plan to be too busy to feel lonely.'

But she knew immediately this wasn't the right response. It didn't answer the unasked question he was posing—the question of, as he had put it, the electricity that sometimes sizzled between them. Even now it was there between them as he stood watching her, so tall, so— She sought for the right expression. So dynamic that she couldn't help being physically moved by him— moved and made to wonder what it would be like to be in his arms.

She actually felt all the little hairs on her body stand up as she wondered this, and realised to her amazement that she'd given herself goosebumps again.

But there was more.

Lonely, she thought on a sudden indrawn breath.

She'd been lonely for years. Lonely for that special companionship with a man who was your lover. And she had no doubt that Cameron Hillier would meld those two roles brilliantly. For how long, though, before another Portia crossed his path? Well, maybe not a Portia, but— Stop it! she told herself. Don't go there…

'Liz? Are we going to play games about this?'

She trembled inwardly, but it struck her that she'd only ever been honest with this man, and she'd continue to be so.

'If you mean am I going to deny that an attraction exists for me? No, I'm not. But…' She paused and rubbed her palms together, then laced her fingers. 'I can't let it affect me. I made one terrible mistake in the name of what I thought was love, but it turned out to be only a passing attraction. I'm still trying to pick up the pieces—the pieces not only of my life but of my—my morale, maybe.'

She stopped, and didn't know that a terrible tension was visible in her expression. She did try to lighten her tone. 'You'd think five years would be enough to get over it.' She smiled briefly. 'But not so. And then, if you'll forgive me, Mr Hillier, there's you.'

'Go on,' he invited dryly. 'Or can I guess? You don't know whether my intentions are honourable or the opposite?' He paused, then said deliberately, 'I certainly wouldn't be so heartless as to leave you pregnant and alone.'

'I did…walk out on him,' she whispered.

'Liz, you're twenty-four now. That means you would have only been *nineteen* when it happened. Right?' he said interrogatively.

'Well, yes. But—'

'How old was he?' he continued. 'Older, I gather?'

'He—he was thirty-five.'

'And who was he? I don't want names,' he added as she took a quick, tempestuous breath. 'What was he in your life?'

Her shoulders slumped. 'One of my tutors.'

He studied her for a long moment. 'That's an old, old story, Liz,' he said. 'An older man in some sort of authority. A young, possibly naïve, starstruck girl. He shouldn't have walked out of your life without a backward glance when things came right for him with another woman. He should have known better *right from the start*.'

Liz fiddled with her bangles for a long moment and found that breathing was difficult. Why? she questioned herself. Because those had been her own bitter sentiments even while she'd changed courses and campuses and finally finished her degree as an external student?

'Look,' she said in a strained voice to match the expression in her eyes, 'for whatever reason—I mean legitimate or otherwise—I'm not ready to go down that road again.'

'Why are you taking the job, then?'

She gestured. 'It's the only opportunity that's come my way so far to climb out of the hole Scout and I are stuck in. And...' She stopped.

'Go on?' he prompted.

She moistened her lips. 'This may sound strange, but seeing you with Archie sort of—made up my mind. But if it's going to...' She hesitated.

'Going to what? Make my life uncomfortable?' he suggested.

Liz coloured. 'I don't— I mean I—' She bit her lip.

He crossed to the desk and dropped into his chair. 'Perhaps I should take up wood-chopping?' His lips twitched.

'Seriously,' Liz said quietly, 'perhaps we should forget all about it?'

He swung his chair round so he was facing her, and she could see suddenly that he was stone-cold sober. 'No. You seem convinced you can handle it, so I'll do the same.'

'I still don't quite understand why you've offered me the position if—' She stopped a little helplessly.

'If I'm not going to get you down the slippery slope into my bed?' He looked coolly amused. 'I think it's because of my sister,' he went on. 'One reason, anyway. Hers was a similar story to yours, but we never got to know who Archie's father was. She refused to say, but she was obviously traumatized. She was bitter, and she felt she'd been betrayed. I sometimes wonder if she thought I would—' he gestured '—take matters into my own hands if she told me who he was. Then she was killed on a skiing holiday in an avalanche when Archie was three, and the secret died with her.'

'Would you have?' Liz asked round-eyed. 'Taken matters…?'

Cam Hillier looked away, his mouth set in a hard line. 'I don't know what I might have done. I hated seeing her so distressed.'

'So you had absolutely no idea who he was?'

'No. She was overseas at the time.'

'Oh. I'm sorry.'

He stared past her, his eyes bleak, then he shrugged. 'So we're on, Miss Montrose?'

Liz hesitated.

'Don't worry. I won't impose on you.'

He was not to know that his promise not to impose on her had sent an irrational—*highly* irrational—shiver down her spine, although she ignored it.

'Yes,' she said at last.

'OK. I'll get things underway. Now, let's see what the diary holds for today.'

Liz hesitated, then reached for the diary and went through his appointments one by one.

At the end of it he told her what he wanted her to arrange for him in the next few days, and it was all normal and businesslike as Liz made notes. Finally she stood up, saying, 'I'll get on to it.' She turned away.

It was as she was almost at the door that he said her name.

She turned back with her eyebrows raised.

He paused, then said quietly, 'You can always talk to me, you know. If you need to—or want to.'

Liz stared at him, and to her horror felt tears rising to the surface. She blinked several times and cleared her throat. 'Thanks,' she said huskily. 'Thank you.' And she turned away quickly, praying he would not notice how she'd been affected by a few simple words of kindness…

Lying in bed that night, though, she wondered if it was that unexpected streak of kindness in him that she—loved? No—not that, surely? But it was something that drew her to him.

CHAPTER SIX

A MONTH after she'd started work at Yewarra, Liz had
to concede that Cam Hillier had kept his promise.

It had been a hard-working but satisfying month.
She'd settled into the cottage, which wasn't far from
the house and, although small, was comfortable, with
its own fenced garden. It was not only comfortable but
picturesque, with some lovely creepers smothering its
white walls. There was also a double swing seat with
a canopy in the garden that just invited you to relax on
it.

Probably because of having lived in an apartment
all her life Scout loved the garden, and Liz loved the
fact that when she could work from the cottage, in an
inglenook converted to a small office, she could keep
an eye on Scout through the window.

It also gave Liz her own freedom. Although she
sometimes accepted Mrs Preston's invitation to eat up at
the house, she more often cooked for herself and Scout.
And when Cam was in residence and entertaining she
had a place to retreat to.

At the same time—and she hadn't thought it possible—Scout was weaving her way more and more into

her heart. She tried to analyse why, and decided it had something to do with she herself being under much less stress and being able to spend much more time with Scout.

They'd got into the habit of Scout coming into her bed every morning, bringing her favourite doll, Jenny Penny.

One morning Scout said to Liz, 'You've got me and I've got Jenny Penny. We're lucky, Mummy!'

'Sweetheart,' Liz responded, giving her blue-eyed, curly-haired daughter half a hundred kisses—a game they played— 'I am so lucky to have you I can't believe it sometimes!'

She *had* been aware that she'd been under discreet surveillance as she'd fitted into the job. Mrs Preston might be a motherly soul, and Bob might be a friendly bear of a man, but that hadn't stopped them from monitoring her progress—especially where Archie was concerned.

It hadn't annoyed her. It had made sense.

Mary had come up for a couple of weekends, and appeared satisfied that her daughter and granddaughter were in a good place. At the same time Liz had been happy to see that her mother was in high spirits— excited, and full of ideas for the costumes she was designing. Plus, Liz thought she'd detected that Mary might have a man in her life, from the odd things she'd let drop about how this or that had appealed to Martin.

But Liz's enquiries had only sent her mother faintly pink at the same time as she shrugged noncommittally.

Mary had also met Cam a couple of times and been visibly impressed. Not that that was so surprising, Liz acknowledged. What *was* surprising—although Mary had always been intuitive—was her mother's discreet summing up of the situation between her daughter and her daughter's employer.

She knows, Liz thought with an inward tremor. Somehow she's divined that things aren't quite as they seem between Cam and me.

Mary had said nothing, however, and Liz was more than happy to allow it to lie unspoken between them and, hopefully, to sink away into oblivion.

As for the work side of Liz's life—she'd gone through the big house and identified what needed repairing, replacing or upgrading, and she'd set it all in motion. She'd had a section of the stable driveway repaved where it had badly needed it, and she'd personally checked all the fence lines on Yewarra.

She'd done this on a quiet mare Bob had told her she could ride whenever she wanted to. She'd thoroughly enjoyed getting back into the saddle, and she loved the country air and the scenery.

Setting up a computer program for the stables had come easily to her, and had provided a source of great pleasure for Scout and Archie as she often took them with her to check out the foals born on Yewarra. They made up names for them as they watched them progress from stiff-legged newborns to frisky and confident in an amazingly short time.

There had been some moments of unease for her,

however, during the month. Faint shadows that had darkened her enjoyment and sense of fulfilment...

Don't get too used to this, she'd warned herself. Whatever you do, don't get a feeling of *mistress of all she surveys*. Don't let yourself feel too much at home because sooner or later you'll have to move on.

She'd reiterated those warnings to herself a couple of times, when Cam had been home with a party of guests, but from a slightly different angle. It was one thing to work with Mrs Preston and the household staff to make sure everything went like clockwork. It was another to watch from the sidelines and feel a bit like Cinderella.

And it was yet another again to find herself keeping tabs on her employer—no, not that, she thought with impatience. Surely not that! So what? To have a sixth sense whenever he was home as to his whereabouts? To feel her skin prickling in a way that told her he was nearby?

To—go on: admit it—feel needled by the way he kept his distance from her? How ridiculous is that? she asked herself more than once.

Then there was Archie.

A serious, sensitive little boy, with grey eyes and brown hair that stuck up stubbornly from his crown, he worried about all sorts of things—when five of Wenonah's puppies were sent to their new homes he hardly ate all day and couldn't sleep that night. And he pulled at her heartstrings at times when she thought about him being motherless and fatherless. When she could see how he hero-worshipped Cam, who tried to temper the little time he could spend with the boy by sending him postcards and books and weird and wonderful things from different parts of the country and overseas—things that Archie took inordinate pride in and kept in a special cabinet in his room.

'Of course they're not all suitable for a five-year-old,' Archie's nanny said to her once, when they were looking through them. 'Take this.' She pulled down a full-size boomerang from a shelf Archie couldn't reach. 'Archie didn't realise he shouldn't experiment with it inside and he threw it through a window, breaking the glass. He was really upset—until Mr Hillier found him a song about a man whose boomerang wouldn't come back. Archie loves it. It really cracks him up and it made him feel much better.'

'I—I know it,' Liz said with a smile in her voice, and she thought, so that explains *that*!

She couldn't deny that she was getting very fond of Archie.

As for Scout, although she'd missed Mary for a time, she'd taken to Daisy Kerr, Archie's nanny, and so had Liz. Daisy was a practical girl, very mindful of her responsibilities, but with a streak of romance and nonsense in her that lent itself to the magical world kids loved.

And, between them, Liz and Daisy had soon joined forces to occupy the children with all sorts of games.

One memorable one had been the baby elephant walk. When a real baby elephant had been born at Taronga Zoo, they'd watched its progress avidly on the internet, and Liz had found a recording of Henry Mancini's "Baby Elephant Walk" from the movie *Hatari*.

She and Daisy had mimicked elephants, and with one

arm outstretched for the trunk and one held behind the back they'd paced around the playroom to the music. Scout and Archie had quickly caught on, and it had become a favourite game.

None of them had realised that Cam was watching one day, unseen from the doorway, as they shuffled their way around and then all fell in a heap, the kids screaming with laughter. Liz had coloured at the indignity of it as she'd hastily got to her feet and patted herself down, but her boss had been laughing and she'd caught a glint of approval in his blue gaze.

Scout had been a little wary of Archie to begin with. It was plain Archie saw himself as the senior child on Yewarra, not to mention owner and architect of the menagerie. As such he dictated what they should do and what they should play.

Scout bore it with equanimity until one day, almost a month on, when Archie removed a toy from her. She screamed blue murder as she wrested it back, and then she pushed him over.

'Scout!' Liz scolded as she picked up the astonished Archie and gave him a hug.

'Mine!' Scout declared as she clasped the toy to her chest and stamped her foot.

'Well...' Liz said a little helplessly

'Like mother like daughter,' Cam Hillier murmured, causing Liz to swing round in surprise.

'I didn't know you were here!'

He straightened from where he'd propped his wide shoulders against the playroom doorframe. 'Just arrived.

I drove up. So she's got a temper and a mind of her own, young Scout?'

Liz grimaced. 'Apparently. I've never seen her react like that before.' She turned back. 'Scout, you mustn't do that. Archie, are you all right?'

Daisy took over at this point. 'You'll be fine, won't you, Archie? And we'll all be friends now. I know—let's go and see Wenonah and her puppy.'

Liz and Cam watched the three of them head off towards the stables, peace and contentment restored, although Liz felt somewhat guilty.

'Thank heavens for Wenonah and her puppy—look, I'm sorry,' she said. 'They usually get along like a house on fire.'

He shrugged. 'It probably won't do Archie any harm to learn from an early age that the female sex can be unpredictable.'

Liz opened her mouth, closed it, then chuckled. 'But you must admit I don't go around pushing people over. Or screaming at them,' she said humorously.

He glanced down at her quizzically as they walked side by side into the kitchen.

Liz clicked her tongue. 'Well, maybe I *did* threaten you once—but under extreme provocation, and I would never have carried it out! I didn't scream either.' She stopped and had to laugh. 'I would have loved to, though.'

'Oh, good. There are some things I did want to speak to you about. When would you like to have a tour?'

'I think I'm going to hit the sack after this. How about tomorrow morning?'

'Fine.' But she said it slowly and looked at him rather narrowly.

'What?' he queried.

'Are you feeling OK? I only ask,' she added hastily, 'because I've never seen you less than…well, full of energy.'

Cam Hillier drummed his fingers on the table, then raked a hand through his hair and rubbed the blue shadows on his jaw. He wondered what she would say if he told her the truth.

That he was growingly plagued by thoughts of her. That when he allowed himself to step into his imagination he could picture himself exploring the pale, satiny, secret places of her slim elegant body. He could visualise himself, with the lightest touch, bringing her to the incandescence he'd seen in her once or twice—but much more than that, more personal, more physical, more joyful.

He could see her, in his mind's eye, breathless, beaded with sweat, and achingly beautiful as she responded to his ardour with her own…

How would she react if she knew that to see her apparently blooming when he was going through all this was actually annoying the hell out of him?

That, and something else. He was the one who had visualised a family unit. He was the one who'd dug into his subconscious and realised his business life had taken over his whole life—to its detriment—but he didn't seem to be able to change gears and slow down. It had been *his* somewhat shadowy intention to see how

Liz fitted into Yewarra, and therefore by extension his life, to make it work better for him—for both of them.

Yes, he'd kept his distance for the last month, to give her time to settle in and because he'd made her a promise, but it had become an increasing hardship. What he hadn't expected was to find that the family circle had been well and truly forged—Liz, Scout and Archie— and *he* now felt like an outsider in his own home.

Was there any softening in her attitude towards men, and towards him in particular? he wondered, and was on the point of simply asking her outright. Take it easy, he advised himself instead. Don't go crashing around like a bull in a china shop. But he grimaced. He knew himself well enough to know that he would bring the subject up sooner or later…

'I'm OK,' he said at length. 'Thank you for your concern,' he added formally, although he couldn't prevent the faintest hint of irony as well. 'I should be back to fighting fit by tomorrow.' And the sooner I get out of here the better, he added, but this time to himself.

Liz might not have been privy to her employer's thoughts, but she found she was curiously restless after their encounter.

Restless and uneasy, but not able to say why.

The next morning she told herself she'd been imagining things as they toured the house and she pointed out to Cam what she'd organised for it.

He appeared to be back to normal. He looked refreshed, and his manner was easy. He also looked quintessentially at home on his country estate, in jeans and a khaki bush shirt. And he'd already—with Archie and Scout's assistance—been on a tadpole-gathering exercise in a creek not far from the house, to add to the menagerie's frog population.

Scout, who'd been a bit awestruck when she'd first met Cam Hillier, had completely lost her reserve now, Liz noted. And that led her to think, still with some amazement, about the two sides that made up her employer: the dictatorial, high-flying businessman, and the man who was surprisingly good with little kids.

'This is the only room where it seemed like a good idea to start from scratch,' she said as they stood in the doorway of the veranda lounge, which was glassed in conservatory-style, with a paved area outside and views of the valley. It was the focal point for guests for morning and afternoon tea. As such, it got a lot of use—and was showing it.

Cam had already approved the upgrading of two guest bedrooms, the new plumbing she'd ordered for some of the bathrooms, the new range she'd ordered for Mrs Preston, and he'd waved a hand when she told him about the linen, crockery and kitchenware she'd ordered.

'I got a quote and some sketches and samples from an interior decorating firm,' she told him, 'but I thought you'd like the final say.'

'Show me.'

So she displayed the sketches, the pictures of furniture and the fabric samples.

Cam studied them. 'Got a pin?'

She frowned. 'A pin?'

'Do you always repeat what people say to you?' he enquired.

'No,' she retorted.

'You seem to do it a lot with me.'

'That's because you consistently take me by surprise!' she countered. 'What on earth—?' She paused and stared at him. 'Don't tell me you're going to choose one with a pin?'

He laughed at her expression. 'It's not sacrilege, and since I don't have a wife to do it for me, what's left? Or why don't you choose?'

'Because I don't have to live with it. Because I'm not...' She stopped and stared at him as a vision she'd warned herself so often against entertaining raced through her mind.

'Because you're not my wife? Of course I know that, dear Liz,' he drawled, and once again couldn't help a certain tinge of irony.

She might have missed it yesterday, but Liz didn't miss it now. She blinked as she became aware of a need to proceed with caution, of dangerous undercurrents between them that she didn't fully understand—or was that being naïve?

Of course it was, she chastised herself. She could feel the physical tension between them. She could feel the heat...

They were standing facing each other, separated by no more than a foot. His shirt was open at the neck and she could see the curly black hair in the vee of it. She took an unexpected breath as she visualised him without his shirt, with all the muscles of his powerful, sleek torso exposed. She felt her fingertips tingle, as if they were passing over his skin, tracing a path through those springy black curls downwards...

She felt her nipples tingle and she had a sudden, mind-blowing vision of his hand on her, tracing a similar path downwards from her breasts.

Worse, she was unable to tear her gaze from his—and she had no doubt he'd be able to read what was going through her mind as colour mounted in her cheeks and her breathing accelerated. She was not to know he could also see a pulse fluttering at the base of her throat, but she did see a nerve suddenly beating in his jaw—something she'd seen before.

She swallowed desperately and opened her mouth to say she knew not what—anything to defuse the situation—but he got in first.

'You are a woman of taste and discrimination, wouldn't you say?' His gaze wandered up and down her in a way that she thought might be slightly insolent—why?

But it did help her regain some composure. 'I guess that's for others to decide,' she said tartly, and for good measure added, 'If you really want to know, I don't like any of these ideas.'

She turned to look around at the veranda room. 'It's a room to be comfortable in—not stiff and formal, as these sketches are.' She gestured to the drawings. 'It's not a room for pastel colours and spindly furniture. You need vibrant colours and comfortable chairs. You need some indoor plants. You need—' She broke off and put her fingers to her lips, realising that in her confusion and everything else she'd got quite carried away. 'Sorry. That's only my—thinking.'

He watched her with a glint of amusement. 'Do it,' he said simply.

'What?' She raised an eyebrow at him. 'Do what?'

'Liz, you're doing it again,' he remonstrated. 'Decorate it yourself, along the lines you've just described to me. I like the sound of it. I won't,' he added deliberately, 'confuse you with a wife.'

Liz opened her mouth, but Mrs Preston intervened as she came into the room.

'Liz—excuse me, Mr Hillier—I just wanted to check with you whether the barbecue is going ahead this afternoon?'

'Oh!' Liz hesitated, then turned to Cam. 'I was going to have an early barbecue for the kids—round about five this afternoon, in my garden. We've done that a couple of times lately and they both really enjoy it. But you might like to have Archie to yourself?'

'What I'd like is to be invited to the barbecue,' Cam Hillier said blandly.

'So I don't need to cater for you this evening, Mr Hillier?' Mrs Preston put in—a little hastily, Liz thought with an inward frown.

Cam raised his eyebrows at Liz.

'Uh—no. I mean, yes. I mean…' Liz stopped on an edge of frustration. 'No, you don't, Mrs Preston. Please do come to the barbecue, Mr Hillier.'

'If you're sure it's not too much trouble, Miss Montrose?' he replied formally.

'Not at all,' she said, with the slightest edge that she

hoped wasn't apparent to Mrs Preston. But she knew she was being laughed at and couldn't help herself. 'We specialise in sausages on bread.'

'Oh!' Mrs Preston had turned away, but now she turned back, her face a study of consternation. 'Oh, look—I can help out, Liz. You can't give Mr Hillier kids' food.'

'I was only joking, Mrs Preston,' Liz said contritely, and she put her arms around that troubled lady. 'I've got—let me see...' She paused to do a mental run-through of her fridge and pantry. 'Some prime T-bones, and I can whip up a potato gnocchi with bacon and some pecorino cheese, and a green salad. How does that sound?'

Mrs Preston relaxed and patted Liz's cheek. 'I should have known you were teasing me.'

'But were you?' Cam Hillier murmured when his housekeeper was out of earshot.

'What do you mean?' Liz queried.

'*Were* you teasing her? I can actually see you deliberately condemning me to sausages on bread,' he elucidated.

Liz gathered all her sketches and samples before gainsaying a reply. 'Have you got nothing else to do but torment me?'

'*You*—' he pointed his forefingers at her pistol-wise '—are supposed to be giving *me*—' he reversed his hands '—a tour of all the great things you've done or plan to do for Yewarra.'

Liz caught her breath. 'If—' she said icily.

'Hang on—let me rephrase,' he interrupted humorously.

'Don't bother,' she flashed.

'Liz!' He was openly laughing now. 'Where's your sense of humour?'

'To quote you—flown out of the window.' She stopped and bit her lip frustratedly, because the conversation where he'd used that phrase was the last thing she wanted to bring to mind. The day he'd told her that professionalism between them had flown out of the window...

She was saved by his mobile phone.

He pulled it out of his pocket impatiently, and spoke into it equally impatiently. 'Roger, didn't I tell you not to bother me? What? All right. Hang on—no, I'll ring you back.' He flicked the phone off.

'You'll be happy to know you're released for the rest of the day, Miss Montrose,' he said dryly. 'Something has come up, as they say.'

'Oh? Not bad news?' she heard herself ask.

'If you call the potential acquisition of another company via some delicate negotiations that require my expert touch bad news, no.'

Liz blinked confusedly. 'You don't sound too happy about it, though.'

He moved his shoulders and grimaced. 'It's more work.'

'Surely—surely you could cut back?' she suggested. And with inner surprise heard herself add, 'Do you *need* another company?'

'No. But it gets to be a habit. I'll see you at five.'

Liz stared after him as he strode out of the veranda room and found herself prey to some conflicting emotions. Surely Cameron Hillier didn't deserve her sympathy for any reason? But *was* it sympathy? Or a sort of admiration tinged with—? Don't tell me, she reprimanded herself.

Surely I'm not joining the ranks of his devoted staff?

She sat down suddenly with a frown as it occurred to her that the frenetic pace her boss worked at might be a two-edged sword for him. He hadn't sounded enthusiastic at the prospect of another take-over. He'd admitted it was habit-forming in a dry way, as if to say he did it but he didn't exactly approve.

Did he have trouble relaxing? Was he unable to unwind? And if so why?

She blinked several times as it crossed her mind that she was not the only one with burdens of one sort or another. She blinked again as this revelation that Cam Hillier might need help made him suddenly more accessible to her—closer. As if she wanted to be closer, even able to help.

But what about what had gone—before she'd felt this streak of sympathy for him? What about the simmering sensual tension that had surrounded them? Where had it exploded from? In the month she'd been at Yewarra he'd given no sign of it during his visits, and she'd been highly successful at clamping down on her feelings. Or so she'd thought…

So how, and why, had it escaped from the box today, over an interior decorating issue?

Not that at all. It had been the mention of not being his wife, she suddenly realised. It was the thought of *being* his wife that had raced through her mind and opened up that flood of pure sensuality for her.

She looked around, looked at the samples and sketches she'd folded up neatly, and thought of her brief to redecorate the room. But none of those thoughts could chase away the one that underlined them. Why did she feel like a giddy schoolgirl with an adolescent crush?

The barbecue, although Liz had been dreading another encounter with Cam Hillier, and was feeling tense and uneasy in consequence, was going smoothly—at first.

She'd loaded the brick barbecue with paper and wood, and ensured the cooking grid was clean. She'd put a colourful cloth on the veranda table, along with a bunch of flowers she'd picked, and she'd lit some candles in glasses even though the sun hadn't set, to add a festive note to an occasion that the kids loved.

She'd showered, and changed into a grey short-sleeved jumper and jeans, and—as she usually did on these occasions—she'd devised a treasure hunt through the garden for Scout and Archie. Something they also loved.

As promised, she'd produced steaks, potato gnocchi and a salad, as well as sausages on bread. There was also a chocolate ice cream log waiting in the freezer.

Although all set to do the cooking on the barbecue herself, when Cam arrived with Archie Liz found herself manipulated by her boss into releasing the reins after he'd taken one shrewd glance at her. He'd brought a bottle of wine and he poured her a glass and told her to relax.

She sat down in two minds at first, but the lengthening shadows as the lovely afternoon slid towards evening, the perfume from the garden and the birdsong got to her, and she found herself feeling a little better.

He was a good cook, and he handled the fire well, she had to acknowledge when the steaks and sausages were ready. Nothing was burnt, and nothing was rare to dripping blood. It was all just right. And not only Scout and Archie, sitting on a rug on the lawn, tucked in with gusto, so did she.

Then came the chocolate ice cream log, and with it an extra surprise. Liz had stuck some sparklers into it, causing round-eyed wonder in to the kids when she lit them.

'Wow! Now it's a real party,' Archie enthused. 'Don't be scared, Scout,' he added, as Scout stuck her thumb in her mouth. 'They won't hurt you—promise. Yippee!' And, grabbing Scout by the hand, he danced around the garden with her until she forgot to be nervous.

But that wasn't the end of the surprises—although the next one was for Liz. When the kids had finished their ice cream and quietened down, could even be seen to be yawning, although they tried valiantly to hide it, Mrs Preston and Daisy appeared, with the suggestion that Scout might like to spend the night in the nursery up at the big house tonight.

Scout said, 'Yes, please—pretty please, Mummy,' before Liz had a chance to get a word in, and Archie added his own impassioned plea.

So she agreed ruefully.

It was after she'd collected Scout's pyjamas and was about to head up to the big house that Mrs Preston said, 'You two relax, now. Oh, look—you haven't finished the wine!'

Thus it was that peace and quiet descended on the garden, and Liz found herself alone with Cam and with a second glass of wine in her hand. A silver sickle moon was rising, and there was a pale plume of smoke coming from the barbecue as it sank to a bed of ashes. There were fireflies hovering above the flowerbeds, fluttering their delicate wings.

She frowned, however. 'They didn't have to do that.'

He grimaced, and went to say something in reply, she thought. But all he said in the end was, 'They do get on well, the kids.'

'I guess they have quite a bit in common. They're pretty articulate for their ages—probably because they're single kids, so they get a lot of adult attention. They have that in common. I think Archie is particularly bright, actually. And quite sensitive.'

'I think he's certainly appreciated having you and Scout around. He seems…' Cam paused, then grimaced. 'I know it sounds strange for a five-year-old, but he seems more relaxed.'

'Except when he gets shoved around—but it hasn't happened again. I've asked Daisy to watch out for it.'

'They've probably established their parameters. Their no-go zones.' He glanced at her. 'As we have.'

Liz looked down at her wine and sipped it.

'What would you say if I suggested we move our parameters, Liz?'

She opened her mouth to ask him what he meant, but that would be unworthy, she knew. In fact it would be fair to say their parameters had moved themselves of their own accord, only hours ago.

'I—I thought it was going so well,' she said desolately at last.

CHAPTER SEVEN

'IT IS GOING well, Liz,' he said dryly.

'Not if we keep—' She broke off, floundering.

'Finding ourselves wanting each other? So I wasn't imagining it earlier?'

She glinted an ironic little glance at him.

'Dear Liz,' he drawled as he interpreted the glance, 'you're not always that easy to read. For example, I arrived in your garden tonight to find you in chilly mode—prepared to hold me not so much at arm's length but at one hundred feet down a hole. Or—' he paused and inspected his glass '—prepared to scratch my eyes out if I so much as put a foot wrong.'

Liz sat up with a gasp. 'That's not true!'

He shrugged. 'Uptight, then. Which made me wonder.'

She subsided.

He watched her thoughtfully. 'Don't you think it's about time you admitted you're human? That you may have had good cause to freeze off any attraction under the weight of the betrayal you suffered but you can't go through the rest of your life like that?'

'So…so…' Her voice shook a little. 'You think I'm being melodramatic and ridiculous?'

'I didn't say that, but it is a proposition I'm putting to you. Take courage is what I'm really trying to say.'

'By having an affair with you?' She said it out of a tight throat. 'I—'

'Liz, I'm not going to get you pregnant and desert you,' he said deliberately. 'But we can't go on like this. *I* can't go on like this. I want you. I know I said I wouldn't but—' He stopped frustratedly.

'It will spoil everything, though.'

'Why?'

She licked her lips. 'Well, it would have to be sort of clandestine, and…'

'Why the hell should it be? You're probably the only one around here who doesn't believe it might be on the cards.' He lifted an ironic eyebrow at her. 'Why do you think we've been left alone in a romantically moonlit garden?'

Liz's eyes widened. 'You mean Mrs Preston and Daisy…?'

He nodded. 'They've both given me to understand you and I would be well-suited.'

'In so many words?' Liz was stunned.

He shook his head and looked amused. 'But they never lose an opportunity to sing your praises. Bob's the same. Even Hamish.' Hamish was the crusty head gardener. 'He has allowed it to pass his lips that you're "not bad for a lass". Now, that's a *real* compliment.'

Liz compressed her lips as she thought of the gossip that must have been going on behind her back.

'And Scout and Archie are too young to be affected,' he went on. 'If you're happy to go on in your job there's no reason why you shouldn't.'

Liz got up and paced across the lawn, with her arms folded, her glass in her hand.

He watched her in silence.

She turned to him at last, her eyes dark with the effort to concentrate.

'Liz,' he said barely audibly, 'let go. For once, just let go. The last thing I want to do is hurt you.' He put his glass down on the lawn and got up. 'Give me that.' He took her glass from her and put it down too. Then he put his hands around her waist loosely, and drew her slowly towards him.

Liz stiffened, but as she looked up into his face in the moonlight she suddenly knew she couldn't resist him. She raised her hand tentatively and touched her fingertips to the little lines beside his mouth—something she realised she'd wanted to do for ever, it seemed. Just as she'd wanted to be drawn to the flame of this tall, dangerously alive, incredibly exciting and tempting man for ever...

He turned his head and kissed her fingers, ran his hands up and down her back, then down to the flare of her hips. She breathed raggedly as her whole body came alive with delicious tremors.

He bent his head and started to kiss her.

Some minutes later, he picked her up and carried her to the swing seat, sat down with her across his lap.

'Forgive me,' he said then, 'but I've been wanting to do this for some time. And so have you, I can't help feeling. Maybe that's all we should think of?' And he cupped her cheek lightly.

Liz was arrested, with her lips parted, her eyes huge. And if she thought she'd been affected by him on a hot Sydney pavement, in his car, in his office, in his veranda room it was nothing to the mounting sensations she was experiencing now, in his arms.

She could literally feel her body come alight where it was in contact with his. She felt, to her astonishment, a primitive urge to throw her arms round his neck and surrender her mouth, her breasts, her whole body to him, to be played in whatever key he liked. But what she would really like, she knew, would be for him to mix his keys. To be gentle, although a little teasing, to be strong when she needed it, to be in charge when she was about to explode with desire—because she just knew he could do that to her…make her ignite.

She groaned and closed her eyes, and when she felt his mouth on hers she did put her arms around his neck and draw him closer.

He did just as she'd wished, as if he'd read her mind. He ran his fingers through her hair, then down her neck and round her throat, and that was nice. It made her skin feel like silk. But when he slipped his hand beneath her jumper and beneath her bra strap it was more than nice. It was exquisite. And tremors ran up and down her because it was almost too much to bear.

As if he sensed it, he removed his hand and stopped kissing her briefly to say, 'This can be a two-way street.'

A smile curved her lips, and she freed her hands and slid them beneath his shirt.

It was glorious, she found. A glorious warmth that came to her as she held him close. It was a kinship that banished the lonely years—but a kinship with an exciting, dangerous edge to it, she thought. A blending of their bodies—a transference, as his hands moved on her and hers moved on him, of lovely sensations and rhythms that had to lead to the final act they both not only sought but needed desperately.

But that was where the danger lay, she knew. Not only because of the consequences that could arise— she would never allow that to happen to her again—but could she afford the less tangible consequences? The giving of her soul into a man's keeping with this act, only to have it brutally returned to her?

She faltered in his arms.

He raised his head. 'Liz?' Then he smiled down at her. 'Not an Ice Queen at all. The opposite, if anything. I—'

But he never did get to say it, because she freed herself and fell off his lap.

'Liz!' He reached for her. 'What's wrong?'

She scrambled up, evading his hands and smoothing her clothes. 'You make it sound as if I'm in the habit of doing this.'

'I didn't say that.'

'You didn't have to.' She dragged her fingers through her hair.

'Liz.' He pushed himself off the swing seat and towered over her. 'You are being ridiculous now. Look, I know you might have cause to be sensitive about what men think of you, but—'

'Oh, I *am*.' She retreated a few steps. 'Sorry, but that's me!'

'Despite the fact you light up like a firecracker in my arms? No,' he said as she gasped, 'I'm *not* going to sugar-coat things between us just because you had one lousy experience.'

'Sugar-coating or not, you'll be talking to yourself. I'm going in!' And she ran across the dew-spangled lawn and into the house.

He made no attempt to follow her.

The next morning she studied herself in the bathroom mirror and flinched.

There were dark shadows under her eyes, she was pale, and she looked—not to put too fine a point on it—tormented.

She took a hot shower and dressed in navy shorts and a white T-shirt. She didn't even have Scout to distract her, she thought dismally, as she made coffee and poured herself a mug. But coffee would help, she assured herself as she picked up the phone that had a direct line to the house. Help her to do what she knew she had to do.

Two minutes later she waited for Mrs Preston to put the house phone down, then she slammed hers into its cradle and wouldn't have given a damn if it never worked again.

She took her coffee to the kitchen table, and to her horror found herself crying again. She licked the salty tears from her lips and forced herself to sip her coffee as she wondered what to do.

Her plan had been to offer her resignation to Cameron Hillier via the telephone, and not take no for an answer. That was not possible, however, because according to Mrs Preston he'd driven away from Yewarra last night.

Had he left any messages? Any instructions? Had he said when he'd be back? No, no and no, had been Mrs Preston's response. All he'd left was a note, telling her what he'd done. There'd been a puzzled note in Mrs Preston's voice—puzzled and questioning at the same time. Liz had understood, but had had no answer for her.

Typical of the arrogant man she knew him to be, she thought bitterly. How could he not know that with one short observation he'd made her feel cheap last night? How could he not know that, for her, when she gave herself to a man it could never be just sex? It was a head over heels, all bells and whistles affair for her. It was the way she was made and it had taken one awful lesson to teach her that.

On the other hand, was he entitled to be angry with her? Had she overreacted?

She paused her thoughts and got up to look out of the kitchen window. It was an overcast morning, as grey as she felt. Not only grey, but down in the dumps and… hopeless.

What if she'd said yes? Would she have spent her life feeling as if she was treading on eggshells in case it didn't last and he turned to some other woman? After all, despite his explanation of the situation that had developed between him and Portia Pengelly, she couldn't help feeling a streak of sympathy for Portia.

She also flinched inwardly because she knew herself well enough to know that she might *never* feel safe with a man again, despite the irrationality of it. It too was the way she was made. No half-measures for Liz Montrose, she thought grimly. Could she change?

But even if she did there was something holding her back—something she couldn't quite pin down in her mind. Unless…?

She stared unseeingly out of the window and thought suddenly, *Of course!* It was her reputation that was troubling her so deeply. Living with a man in an informal relationship, as opposed to Scout's father who was solidly married—could she ever feel right about that? Not so much not right, but secure in her position as the most suitable parent for Scout?

She folded her arms around her, trying desperately to find some comfort and some solution.

If she didn't agree to move in with Cam Hillier, what on earth was she going to do? Walk away? Uproot Scout? Leave Archie? Go back to living with her mother—who definitely had a man in her life and was loving every minute of it, as well as her costume-designing project?

But how could she stay…?

She reached for the other phone, the one with an outside line, and rang Cam Hillier's mobile. She couldn't allow things to simply hang, but perhaps she could offer him a week's notice so as not to destabilise his house-hold completely?

What she got was a recorded message advising callers that he was unavailable and they should contact Roger Woodward if the matter was urgent. It wasn't even his own voice. It was Roger's.

She pressed her lips together as she put the phone down, and thought, *All right!* She had no choice but to go on as usual—for the time being.

Several days later Cam stared around his office in the Hillier Corporation's premises and knew he was in deep trouble.

He'd just signed the final document that had acquired him another company and he couldn't give a damn. Worse than that, he hated the drive within him that had seen him add another burden to his life—a life that was already overburdened and completely unsatisfactory.

He'd been more right than he knew when he'd posed that question to himself—what if a tortured Ice Queen was the one woman he really wanted and couldn't have?

What if?

He'd turn into a more demented workaholic than ever. He'd turn into a monster to work for. He'd...

He threw his pen down on the desk and ground his teeth. There had to be a way to get through to Liz. He knew now they set each other alight physically—it certainly wasn't one-sided—but how to make her see there was so much more they could share? How to make her see he needed her?

He shrugged and thought with amazement that Liz Montrose had planted herself in his heart probably from the moment he'd caught her climbing over his wall. That was the way it had happened, and he was helpless to change it.

And the irony was she loved Yewarra and Archie, and Scout loved…

He sat up suddenly. Archie and Scout—would they get through to Liz where he had failed?

He came back with a house party.

It was an impromptu party in that it had somehow been missed in both his office and the Yewarra diary until it was too late cancel. And Liz and Mrs Preston had only had a couple of hours and their work cut out to have everything ready for six overnight guests.

As for her own *contretemps*—how she was going to face Cam Hillier—Liz had no idea. But she comforted herself with the thought that at least she could stay very much in the background, as she usually did when there were guests.

An hour before dinner was due to be served she learnt that she was to be denied even that respite.

She got an urgent call from Mrs Preston with the news that her offsider, Rose, who acted as a waitress, had cut her hand and wouldn't be able to work. Could Liz hand Scout over to Daisy for the night and take her place?

Liz breathed heavily, but she could tell from Mrs Preston's voice that the housekeeper was under a lot of pressure. 'Sure,' she said. 'Give me half an hour.'

* * *

She showered, and changed hastily into a little black dress and flat shoes.

She hesitated briefly in front of the bathroom mirror, then swept her hair back into a neat, severe pleat and applied no make-up. She thought of replacing her contact lenses with her glasses, but decided she didn't need to go to extremes.

Then she gathered up Scout, and everything she needed, and ran over to the big house. Archie was delighted with the unexpected change of plan, and proudly displayed the latest curiosity Cam had brought home for him: a didgeridoo that was taller than Archie himself.

Liz glanced at Daisy, who raised her eyes heavenwards.

'Problem is I can't play it—and girls aren't allowed to, Cam said.' Archie suddenly looked as troubled as only he could at times.

Liz squatted down in front of him and put an arm round him. Scout came and snuggled into her other side. She dropped light kisses on their heads. 'It's very hard,' she said seriously, 'to play a didgeridoo. You need to learn a special kind of breathing, and you need to be a bit bigger and older. So until that happens, Archie, what say we find out all about them? How they're made, where this one may have come from, and so on.'

Archie considered the matter. 'OK,' he said at last. 'Will you help me, Liz?'

'Sure,' Liz promised. 'In the meantime, goodnight to both of you. Sleep tight!' She hugged them both, and to

Daisy added, 'I took them for a run through the paddock this afternoon to check out the new foals, so they should be happy to go to bed PDQ!'

Mrs Preston was standing in the middle of the kitchen still as a statue, with her fists clenched and her eyes closed, when Liz got there.

'Mrs P! What's wrong?' Liz flew across the tiled floor. 'Are you all right?'

Mrs Preston opened her eyes and unclenched her fists. 'I'm all right, dear,' she said. 'It must be the late notice we got that's making me feel a bit flustered. And, of course, Rose cutting her hand like that.'

'Just tell me what to do. Between us we can cope!' Although she sounded bright and breezy, Liz swallowed suddenly, but told herself it was no good both she *and* Mrs Preston going to water. 'What delicious dishes have you concocted tonight?'

Mrs Preston visibly took hold of herself. 'Leek soup with croutons, roast duck with maraschino cherries, and my hot chocolate pudding for dessert. The table is set. I'll carve the duck and we'll serve it with the vegetables buffet-style on the sideboard, so they can help themselves. Could you be a love and check the table, Liz? Oh, and put out the canapés?'

'Roger wilco!'

The dining room looked lovely. The long table was clothed in cream damask with matching napkins, and a centrepiece of massed blue agapanthus stood between two silver-branched candlesticks.

Liz did a quick check of the cutlery, the crystal and

the china and found it all present and correct, then carried the canapé platters through to the veranda room. There were delicate bites of caviar—red and black—on toast, and anchovies on biscuits. There were olives and small meatballs on toothpicks, with a savoury sauce in a fluted silver dipping dish. A hot pepperoni sausage had been cut into circles and was accompanied by squares of cool Edam. There were tiny butterfly prawns with their tail shells still attached, so they could be dipped into the thousand island sauce in a crystal bowl.

It was the prawns that reminded Liz of the need for napkins for the canapés. She found them, and jogged back to the veranda room—not that they were running late, but she had the feeling that the less time Mrs Preston was left alone tonight, the better.

She deployed the napkins and swung round—to run straight into Cam Hillier.

'Whoa!' he said, and steadied her with his hands on her shoulders, as he'd done once before on a hot Sydney pavement—an encounter that seemed like a lifetime away as it flashed through Liz's mind.

'Oh!' she breathed, and then to all intents and purposes was struck dumb, as the familiar sensations her boss could inflict on her ran in a clamouring tremor through her body.

'Liz?' He frowned, giving no indication that he was at all affected as she was. 'What are you doing?'

'Uh…' She took some quick breaths. 'Hello! I'm filling in for Rose. She had an accident—she cut her hand.'

His gaze took in her pinned-back hair and moved

down her body to her flat shoes. 'You're going to waitress?'

She nodded. 'Don't worry,' she assured him, 'I don't mind! Mrs Preston really needs a hand and—'

'No,' he interrupted.

Liz blinked. 'No? But—'

'No,' he repeated.

'Why not?' She stared up at him, utterly confused. He was wearing a crisp check shirt open at the throat, and pressed khaki trousers. She could smell his faint lemony aftershave, and his hair was tidy and slightly damp.

'Because,' he said, 'you're coming to this dinner as a guest.'

He removed his hands from her shoulders and with calm authority reached round her head to release her hair from its pins, which he then ceremoniously presented to her.

Liz gasped. 'How…? Why…? You can't… I can't do that! I'm not dressed or anything.' She stopped abruptly with extreme frustration. What she wore could be the least of her problems!

'You *are* dressed.' He inspected the little black dress. 'Perhaps not Joseph's amazing coat of many colours, but it'll do.'

Her mouth fell open—and Daisy walked into the veranda room, calling her name.

'There you are, Liz! Oh, sorry, Mr Hillier—I was looking for Liz to tell her that she was right. Both Archie and Scout are fast asleep!'

'That's great news, Daisy,' Cam said. 'Daisy, I have

a huge favour to ask of you,' he added. 'We seem to be short-staffed—would you mind helping Mrs Preston out with dinner tonight? Liz was going to, but I'd like her to be a guest.'

Daisy's eyes nearly fell out on stalks, but she rallied immediately. 'Of course I wouldn't mind. But...' She trailed off and looked a little anxiously at Liz.

'I look a mess?' Liz said dryly.

'No, you don't!' Daisy said loyally. 'You always look wonderful. It's just that your hair needs a brush! I'll get one.' And she twirled on her heels and ran out.

Leaving Liz confronting her employer with a mixture of sheer bewilderment and disbelief in her eyes.

'Why are you doing this?' she asked, her voice husky with surprise and uncertainty.

'Because if you ever do agree to live with me, Liz Montrose, I'd rather not have it bandied about that you were once one of my kitchen staff. For your sake, that is. *I* don't give a damn.'

Five minutes later, with her hair brushed but still no reply formulated to what her boss had said to her, Liz was being introduced to the house guests as his estate manager.

Half an hour later she was seated on his right hand, with her spoon poised to partake of Mrs Preston's pale green leek soup that was artistically swirled with cream.

It was going amazingly well, this dinner party that she had gatecrashed.

The guest party comprised two middle-aged couples,

a vibrant woman in her early thirties, and Cam's legal adviser in an unofficial capacity. The talk was wide-ranging as the duck with its lovely accompaniment of glowing maraschino cherries was served, and Liz was gradually able to lose her slightly frozen air.

And then the talk became localised—on horses. On breeding, racing, and buying and selling horses.

Thanks to the computer program Liz had set up for Bob, and her involvement in the stables, it wasn't all double Dutch to her. She was even able to describe several of the latest foals that had been born in the past few weeks.

That was when she realised that all the guests had come to view the latest crop of yearlings Yewarra had bred.

It grew on Liz that the vibrant woman—her name was Vanessa—with her golden pageboy hair, her scarlet lips and nails, her trim figure and toffee-coloured eyes, was a little curious about her. Twice she had surprised those unusual eyes resting on her speculatively.

And twice Liz had found herself thinking, *If you're wondering about me in the context of Cam Hillier, Vanessa, that's nothing to my utter confusion on the subject! But what are you doing here? A new girlfriend? No, that doesn't make sense. But...*

Finally the evening came to an end, and all the guests went to bed.

Liz retreated to the kitchen, to find it empty and gleaming. She breathed a sigh of relief and poured herself a glass of water. Daisy had obviously been a tower of strength in the kitchen tonight.

Something prompted her to go out through the kitchen door and wander through the herb garden that was Mrs Preston's pride and joy until she came to the lip of the valley.

It was only a gradual decline at that point, but it was protected by a low hedge and was an amazing spot to star-gaze. There was even a bench, and she sank down onto it and stared upwards, with her lips parted in amazement at the heavenly firmament above her.

That was how Cam Hillier found her.

'One of my favourite spots, too,' he murmured as he sat down beside her. 'I was looking for you. Put your glass down,' he instructed.

Liz opened her mouth to question this, but did as she was told instead, and he handed her a glass of champagne.

'You hardly had a mouthful of wine at dinner, and there's a refreshing quality to a glass of bubbly at the end of the day. Cheers!' He touched his glass to hers.

'Cheers,' Liz repeated, but sounded notably sub-dued—which she was. Subdued, tired, and entirely unsure how to cope with Cam Hillier.

'What's up?' he queried.

Liz took a large sip. 'Brrr...' She shook her head, but found her tongue suddenly loosened. 'Up? I don't know. I have no idea. If you were to ask me what's going on I wouldn't be able to tell you. I'm mystified. I'm bothered and bewildered. That's what's up,' she finished.

He laughed softly. 'OK, I'll tell you. We got into a verbal stoush the last time we met.'

She made a slight strangled sound.

He stopped, but she said nothing so he went on. 'Yes, a war of words after a rather lovely interlude, when I made an unfortunate remark which incensed you and you slammed your way inside, whilst I slammed my way back to Sydney in the dead of night, where I remained, incensed, for some days.'

He paused and went on with an entirely unexpected tinge of remorse, 'I don't very often get said no to—which may account for my lack of graciousness or my pure bloody-mindedness when it does happen. What do you think?'

'I...' Liz paused, then found she couldn't go on as a lone tear traced down her cheek. She licked the saltiness off her upper lip.

'I mean,' he went on after a long moment, 'would I be able to mend some fences between us?'

'I can't...I can't move in with you,' she said, her voice husky with emotion. 'Surely you must see that?'

'No, I don't. Why not?'

'I'd...' She hesitated, and breathed in the scent of mint from the herb garden, 'I wouldn't feel right. Anyway—' She stopped helplessly.

'Liz, surely by now you must appreciate that you have a rather amazing effect on me?'

'You don't show it.' It was out before she could help herself.

'When?'

'Earlier. When we first met.' She clicked her tongue, because that wasn't what she'd meant or wanted to say, and moved restlessly. 'I even wondered if you'd brought Vanessa up here to...to taunt me.'

'Much as I don't mind the thought of you being jealous of Vanessa,' he said dryly, 'she's happily married to a champion jockey who rarely socialises on account of his weight battles.'

Liz flinched. 'Sorry,' she murmured.

'Have another sip,' he advised. 'What would you do if I told you that, along with wanting to stick pins into an Ice Queen effigy, I haven't been able to sleep. I've been a monster to work with. I kept thinking of how good you felt in my arms. I kept undressing you in my mind. Incidentally, how have *your* few days been?'

Liz swallowed as she recalled her days—as she thought of how she'd exchanged the swings for the roundabouts in her emotions. Round and round, up and down she'd been, as she'd alternated between maintaining her anger and wondering if he was right. Was it time to let go of her past and try to live again? Was she being unnecessarily melodramatic and tragic? But of course that hadn't been all she'd grappled with over the week.

There'd been memories of the pleasure he'd brought to her, memories of the man himself and how he could be funny and outrageously immodest when he wasn't being an arrogant multi-millionaire. How he was so good with kids—the last thing she'd have suspected of him when she'd gone to work for him. All the little things she couldn't banish that made up Cam Hillier.

'I was…a little uneven myself,' she admitted, barely audibly.

'Good.'

She looked askance at him. *'Good?'*

'I'd hate to think I was suffering alone.'

For some reason this caused Liz to chuckle—a watery little sound, but nonetheless a sound of amusement. 'You're incorrigible,' she murmured, and with a sigh of something like resignation she laid her head on his shoulder.

But she raised it immediately to look into his eyes. 'Where do we go from here, though?' There was real perturbation in her voice. 'I still can't move in with you.'

'There is another option.' He picked up her free hand and threaded his fingers through hers. 'You could marry me.'

Liz stiffened in disbelief. 'I can't just *marry* you!'

'There seems to be a hell of a lot you can't do,' he said dryly. 'What *can* you do?'

She went to get up and run as far away from him as she could, but he caught her around the waist and sat her down. He kept his hands on her waist.

'Let's not fight about this, Liz,' he recommended coolly. 'You said something to me once about two sane adults. Perhaps that's what we need now—some sanity. Let's get to the basics.'

He watched the way her mouth worked for a moment, but no sound came and he went on. 'I need a mother for Archie. You need a father for Scout and a settled background.' He raised his eyebrows. 'You couldn't find a much more solid background than this.'

Liz stared at him with her lips parted, her eyes stunned.

'Then there's you.' He tightened his hands on her

waist as she moved convulsively. 'Just listen to me,' he warned. 'You've settled into Yewarra and the life here as if you were born to it. If you don't love it, you've given a very good imitation of it. Has it been an act?' he queried curtly.

'No,' she whispered.

'And Archie?'

'I *love* Archie,' she said torturedly. 'But—'

'What about us?' His gaze raked her face, and his eyes were as brooding as she'd ever seen them. 'Let's be brutally honest for once, Liz. We're not going to be a one-night wonder. We wouldn't have felt this way for two crazy months if we were.'

She licked her lips.

'And they *have* been two crazy months, haven't they? Like a slow form of torture.'

She released a long, slow breath. 'Yes,' she said at last. 'Oh, yes.'

His hands relaxed at last on her waist. He took them away and drew her into his arms. 'Maybe we need a couple of days on our own—to get used to this idea. Would you come away with me for a while?'

'What about the kids?'

'I only meant a few days, and Archie is used to that. Perhaps your mother would come up to be with Scout?'

She took a breath. 'Well…'

'Well?' he repeated after a long moment.

It occurred to Liz that one of her hurdles in this matter was getting to the core of Cam Hillier. Discovering whether she could trust him or not. Finding out what was really behind this amazing offer of marriage.

'I—if I did it,' she said hesitantly, 'I couldn't make any promises. But you've been very good to me,' she heard herself say, 'so—'

'Liz.' His voice was suddenly rough. 'Do it or don't do it—but not out of gratitude.'

She sat up abruptly. 'I *am* grateful!'

'Then the offer's withdrawn.'

She sucked in a large amount of air. 'You're not only incorrigible, you're impossible, Cam Hillier,' she told him roundly.

'No, I'm not. Be honest, Liz. We want each other, and gratitude's got nothing to do with it.'

She opened and closed her mouth several times as her mind whirled like a Catherine wheel, seeking excuses, twirling round and round in search of escape avenues. But of course he was right. There were none.

'True,' she breathed at last. 'You're right.'

His clasp on her hand tightened almost unbearably. 'Then the offer's open again.'

'Thanks. I'll—I'll come.'

He released her hand and put his arm round her shoulders.

Liz closed her eyes and surrendered herself to the warmth that passed between them. At the same time she was conscious that she'd put her foot on an unknown path—but she just didn't seem to have the strength of mind to resist Cam Hillier.

She took refuge in the mundane, because the enormity of it all was threatening to overwhelm her.

'I'm a bit worried about Mrs Preston. She got herself into quite a state tonight.'

'I'll get her some help before we go. Don't worry. You're worse than Archie.' He slipped his fingers beneath her chin and looked down into her eyes. 'In fact,' he murmured, 'don't worry about a thing. I'll take care of it all.' And he started to kiss her.

CHAPTER EIGHT

HE TOOK HER to the Great Barrier Reef three days later.
He'd told her that much, but said the rest would be a
surprise.

They flew to Hamilton Island, just off Queensland's
Whitsunday coast, on a commercial flight. She was quiet
at first—until he put his hand over hers.

'They'll be fine—the kids.'

She looked quickly at him. 'How did you know I was
thinking about them?'

'It was a safe bet,' he said wryly. 'Unless you're re-
gretting coming away with me?'

'No...'

He narrowed his eyes at her slight hesitation, but
didn't take issue with it.

She marvelled as the jet floated over the sparkling
waters, the reefs, the islands of the Whitsunday Passage
and right over the marina, with its masts and colourful
surrounds, to land. Then she discovered they were not
staying on Hamilton, although they walked around the
busy harbour with its shops and art galleries, its cafés.
Their luggage—not that there was a lot—seemed to
have been mysteriously taken care of.

Her discovery that they weren't staying on Hamilton came in the form of a question.

'Have you got a hat?' he asked, as they stopped in front of a shop with a divine selection of hats. 'You need a hat out on the water.'

'Out on the… No, I don't have one I can squash into a suitcase. Out on the water?' she repeated.

'You'll see. Let's choose.' So they spent half an hour with Liz trying on sunhats—half an hour during which the two young, pretty shop assistants got all blushing and giggly beneath the charm and presence of Cameron Hillier.

But it was light-hearted and fun, and Liz found herself feeling light-hearted too. It was as if, she thought, all the pressure from all the difficult decisions was flowing out of her system under the influence of the holiday spirit of the island.

She chose a straw hat with a wide brim, and wore it out of the shop. They stopped at a café and had iced coffees, and shared a sinfully delicious pastry. Then, swinging her hand in his, he led down to the marina to a catamaran tied up to a jetty.

Its name was *Leilani*, and she was the last word in luxury: a blend of glossy woodwork, thick carpets, beautiful fabrics, bright brass work and sparkling white paint. The main saloon was huge, with a shipshape built-in galley. The staterooms—there were three—were wood-panelled and had sumptuous bed clothing.

There were two decks—one that led off the saloon, and an upper deck behind the fly-bridge controls.

Liz was wide-eyed even before she got to see *Leilani*'s interior. A young man in whites named Rob welcomed them aboard with a salute, and showed her to her stateroom. He returned upstairs and she heard him talking to Cam, but not what was said. When she got back on the upper deck the conference was over, and to her surprise the young man whom she'd assumed was the skipper hopped off onto the jetty as Cam started the engines and untied the lines.

'He isn't coming?' she queried.

Cam looked over his shoulder as the cat started to reverse out of the berth. 'Nope.'

She blinked. 'Do you know how to handle a boat this size?'

'Liz, I virtually grew up on boats.' He cast her a laughing look. 'Of course I do.'

She chewed her lip.

This time he laughed at her openly. 'You're getting more and more like Archie,' he teased, as he turned *Leilani* neatly on her own length and headed her for the harbour mouth. 'I'll show you how to do it—but maybe not today.'

'Do you own her—is she yours or have you borrowed her?'

'I own her.'

'I'm surprised she hasn't got a Shakespearean name!'

He said wryly, 'She was already named when I got her. It's supposed to be unlucky to change a boat's name. But funnily enough Leilani was a famous racehorse. OK. I'll need to concentrate for a few minutes,' he added as they cleared the harbour entrance.

'Where are we going?'

'Whitehaven,' he said. 'We should be there in time to see the sun set. There's nothing like it.'

He was right.

By the time the sun started to drop below the horizon they'd anchored off Whitehaven Beach, Liz had unpacked, and she was starting to feel more at home.

She'd been helped in this by the fact that once Cam was satisfied the anchor was set, and he'd turned off the motors and various other systems, he'd followed her down to the lower deck and taken her into his arms.

'A difficult few days,' he said wryly.

She could only nod in agreement. They'd decided to maintain a businesslike stance at Yewarra in front of staff and children alike—even Liz's mother, when she arrived. 'It's nothing to do with anyone but us,' he'd said. 'And we'll tell them it's a business trip to do with real estate.'

'But they'll probably be dying of curiosity,' she'd responded. 'Not the children, but…'

'Would you rather I kissed you every time I felt like it?' he'd countered.

Liz had blushed brightly and shaken her head.

'Thought not,' he'd said, with a glint of sheer devilry.

In the event he'd spent quite a bit of those three days in Sydney tidying up loose ends before going away. And Liz had spent the time he was away feeling like pinching herself—because, hard as it was to remain unaffected in his presence, it was harder to feel she'd made a rational decision when he wasn't around.

The one argument she'd bolstered herself with was that she owed it to Cam Hillier to at least try to understand him. It might be close to gratitude, but she couldn't help it; she certainly wouldn't be telling him that, though.

Now, anchored off Whitehaven Beach on his beautiful boat, he put his hand on her waist from behind and swung her round. 'I'm sorely in need of this,' he said huskily.

Liz smiled up at him and relaxed against him. 'You and me both.'

He released her waist and gathered her into his arms, making her feel slim and willowy, and said against the corner of her mouth, 'No desire to fight me or call me a menace?'

Liz suffered a jolt of laughter, but said ruefully, 'I don't know where it all went.'

'All the hostility?' He nuzzled the top of her head and moved his hands on her hips.

'Mmm… Could be something to do with—I mean it's very hard to say no to a guy with a boat like this!'

He laughed down at her and she caught her breath, because in all his dark glory he was devastatingly attractive and he made her heart beat faster and her pulses race.

'Tell you what.' He kissed her lightly. 'Why don't you change into something more comfortable whilst I whip up the sundowners that are traditional in this part of the world?'

She drew away and looked down at her clothes. She

was still wearing the jeans and top she'd travelled in. 'I guess I could. It *is* warm. How about you?'

'I'm going to sling on some shorts—but don't be long. The sun goes fast when it makes up its mind to retire.'

'Just going!' She clasped his fingers, then went inside and down to her stateroom.

'A maxi-dress! You *must* have a maxi-dress,' had been her mother's emphatic response upon learning her daughter was going to Hamilton Island in the Whitsundays, even if it was on business. 'They're all the rage. I'll bring you one!'

And despite the short notice she'd done just that—a lovely long floaty creation in white, with a wide band of tangerine swirls round the hem. It was strapless, with a built-in bra, and had a matching tangerine and white scarf to drape elegantly around her neck.

Liz slipped it on and discovered the lovely dress had a strange effect on her. It made her feel as light as a feather. It made her feel flirty and young and desirable.

In fact she stretched out her arms and did a dancing circle in front of the mirror. Then, mindful of the sun's downward path, she brushed her hair, shook her head to tousle it, put on some lipgloss and, barefoot—because that seemed to fit the scene—moved lightly up to the saloon and out on to the back deck.

Cam was already there, changed into navy shorts and a white T-shirt. He was sitting with his long legs propped up on the side of the boat. On the table beside him stood two creamy white cocktails, complete with paper parasols. There was also a pewter tray of smoked salmon canapés, topped with cream cheese and capers.

'You're a marvel, Mr Hillier!' She laughed at him with her hands on her hips. 'I had no idea you were so domesticated.'

He turned to look at her, and it was his turn to catch his breath—although she didn't know it.

Nor could she know that it crossed his mind that she'd never looked so lovely—slender, sparkling with vitality, and absolutely gorgeous...

He stood up. 'I cannot tell a lie. I did make the cocktails, but Rob organised the canapés along with a catering package. You—' he held out his hand to her '—are stunning.'

She laughed up at him as he drew her towards him. 'I also cannot tell a lie. I *feel* stunning. I mean, not that I look stunning, but I feel—'

'I know what you mean.' He bent his head and kissed her. 'OK.' He released her. 'Sit down. Cheers!' He handed her the cocktail. 'To the sunset.'

'To the sunset!' she echoed, and stared entranced at the white beach so well named and the colours in the sky as the sun sank below the tree-lined horizon.

That wasn't all there was to the sunset, though. The sky got even more colourful after the sun had disappeared, with streaks of gold cloud against a violet background that was reflected in the water, and a liquid orange horizon.

There were several other boats at anchor, and as the sunset finally withdrew its amazing colours from the sky they lit their anchor lights. Cam did the same, and then went to pour them another Mai Tai cocktail.

Liz stayed out on the deck, enjoying the warm, tropical air and the peace and serenity. It was a calm night, with just the soft lap of water against the hull.

'You could get addicted to this lifestyle,' she said with a grin when he brought their drinks out, then she sat up, looking electrified, as soft but lively music piped out onto the deck. 'How did you know?'

'Know what?'

She cocked her head to listen. 'That I was a frustrated disco dancer as a kid? I haven't danced for years. Except with Scout. She loves dancing too.' She smiled and sat back. 'I feel young all of a sudden.'

'You *are* young.' He pulled up his chair so that they were sitting knee to knee, and leant forward to fiddle with the end of her scarf. 'Actually, you make *me* feel young.'

Liz looked surprised. 'You're not old. How old are you?'

He grimaced. 'Thirty-three. Today.'

Liz sat forward in surprise. 'Why didn't you tell me?'

He lifted his shoulders. 'Birthdays come and go. They don't mean much when you start to get on. What would you have done, anyway?'

She thought for a moment. 'You seem to have everything that opens and shuts—so a present might have been difficult. But at least a card.'

'To put on my mantelpiece?' He looked amused.

'No,' she agreed ruefully. 'OK, here's my last offer.'

She leant right forward and kissed him lightly. 'Happy Birthday, Mr Hillier!'

'Miss Montrose—thank you. But I hope that was only an appetiser,' he replied wryly.

Liz trembled as she saw a nerve beat in his jaw— she'd seen it before, and she knew that under the light-hearted fun there lurked a rising tide of desire. It caused her nerves to tighten a fraction—not that she was feeling like a block of wood herself, she thought dryly, but was she ready for the inevitable?

He didn't press the matter. Whether he sensed that slight nervous reaction or not, she didn't know, but he merely kissed her back lightly and handed her a cocktail."

'Finish that. Then we have a veritable feast to get through.

A feast it was: a seafood platter heaped with prawns, crab, calamari and two lobster tails. There was also a side salad, and there was white wine to go with it. It was the kind of meal to eat slowly, often using fingers and not being too self-conscious about the smears left on your glass, despite the fingerbowl and linen napkins.

It was the perfect feast to eat on the back deck of a boat surrounded by midnight-blue sea and sky—al-though she could just make out the amazing sands of Whitehaven Beach.

It was a meal that lent itself to talking when the mood took them, about nothing very much, and to not feeling awkward when a silence grew. Because—and Liz grew more aware of it—there seemed to be a mental unity between them.

'That was lovely,' she said as he gathered up their plates and consigned their food scraps overboard. She got up and helped him carry the plates and accoutrements back into the galley, then washed her hands.

He did the same. 'Coffee?'

'Yes, please—I don't believe it!'

He raised an eyebrow at her.

'It's eleven o'clock.'

He grinned. 'Almost Cinderella time. Sit down. It's getting a bit cool outside. I'll make the coffee.'

Liz sank down on to the built-in settee that curved around an oval polished table. The settee was covered in mushroom-pink velour that teamed well with the cinnamon-coloured carpet, and there were jewel-bright scatter cushions in topaz, hyacinth and bronze.

She looked around. There were two lamps, shedding soft light from behind their cream shades, and beyond the saloon up a couple of steps was the wheelhouse, almost in darkness, but with a formidable array of instruments and pinpricks of light. A faint hum echoed throughout the boat.

Where she sat was superbly comfortable, and she could see across to the galley where her boss—she amended that. Her lover-to-be?—was making coffee.

'I could have done that,' she said.

'I can make decent coffee.' He reached for a plunger pot from the cabinet, then a container of coffee from the freezer. 'I have it down to a fine art,' he continued. 'Same coffee, same size measuring spoon and I can't go wrong.' He took down two Wedgwood mugs, spooned the coffee into the pot, poured boiling water on and balanced the plunger on top. 'Four minutes, then plunge.'

Liz couldn't help herself. She started to laugh softly. 'So you have an identical set-up in all your houses?'

'Yep. But I only have two houses.'

'And a boat?'

'And a boat. Actually...' He assembled cream, sugar and spoons on a tray with the mugs and pot, and brought it over to the table. 'I wasn't prevaricating about the real estate aspect of this trip. I'm looking at a house on Hamilton.'

'Oh, so you're combining pleasure with a bit of business?' she teased. 'Or maybe a bit of pleasure with a lot of business?'

'Not at all,' he denied. 'I'm relying on your judgement in the matter.'

Liz sobered. 'Really? I mean—do you *need* another house?'

'Really?' He sat down and plunged the coffee, and a lovely aroma rose from the pot. He poured it and moved her mug towards her. 'Help yourself. Do I need another house? No. But at least it's not another company.'

Liz digested this with a frown. 'Are you—do you— are you happy? With your life, I mean?'

He studied his coffee, then stirred some sugar in. 'I have a few regrets. Apart from Archie and Narelle I have no close relatives left. No one to benefit from the fruits of my labours, you might say.' He shrugged. 'No one to wish me happy birthday.' He looked humorous and held up a hand. 'I don't really care about that. But

I do sometimes care—greatly—that my parents didn't live to see all this.' He looked around. 'And Amelia, my sister.'

'So…' Liz hazarded. 'Are you saying…?' She paused to gather her thoughts better.

'Do I sometimes feel like saying stop the world I want to get off? Substitute the Hillier Corporation for the world? Yes.' He shrugged.

'Why—why don't you?' she breathed.

'Liz.' He looked across at her. 'It's not that easy. I employ a lot of people. And I don't know what I'd do with my time, anyway.'

He looked across at her and she could suddenly see something different about him. She could see the stamp of inner tension on the lines of his face and in his eyes.

Then he shrugged and added, 'Perhaps there's a side of me that could never sit and twiddle its thumbs? Perhaps it's the way I'm made?'

'Perhaps not,' she said huskily at length. 'Maybe it's the way things have happened for you.' She grimaced. 'Like me.'

He opened his mouth to say something, but there was a whir as an unseen machine in the wheelhouse came alive.

She looked a question at him.

'It's the weather fax,' he said with a faint frown. 'Any change in the forecast comes through automatically.'

A smile curved Liz's lips. 'Go and have a look. I know you won't rest easy until you do.'

He raked a hand through his hair and got up. 'I will.

Contrary to what you may believe about me in a car, I'm a very cautious seaman. I'll only be a moment.'

But he was a bit longer than that, and Liz leant back in a corner and curled her legs up beside her. She fell asleep without even realising it.

Cam came back with a piece of paper in his hands and the news that they'd need to change their anchorage tomorrow because of a strong wind warning.

He stopped as he realised she was asleep, and let the sheet of paper flutter to the table as he stared down at her.

He looked at the grace of her body beneath the long dress, her hand beneath her cheek, and thought that she must be really tired. Perhaps two Mai Tais and a couple of glasses of wine had contributed? Perhaps the trauma of it all…?

His lips twisted as he pulled the table away and bent to pick her up in his arms. She made a tiny murmur, but didn't wake as he carried her to her stateroom.

He put her down carefully on one side of the double bed and rolled a light-as-air eiderdown over her.

He stood looking down at her for a minute or so. Then he said, 'Goodnight, Cinderella.'

Liz slept for a few hours, then a nightmare gripped her and she woke with no idea where she was. There were different unaccountable sounds to be heard, and the terrifying conviction that she'd lost Scout.

She thrashed around on a bed she didn't know, grappling with an eiderdown she didn't remember, and was drenched in ice-cold sweat as she called Scout's name...

'Liz? Liz!' A lamp flicked on and Cam stood over her, wearing only sleep shorts. 'What's wrong?'

'I've lost Scout,' she gasped. 'Where am I?'

He sat down on the bed and pulled her up into his arms. 'You haven't lost Scout, and you're safe and sound on my boat. Remember? *Leilani* and Whitehaven Beach? Remember the sunset?'

Shudders racked her and her mouth worked.

'Scout is safe at home with Daisy and Archie and your mother at Yewarra.'

Very slowly the look of terror left her eyes and she closed them. 'Oh, thank heavens,' she breathed. Her lashes flew up. 'Are you sure?'

'Quite sure.' He said it into her hair. 'Quite sure.'

'Hold me—please hold me,' she whispered. 'I couldn't bear it if I lost Scout.'

'You're not going to lose her,' he promised. 'Hang on.' He unwound the eiderdown and lay down with her in his arms, pulling it over them. 'There. How's that?'

Liz moved against him and found the last remnants of the nightmare and her sense of dislocation leave against the security of the warmth and bulk of his body, the strength of his arms around her.

'That's wonderful.' She laid her cheek on his shoulder. 'Do you still want to marry me?'

'Liz...?' He lifted his head to look into her eyes. 'Yes. But—'

'Then do it—please. Don't take any nonsense from

me. I can be stubborn for stubborn's sake sometimes. Don't let me go—oh! I'm still dressed!'

'Liz, stop.'

He held her close, staring into her eyes with his mouth set firmly until she subsided somewhat, although she was still shivering every now and then.

'Yes, you *are* still dressed,' he said quietly. 'I don't take advantage of sleeping girls. And I don't think we should make any earth-shattering decisions right now, either. You were over-tired, overwrought, and you got a fright. So let's just take things slowly,' he said dryly, and moved away slightly.

She flinched inwardly, because whatever she might have been one thing had become crystal-clear to her through it all. Cam Hillier was her answer. Not for Scout's sake—for her sake. He not only made her feel safe, he attracted her like no other man ever had...

'Do you mean share this bed chastely?' she said huskily. 'I don't think I can. I think I've gone beyond that. You can always claim I seduced you if—if it's not what you want, too.'

He took a ragged breath. 'Not what I *want*?' he repeated through his teeth. 'If you had any idea, Cinderella...'

'Cinderella?' Her eyes widened.

He shrugged. 'It wasn't so far from midnight when I put you to bed.'

'Damn,' she said.

He lifted a surprised eyebrow at her.

'I was planning—well, I was thinking along the lines of being a birthday surprise for you. If things fell out that way. I mean, it wasn't a set-in-concrete kind of plan—more just a thought.' She trailed off, thinking that—heaven help her!—it was true.

He was silent for so long she looked away and bit her lip.

Then he said, 'Liz, I'm not made of steel.'

She looked back. 'Neither am I,' she said, barely audibly, and laid her hand on his cheek. 'I want to be held and kissed. I want to be wanted. I want to be able to show you how much I want you. Do you know when you first brought me out in goosebumps? A few days after I started working for you, when I tripped on the pavement and you caught me. Remember?'

She waited as his eyes narrowed and she saw recognition come to them.

'So I've actually been battling this thing between us longer than you have. Think of that.'

He groaned and pulled her very close. 'Don't say I didn't put up a fight,' he warned, and buried his face in her hair.

'I knew it would be like this,' Cam said.

'Like what?'

They were lying facing each other. The eiderdown had hit the carpet, along with Liz's maxi-dress and her bikini briefs—all she'd worn under it.

Her hair was spread on the pillow and looked almost ethereally fair in the lamplight.

He drew his fingers down between her breasts. 'That you'd be pale and satiny, as well as slim and elegant and achingly beautiful.'

She caught his hand and raised it to her lips. 'I sort of suspected you'd be the stuff a girl's dreams are made of. As for these—' she kissed his hand again '—I love them. They've played havoc with my equilibrium at times. They are now.'

'Like this?' He took his hand back and traced the outline of her flank down to the curve of her hip.

She caught her bottom lip between her teeth as his hand strayed to her thigh. 'Yes, like that,' she said, as those exploring fingers slid to an even more intimate position on her body. She gasped and wound her arms round his neck as all sorts of lovely sensations ran through her.

'Cam...' she said on a breath, and all playfulness left her—because she was body and soul in thrall to what he was doing to her, and because she knew he wanted her as much as she wanted him.

She could feel them moving to the same drumbeat as their bodies blended together. She could feel the powerful chemistry between them. She could glory in all the fineness of Cam's sleek powerful body, and she did. She traced the line of that dark springy hair down his torso, as she'd pictured herself doing not many days ago. She pressed her breasts against the wall of his chest and slid her leg between his.

She was overtaken by a feeling of joy as they touched, tasted and held each other. She felt like a flame in his arms—hot and desirable, then light as quicksilver. She felt wanton in one breath and irresistible to him in the next—incandescent, and totally abandoned to the pleasure he was bringing her.

Their final union brought her close to tears as the pleasure mounted to a star-shot pitch, but he held her and guided her with all the finesse and strength and control she'd probably always known Cameron Hillier would bring to this act. So that even while she was helpless with pleasure she knew she wasn't alone. She felt cherished at the same time…

'Mmmm,' he said when they were still at last. 'That was worth the wait.'

Liz put her hand on his shoulder and kissed the long, strong column of his throat. 'That was… I can't tell you… It was too wonderful to put into words.'

He traced the outline of her mouth with one long finger and looked consideringly into her eyes. 'I could try. You, my sweet, prickly, gorgeous-all-rolled-into-one Liz, created a bit of heaven on earth for me.'

She smiled and smoothed her palm on his shoulder. 'Thank you.' A tiny glint of laughter lurked in her eyes. 'But I couldn't have done it without you.'

She felt the jolt of laughter that shook him. 'No?'

'No. And you do know I'm teasing you, don't you? Because I was utterly at your mercy, Mr Hillier.'

'Not so, Miss Montrose. Well,' he amended, 'let's split the credit.'

'Sounds fair enough,' she said gravely, but all of a sudden she sobered as it came back to her—what she'd said about marrying him.

'Liz?'

She looked up into his eyes to see that he too had sobered, and that there was a question mark in their blue depths. For a moment it trembled on her lips to tell him that she'd fallen deeply in love with him—that she probably had way back, despite everything to the contrary she'd told herself.

But a remnant of fear generated from her past held her silent. Just take it slowly, she thought. Yes, she'd done it again—given herself to a man. And it was so much more than sex for her, but—for the time being anyway—should she protect herself by being the sole possessor of that knowledge?

'Nothing,' she breathed, and buried her face in his shoulder.

They had two more days on *Leilani*.

They moved the next morning to an anchorage protected from the strong winds predicted—this time to a rocky bay with turquoise waters and its own reef.

They swam and fished. They went ashore in the rubber dinghy and climbed to a saddle between the hills, from where they could see a panoramic view of the Whitsundays. They snorkelled over the coral. They paddled the light portable canoes *Leilani* carried.

Liz almost lived in her ice-blue bikini. She wore a borrowed baseball cap when they streaked across the water in the dinghy. She donned a long-sleeved white blouse as protection against the sun, and wore her sunhat on the boat. She reserved her maxi-dress for the evening.

The one thing they didn't do was discuss marriage again.

It puzzled Liz—from both their points of view. Her

unwitting reluctance to bring the subject up, and whatever reason Cam had for not doing so either. In fact a couple of times she caught him watching her with a faint frown in his eyes, as if he couldn't quite make her out. On both occasions she felt a little tremor of unease. But then he'd be such a charismatic companion she'd forget the unease and simply enjoy being with him on his beautiful boat.

One thing she particularly enjoyed was seeing him relax, and the feeling that had already occurred to her came alive in her again—Cam Hillier needed rescuing from himself. Could she do it on a permanent basis? Could she find the key to making a life with him that would be satisfying enough to ease him from the stratosphere he inhabited and which she had the strong feeling he was growing to hate?

She had to smile dryly at the thought, however. Who was to say her demons would ever let her go enough to be able to share *any* kind of a life with him?

And then it all came apart at the seams...

He said to her, apropos of nothing, 'There's no one else anchored here today.'

They were lying on loungers on the back deck. Liz looked around. 'So there isn't.' Then she sat up with a faint frown. 'You said that with a peculiar sort of significance.'

He moved his sunglasses to the top of his head. 'I have this fantasy.' He shrugged. 'I suppose you could say it involves mermaids.'

Liz studied him, but he was looking out over the

water. 'Go on. What has that to do with no one else being here?'

'We could skinny-dip.'

She took a breath. 'But we're not mermaids—or mermen,' she pointed out.

'All the better, really.'

'Cam—' She didn't go on.

'Liz?' He waited a moment. 'The problem is—my problem is—I'd love to see your naked body in the water.'

Liz looked down at herself. 'It's not a hugely camouflaging bikini.'

'Still…'

She looked out over the water. It looked incredibly inviting as it sparkled under a clear sky and a hot sun. Why not?

She rose noiselessly, stepped out of her bikini, and climbed down to the duckboard where she dived into the water before Cam had a chance even to get to his feet.

'Come in,' she called when she surfaced. 'It feels wonderful.'

It did, she thought as she floated on her back, but not as wonderful as when he dived in beside her and took her in his arms.

'Good thinking?' he asked, all sleek and wet and tanned, and strong and quite naked.

'Brilliant thinking,' she conceded. 'I feel like a siren,' she confessed as she lay back in the water across his arm.

'You look like one.' He drew his free hand across

the tips of her breasts, then put his hands around her waist and lifted her up. She laughed down at him with her hands on his shoulders as she dripped all over him. Then she broke free and swam away from him.

'You swim like a fish,' he called when he caught up with her. 'And you make love like a siren—come back to the boat.'

'Now?'

'Yes, now,' he said definitely.

Liz laughed, but she changed direction obediently and swam for the boat.

He followed her up the ladder, and when they reached the deck he picked her up and carried her, dripping wet, down to his stateroom, where he laid her on the bed.

'Cam,' she protested, 'we're making a mess.'

'Doesn't matter,' he growled as he lay down beside her and took her in his arms. 'This—what I desperately want to do with you—is not for public consumption.'

'There was no one there—and it was your idea anyway.'

'Perhaps—but not this. There. Comfortable?' he asked as he rolled her on top of him.

Liz took several urgent breaths, and her voice wasn't quite steady as he cradled her hips and moved against her. 'I don't know if that's the right word for it. It's…' She paused and bit her bottom lip. 'Sensational,' she breathed.

He withdrew his hands from her hips and ran them through her hair, causing a shower of droplets. They both laughed, then sobered abruptly as they began to kiss each other and writhe against each other with desperate need.

It was a swift release, that brought them back to earth gasping. Liz, at least, was stunned at the force of the need that had overtaken them. She was still breathing raggedly as they lay side by side, holding each other close.

'Where did th-that come from?' she asked unsteadily as she pulled up the sheet.

He smoothed her hair. 'You. Being a siren.'

'Not you? Being a merman?'

'I don't think there is such a thing.'

'All the same, do you really mean that? About me being a siren? It's the second time you've—well, not *accused* me of it, but something—' she hesitated '—something similar.'

She felt the movement as he shrugged, but he said nothing. In fact she got the feeling he was somewhat preoccupied. She got the feeling from the way he was watching her that he was waiting for something...

She pushed herself up and rested her elbow on the pillow, her head on her hand. 'Is something wrong?' She slipped her fingertips over the smooth skin of his shoulder.

He stared expressionlessly into her eyes, then he said, 'You're right. We have made a mess. Let's strip the bed and remake it. But have a shower first.' He threw back the sheet and got up.

Liz hesitated, feeling as if she'd stepped into a minefield. She studied his long, strong back for a moment as he reached into a cupboard for clothes. Then, with a mental shake of her head, she got up in a few quick movements and slipped past him into her stateroom, with its *en-suite* shower. She closed the door—something she wouldn't usually have done.

He didn't take issue with it.

They remade the bed in silence.

Liz had put on a pair of yellow shorts with a cream blouse and tied her hair back. He'd also donned shorts, and a black T-shirt. The tension that lay between them was palpable.

How? Why? Liz wondered.

She didn't get the opportunity to answer either of those questions as his phone rang—it was never far away from him. It was Roger, and when Cam clicked it off she knew from his expression and the few terse questions he'd posed that it was something serious.

She clutched her throat. 'Scout?' she whispered.

'Liz, *no*. She's fine. So is Archie. But Mrs Preston had been hospitalised with heart problems. I made her promise to get a check-up when you said you were worried about her.'

Liz's hand fell away. 'Oh,' she breathed, in a mixture of intense relief and concern.

'There's more. Daisy's got the flu.'

'Oh, no! So who…?'

'Your mother has taken command, with the help of Bob's wife, but I think we should go back as soon as we can.'

'Of course.' Liz looked around a little helplessly. 'But how soon can that be?'

He was already on his mobile. 'Roger's organising a flight from Hamilton. Hello, Rob?' he said into the phone. 'Listen, mate, I need to get home ASAP. Organise a chopper to pick us up off Whitehaven Beach. Come on it yourself, and you can sail *Leilani* back to Hamilton.'

Liz's mouth had fallen open at these instructions. She closed it but got no chance to comment.

'OK,' Cam said, 'let's up anchor. It'll take us about half an hour to get to Whitehaven.'

'What if there are no helicopters available?'

He looked at her, as if to say, *You didn't really say that, did you?* 'Then he'll buy one.'

'Oh, come on!' Liz clicked her tongue. 'You don't expect me to believe that?'

'Believe it or not, Ms Montrose, it's something I have done before.' He paused and looked around. 'Would you mind packing for both of us?'

Liz stared at him, but she recognised this Cam Hillier, and she turned away, saying very quietly, 'Not at all.'

She didn't see him hesitate, his gaze on her back, or see his mouth harden just before he left the stateroom.

Liz stood in the same spot for several minutes.

She heard the powerful motors fire up. She heard above that the whine of the electric winch and the rattle of the anchor chain as it came up. All sounds she knew now.

She felt the vibration beneath her feet change slightly as he engaged the gears and the boat got underway...

She licked a couple of tears from her upper lip—because something had gone terribly wrong and she had no idea what it was. *Ms Montrose*, she thought. Had she gone back to that? *Why* had she gone back to that?

Why this almost insane rush to get home? Yes, when he made up his mind to do something he often did it at a hundred miles an hour—and it wasn't that she didn't want to get home as soon as possible—but *this*?

Wouldn't they be alone together any more? What about that fierce lovemaking? Where did that fit in?

She buried her face in her hands.

They got back to Yewarra after dark that same evening.

Roger had organised a flight for them on a private jet from Hamilton Island with a business associate of Cam's. The associate was on the flight, so there'd been no chance of any personal conversation. And they'd flown from Sydney to Yewarra on the company helicopter—ditto no personal conversation.

Liz was unsure whether it had been fortuitous or otherwise.

Both Scout and Archie were already in bed and asleep, but Mary Montrose was there to greet them. And she had assurances that Daisy was resting comfortably and so was Mrs Preston, although she was still in hospital.

Liz hugged her mother and Cam shook her hand.

'Thanks so much for stepping into the breach, Mrs Montrose,' he said to her, and Liz could see her mother blossoming beneath his sheer charm. 'I hope you've moved into the house?'

'Yes,' Mary said, 'along with Scout. Although only

into the nursery wing. I guess you'll stay there too?' she said to Liz.

'Uh—actually,' Cam said, 'Liz and I have some news for you. We've agreed to get married.'

CHAPTER NINE

'HOW COULD YOU?'

They were in his study with the door closed. It was a windy night, and she could hear trees tossing their branches and leaves outside, as well as occasional rumbles of distant thunder

Liz was stormy-eyed and incredulous, despite the fact that her mother had greeted Cam's news with effusive enthusiasm before faltering to an anxious silence as she'd taken in her daughter's expression.

Then she'd said, 'I'll leave you two alone,' and gone away towards the nursery wing.

'It's what you told me to do,' he countered, lying back in his chair behind the desk. '"*Don't take any nonsense from me,*"' he quoted. '"*I can be stubborn for stubborn's sake.*" Remember, Liz?' He raised a sardonic eyebrow at her and picked up his drink—he'd stopped to pour them both a brandy on their way down to the study.

Despite the drink, Liz couldn't help feeling that to be back in his study, on the opposite side of his desk from him, was taking them straight back to an employer/employee relationship, and it hurt her dreadfully.

'There's nothing wrong with my memory,' she said

helplessly, then took a breath to compose herself. 'I also remember—not that many hours ago—being all of a sudden being frozen out after we'd slept together as if we'd never get enough of each other. The last thing I expected after that was to be told I planned to marry you.'

'But you do, don't you, Liz? Because of Scout.'

Liz paled. 'But you knew,' she whispered. 'You yourself told me that you needed a mother for Archie and I needed security for Scout.'

He got up abruptly and carried his glass over to the paintings on the wall. He stared at one in particular—the painting of a trawler with the name of *Miss Miranda*. 'I didn't know I was going to feel like this.'

She stared at him. He was gazing at the picture with one hand shoved in his pocket and tension stamped into every line of his body. Even his expression was drawn with new lines she'd never seen before.

'Like what?' she queried huskily.

He turned to her at last. 'As if I've got my just desserts. As if after playing the field—' his lips twisted with self-directed mockery '—after having a charmed life where women were concerned, being able to enjoy them without any deep commitment, I've finally fallen for one I can't have.'

Her eyes grew huge and her lips parted in astonishment. 'C-can't have?' she stammered.

He smiled briefly, and it didn't reach his eyes. 'You're doing it again, Liz. Repeating things.'

'Only because I can't believe you said that. You have—we have—I don't know how much more you could want.' Tears of confusion and desperation beaded her lashes.

He came back and sat down opposite her. 'I thought it would be enough to have you on any terms, Liz. That's why I lured you into the job up here at Yewarra. That's why—' he gestured '—I played on your insecurity over Scout. Only to discover that when you agreed to marry me you had Scout on your mind, not me. I didn't want that.'

She gasped, and her mind flew back to the first time they'd made love—to their first night on the boat and the nightmare she'd had. Flew back to his initial resistance that she, in her unwisdom, had not given enough thought to.

'You should have told me this then.'

'I nearly did. I *did* tell you I wasn't made of steel,' he said dryly. 'I didn't seem able to also admit that I was a fool—an incredible fool—not to know what had happened to me.'

'What about this morning? Was it only this morning?' she breathed. 'It seems like an eon ago.'

'This morning?' he repeated. 'What I really wanted this morning was to hear you say you loved me madly, in a way that I could believe it.'

Liz let out a long, slow breath. 'What I don't understand now is why you told my mother we were planning to marry.'

He drummed his fingers on the desk. 'That was a devil riding me. But I am prepared to give you the protection of my name if you feel it will safeguard Scout from her father. It'll be a marriage of convenience, though.' He shrugged.

'Is that what you think I want?' she whispered, paper-pale now.

He raised an eyebrow. 'Isn't it?'

Her lips trembled, and she got slowly to her feet as every fibre of her being shouted at her to deny the charge. Why couldn't she say no? It's *not* what I want. Why couldn't she tell him she'd fallen deeply and irrevocably in love with him?

Because she had no proof? Because she saw now in hindsight that the way things had played out it *did* look as if she'd been angling for marriage because of Scout?

Because she was still unable to bare her soul to any man?

'No, it's not what I want,' she said, barely audibly. 'Cam.' She swallowed. 'It's over. We'll leave first thing tomorrow morning. It—it could never have worked between us. Too many issues.' She shook her head as a couple of tears coursed down her cheeks. 'I told you once you'd be mad to want to get involved with me. I was right. Not that I blame you for the mess I…I am.' She turned away, then turned back. *'Please,'* she begged, 'just let me go.'

'Liz—' he said harshly, but she fled out of the study.

CHAPTER TEN

'WHERE'S ARCHIE?' Scout said plaintively. 'And where's 'Nonah's puppy? Why can't I play with them any more?' She looked around her grandmother's flat discontent-edly. 'I don't like this place.'

Liz sighed inwardly.

It was three weeks since they'd left Yewarra—a heart-wrenching move if ever there'd been one, as she'd thought at the time.

She could still see in her mind's eye Archie, stand-ing at the dolphin fountain waving goodbye, looking pale and confused. She could still see Cam, standing beside him but not waving, as she'd driven Scout and her mother away.

She could still remember every word of the stilted last interview she'd had with Cam, during which he'd insisted on paying her three-month contract out.

She could particularly recall the almost irresistible urge she'd had to throw herself into his arms and beg him to take her on any terms, even if she was unable to tell him what he wanted to hear. She closed her eyes in pain every time she thought of it…

She couldn't get out of her mind the thought of Cam

Hillier needing help to stabilise his life and how she was too emotionally crippled to give it to him.

In the three weeks since that parting she'd lost weight, she'd slept little, and she'd done battle with herself over and over. Had she walked away from a man who loved her for no good reason? On the other hand, would he ever trust her?

Her mother had been an absolute stalwart, doing her very best to make the dislocation more bearable for both her and Scout, but Liz knew she would have to make some changes. She couldn't go on living with her mother in the way she had. Mary was obviously very close to her new beau, Martin. She was also knee-deep in concert costumes.

But it had been a week before Liz had even been able to pull herself together and start looking for an alternative life and a job.

She'd got in touch with the agency she'd worked for and put herself back on their books. So far nothing had come up, but she had got her old weekend job as a restaurant receptionist back. Next thing on her list was a flat of her own.

It was not long after Scout had made her displeasure with their new life known that the phone rang. It was the agency, with an offer of a diary secretary position for two weeks starting the next day.

Liz accepted it after consulting her mother, although she was dreading getting back on the old treadmill. And the next morning she presented herself at a suite of offices in the city, the home of Wakefield Inc—a company that operated a cargo shipping line.

She was, she'd been told, replacing the president's diary secretary, who had fallen and broken a leg. That was all she knew.

As always for work, she'd dressed carefully in a fresh suit with a pretty top. But her hair was tied back and she wore her glasses.

She was greeted by a receptionist, whose name-plate labelled her as Gwendolyn, as she stepped out of the lift, and was ushered immediately towards the president's office when she'd explained who she was.

'In you go,' Gwendolyn said cheerfully. 'He's asked to see you immediately.'

Liz took a deep breath and hesitated. She could partly see into the office, and it looked quite different from the last office she'd worked in. No pictures of horses and trawlers that she could see, and a completely different colour scheme—beige carpet, beige walls and a brown leather buttoned settee. The desk was hidden from her, and she took another deep breath and walked through the door—only to find herself almost fainting from sheer shock.

Because it was Cam Hillier who sat behind the desk belonging to the president of Wakefield Inc—a company she'd never heard of before yesterday.

She stopped as if shot.

He got up and came round the desk towards her. 'Liz,' he said quietly. 'Come in.'

'Y-you?' she stammered. 'I don't understand.'

He smiled briefly. 'It's the company I bought while you were up at Yewarra. Remember?'

Her eyes were huge and her face was pale as her lips

worked but no sound came. She stared at him. He was formally dressed, in a navy suit she recognised. He was as dynamic and attractive as he'd ever been—although she thought he looked pale too.

'I—I don't understand,' she repeated. 'I'm supposed to be temping for someone who's broken a leg.'

'I made that up. I also asked for you personally.'

She blinked. 'You…you got me here deliberately? Why?' she asked hoarsely.

'Because I can't live without you. I need you desperately, Liz.' He put a hand out as she rocked on her feet, and closed it around her arm to steady her. 'Archie can't live without you. None of us can. So we'd be grateful for anything you can give us, but you have to come back.'

'Anything?' she whispered.

And whether it was the shock of seeing him again when she'd never expected to, or the shock of discovering he'd sought her out, it was as if some unseen hand had turned a key in her heart and everything she'd longed to say but been unable to came pouring out…

'Don't you understand? I would never have slept with you if I didn't love you. That's the way I'm made. I know—I know it looked as if it was all about Scout, but it wasn't. It was *you*. It was you from way back.'

Tears were pouring down her cheeks and she was shaking.

'Liz.' He put his arms around her, and despite her tears she could see that he was visibly shaken too, 'Liz, my darling…'

'I don't know why I couldn't say this before,' she wept. 'I *wanted* to, but—' She couldn't go on.

'I understand. I always understood,' he said softly. 'I just couldn't help myself from rushing my fences at times.'

'I'm surprised you don't hate me,' she said, distraught.

His lips twisted. 'Maybe this will reassure you more than any words,' he murmured, and took off her glasses. He started to kiss her—her tear-drenched cheeks, her brow and her mouth.

When they finally drew apart Liz was breathless, but her tears had stopped and she looked up at him in wonderment. 'It—it *is* real,' she said tentatively.

'I really love you,' he said. 'I've never felt this way before. As if I'm finally making the right music. As if the rest of the world can go to hell so long as I have you.'

He traced the outline of her swollen mouth with his forefinger. 'I never told you this—I've never told anyone this—but my parents were soul mates, and I've been looking for my soul mate for a long time. So long I didn't think it was going to happen. Until I met you.'

Liz moved in his arms. 'I had no idea.'

'Remember when you offered to take me apart?' he asked, with a wryly lifted eyebrow.

'I didn't! Well—' she shook her head '—if you say so.'

He grinned. 'That was when the danger bells started to ring for me. Although, to be honest—' he looked rueful '—when you climbed over my wall I had an inkling there could be something special about you.'

Liz gasped. 'But...'

He shrugged. 'Don't ask me why. I guess it's the way these things happen. But by the time I got you to Yewarra it was more than danger bells. It was the growing conviction that you and you alone were going to be that special one for me—if only I could get you to see it—if only I could get you to trust me.'

Liz closed her eyes and rested her head on his shoulder. 'I'm sorry.'

He kissed her lightly, then took her hand and drew her over to the buttoned settee, where they sat down with their arms around each other.

'Don't be sorry,' he said. 'Marry me instead.'

Liz laid her cheek on his shoulder. 'I can't think of anything I would rather do, but—' she sat up suddenly, and looked into his eyes with a tinge of concern in her own '—I do know I can be difficult—'

'So do I,' he interrupted. 'I've seen it. Outspoken, for example. Fighting mad at times. However, since I'm such a model of patience, so easy-going, so tolerant, so predictable, et cetera, we should complement each other.'

'Patient? Tolerant? Predictable?' Liz stared at him in disbelief, then she started to laugh. 'For a moment I thought you actually believed that,' she gurgled. 'Oh, Cam, you can be totally unpredictable, intolerant and impatient, but you can also be—in lots of ways—my hero, and I love you so very much!'

He held her as if he'd never let her go. And the magic started to course through her—the assault on her senses, the thrilling, magnetic effect he'd had on her almost from the beginning claimed her.

They could have been on the moon, she thought, as they revelled in each other. It was as if the world had melted away and all that mattered was that they'd found each other.

It was when they finally drew apart that Cam said, 'We need to get out of here.'

'Yes.' Liz pushed her hair back—he'd taken it down, and there were clips scattered she knew not where. 'Yes. But it might look—funny.'

'No, it won't.' He helped her to her feet and patted her collar down. 'Well, you did come in looking all Ice Queen, but now you look gorgeous so I don't suppose anyone will mind.'

'Cam,' she breathed, as colour came into her cheeks, but said no more as he kissed her, then took her hand and led her to the door—and once more demonstrated how unpredictable Cameron Hillier could be.

There were several people in the reception area, grouped around the reception desk. They all greeted Cam with the deference that told Liz they were employees.

He returned the greetings and rang for the lift then said to Gwendolyn, 'Gwen, may I introduce you to my future wife? This is Liz. Oh, and by the way, I won't be in for a couple of weeks, maybe even months. If anything seems desperate get hold of Roger Woodward at Hilliers, he'll sort it out.'

There was dead silence and several mouths hanging open for a couple of seconds then Gwen shot up and scooted round her desk to shake Liz's hand as well as Cam's. 'I'm so happy for you both!' she enthused. 'Not

that I realized—or knew anything about it—still, all
the very best wishes!' And she pumped Cam's hand
again.

Another devoted employee in the making, Liz thought
wryly but she was warmed as everyone else shook hands
and they finally stepped into the lift.

'Poor Roger,' she said as they descended to the car
park.

Cam looked surprised.

'He'll probably be tearing his hair out soon. I know
the feeling,' she explained.

He took her hands. 'I apologize for all my former
sins,' he said gravely. 'But there was one thing I nearly
did that I narrowly, very narrowly, restrained myself
from doing.'

She looked up at him expectantly.

'This.' He took her in his arms then buried a hand in
her hair and started to kiss her.

They didn't notice the lift stop or the doors open, they
noticed nothing until someone clearing their throat got
through to them.

They broke apart to discover they had an audience
of four highly interested spectators, one of them with
his finger on the open button.

'Different lift but that's exactly what I wanted to do,'
Cam said to her then taking her hand again led her out
into the car park, adding to the small crowd, 'Forgive
us but we've just agreed to get married.'

And their little crowd of spectators burst into spontaneous applause.

Liz was pink-cheeked but laughing as they made their way to the Aston Martin. Laughing and full of loving.

They flew up to Yewarra the next morning. Mrs Preston and Daisy were there to greet them, both with tears in their eyes. Bob and his wife were at the helipad—even Hamish the head gardener was there. But it was Archie who really wrung Liz's heartstrings.

He hugged Cam first, then he hugged Scout but he stood in front of Liz looking up at her with all the considerable concern he was capable of and said, 'You won't go away again, will you, Liz? You won't take Scout away again, will you? 'Cause nothing feels the same when you're not here.'

Liz sank down on her knees and put her arms around Archie and Scout. 'No. We won't go away again, I promise.'

Archie stared into her eyes for a long moment and then, as if he'd really received the reassurance he wanted, he turned to Scout. 'Guess what, Golly and Ginny have had more kids! Want to see them?'

Scout nodded and they raced off together towards the menagerie.

Liz rose to her feet and Cam took her hand. 'Thanks,' he said huskily. 'Thanks.'

They were married on Whitehaven Beach several weeks later.

Liz and Cam, with Archie and Scout and the marriage celebrant, arrived by helicopter. The guests had set out on *Leilani* and another boat from Hamilton Island earlier and were ferried to the beach by tender.

The bride wore a dress her mother had made, a glorious strapless gown of ivory lace and tulle and she had flowers woven into her hair. The bridegroom wore a cream suit. Scout and Archie both wore sailor suits. Everyone was shoeless.

Mary Montrose couldn't have looked happier. Narelle Hastings with bronze streaks in her hair to match her outfit looked faintly smug and she mntioned several times to anyone who'd listen that she'd known this was on the cards right from the beginning. Daisy and Mrs Preston were tearful again but joyfully so. So was Molly Swanson. Even Roger Woodward upon whose shoulders the organization of this unusual wedding had fallen looked happy and uplifted.

Although, he still had to get everyone safely back to Hamilton apart from the wedding party, he reminded himself, and who would have thought Cameron Hillier and Lizbeth Montrose would be so unconventional?

He clicked his tongue then had to smile as he recalled their faces when they'd told him what they wanted. They'd both been alight with love and laughter.

And now, as the sun sank, they were pronounced man and wife and as a hush fell over the guests, they stared into each other's eyes and it was plain to see that at that moment they only existed for each other as the sky turned to liquid gold and so did the water.

Then the spell was broken and the business of ferrying everyone back to *Leilani*, where a feast awaited them, began.

* * *

Several hours later, Cam and Liz farewelled their guests, who were returning to Hamilton Island on the second boat, all but two that was. Archie and Scout, both asleep now, would stay with them as they cruised the Whitsundays for the next couple of weeks.

They stood side by side as the second boat identifiable by its running lights negotiated the Solway Passage and disappeared from sight. All the guests were to spend two nights at the resort on Hamilton.

'So,' Cam put an arm around her, 'it went well. Even Roger managed to enjoy himself.'

Liz gurgled with laughter. 'Poor Roger! Yes, it went well.' She leant against him. 'Do you feel married?'

He looked down at her somewhat alarmed. 'Don't you?'

'I do.' She turned her face up to him. 'I really do.'

He cupped her cheeks, kissed her lightly, then swept her into his arms.

Twelve months later Yewarra was looking its best after good rain that had given all the gardens a boost for their final late summer flowerings.

Liz was wandering through the beds of massed roses, inhaling their delicate perfume when Cam came looking for her and he found her leaning against a tree trunk, day-dreaming.

He'd been away for a few days, and he'd just driven in. He'd discarded his suit jacket and loosened his tie and the sight of him, so tall and beautifully made, still, twelve months on, had the power to send her pulses racing.

'You're back,' she said and lifted her face for his kiss. She wore a floral summer dress that skimmed her figure, and sandals.

'You look good enough to eat,' he murmured. 'I'm not only back, I'm back where I belong.' He kissed her thoroughly then he linked his arm through hers and they started to stroll through the gardens. 'Missed me?'

She nodded but her lips curved into a smile as she thought about the changes in him. How he'd cut his work load down and what he couldn't he did mostly from home so that he was rarely gone from her, and then only for short stretches.

How he was so much more relaxed and able to enjoy their lifestyle. Not, she knew, that he wouldn't need different challenges from time to time but the frenetic pace of his previous life was a thing of the past.

As for herself, she couldn't be happier...

'How come you're so alone?' he queried as they strolled along. 'Not a kid in sight.'

'They were invited to a birthday party down the road. Daisy took them and stayed on to give a hand.'

He stopped and swung her round to face him, and frowned. 'Why do you look—I don't know—secretive?'

'Ah,' Liz said, 'so you noticed?'

His lips twisted. 'I notice everything about you, Liz Hillier. I always did. Hang on, let me guess.' He scanned her from head to toe but his gaze came back to rest on her face, her eyes particularly. 'It's a baby, isn't it?'

'It's a baby,' she agreed gravely.

He paused. 'How do you feel about that?' he asked slowly then.

'I'm over the moon.' She slipped her arms around his neck. 'Can I tell you why?'

'Of course…'

'I used to worry,' she said barely audibly, 'that I could never prove to you how much I loved you, I could only say it. But this is my proof. I want your baby with all my being.'

'Oh, Liz,' was all he said but she could see his heart in his eyes, and she knew that he really believed her.

He caught his breath as he saw the joy in her. 'Come,' he said, and she knew exactly what he had in mind.

They turned and walked away through the gardens to towards the house, hand in hand again.

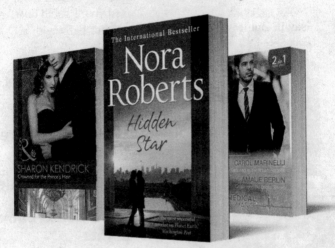